Praise for

To Bargain with Mortals

"An absolute triumph of epic fantasy and searing political drama, introducing a stunning new voice to the genre. Basu's debut is a profound and intricate tale of rebellion and a meditation on the nature and nuances of power. *To Bargain with Mortals* demands both your love and your outrage. I devoured it."

—Ava Reid, *New York Times* bestselling author of *A Study in Drowning*

"Full of cinematic South Asian world-building, complex colonial politics, and a clever magic system, *To Bargain with Mortals* is an incredible, ambitious debut. R. A. Basu has a gift for epic storytelling and an incisive eye for character dynamics that make this novel shine."

—Vaishnavi Patel, *New York Times* bestselling author of *Kaikeyi*

"Basu delivers a gripping tale of resilience in a gritty but unflinching world for fans of Fonda Lee. Set in a vividly imagined, magical country scarred by colonization and exploitation, Basu's novel explores the devastating price of freedom—and the audacious hope it requires of the people who demand their fate, stolen by their oppressors. A timely novel that is impossible to put down!"

—Sarah Mughal Rana, author of *Hope Ablaze*

"*To Bargain with Mortals* is a sharp and nuanced takedown of colonialism and forced assimilation, wrapped up in magic. R. A. Basu explores colliding cultures with a deft hand. Her gorgeously cinematic writing swept me away from the start, and the smoldering chemistry between Poppy and Hasan gripped me until the end. With complex familial relationships woven into the twists and turns of the plot, every page packs an emotional punch. For readers looking for an intricate and layered world, fresh magic system, and resourceful FMC [female main character], this is not a book to be missed!"

—Eli Snow, author of *The Divine Gardener's Handbook*

"On its surface, *To Bargain with Mortals* is an exhilarating tale about the cost of revolution and legacy, rife with cleverly woven political intrigue. At its heart, it is a love letter to brown women who have sought love in places that will never love them back. This magnificent debut healed something in me."

—S. Hati, author of *And the Sky Bled*

To Bargain with Mortals

To Bargain with Mortals

BOOK ONE

• *The Reckoning Storm* •

R.A. Basu

Published by Skies Press, an imprint of Bindery Books, Inc., San Francisco
www.binderybooks.com

Acquired by Emma Skies
Edited and designed by Girl Friday Productions
www.girlfridayproductions.com

Cover: Charlotte Strick
Cover illustration: Dan Funderburgh

ISBN (paperback): 978-1-964721-68-2
ISBN (ebook): 978-1-964721-67-5

Library of Congress Cataloging-in-Publication data has been applied for.

First edition
10 9 8 7 6 5 4 3 2 1

Printed in China

For my grandparents

Prologue

Stories of Heresy

SEVENTEEN YEARS AGO

The storm was going to tear the mansion apart. Howling, the winds drove sheets of rain, pounding the stone walls like fists. Outside, the sea threw itself on the beach, again and again, reaching for the house as if seeking to pull it in and drown it. A flash of lightning outside lit up the servants' quarters of the Sutherland mansion, revealing, for a split second, the barefoot six-year-old girl wandering through the corridors. Though the servants' quarters were pitch black, Poppy navigated her way deftly until she reached a door at the end of the hallway. She pushed it open tentatively.

"Nanny," Poppy whispered as thunder shook the house, "can I sleep with you?"

Poppy's nanny sat upright in her cot, rubbing her eyes as the sheet fell away from her. To her right, a small form stirred—Nanny's own four-year-old daughter, Samina.

"What are you doing down here, Poppy?" Nanny asked. "You know you're not supposed to be in the servants' quarters."

"Mother said I'm too old to sleep with her." Poppy sniffled. "She said I'm a big girl now. But I'm still scared."

Nanny sighed and patted the left side of the cot. "Come, child."

Poppy didn't have to be told twice. She scrambled up into the cot, tucking herself in against Nanny's soft, comforting body. Though her father had hired Nanny years ago with the explicit instruction to teach Poppy Welkish, sometimes, when it was just the two of them, she still spoke to her in Virian. She did so now, her rolling consonants and vowels just as comforting as her hand stroking Poppy's hair.

"You don't have to fear the storm, Poppy."

"It's so angry." Poppy cringed at another clap of thunder. "What if Viryana sinks?"

"It will not," Nanny said firmly. "The rains are good, a gift to the land so that things can grow. This happens every year. We've had storms like this as long as our people have lived on the island."

Even though Nanny was a servant, and Poppy's father, the Duke of Cloudcliff, was the viceroy, she didn't view Poppy as any different from herself. *Our people,* she said. *Virians.*

"But how come the storms never destroy the island?" Poppy asked. "How have people survived so long?"

Nanny smiled, teeth bright against her warm-brown skin. "Let me tell you a story. Once, over a thousand years ago—"

"A thousand? Was the Founder there?"

"No, child. This story takes place long before the Founder's empire was created, before the man himself was born."

Poppy couldn't imagine a world before the empire, but she remained silent as Nanny continued.

"Over a thousand years ago, disasters plagued the island of Viryana. The storms raised the seas, and the skies flooded the lands, drowning the people. The volcano spewed fire and ash, burning and choking those nearby. Strong winds would catch fishermen's boats and dash them against the rocks. The earth itself would slide in great heaps or tremble and quake, destroying whole villages at a time. All this was caused by divine energy, the restless nature of the gods.

"But the people of the island cried out to the gods and begged for mercy. All they wanted was to live on the island, to be safe and prosperous. The gods listened to the cries of the holiest few, and on them, they bestowed the gift of control over the four respective elements of water, fire, air, and earth. Those with the gift used it to tame the sea and the sky, quiet the volcano, calm the winds, and steady the earth. With control over the elements, humans were able to flourish on Viryana. Those who could control the elements were considered gods-blessed, and so the people made them maharajas and maharanis, kings and queens, whose job was to protect their subjects, who did not have power of their own.

"And so, the people of Viryana lived safely and happily, with the gods-blessed maharajas of old watching over them, for many generations."

Poppy yawned, her fear of the storm forgotten. "Nanny, isn't controlling the elements like doing magic? Father says magic is unnatural. He says it's *heresy*." She sounded out the last word carefully, breaking it into three: *hair-is-see.*

"Different people sometimes see things differently, and they may use different words to describe and explain things that are actually the same. This divine energy comes from our gods, our land; it is very much a part of nature. It only came to be called 'heresy' or 'magic' under the emperor's rule. But for our people, 'magic' really isn't bad at all—it's a divine gift."

"There are no more kings in Viryana," Poppy said. "Does that mean there's no more divine energy?"

For a long stretch, Nanny was quiet. Poppy's eyelids had grown heavy and had already slid shut when she heard Nanny respond. "No," she whispered. "There are still Virians with that gift, Poppy, but many of them hide it."

"Because it's heresy?"

"Because the Welkish have declared it heresy," Nanny said. "There is no gift more dangerous to them than one they cannot control. But just because they have said it is so doesn't always mean that it is. Do you understand?"

Poppy did not respond to that; at last, sleep had pulled her under.

• • •

Over the course of the next year, whenever Poppy was hurt or scared, Nanny would tell her a new story about the old kings and queens, or sometimes about the gods who had given them their powers. There were the goddess of the ocean and the goddess of the volcano, who, despite their opposite natures, were sisters who had created the island of Viryana. There was the story of the maharaja who had designed the first temples to the gods, leveling the land with his earth power to create a smooth foundation. Nanny would explain how there used to be so many people with divine power, that those who were not royalty would become priests who would use their powers to help with tasks such as farming and fishing. Sometimes, Samina would sit and listen to the stories too. Each time, Nanny reminded Poppy not to repeat the stories to anyone else—not even the other girls who sometimes came to visit Poppy, children of her parents' friends.

"You don't have to worry about that," Poppy grumbled.

"Everyone just kind of whispers and stares, even the adults. No one really wants to play with me anyway."

"I do," Samina piped up helpfully.

Poppy brightened considerably at that. Dark-haired and brown-skinned, she knew she *looked* different from the other daughters, but she didn't understand why that brought out such strong reactions in them. At least she had a friend in Samina. On hot summer afternoons, the pair would go to the kitchens and steal food when the cooks weren't looking, fruits and mince pies and tea biscuits. They would take their loot onto the lawn behind the mansion, where they would enjoy their spoils in the shade of the pavilion, safely out of the scorching sun of Viryana's dry season.

But the monsoon season returned again, and with it, Poppy's old fears. The black skies tugged on something in her chest, leaving her feeling unbalanced. One night, when the storm's rage was especially vicious, she remembered Nanny's stories about the kings and queens with the ability to control water. She opened the window and looked out at the churning sea. The clouds snarled, lightning splitting the horizon. Cold rainwater stung her cheeks, but she forced herself to stand tall. Pretending she was like one of those kings of old, she shouted, "Calm down!"

The storm, of course, did not listen, but giving it a command had made her feel slightly better. Pretending she had control was almost as good as being in control itself, and so she tried again. "Rain, quiet!" She lifted her hands, waving them in the air as though dispelling the clouds.

"Poppy?" Poppy turned to see her father, Clarence Sutherland, standing in the doorway with his night-robe wrapped tight around him, his mouth pressed together in an exasperated line. "Why, in the name of the Founder, are you yelling out of your window in the middle of the night?"

He crossed the room, grabbing the window and pulling it shut.

"I'm trying to control the storm." Poppy looked at her soaked nightgown as she spoke, feeling slightly foolish now.

Her father paused. "And who," he asked, looking down at her sternly, "did you get that idea from? Tell the truth."

"The old kings," she answered. "Some of them had the power to control water. If they were here today, they could stop the storm. I want to save the island from drowning."

A long silence filled the room. Then, her father asked, "Is Nanny telling you stories, Poppy?"

"Yes," Poppy said, hesitating before adding defensively, "I like them."

He nodded once, very slowly. He kneeled, picked her up, and deposited her back in her bed. "Go back to sleep, Poppy."

• • •

Nanny was dismissed the next day. Without so much as a good-bye, she and Samina had already left the Sutherland mansion by the time Poppy arose. The storm from the previous night had dissipated, but turmoil roiled within Poppy nonetheless; she bawled so much when her parents had broken the news that her mother had left her room in a huff.

"Why?" Poppy asked, again and again. "Why did you let her go?"

"Because," her father said, "when we adopted you, you could only babble in Virian. Her job was to translate and teach you Welkish. But she was teaching you things that she should not have, and for that we had to let her go."

"They were just stories," Poppy protested.

"Those stories were heresy," her father corrected her sharply.

"The glorification of false gods and unnatural power is a crime against the empire. Who is the ultimate power in the empire, Poppy?"

"The Founder," she mumbled.

"And what did the Founder have to say about magic?"

"But Nanny didn't tell me tales of magic! The kings' powers were given to them by the old gods."

"The Virian gods do not exist," her father snapped. "I won't ask you again, Poppy. What did the Founder have to say about magic?"

Poppy shrank down. "It's corruption," she said, repeating what her mother had taught her, what she had heard at the Marnapur Cathedral at every service. "Those who use magic are unnaturals. They're a danger to everyone else. For the safety and prosperity of the empire, all must be equal in ability."

Her father nodded. "When I adopted you, I swore to raise you with these values. The fact that you see nothing wrong with what Nanny was teaching you reflects a failure on my part."

He rose from the foot of her bed and paced the room slowly. "In my life, I have triumphed over every challenge I faced," he said. "But when I made you my daughter, everyone told me I would fail. They told me that I could not raise a Virian orphan into a Welkish noblewoman. I didn't listen to them, because I was so confident in myself—and in you. After today, however, my confidence is shaken."

Her throat closed. *What is Father saying?*

"I will try, one last time, to have you educated," he continued. "I will personally select your governess and tutors myself. But if you give me any cause to believe that it is not succeeding, I am not beyond sending you to a boarding school in Welkland for a *true* education in Welkish manners."

Poppy's head spun, the sound of her own heartbeat loud in her ears. A boarding school in Welkland? Viryana was the only home she had known, the place she was born. She had just lost Nanny; she could not lose everyone else in her life too. "Please don't," she said, tears in her eyes. "I don't want to be sent away, Father, please."

Her father softened. He approached the bed slowly and sat down beside her. "I don't wish to send you away, either." He rested a hand on her knee. "But heed my words, Poppy: If you do not accept the Founder and his teachings and reject all that goes against them—even if it is just *stories*—then you have no place among Welkish nobility, and you are better off returning to where you came from. Am I understood?"

His words stunned Poppy, and the threat of abandonment dug sharp claws into her heart. She had come from nowhere—she could not return to that. She had to be the perfect Welkish daughter, or she would be no one at all. "Yes, Father," she choked out. "I understand. I won't let you down again, I promise."

And she didn't—not until the year she turned sixteen.

Chapter One

A Changed Woman

SALTCREST, WELKLAND

PRESENT DAY

Headmistress Thornhaven's gray eyes bored into Poppy's brown ones from over her teacup. Poppy lifted her own with great caution—it wouldn't do to spill it—and took a sip herself. Thornhaven watched closely, tracking her movements like a falcon does a field mouse, from the moment she bent to drink to the moment she returned the cup to its fragile saucer.

"Miss Sutherland," Headmistress Thornhaven began. Poppy tensed. *Here comes the criticism.* "I must confess that when you first arrived in my office seven years ago, I was not expecting much from you."

She could hear everything the headmistress wasn't saying: backward, Virian, *brown.*

Color me surprised. Poppy could still recall how the headmistress's pale face had curdled when she'd washed up at the door to Thornhaven College for Fine Ladies, drained from six weeks at sea. All of the clothes Poppy packed had been made for the golden heat of Viryana, not the gray Welkish damp.

As she'd shivered in the college's foyer, the headmistress

sneered. "I am not in the business of taming wild animals," she'd said. "However, I'll give this my best effort. We wouldn't want His Grace to have spent his funds in vain on a . . . thing . . . like you, would we?"

The memory of her cruelty swelled inside Poppy's throat, but she forced it down with another deep sip of tea.

"Pleased with my handiwork," Headmistress Thornhaven was saying. "Who would have thought that the ragged creature that was dumped on my doorstep, reeking of brine, could be the same woman sitting in front of me, with perfect posture, drinking tea like a lady!"

Poppy bent her head, pretending to consider the assortment of sandwiches and biting her lip to keep from speaking out. The metallic tang of blood mixed with the aftertaste of the tea. Headmistress Thornhaven met with every girl twice each semester to discuss their studies and progress—though Poppy was certain that she was the only girl whom the headmistress dared to insult so openly.

"Miss Sutherland, do pay attention. I'm speaking."

Reluctantly, Poppy lifted her gaze back to the headmistress, whose thin lips curved in a satisfied smile. She knew her words had found their mark. When it came to insecurities, she had a bloodhound's nose. Headmistress Thornhaven was the kind of woman who only grew sharper with age, the passing years like a whetstone against the keen blade of her intelligence. For this reason, the other girls at the college often referred to her as the Hawk—though only when they were certain they were out of the wide radius of her earshot. Though the headmistress could be terrifically cruel with her words, she was not above also using her cane.

"My sincerest apologies, Headmistress," Poppy managed. "Do continue."

The headmistress smoothed out her gown. "Where was I? Ah yes, your miraculous transformation. Well, I should never have doubted myself. If there was anyone who could have tamed you, it was me. I should think that of all the girls I have educated at this school, you are one of my greatest accomplishments. A Virian—one born on the streets, at that—turned into a pious, well-educated lady, with perfect Welkish manners."

On hearing this, Poppy's head whipped up. "Pardon me, Headmistress," she said before she could stop herself, "but your immodest bragging is *quite* vulgar."

Silence filled the salon. Poppy snapped her mouth closed, but the deed was done.

The Hawk swooped, seizing control of the situation in her talons. "But, of course, my work is not finished." She sniffed, deflecting Poppy's barb without acknowledging it. "You are still far too defiant. Your father will be most disappointed when I write to tell him that even after seven years, his daughter has still not changed. Perhaps you never will—most of your kind never escape the nature of your race. That is why the Founder asks us to go and guide them, so that we can save them from their savagery."

Despair twisted in Poppy's chest, sharp claws cutting into her heart. A scream swelled in her throat: *I have changed!* She was no longer the same girl she'd been at sixteen, no longer the same girl whom her father had exiled overseas for a single careless trespass. She had tried, every single day for the last seven years, to be different. To become more elegant, more diplomatic, more respectful. To become the Welkish lady others refused to see in her. To become more. Poppy wanted to believe that she was more, even as the headmistress—and everyone else—condemned her to a life of being lesser.

Pressure built behind her eyes. She forced herself to blink once, slowly, pushing it back. From across the tea tray, Headmistress Thornhaven was still watching her, searching to see if her blow had landed, a shark looking for blood in the water. When she found no evidence of it, she sat back and selected a sandwich. Poppy knew this tactic well—she was holding back her dismissal. The trap was obvious: The headmistress was waiting for her to crack, apologize, and grovel for another chance. But Poppy was no new girl. After seven years, she had memorized the Hawk's rules, and *ladies do not whine like children.*

Instead, Poppy mirrored her, picking up a sandwich of her own and taking a polite-sized bite. She hoped the headmistress couldn't tell how much effort it took to force it past the lump in her throat.

• • •

Two months later, Poppy found a pair of envelopes at the foot of her door. The collage of stamps announced that the letters had been delivered from overseas. From home.

She waited for the joy to bubble up, but dread sank through her instead as she recalled Headmistress Thornhaven's threat. She'd promised to report that teatime outburst. Could the letters be about this? She gripped the first envelope, the Duke of Cloudcliff's seal glaring at her like the Hawk's stare.

Maybe it wouldn't be so bad. Maybe he would understand. The lie fell flat, even in the confines of her head. The Hawk would have portrayed her in the least sympathetic light, and her father would have no cause to believe that she was lying.

She put the envelope down, her heart immediately lifting at the name on the other: Mrs. Catherine Montrose-Oakbury, her best—and only—friend from back home. Catherine and Poppy's relationship had bloomed on the sidelines of every ball and social gathering. When Poppy had been shipped off to college, she'd expected the friendship to wither, but Catherine wrote dutifully each month, sometimes even sending packages with her letters. Poppy tore into Catherine's new missive first.

> *Sweet Poppy,*
>
> *I was so jealous upon receiving your last letter. I still cannot believe you get to shop at some of the most fashionable boutiques in all of Welkland! Though I feel your absence every day, I remind myself that it would be selfish of me to wish for you to return from your time at school just so that we might visit the shops here together.*

A pang of nostalgia and yearning cut through her. She'd been forced to go on that shopping trip all alone after one of the other college girls had purposely spilled wine on her gown. Shopping was miserable without Catherine, Welkish boutique or not, but it would have been churlish of Poppy to complain.

> *Since I last wrote you, much has happened. Theo is in quite the state. Richard's men have blocked him . . .*

Poppy read the rest of the letter, commiserating with her old friend as she detailed how her elder brother, Richard, had gotten into another tiff with her husband, Theodore, over some business of Theodore's. Far too soon, Catherine's missive was over. Now there was nothing left for Poppy to do but read the one from her father. *Best to get it over with.* She gripped her letter opener, took another breath, then dragged the blade across the envelope and pulled out its contents.

To her surprise, she found not her father's neat script but Demetria's lacy scrawl. Her mother was rarely a disciplinarian—that task had been left to Poppy's governess or, for more serious transgressions, her father. This letter, then, could not be about that tea with the headmistress. With a renewed sense of interest, she began to read.

Dearest Poppy, she had written. *Please do not be alarmed.*

Poppy huffed in amusement. *A bit late for that, Mother.*

> *Your father has suffered a minor stroke. I wanted to send you a telegram the moment it happened, but he forbade me from doing so. He wishes me to stress to you that this is a trifling matter and no cause for concern. If he had it his way, he would not have mentioned it at all. However, I knew you would be hurt if we did not tell you.*
>
> *Dr. Bluefinch has assured us that your father will make a full recovery. I am certain that by the time you receive this letter, he will already be back on his feet, holding council meetings and fighting the epidemic of crime that has arisen in the slums. The doctor has insisted that the stroke was not caused by any underlying illness but is likely a result of overworking himself. He has been advised to plan for retirement, but in the interim, modifications to his lifestyle will be made as a preventative measure. He will use a cane . . .*

Her fingers went numb, and the letter fell from her grasp.

The only thing worse than enduring a reprimand from her father was learning that he had been too unwell to admonish her. Despite the reassurance that he was recovering, the stroke bothered her deeply.

Her fingers brushed over the word *retirement* once more. For years, she had pictured her father exactly as he'd been the day he'd bid her farewell at the Marnapur docks so long ago: sharp, indomitable, a man in his prime. The man in this letter—planning for retirement, adjusting to a mobility aid—was not the same man who'd clenched Poppy's hands between his own until the last minute before her departure.

The terrifying reality hit her. Her father was *old.* No longer an invincible ruler but a mere mortal. It hadn't occurred to her that while she was here, growing, changing, her father was also undergoing a transformation of his own. Who would she be without him?

The ugly truth came easily: no one.

Without the viceroy, she would have no status, no legacy to claim as her own. She would not even have a title—the fact that her father's own cousin was the king of Welkland and emperor of the Founder's territories would mean nothing, not when the Imperial Family refused to acknowledge her. Sure, she would have her mother, but she had no male next of kin. When her father passed, her family would become her husband—and therein lay the problem.

Poppy had no husband. If her father dropped dead tomorrow, nothing would keep her secured in society. She'd be forgotten, relegated to some crumbling estate for the rest of her days.

The paper crackled in protest as Poppy's fingers crushed the edge. Once, the idea of a life outside the nobility would have appealed to her. But now, after seven years of laboring to transform into the epitome of a Welkish lady in all but skin, Poppy would not be erased so easily. She had mastered watercolor painting, embroidery, horseback riding, and piano. She could treat minor injuries and could do sums in her head. She spoke fluent Welkish, all traces of her Virian accent purged from her tongue.

She had changed, despite whatever lies Headmistress Thornhaven tried to feed her. Her father had promised Poppy that a Welkish education would earn her a place in society, and she would be damned if she was going to lose it now.

She could write to her father and ask him to ask the headmistress to release her from Thornhaven. But that process would take time—time he might not have. It would be *at least* two more months, months that would occur in the scorching Virian summer, where he could easily fall prey to numerous ailments. She could not send him a telegram, for Saltcrest was a full day's travel away from the nearest telegraph office, in Cloudcliff. She would never get permission to leave the school grounds, especially not to send a telegram. When Poppy had been in first year, one of the other girls had asked, and the Hawk had chastised her so thoroughly, Poppy had never forgotten it.

"Ladies do not send telegrams," the Hawk had declared. "Telegrams are so . . . mercenary. The shorthand strips messages of character and integrity. A lady's word means nothing if it is not written in her own hand and sealed with the stamp of her family crest. Indeed, ladies, the art of the handwritten letter is irreplaceable."

Poppy's gaze fell to the ducal seal stamped on the torn envelope, the crossed scepters still intact in crimson wax. The pieces of a plan began to stitch themselves together. Her fingers curled around the handle of her letter opener. She reached slowly for the discarded envelope. For a moment, she hesitated—*forgery is unladylike*—but then she pushed forward, sliding her letter opener between the wax and the paper, gently prying it free.

Then Poppy selected her cherished fountain pen and the best sheet of paper from her lettering kit. Headmistress Thornhaven was familiar with her father's penmanship, so the letter must be delivered from Demetria. She flattened out her mother's letter beside the blank page and put the tip of the pen to paper.

Dear Headmistress Thornhaven, she began, doing her best to imitate her mother's thin, curling letters. *His Grace, my husband, has taken ill . . .*

When Poppy finished the letter, she folded it twice along crisp lines and put it aside. She then took up her mother's envelope, considering the way it had been addressed:

> *POPPY SUTHERLAND*
> *Thornhaven College for Fine Ladies*
> *1 College Court, Saltcrest, Welkland*

There was nothing she could do about her name on the envelope; however, she had to use this one if she wanted to retain the authentic postmarks. In the same forged script, she made her own additions to the envelope:

> *HEADMISTRESS N. THORNHAVEN*
> *RE: POPPY SUTHERLAND*
> *Thornhaven College for Fine Ladies*
> *1 College Court, Saltcrest, Welkland*

There. Now the envelope looked genuine. Retrieving her forged letter, she slid it inside the tampered envelope. She lit a candle and heated the seal over it until it was tacky. Then she pressed it against the envelope firmly, holding her breath as the wax cooled. When she lifted her trembling fingers away, the flap stayed shut.

The sight of the forged letter sent electricity through Poppy's veins, thrilling and uncomfortable all at once. She swept it into her purse before she could lose her nerve and toss it in the waste bin. She would give the letter to the headmistress tomorrow with a story about their mail getting mixed up, which was not an uncommon occurrence given the number of girls and the sheer volume of correspondence that flowed through the school.

That sorted, Poppy picked up a fresh piece of paper and began a second note, this one intended for a much longer journey:

> *Dear Mother and Father,*
>
> *While I am surprised and saddened to hear about Father's ailment, I am relieved to know that his recovery has been swift. Being away all these years has given me an education in not only manners but in perspective as well. I have been away from home for too long. I intend to return now, my education having achieved its purpose: I am prepared for my future in society. Upon my return, given that Father has recovered well, I wish to select a husband and do my part to ease some of the burden from Father's shoulders.*
>
> *Your loving daughter,*
>
> *Poppy*

Poppy's lips tugged up as she considered the irony of the situation. Her disregard for the rules had been the cause of her exile. Now, it would be the thing that brought her home.

Chapter Two

The Jackal's Tithe

MARNAPUR, VIRYANA

Hasan Devar did not believe in the Welkish concept of hell, but if it existed, the summer heat had him convinced that he was already there. Though it was dusk, the air was blistering. It was the kind of dry, withering heat that made the fingers swell and the tongue shrivel with dehydration. With not a cloud in the sky, the rainy season seemed in no hurry to arrive. It was bad news for everyone, but it felt particularly damning to Hasan.

He dwelled on it as he stalked through the back alleys of Marnapur's slums. In his state of inattention, he nearly tripped over a scrawny, half-nude child running across his path. Before he could speak, an arm reached out and ripped the boy away.

"Can't you see the Jackal is coming?" the man hissed at the boy. He bowed his head to Hasan. "I apologize for my son. Please, he's only seven."

Now that Hasan was paying attention, he observed the boy was indeed no more than seven, though malnutrition had stunted his growth so badly, he could have easily passed for five. Hasan's gaze lingered on the boy's ribs, jutting prominently through his ashy skin. It was impossible to tear his eyes away from that kind of suffering, but the father stepped in front of his boy, fear evident on his face. Hasan blinked, becoming aware of his surroundings again. A crowd had gathered around them, all waiting to see what the Jackal would do next.

"You're forgiven," Hasan barked. "Watch where you're going next time."

He shoved through the crowd, disappearing into the winding labyrinth of the vasudhakt slums, cursing quietly. Tonight of all nights, he had needed stealth on his side, even resorting to coming without a crew of his men. Now the streets rustled with whispers, all of them asking the same thing: *Who is the Jackal hunting?*

His prey tonight was a particular man, one who had eluded paying his debt twice now. Hasan had a reputation to uphold, and if he didn't catch his debtor tonight, people were going to say he was getting lenient.

He stopped in front of the mark's house, observing it from across the narrow lane. With its dirty walls and battered wooden door, it looked like every other shack in the slums.

Hasan's eyes roved to where an old beggar squatted farther down the street, smoking and reading a newspaper that covered half his face. He resisted the urge to grin; Vinay had always been talented at disguises. He approached his man casually, putting a coin in the small tin in front of him.

Vinay lowered the newspaper. "Thank you, son," he said, bowing his head so exaggeratedly, Hasan had to tighten his jaw against a laugh. "May Baghia smile upon you."

"Is the target in?" Hasan asked, keeping his voice low.

"I've been here twelve hours, and I haven't seen him leave. My scouts haven't spotted him anywhere else, either. He *must* be here."

Hasan turned and eyed the house. Then he saw it, behind the curtain on the main floor—a moving shadow. Proof that Vinay was right. Darsh Jana was at home.

"Stay here," he said, "and wait until I come out."

With that, Hasan strode forward and knocked on the door.

The woman who answered was not Darsh Jana but his sister, Daria. She was young—barely in her twenties, if at all—and pretty in a way that was too delicate for the slums, like a wildflower that had grown through a crack in the pavement.

"Hasan?" Daria opened the door a fraction. He caught a glimpse of a threadbare blue dressing robe. "I wasn't expecting you."

"Are you home alone?"

She nodded.

Very well, if Darsh Jana wasn't here, then Hasan could wait. He had all night. "Might I come in?" he asked. It was a formality, not a request.

Daria opened the door fully, stepping aside so he could cross over the threshold. "Come. Let me make you some chai."

The inside of the house was even more decrepit than the outside. Though a broom was propped up against the wall, the bare floor was still grimy. A layer of dust coated the stiff, threadbare furniture. He moved quietly around the cramped room, inspecting the faded picture of Darsh's parents hanging on the wall, a limp garland of dead flowers draped over it.

In the kitchen, Darsh's sister was making a racket as she prepared tea for the two of them.

"Where's your brother tonight?" he called, running a finger over the dusty frame.

"Oh, I wouldn't know." Daria laughed a little. "He's always working, my brother. Does every odd job he can find. He's not gotten a moment's rest since Mama and Baba passed."

Touching, but entirely untrue. Hasan doubted that Darsh Jana had done a single day's honest labor since a rickshaw accident claimed both his parents' lives. Behind him, Daria came in with a steel teapot and two glass cups balanced on a tray. She put the tray down carefully on a crate masquerading as a coffee table.

"Please," she said, "sit."

Hasan gingerly took a seat on the rickety couch. As Daria poured, he asked her again, "So where is Darsh working this evening?"

Daria shook her head. "I told you, I don't know where he is." The stream of black tea wavered slightly, spilling over the lip of one glass.

"He's your brother. Your only remaining family. And you expect me to believe that you don't know what he's doing?"

The girl shrugged as she put Hasan's cup down in front of him. He seized her wrist so swiftly, she had no time to pull back. Hot tea sloshed out of the cup and ran down his forearm, but he barely felt the burn.

"Your brother owes me a lot of money, you know," he said softly, as though he were trying to coax a stray cat out from under his car. "Where does a man with no money to his name spend his evenings?"

Daria stayed silent, her gaze locked on where his long fingers had wrapped around her wrist like manacles.

"Hiding." Hasan answered his own question. "I know when someone is lying to me. I have eyes all over the city. If my men find him first, I won't hold back. But if you tell me the truth tonight, I'll show him mercy."

Daria wavered; Hasan pounced. "Last chance, Daria: Where is Darsh?"

"I don't know anything," she insisted. Then she looked up at him through her lashes, her calf eyes wide and innocent. "But if my brother is in your debt, then perhaps I can repay it."

As though her meaning were not already clear, Daria placed her free hand on top of where Hasan still held her wrist, trying her best to change the meaning of his grip into something more intimate. While she reached across, she bent a little lower, letting the front of her robe hang open, a window of temptation for most men.

But Hasan was not so easily tempted as most men.

He didn't bother to hide his disdain as he pulled back. "It's money I want. Nothing else."

"Are you sure?" Daria purred, though the noise sounded more like the mewling of an alley cat than the seduction of a sultry vixen. She pushed down one sleeve of her dressing robe, exposing first her collarbone, then her shoulder. It became painfully obvious to Hasan that she had planned to seduce him from the start.

"I'm certain," he said, his voice cool and detached as he rose from the couch.

She blocked his path, fumbling with the tie holding her robe closed. "You don't sound certain."

Hasan seized both her wrists in one of his hands and thrust her back firmly. "Look. I don't have time for *pleasantries*," he said. "Tell Darsh he cannot avoid me forever. I will catch him eventually. Each time I have to come calling, I will double his debt. Starting today."

With that, he released her. Turning on his heel, he made to leave one last time. Daria caught his arm again, and he nearly swore.

"Wait!" Her voice cracked.

Damn if the girl wasn't stubborn. But when he turned around, there were tears in her eyes, and the tip of her nose was turning red. "We don't have the money. He's trying, I swear. Just give us one more week. One more chance."

Godsdamn it. "Your brother is already two weeks late. He's run out of chances. You know what happens now, don't you?"

Daria burst into tears. "Please, Hasan. You said you'd show mercy if I was honest."

Hasan's heart stirred against his will. For a moment, he hesitated, mercy and duty fighting against one another. A deadline was a deadline. Though it seemed cruel to withhold mercy, it would have been unfair to his other debtors, who had either paid on time or suffered the consequences. Plus, if word got around that he had given an extension to Daria, then every Raj, Kumar, and Anil who owed him money would be flinging their sisters into his path. Zeyar would have said that they weren't running a charity—and though Hasan was rarely in agreement with his brother, he couldn't disagree with facts.

He looked at Daria again. She sobbed loudly, like one of the village performers his grandfather used to take him to see as a boy. His mouth flattened into a thin line. As unfair as it was to his other debtors, it would have been even more unfair to Daria to punish her for her brother's mistakes, especially when he *had* promised to be merciful.

"Two more nights," Hasan ground out. "That's all. Then I burn this place down, no matter who's inside."

Daria gasped a sigh of relief. As she started a fresh wave of waterworks, Hasan ducked around her, slamming the wooden door shut behind him. Vinay lowered his paper and made to stand, but Hasan shook his head discreetly. Vinay sank back down.

Hasan pretended to head toward the street, then ducked into

the gap between two homes and came around the side of the Jana house, squatting beneath the window.

As he strained his ears, he heard a commotion coming from inside the house.

"Useless! You were supposed to seduce him," a familiar male voice roared. Glass shattered in a resounding crash, punctuating the shout.

"I tried," Daria sobbed. "I e-even t-tried undressing in front of him. . . ."

"Well, clearly you weren't appealing enough," Darsh Jana jeered at his only sister. "What good are you? I ask you to do one thing—persuade the Jackal to forgive a debt—and you can't even do that! You have no marriage prospects, no useful talents—you'll be a spinster all your life, a burden in my household."

Hasan opened the door and came back inside, but Darsh, so caught up in his fit of rage, didn't seem to notice him. Daria kneeled in front of Darsh, who stood with his back to Hasan. The tea tray had been overturned, the glasses shattered, chai running in rivulets across the floor. Daria looked up from where she was picking glass off the floor and caught sight of Hasan. Her eyes widened. Before Darsh could turn, Hasan grabbed him by his collar and wrenched him around so that he was facing the photograph of his dead parents.

Hasan met Darsh's eyes in the frame's reflection. "What kind of brother whores out his younger sister in the presence of their parents' image?"

"H-Hasan?" He'd gone pale as a Welk, shaking hard. "If this is about the money, I'll have it next week, I promise—"

"You've run out of time." Hasan shook his head. "I'm here to collect. If you don't have money, then I'll take something else."

"But I have nothing else!"

"Untrue." Hasan smiled. "You were willing to give me your sister."

Darsh stilled. "Surely you don't mean Daria—"

"Oh, I do," Hasan promised. "She'll come with me."

He released Darsh and spun, catching Daria by the wrist. "You have three minutes to get dressed, and then we're leaving regardless of what you're wearing. Make it count." The second he released her, she ran from the room.

"You can't take Daria," Darsh said. "She's my sister."

"Your sister?" Hasan laughed. "And what kind of brother have you been to her? You are a burden. Instead of paying off your own debts, you try and sell her innocence. Instead of finding her a caring husband, you force her to lie with your own mistakes. Why is it that you protest to my taking her? Is it because you care for her well-being? Or is it because you can no longer use her for your own ends?"

Darsh was silent, struggling to choke down his misplaced pride, no doubt. Finally, he gritted out, "I'll be a better brother. I'm sorry."

"It's not me you should apologize to. It's her." Hasan jerked his chin at Daria, who had reentered the room in a worn-out salwar kameez.

"I'm sorry," Darsh said, not quite looking Daria in the eye.

She reached for him and rested a hand on his shoulder. "It's okay."

"Great," Hasan said. "Truly heartwarming. Now let's go." He seized Daria's wrist again, but her brother leaped in their path.

"But I apologized!"

"The apology was for her, not me," Hasan snapped. "An apology is not going to replace the fifty thousand gold crowns you owe me."

Darsh lunged at Hasan, fists balled, but Hasan had seen this coming a mile away. Without releasing his hold on Daria's arm, he swung his free hand through the gaping hole in Darsh's stance and struck him squarely in the chin. Daria cried out as Darsh hit the floor. He didn't get up.

When they were outside, Hasan whistled through his teeth. Immediately, Vinay threw down his paper and stood, crushing his cigarette under his heel before coming to Hasan's side.

"Hold her," Hasan said, "but be gentle."

Vinay had a hundred questions in his eyes as he pried Daria from Hasan's side, but Hasan knew he wouldn't ask them. Vinay's time in the gang had taught him that there was a time and place to question the boss, and this situation wasn't one of them.

Hasan kneeled at the foot of the door, grateful that he'd made a large enough offering to Aganath that morning. Flexing his hand, he reached for the energy humming against his skin and concentrated, warmth flooding up into his shoulder and down his arm. He channeled his daivyakhi through the tips of his fingers until it flickered to life, forming a ball of fire the size of a pomegranate. He held it to the base of the wooden door until the flames caught onto the dry wood. In the scorching heat, they grew without much encouragement from him. He stepped back, satisfied.

"Stop!" Daria shrieked, thrashing in Vinay's grip. "My brother's inside!"

"He knew this would happen if he didn't pay," Hasan said.

"You said you'd be merciful!"

"I *was* merciful. That's why you're not in there with him." As the meaning of his words sank in, Daria stopped struggling. Hasan dusted off his hands on his pants. "I wouldn't worry about him, anyway. If there's one thing a weasel like him knows, it's how to wriggle out of tight spaces. Come on. Let's go, before the crowds gather."

With that, they left Darsh Jana's house, smoke filling the alleyway behind them.

"I won't ask you if you know what you're doing," Vinay said, too quietly for Daria to hear over her own keening. "The real question is whether your brothers know."

"What do you think?" Hasan whispered back. The mission had been to collect fifty thousand crowns. Instead, they'd scavenged a frightened, grieving girl.

Zeyar was going to be pissed.

Chapter Three

The Devar Brothers

"Honestly, Hasan, what the hell were you thinking?" Zeyar's black eyes, the same color and shape that all the brothers shared, bored into Hasan's face. Hasan had borne Zeyar's censure so many times it barely stung. "You were *supposed* to collect fifty thousand crowns, not a *useless* vasudhakt girl."

Hasan glared back at Zeyar. Although they were sitting at opposite ends of the table, the distance only tightened the wire of tension between them.

"Hey now," Paranjay said. The smell of sea brine accompanied him as he walked into the room. While both Hasan and Zeyar were well dressed, Paranjay was in his typical uniform of denim trousers and a well-worn cotton shirt that showed off the tattoos and scars decorating his muscular arms. "Let's not bring caste into this. Nor should we be so quick to judge the girl when she's clearly at her worst."

Zeyar turned his glower on Paranjay, who held his gaze evenly. Finally, Zeyar acquiesced, lowering his eyes to fish out a pack of smokes in his tailored gray blazer. Hasan allowed his glare to morph into a smug grin.

The expression quickly fell off his face as Paranjay continued.

"However, I have to agree with Zeyar. What were you thinking, Hasan?"

"Darsh didn't have the money. I had to burn down the house. Those are the terms of the loan. It wasn't fair to trap Daria inside when it happened."

"Fair?" Zeyar repeated. "We're not a courtroom. We're a business. *Fairness* is not a line item on a balance sheet or income statement, last I checked."

He clicked his lighter, raising his right eyebrow mockingly as he lifted his cigarette to the flame. A scar split the brow, dividing it into two. It was one of the only scars Zeyar had, and Hasan had been the one to put it there. As a teenager, he'd tackled Zeyar in a fit of pride and anger—over what, he couldn't recall. He hadn't walked away unscathed. When his skull had collided with Zeyar's, both of their brows had split. Now, Hasan wore the twin scar on the left side of his face. It was one of many on his body, but one of the rare few whose origin he remembered.

"Darsh was mistreating Daria." Hasan's mouth twisted with disgust. "He tried to pimp her out to evade paying me."

"Did you hear what I said?" Zeyar asked, puffing smoke out. "We're not a women's shelter. We do things for profit. That means we need to gain assets, not liabilities. Guess which category the girl fits into."

Hasan gritted his teeth at Zeyar's crude, profit-oriented logic. True, they didn't run a charity or a shelter. No, they weren't in the business of fairness. But their business was composed of people—primarily, vulnerable ones—and Hasan hated it when his brother oversimplified like this. They'd had *that* argument countless times before, and it had gotten Hasan nowhere.

He paused, choosing his words carefully, trying to spin the situation in a way that would make Zeyar agree with him. "We could get her a job with us. Turn her into an asset. Do you need a seamstress?"

Zeyar huffed out another cloud of smoke. "No, I do not. Besides, we'd have to pay her if we hired her. That's a drain on our resources. We don't need another mouth to feed. We have to take care of ourselves."

"I could make her a spy."

"You already have nearly three hundred spies," Zeyar snapped. "You don't need another. The problem isn't where we're going to place the girl. The problem, as always, is you."

Hasan opened his mouth to fire back, but Zeyar jabbed his cigarette at him menacingly, half rising from his seat.

"No, listen to me. This week, you bring home Daria. Last week, you *struck a police officer* over a dispute about a pickpocket who was stupid enough to get caught."

"He was a child!" Hasan protested. "And he was stealing food, so he was obviously desperate. I told you, the cop was part of Montrose's squadron. Violence was the only way."

Hasan's scowl deepened as he recalled the incident. He'd been on his way to collect a debt when he'd seen the commotion: a police officer, holding a boy by his ear, while a shopkeeper looked on with his hands on his hips. Hasan hadn't needed any more context. At first, he'd tried talking to the officer. Zeyar had spent a significant amount of funds bribing the cops to look the other way from the Devars, but there was one squadron, led by Captain Richard Montrose, that was utterly impervious to bribes. They hated Virians, and by extension, they hated Virian wealth. No amount of money could make them forget that it was a brown hand offering it. When it became clear that both words and money were ineffective, Hasan had used his quick wit and even quicker fists to incapacitate the man long enough for the thief—and Hasan—to escape. Still, word of the Jackal's brawl with the police had made its way back around to Zeyar, who had been almost as infuriated that evening as he was now.

"It would have been best if you had just left that officer well enough alone." Zeyar shook his head. "Now our operations will be scrutinized more than ever as that bastard tries to get even with us. It's in our best interest to keep the police happy or, at the very least, ignorant."

"Why are you so determined to please the pigs?" Hasan wrinkled his nose. "They brutalize us without hesitation, yet when I return the favor, you chastise *me*?"

"*They* hold the power," Zeyar said. His words were tauntingly slow, as though he were explaining something to a child. "Befriending them means *we* get access to that power."

"We have power of our own."

"Our business will never have as much power as the legitimate hierarchy," Zeyar said emphatically. "Until we can make ourselves part of it, it's in our best interest to placate it."

Hasan scoffed. "We'll never be part of it."

"We deserve to be," Zeyar insisted. "We're daivyakt. Our blood can channel the power of the gods. The power we have now is a shadow of what we were born to wield."

Paranjay, as if sensing that the conversation was about to plunge into the rut of an oft-argued topic, intervened again. "I agree that it's best to avoid police scrutiny. However, I think even if Hasan had not interfered, we would still be seeing an increased police presence. The famine has led to reckless acts—highway robberies, countless pickpocketings, burglaries. The police will catch the desperate. Will you rescue them all, Hasan?"

"I don't care who he rescues," Zeyar muttered loud enough

for Hasan to hear, "as long as he doesn't bleed out the rest of us to do it."

"It's not about rescuing." Hasan turned to Paranjay. "We may not have the legitimate power that Zeyar thinks we deserve, but as the leaders of this gang, we have more power than most. When we create contracts, they're law. When our rules are broken, we punish the offender. We have a responsibility to behave justly. To do what's right."

"Noble, but untrue," Zeyar drawled, stubbing out his cigarette. "We do what makes us money. When there are shortages of food and water, and the price of basic commodities has doubled, do you think honor will put food on the table?"

Hasan put his hands over his face, trying to find the right words to convey his argument. It wasn't about *nobility.* Those kinds of lofty ideals were reserved for men who could afford to pay others to get their hands bloodied for them. But when you were the one pulling the trigger, it was easy to lose sight of the meaning behind the violence. Their gang had the ability to affect real change through violence—or mercy. But the only change Zeyar would ever acknowledge was in the figures in his bookkeeping.

"I don't think this is about money, actually." Paranjay palmed a sun-browned hand over his thick beard. "This is about family—has always been. We do this so we can take care of each other. And to Zeyar's point, we cannot do this if we aren't turning a profit, and we can't turn a profit if we aren't unified in the way we're running our business. So the problem tonight is not Daria or the police or money; it's Hasan. Hear me out," he added, catching Hasan's incredulous look. "We're a family business, but you aren't acting like it. Twice now, you've made rash decisions that impact the business without consulting us. You need to stop."

Hasan tried to look away, but Paranjay held his gaze firmly. Hasan noted that his second brother was alarmingly like their mother when he needed to be. "Fine," he said at last. "I will consult you both before I deviate from the plan."

"Finally," Zeyar said, pushing his chair back. "Glad we sorted this. If you'll excuse me, I've got—"

"Not so fast." Paranjay kicked Zeyar's chair back under him. The edge of the seat hit the eldest Devar brother behind the knees, reflexively forcing him to sit.

"There's also the matter of Daria. At this point, it doesn't matter if she's an asset or a liability. She's with us, and we can't send her back to the ashes of her home in cold blood. We will find her a job in one of the textile factories that we patronize, and the owner will give us a cut of her wages until Darsh's debt is paid off." Paranjay looked at each brother. "Are we agreed?"

It would take Daria a decade to repay the debt, but at the end of the day, Hasan's brothers were right: This was a business, and if he had to worry about how every single person who owed the Devar brothers money intended to finance their loan, he would go mad.

"Okay," Hasan relented.

"Fine," Zeyar said, looking considerably less pleased than he had a minute ago.

"Good." Paranjay grinned, light as a sea breeze. "Because I'm starving, and it's breakfast time. Who wants chai?"

As Paranjay turned on the gas stove and rummaged in the drawers for a pot, Hasan privately thought that his second brother often played far more than just his role of smuggler. He was a mediator—a bridge between the islands that were Hasan and Zeyar, the fulcrum on a scale. They were an odd number, the three of them, but without Paranjay, they were unbalanced.

• • •

A month later, Hasan and his brothers ate what would be their last meal together in a very long time. Tomorrow, Paranjay would set sail for Welkland, his cargo full of opium.

While Hasan had inherited his control over fire from his mother's side of the family, Zeyar and Paranjay had taken after their father, with the ability to control the air. Paranjay, like their father, used his skills when sailing to maximize speed and agility. These traits, plus Paranjay's own love of the sea, lent themselves well to his role as a smuggler in the Devars' criminal business. While the Devars transported everything from tea to tobacco, their most profitable—and most frequent—cargo was opium. While the plant was still grown in various colonies, including Viryana, it was illegal in Welkland, which only boosted demand. Paranjay made triple the markup on opium than on anything else.

"Are you headed out?" Zeyar asked. He and Hasan hovered as Paranjay lugged his trunk toward the door.

"Yeah." Paranjay set it down. "I'm already late, though. Let's make this quick."

Paranjay gripped Hasan's hand, pulling him into a hug. Hasan sighed but reciprocated, wrapping his arms around Paranjay. Though he'd never admit it, he was distrustful of the sea. He couldn't imagine being in the middle of its vast expanses, trapped between the rolling depths and endless skies. It didn't help, either, that their father had died like that, caught in a storm that he didn't have enough power to fight.

"Try not to get killed," Hasan said.

"Try not to kill each other," Paranjay shot back, releasing Hasan and reaching for Zeyar. This had become their standard farewell.

"I make no promises." Zeyar made a big show of cringing away as Paranjay turned their handshake into a hug, but that was part of their routine. Zeyar thumped Paranjay once on the back. "Bring us a souvenir?"

Paranjay chuckled. "Whatever you want." He bent and picked up his trunk. "I'm ready."

Zeyar frowned, and he and Hasan exchanged a glance. "Aren't you going to make an offering to Neelam, or at least to Nathria?"

Hasan couldn't remember the last time Paranjay had visited the pantheon. He couldn't have had enough daivyakhi left in him to fly a kite.

Paranjay glanced at his watch. "No time. I'm late, and if we aren't done loading the ship and out on the horizon before sunrise, we're going to run into problems."

Hasan took a step forward. "You should still—"

"I can do it on the ship," Paranjay said. "We've got the faces of the gods carved into the mast, remember?"

Hasan's and Zeyar's faces creased in identical expressions of displeasure—a rare moment of alignment, Hasan thought. When it came to Paranjay's safety, they were both on the same page.

Paranjay, however, remained unmoved. "I don't need the power of the gods to load crates." He softened for a moment, then added, "You don't need to worry about me. I've done this plenty of times before. I'll be home soon."

Then he shouldered past Hasan and Zeyar, through the doorway, and out to the docks. Hasan stared at the door as it swung shut, hoping that the sea Paranjay loved so much would keep him safe for the next two months.

Chapter Four

The Twelfth Man

The telephone rang before dawn. Hasan ignored it, shutting his eyes harder and putting his pillow over his head to muffle the awful metallic shrieking. A soft bang echoed through the hall as Zeyar opened his door and shuffled out to the living room. He spoke softly, his words dampened by the wall and the pillow that Hasan still held pressed to his ear.

Zeyar burst into his room a moment later, ripping the pillow off Hasan's head. "Get up," he said. "Our ship was raided last night."

Zeyar might as well have doused him in a bucket of ice water. He sat up immediately, his back ramrod straight. "What about Paranjay?"

"I don't know," Zeyar said, his face pale. "Raman said it was better to discuss in person."

An hour later, Hasan and Zeyar had convened in a shabby, unremarkable office, "Devar Brothers Shipping Co." printed on the awning in faded red letters. Dawn light filtered in through the slats covering the windows, illuminating those in attendance: the Devars' most trusted subordinates. First, there were Kaushal and Jayendhra, two of their cousins, from their paternal and maternal sides, respectively. While Kaushal didn't attach too much importance to their blood ties, Jayendhra was relentless, constantly pushing to be favored over the others. Hasan regretted the day he'd let his mother talk him into promoting him, but the deed was done.

Then there was Raman, a gruff, dark-skinned man who'd lost his left hand in an accident at an automotive manufacturing plant. Though the Welkish company that owned the factory made more money on each car than most Virians would make in a decade, it refused to pay him restitution, and the authorities claimed they could do nothing to compel payment. Raman had joined the gang shortly after to pay his hospital bills and make ends meet.

He sat beside Vinay, one of his oldest gang members, and the man who had helped Hasan on the Darsh Jana job. Hasan hadn't chosen him just for the wisdom that came with his age. By day, Vinay worked as an innocuous rickshaw driver, making him privy to the secrets of streets where Hasan was too conspicuous to go.

The only one better at spying than Vinay was Samina, who was the most recent one to be promoted to middleman. She had joined the gang with her half brother after burning down their orphanage. Despite her petite size, a by-product of childhood malnutrition, she was a force to be reckoned with and had clawed her way up the ranks quickly.

Last to arrive was Harithi, a tall, dark-skinned woman with sharp hazel eyes who took no shit and could do a whole lot of harm. Much like Samina, she'd joined the gang to provide for her younger siblings—but unlike Samina, she refused to speak about them at all, putting up an iron wall whenever asked.

These were the middlemen, all of them daivyakt, managing

their own crew of Hasan's spies and collecting money from most of his debtors, save for the slippery few like Darsh, who required personal home visits from the Jackal. They were the only people in the city privy to the brothers' entire operation.

"What are we doing here?" Hasan demanded.

Zeyar tilted his head at Raman, giving him permission to speak.

"I received intel from one of my spies this morning," Raman announced. "The *Rohini II* was raided, late last night. Her crew was taken into police custody at the main precinct, and even now they are being transported to the city jail."

The room might have fallen silent. It might have erupted into pandemonium. Hasan would never know, because his ears began ringing as though he'd been flung from an exploding building. Paranjay, arrested? It couldn't be. They needed him. *Hasan* needed him. His throat tightened as he tried to picture his brother's last moments as a free man. *A raid.* That meant police officers, pistols and nightsticks, and insatiable egos. Undoubtedly, Paranjay would have fought, which meant that the police would have retaliated. Hasan's fists tightened, unease and rage brewing inside him.

"Who was leading the raid?" Zeyar asked. Though his expression was blank and his posture unchanged, Hasan could tell that his brother was just as disturbed as he was.

Still, he couldn't curb the venom in his voice as he said, "Do you have to ask? There's only one squadron of the Marnapur police you haven't been able to bribe."

"The same squadron *you* insist on antagonizing, you mean?" Zeyar fired back, eyes blazing.

"Wait." Samina's soft voice interrupted them. "Let Raman finish. Is there any more information?"

Raman sighed, pressing his lips together. "My man says that the crew was outnumbered, at least three to one. Perhaps they suspected some of the crew were daivyakt and prepared accordingly. Most of the ship's crew tried to dive into the water and swim away, but the pigs had nets, and reinforcements came by motorboat to round up the rest. The spy counted eleven men taken into custody."

"Eleven?" Hasan sat upright. "Paranjay's crew numbers twelve, including himself. Where's the last man?"

"My team is looking," Raman said. Turning to the other middlemen, he added, "It's likely that whoever escaped will be injured. The officers brought guns with them, and my spy says shots were fired. Tell your crews to keep an eye out for healers' dens. The man won't risk visiting a hospital—not when he knows police are looking for him."

While Raman spoke, Hasan glanced over his head to the back of the room, where Zeyar leaned against the wall, lips pressed into a grim line. He lifted his scarred brow in a mirror of Hasan's expression. Both knew the same thing: If Paranjay was the twelfth man, he'd have already come home.

"The twelfth man will turn up." Hasan fought to keep his voice even. "We have eyes all over the city. But we need to come up with a plan to rescue the other eleven."

"I'll put some funds together," Zeyar said.

"Are you fucking serious?" Hasan stared at him. "You know Montrose can't be bribed. He's the reason we're in this mess."

"Perhaps Montrose and his inner circle can't be bribed," Jayendhra said, "but I seriously doubt that not one man guarding those cells would be impervious to a little windfall."

Hasan shot his cousin a glare, but before he could respond, Vinay asked, "Where do you intend to get the funds? We can afford ransom for two men, maybe three. But eleven?"

For a moment, Zeyar looked startled. His lips parted soundlessly, as though he hadn't considered the logistics, but Hasan knew him better than that. Zeyar never spoke without running some sort of cost-benefit analysis, calculating the return on investment of each word before he said it. His brother hadn't failed to do the math on his bribery scheme. He'd made his calculations with only one target in mind: Paranjay.

"What's the alternative?" Kaushal retorted, saving Zeyar from having to respond. "Attack the police headquarters?"

"Why not?" Hasan said. "If we gather all our fighters, we could overwhelm them."

"They have advanced weapons," Zeyar objected.

"We have daivyakhi."

Zeyar shook his head. "Only the daivyakt. The vasudhakt make up the bulk of our numbers, and they have neither magic nor weaponry. It would be a bloodbath."

"Attacking the precinct is not only risky," Harithi said, speaking for the first time, "but it will ruin our relationship with all of the police officers, including the ones who currently tolerate our operations. Right now, there is no evidence that we have daivyakt among us. A full display of divine power would ensure none of them work with us again."

"*Thank* you," Zeyar said.

"Your idea is preposterous too," Harithi informed him coolly, tossing her black braid over her back. "We could have the funds to ransom fifty men, and it still wouldn't work. Why? We're not bailing out one of our brawlers who got into an ill-advised spat. We're talking about a notorious drug smuggler and his crew, individuals who are connected to the infamous Jackal, who is a suspected heretic to boot. Montrose would hang the man who cost him such a prize. Even if the guards are not handpicked by him, there is no amount of money you could pay them to stick their necks out like that."

"Everyone has a price." Zeyar stared Harithi down.

She held his gaze, unflinching. "Not everyone."

Hasan cleared his throat, uncomfortable with the tension that had filled the room. "Okay," he said. "Since we can't come to an agreement, here's what we'll do. Everyone is to alert their network and ask them if they've seen anything suspicious. Harithi, Raman, I need you to coordinate moving our remaining opium stores to our storehouses in the countryside. Jayendhra, Kaushal, you'll work with Zeyar to check whose debts are coming up soon. See if you can collect early—chip off some interest if you must. Samina, Vinay, I need you to observe the police station. I want to know about the guards, their loyalties, how many officers are in the building—any information that could help us if we were to attack. Questions?"

No one spoke. Hasan nodded. "Okay. We'll regroup once we have more information. Dismissed."

His crew leaders shuffled out of the room without enthusiasm. Hasan couldn't blame them. The gang had suffered a heavy blow, and instead of making a united counterattack, they couldn't agree on a plan of action. They'd have one soon, he swore.

Vinay stopped near the door, resting a wrinkled, sun-browned hand on Hasan's shoulder. He didn't ask if Hasan knew what he was doing. If he felt any doubt at all, he didn't show it. Instead, he said, "I was there, when we lost your father. I know it's not the same, but it's hard nonetheless. I'm here if you need to talk."

Hasan's throat tightened. "We haven't lost Paranjay," was all he said. *Not yet.* The elder man squeezed his shoulder, then left.

Hasan turned around to see Harithi still there, her gaze

pinned on Zeyar. She rose, readjusting the dupatta on her shoulder. "Splitting up is a bad idea," she warned. Turning, she addressed Hasan. "You're wasting your time. You boys will need to get more creative than bribery and violence if you want to get out of this."

Hasan tightened his jaw. On any other day, in any other crisis, he'd have been more appreciative of Harithi's direct counsel. But today, it was all he could do not to make a scathing retort back. "Noted." He tilted his head at the door. "You're dismissed."

She pressed her lips together but left without another word. Zeyar pushed off the wall and collapsed into her empty chair, a cigarette dangling between his lips as he fumbled around for a lighter. Hasan's temper cooled. He reached over and used a pinch of his daivyakhi to light the end of his brother's cigarette.

"Thanks," Zeyar mumbled, inhaling deeply.

Hasan didn't say anything back.

Zeyar exhaled, blowing a thin stream of smoke into the air. With his eyes closed, he said, "I should have insisted that he make naumya before he left. If he'd been at full strength, he wouldn't have been captured."

Hasan's stomach twisted around something sharp. He knew Zeyar had been affected—how could he not be?—but he hadn't imagined that his brother was shouldering blame alone.

"Neither of us knew," he said. "How could we?"

"Well, I should have guessed," Zeyar said, acid in his voice. "After all, I haven't yet bribed all the police in the city. Just another weak spot I left open."

"Zeyar—"

"Don't, Hasan. Just don't."

"Fine." Hasan extended a hand. "At least give me a cigarette, then."

That earned him a raised brow. "You hate smoking," Zeyar said, but he gave Hasan a cigarette anyway.

That much was true. Hasan grimaced around the foul taste of tar. But he'd lost one elder brother, and all he wanted was to be with the other—even if they didn't know how to speak to each other without drawing blood. Cigarettes were safer than words. So, for the length of one cigarette, he sat with his brother, chest aching with grief, and inhaled smoke as the seconds turned to ash.

• • •

Two days later, the telephone rang again. Hasan picked it up on the second ring. On the other end of the line was Azha, a vasudhakt woman who served as one of the gang's healers.

"I've got the twelfth crewmate," she said. "Come quickly."

Hasan and Zeyar wasted no time. Zeyar drove them toward the industrial sector of the city, where a plethora of makeshift healers' dens had cropped up in response to the countless daily factory accidents. The air grew impossibly thicker, the stench of factory smoke clogging their lungs. Eventually, the backstreets grew too narrow, forcing them to get out and walk. Coal dust clung to the soles of Hasan's shoes. Ahead of him, Zeyar meticulously avoided the oil-slick puddles, mouth twisted in distaste.

When they got to the healer's, a dark-skinned woman in her thirties greeted them, her hair tied back into two tight braids.

"Azha," Hasan greeted her. "Where is he?"

"With Madam," Azha said. "The wound was infected. I needed her expertise."

Zeyar and Hasan exchanged an uneasy glance. There was only one woman *Madam* could be, and it was the last person they wanted involved right now: their mother. They'd both agreed not to tell her about the arrest until they'd settled on a plan of action, hoping to spare her—and themselves—for as long as possible. If she knew they had no plan, she would be merciless. Given that she had trained most of the healers affiliated with their gang, they should have known that there would be no excluding her for long.

Azha led the brothers into a den, the makeshift beds separated by an old curtain. Hasan yanked it aside, the curtain rings screeching against the bar.

Sure enough, Hasan's mother sat tending to her patient, strands of her black-and-silver bun coming loose as she bent over him. Rohini Devar was a woman of middling height and a soft build, though none who knew her would ever describe her as such. She'd once been a fearsome fighter in the gang, her intuition sharper than her blades, but as Hasan and his brothers had taken over, she had retired to the countryside, where she'd repurposed her intimate knowledge of human anatomy to teach other women the basics of healing.

His ma straightened to see who had arrived, leaving the patient's face clear: Paranjay's first mate, Sunil. Surprise winded Hasan—not because he was particularly shocked to see Sunil, but because he hadn't realized he was harboring hope like a dagger in his boot, and that misguided optimism had just stabbed him in the foot. He'd known it was impossible for Paranjay to be anywhere but in the clutches of the police, but there had still been opportunity for a miracle.

Not anymore, not with Sunil lying in front of him. An ugly gash on the side of his head wept pus, the stench so putrid that Hasan gagged involuntarily. Sunil whipped his head up at the sound, catching sight of Hasan. A medley of emotions played across his face: shock, guilt, fear, and anger.

"You told them I was here?" he demanded. "What happened to patient confidentiality?"

"Unfortunately, you only get that in a real hospital," Zeyar sneered, falling in line beside Hasan. "Why so nervous, Sunil? We aren't the police."

Sunil pressed his mouth into a flat line. "If you're here to blame me for what happened, then don't bother."

"No one's here to assign blame," Zeyar said. "We want to know what happened."

Sunil crossed his arms over his chest. "Swear you aren't here to punish me."

"We'd only punish you if you did something wrong." Hasan narrowed his eyes. Sunil's caginess reeked worse than his infected wound. "Got something to hide?"

Zeyar held up his hand. "You have my word. We won't harm you. Now, tell us what happened."

Sunil sighed, relenting. "We were loading the ship. It took longer than normal because Paranjay was late, so we had to load his share, and then we had a couple of new boys with us on this trip who were moving slowly. Paranjay was doing the final check in the hold when several cops—maybe twenty, thirty?—came up the dock. Most of them had nightsticks, some had handguns. It wasn't much of a fight. Paranjay tried to use his daivyakt to suffocate the officers, but he ran out quickly, and they overwhelmed him. One of them caught me in the back of the head, but he didn't knock me out fully. I jumped off the dock and swam under the boat. I had enough daivyakhi to create an air bubble there, so I waited—*hey!*"

Hasan launched himself at the first mate, striking him in the face with a satisfying crack.

"No attacking my patients," his ma scolded, shoving him

away. She lifted Sunil's chin, examining Hasan's handiwork as he cursed.

"You gave me your word!" Sunil cried. Blood oozed from both a broken nose and split lip, staining his teeth.

"You *ran away,* you coward!" Hasan moved to strike him again, but Zeyar grabbed him by the back of the jacket. "You could have fought, but instead you chose to save your own sorry hide."

"There was nothing I could do!" Sunil said. "They outnumbered us. What did you want me to do?"

"You could have come to us!"

"That is true," Zeyar said, turning to Sunil. "Why did you hide for two days instead of coming for help?"

"I didn't know what black deal you'd strike with the pigs," Sunil spat at Zeyar. "You'd trade anyone if you stood to profit. Obviously, Paranjay is the same, too, sending his thug brothers after me instead of dealing with me himself."

"He can't come after you because he's in *jail,*" Hasan snapped.

Zeyar winced. His ma went deadly still. Even Sunil gaped in shock, blood continuing to drip unnoticed from his broken nose.

His ma recovered first. "Paranjay is in jail?" she whispered.

"He is." Hasan jabbed a finger at Sunil. "Because this gutless idiot abandoned his crewmates."

"The only people responsible for Paranjay's kidnapping are *you*!" Sunil sat upright, glaring at the brothers. "I told him smuggling that much opium was dangerous, but you lot wanted to make more money per trip. It's your own greed that—"

Sunil stiffened. A scalpel gleamed at the base of his neck, sharp as the look in Rohini's eyes. "Get out of this clinic, before I cut you open to see if you're truly as spineless as you act."

"Madam!" Azha exclaimed. She'd been so quiet the whole

time, Hasan had nearly forgotten she was there. “What about the healer’s code? *Do no damage, take no sides.*”

“Oh, damn the bloody code,” Rohini said, but she lowered her scalpel. “You can finish draining his wound, Azha. I’ve gotten most of it, anyway.” She turned to look at her sons. “I want to speak to you both. Now. Outside.”

“Now you’ve done it,” Zeyar whispered as they followed their ma. “Great job. Magnificent.”

Now that his rage had ebbed, Hasan found himself regretting his outburst. “She was going to find out eventually.”

Rohini stopped in the hall, turning her furious gaze on the two of them. “What’s this about your brother being arrested?”

Zeyar gave Hasan a look that said, *All you, buddy.*

Hasan sighed. “Paranjay was supposed to make another shipment,” he said. He recapped Sunil’s story, combining it with the information Raman had given them to lay out what they knew thus far.

Their ma’s eyes flashed. “You’ve known about this for *two days*, and your first thought wasn’t to call your mother?”

“We didn’t want to worry you until we could get a plan in motion,” Zeyar said.

“And did you?” Rohini put her hands on her hips.

Hasan blinked. “Did we what?”

She narrowed her eyes at them. “Did you get a plan in motion?”

“Yes,” Zeyar bluffed.

“Okay,” she said slowly. “So, what is it?”

“We’re going to raid the precinct,” Hasan announced as Zeyar said simultaneously, “We’re going to bribe the guards.”

Hasan winced. “We have two plans,” he recovered. “Just to cover all our bases.”

"Dual strategies." Zeyar nodded emphatically. "A two-pronged approach."

"Okay," Rohini said. She stared at them dubiously, her sharp-eyed scrutiny piercing through their subterfuge. "I don't know what the hell you boys are doing. But you're adults now, and you have to learn how to take care of each other without my interference."

"We are," Zeyar promised. "We have it under control."

"Good." Their ma smiled dangerously. "Then prove it. Get your brother back, or die trying. Am I understood?"

Hasan swallowed. "Yes, Ma. Understood."

Chapter Five

Return of the Prodigal Daughter

Seven years after Poppy Sutherland's exile, she stood on the deck of the *Lady Audra* as the Marnapur skyline came into view, shimmering in the heat like a mirage. Over the last few days, the ocean skies had warmed rapidly as the ship approached her destination. Poppy closed her eyes and fanned herself in a futile attempt to cool down. How had she ever been used to this climate?

As the *Lady Audra* drew closer to shore, Poppy opened her eyes and peered over the railing. On the dock below, a group of people waited, waving at the ship.

Her breath caught in her lungs when she saw who was standing in front.

Her father had changed more than Poppy could have imagined. What was left of his salt-and-pepper hair had turned pale and wispy, like the clouds on a late-summer afternoon. His wise, stern face had wrinkles and stress lines that hadn't been there before. But the most noticeable change in his demeanor was his posture. The tall, proud man of her childhood had been shrunk by age and circumstance, shoulders sloped sideways as he leaned heavily on the tiger's-head cane in his right hand.

Unbidden, memories of the last time she had seen her father

at these same docks assaulted her. The humid air had pressed down on her skin, her face damp and sticky with tears. Her mother had hissed at her to wipe her swollen eyes before the papers got a photograph of her, she remembered. Officially, no one knew that she was being sent away as punishment, because her father hadn't wanted word of her transgression to get out. She'd given an emerald necklace to a Virian orphan, forgetting, in that moment, what it had been worth to her family.

When her father had found out, he didn't raise his voice at her—he never did—but his naked anger left her shaking. "That necklace belonged to my *mother,* who was part of the Imperial Family," he'd said. "It was a priceless family heirloom, and you all but threw it in the gutters."

And for all her begging and pleading, her father could not be moved from his resolve: The only way to take the Virian sympathies out of Poppy would be to send Poppy out of Viryana.

A crew member touched Poppy's shoulder, bringing her back to the present. The ship was still now, fully docked. He informed Poppy that the anchor had been dropped, and she could now disembark. Her legs trembled all the way down the gangplank. *You've been at sea for six weeks,* she told herself. Naturally she'd be a bit shaky. She needed to get accustomed to land again; that was all.

But she couldn't lie to herself: She trembled because she was scared. She had not been invited home. Boarding the *Lady Audra* was an act just shy of defiance, a willful display of independence when independence was a trait not valued in well-bred women. Would her father be disappointed in her change—or lack thereof?

Poppy's feet touched the sun-bleached wood of the dock. She took a deep breath, then turned to face the viceroy.

For a moment, the two could only stare at each other: father and daughter, separated by a few feet, and yet distant by seven years.

Then her father opened his arms, shaking visibly as he took his weight off his cane. "Poppy," he said, "you're home."

She choked back a sharp sob as she rushed forward, diving into his arms. It was a hug unlike any other that the pair had shared before. Both of them trembled. He was so much smaller than she remembered—or maybe she'd grown bigger. He felt frailer, his shoulders and chest narrower. Though the urge to clutch onto him overwhelmed her, she restrained herself, trying to be as gentle as possible with this new version of her father.

When the two disengaged, they looked at each other again in silence. Her father ran his eyes over her, his sharp gaze cataloging her differences the same way she'd sized him up just minutes ago. Was he pleased, she wondered, by what he saw? Had the last seven years apart been worth it? She opened and closed her mouth again and again, but nothing came out. It was frustratingly counterintuitive—she'd spent nearly a decade yearning to speak to her father in person again, and now that she was here in this long-anticipated, oft-imagined moment, she could not summon a single word.

Her mother saved her from having to speak. She pushed her way out of her husband's shadow and wrapped Poppy in a warm embrace. Poppy stiffened reflexively at the unexpected gesture. Mother had never been prone to physical affection—especially in public. *Coddling is for children,* she'd said. Poppy's throat tightened at the rare display of tenderness. Before her mother could withdraw, she wrapped her arms around her too. The hard knot of tension dissolved, slackening the lines of Poppy's limbs. This was where she belonged, on her island, among her family once again. She'd prepared for this moment for the last seven years, and it did not disappoint.

She only hoped that her parents felt the same about her.

"Come on," her father said roughly. "The car is waiting. Let's go home."

• • •

Although Poppy had just returned after six weeks at sea, Poppy's parents invited the other four First Families to dinner that same evening. The house bustled with activity: servants scrubbing already-spotless floors, grocers arriving with food that would have fed fifteen families, let alone five, and a pair of lady's maids, newly recruited by her mother to wait on Poppy now that she was home.

While one of the women drew a bath, the other began to help Poppy undress, whisking away her traveling clothes to be laundered while she sat in a plush robe, waiting for the tub to fill. Poppy crossed her arms over her chest. She hadn't had maids at Thornhaven, and she was suddenly, painfully aware of how different their bodies were from her own. They were svelte and graceful whereas Poppy was curvier in the bust and hips. Their skin was impossibly smooth, the hair on their arms fine and invisible whereas hers was thick and noticeable, even against her darker complexion.

One of the women freed Poppy's hair from its long braid, brushing out the knots as she sighed enviously. "You have such lovely hair," she gushed. "I would love to have hair even half as thick as this. I could do so much more with it."

Poppy's body relaxed a fraction, warming at her compliment. "I think the way you wear your hair suits you quite well," she told the maid. The other woman ducked her head quickly, but not before Poppy caught a glimpse of a smile.

When the bath was ready, Poppy nearly groaned aloud at how good the water felt. The two women took turns pouring water over her head. One of them massaged her scalp with shampoo, and then when they had rinsed it all away, they turned so that Poppy could get out of the bath and slide back into her robe.

With their help, Poppy dressed in the finest evening gown that she had brought back with her, sewn from heavy blush-pink silk with translucent chiffon butterfly sleeves. Poppy turned to the mirror, taking in her final appearance, admiring the complicated knot of braids at the top of her head. A few pieces had been left to frame her face, softening the look. The maids assisted her with her makeup, dabbing a light pink pigment on her eyelids and covering her face with a beige powder a few shades lighter than her skin.

Poppy's lips curled in satisfaction. She looked dignified. Regal. Against all odds, she looked like she had a place among the nobility. And if there wasn't one, she would carve it out herself.

• • •

The duke was already sitting at the head of the dining table when the Colwicks arrived. This was Welkish custom—no one was permitted to sit unless the highest-ranked person in the room was also seated. Lord Edward III, Earl of Marnapur, approached the duke first. His gangly heir, Edward IV, followed, while his wife and two daughters stood dutifully in their shadows.

"How good to see you, Lord Colwick," Clarence said. "I am glad you could come."

"Poppy grew up with us." The earl put a hand to his chest.

"It would have been like missing the homecoming of my own daughter."

He turned to where Poppy stood, behind the left side of her father's chair. She offered Edward III a gloved hand, which he accepted, kissing the knuckles as was customary. His thick russet mustache scratched the back of her hand even through the silk. "You've become a lovely lady, Poppy." He winked. "Wouldn't you agree, Son?"

The tips of Edward IV's ears turned pink. "She looks nice," he said, his voice muffled as he stared at his feet, awkward in the way teenage boys often were.

"I'm sure you remember my daughters, Lady Cassandra and Lady Olivia?" Edward III beckoned his daughters forward. "You spent many an afternoon with them as a girl."

Poppy tightened her grip on her banal smile before turning her gaze to the elder Colwicks. Olivia's and Cassandra's cherubic childhood features had evolved into hallmarks of Welkish femininity. Their round cheeks had melted into sharp cheekbones, and their matching ginger hair had darkened into auburn tresses.

Poppy had spent many an afternoon at the Colwick house, entirely against her own will. Her parents had insisted, even when she'd cried about how the girls went out of their way to make her feel like an outsider. They had taunted her about many things—her lack of a title, her low birth—but there was nothing that pleased them so much as ridiculing her appearance.

Once, on a picnic, Cassandra had removed her bonnet. "Careful, Cassandra," Olivia had snickered. "Too much sun and you'll become as dark as Poppy!"

If they had been bold enough to say such things to Poppy's face, then she was certain they had said far worse, especially when they'd giggled and whispered to each other and refused to let her in on the joke. All three of them had known that Poppy was the punch line. But no longer.

"Of course," Poppy drawled. "How could I forget?"

The two of them stared at Poppy, but she held their gazes. The girl who had shrunk under their insults was gone. This time when Cassandra and Olivia whispered to each other, there was no giggling.

Good.

In that same manner, the Sutherlands greeted two more families: the Whitecliffs, led by the Earl, Lord Arthur, with his heir Andrew and his younger twin sons, Augustus and Alexander, and then the Viscount Gerald Alderfort, with his wife and heir, James. His daughter, Geraldine, had married a minor lord in Welkland after graduating from Thornhaven a few years ago and rarely visited.

Only three seats remained empty. Before anyone could remark on their absence, the butler announced that the Montroses had arrived.

The Marquess, Lord William Montrose, entered first. Time had not been as harsh on the Montrose patriarch as it had been on Clarence. The only indication of his age was that his thick golden hair had now turned silver, even his eyebrows and well-kept beard. Beside him stood his wife, Lady Elizabeth Montrose. She was nearly unchanged, save for a new set of wrinkles and strands of white running through her chestnut bun.

"Lord Montrose," Clarence said. "Glad you could make it."

"A pleasure," Lord Montrose agreed.

Then their son walked in, and their voices fell away as Poppy's focus locked on him. Here at last was Richard Montrose II: high society's golden boy, the youngest captain on the Marnapur police force in history, and, if the *Miss Marnapur* magazine that

Catherine had regularly mailed Poppy throughout her time at Thornhaven was to be believed, the most eligible bachelor on the island. If Poppy wished to anchor herself to society, there was no stronger rock she could choose than Richard.

She sized him up discreetly, peeking through her lashes. She hadn't had much cause to interact with Richard when they'd been children, save for rare encounters when she visited Catherine. While Poppy's change had been a metamorphosis, Richard had only become more *himself.* His sandy-blond hair had deepened into a rich gold, and the freckles that had once dusted his nose and soft cheeks had given way to perfect, marble skin, with a jawline and cheekbones that could have made a sculpture weep.

Even his personality had grown stronger over the years. His friendly, boyish nature had translated into masculine confidence that made one avert their eyes in respect, the same way one never looked directly at the sun in all its brilliance. Despite his noble disposition, he wasn't cold or haughty. He smiled warmly at the other guests, even offering young Edward IV a brisk handshake that left the younger boy starry-eyed. Poppy could see why his superiors had taken to him so quickly, promoting him not once but *thrice* in the last seven years.

In a way, he reminded her of the man her father had been when she'd left: vital, ambitious, and intelligent. *Miss Marnapur* had not led her astray—if there was ever a man to take as husband, it was this one.

At that moment, Richard turned and caught Poppy staring. She met his gaze, then immediately dropped her eyes, feigning bashfulness. *Gawping is unladylike,* the Hawk had instructed, *but when it comes to gentlemen, a little eye contact goes a long way.*

Richard pulled out the chair closest to Poppy. Her skin warmed under her dress in response. She inhaled, remaining calm and smiling demurely at him before focusing on her plate.

The first course arrived quickly: a fresh salad of dark-green leaves mixed with nuts and sweet oranges, tossed in bitter dressing. As was custom, the table waited for the duke to take the first bite before diving in. The conversation flowed as easily as the wine and food. A lamb roast followed the salad, which was succeeded by sweet rice pudding for dessert.

For the most part, the men carried the conversation. *How interesting, that this dinner was meant to honor my return, and yet no one wants to hear from me,* Poppy thought, but she held her tongue, determined to make the best impression on Richard. He was quiet, too, speaking only when spoken to. His humility was a pleasant surprise, especially given his accomplishments, but she wished he'd speak more, to give her clues on how to win him.

Eventually, Lord Montrose insisted that Richard tell the other guests about a major breakthrough in a case he'd been working on. Richard hesitated, then relented.

"I can't say much right now, as the investigation is ongoing," he cautioned, "but I have good cause to believe that there's a web of organized crime in Viryana that seeks to corrupt Welkland through the drug trade."

Disconcerted murmurs broke out around the table.

"Is it related to the Jackal?" Lady Olivia asked, wide-eyed, causing a second round of chatter.

Poppy blinked, confused but unwilling to expose her ignorance. However, Richard turned to her anyway, explaining, "Since you've been gone, a criminal who identifies himself as 'the Jackal' has risen to notoriety. He's responsible for various grifts, extorting the poor, dealing in contraband, committing murder and arson. What makes him so difficult to catch, however, is the complexity behind his schemes. We estimate his network to include over two hundred people, which would make him the head of the largest organized crime setup in the city, if not the island."

"Crime has certainly spiked," Lord Alderfort said meaningfully. "It was never like this before, was it, Your Grace?"

Poppy recognized the thinly veiled accusation as easily as her father. "Crime rates have gone up with the population," he replied, lifting one brow. "Any man who understands numbers will understand this. As the poverty rate has increased, resources are stretched thin. We need to have a firm hand with these people, just as the Founder would have done."

The Founder was the first Welkish king. Before he'd united Welkland under his banner, the people on the continent had lived in motley villages and towns, with limited trade or interaction. His writings described how he'd rallied the people, flushing out those who wielded the "unnatural and arcane" practice of magic as a means of oppressing and dividing the common folk. With such inequality gone, he raised Welkland to a free society where everyone had a purpose and a place. In the absence of magic, new advancements in medicine and industrialization abounded, allowing Welkland to develop exponentially. His teachings became a manifesto for his successors, who followed one of the final instructions in the book like a commandment: To go and shape other nations in the world so that they might resemble the utopia of Welkland.

Talk of the Founder jostled something in Poppy's brain. She glanced at Richard, at the red stripe of his captain's uniform, then took a deep breath. "If I may, my lords."

The rest of the room turned to stare, but Poppy continued. "The Founder writes that crime is the hobby of an idle man. Instead of using his energy and talent to contribute to a greater society, he uses it to benefit himself. We ought to encourage these men to make better use of themselves than such selfish pursuits."

"And how do you propose we do that, Miss Sutherland?" This question came, as Poppy hoped it might, from Richard. He held her gaze, interest clear in his blue eyes.

"We ought to penalize indolence," she replied, speaking directly to him. "On the drive home, I saw so many men lounging in the streets, unoccupied. These men ought to be fined for loitering. That will motivate them to find other, more productive places to be."

Poppy finished her speech, taking a bite of rice pudding in an attempt to erase the foul taste on her tongue. Her suggestion was repulsive—not to mention illogical. The solution to unemployment was *not* to strip those without income of whatever little funds they might have. But to this audience, poverty was a crime, a moral failing meant to reassure them about the integrity of their own immense wealth while others went without. Punishment would appeal to them, even if it didn't solve the problem.

Her mouth still tasted bitter. Poppy recalled her earlier determination. *If there is no place for me at this table, I will carve it out myself.* No matter what it took.

She picked up her spoon and took another bite of her rice pudding, hyperaware of Richard's eyes roving over her face. She resisted the urge to fidget. The Hawk had beaten that behavior out of her during her first few months at Thornhaven, but between her ugly words and Richard's gaze, the impulse resurfaced in full force.

Finally, his lips curled upward. "An interesting solution," Richard allowed, and Poppy could have sworn that a hint of admiration laced his tone.

She tentatively smiled back, then ducked her head again.

Poise is a must in a lady, the Hawk had preached, *but there is a fine line between being self-assured and being arrogant.*

Cassandra cleared her throat, pulling the attention to herself. She leaned forward, her rouged lips forming a sly smile Poppy recognized from girlhood. "Did you study the works of the Founder when you were in Welkland, *Miss* Sutherland?" she asked, leaning on the common prefix. "I don't recall your being so . . . educated."

Poppy clenched her teeth at the thinly veiled insult but forced herself to smile at Lady Cassandra. "I did. We even had a chance to see the capital and tour the places where he once lived. It was a transformative experience."

"I daresay the whole seven years was transformative," Lord Whitecliff said. "Your Grace, it is no secret that I had my reservations about your decision to adopt a Virian. In fact, I recall a conversation we had where I insisted that it was impossible to change the nature one had been born with, and you would only ever find disappointment by pursuing such a path. It seems, however, that I underestimated the power of a good Welkish education. You have become a rarity, Miss Sutherland."

"Poppy always had it in her." Her father beamed. "In a way, she is the perfect example of what we can achieve on the island. Every Virian has the capacity to become an educated, well-mannered, productive member of society, if only they'd let go of their uncivilized ways. Would you believe that they used to have a barbaric system of segregation? Everything was determined by the circumstances of their birth—the jobs one could hold, the public space one could occupy, even the people one could marry. When we assumed control, we did away with this, naturally, and modernized the law.

"But that core belief, that one can't rise above the caste assigned at one's birth, is what makes the Virian people so averse to self-improvement. It's deeply ingrained in their psyche, this idea that no one can change. But we know better, and it's up to us to use the wisdom the Founder left us to make the island a better place, as Poppy just demonstrated."

"Thank you, Father," Poppy said, though his praise only further stirred her guilt over her vile suggestion. The only thing she could agree with him on was the caste system. Every citizen should have a chance at upward mobility, regardless of the station of their birth—after all, hadn't Poppy herself had that benefit? If she'd been condemned to live out her life confined to the circumstances of her birth, she'd have been a street rat and a thief at best. But the duke had taken a chance by adopting her, and she hoped that he knew how much that meant. In a rare, genuine moment, she blurted out, "I've worked hard to make you proud."

He beamed at her. "You have. You are the best heir I could have hoped for." Poppy's heart swelled, tripping slightly over the word *heir.* "Your use of the Founder's teachings—most men would try and come up with their own solution, but we should all strive to put the wisdom of the Founder first. Though you may be a woman, you're a natural-born problem solver." His gaze swept across the room. "See how she speaks? She commands the attention of others like a true leader. If she were a man, she'd have done well as viceroy." He turned his expression back to Poppy, pride glinting in his eyes. "Even as the next viceroy's wife, she holds the potential to make great change. Any man who weds her would be a fool to exclude her from his office."

By the time her father's speech was done, Poppy didn't know quite where to look. She had to fight the urge to duck her head. She'd never heard him extol her virtues for so long, or so publicly. Old age must have made him more generous. Either that or he'd had a touch too much wine.

As the servants cleared the dessert, her father rose. "Gentlemen, if you'd follow me to my study, we can continue our conversation there. Perhaps with a glass of port?"

Per custom, the women and men began to separate. As Poppy rose to follow the other ladies, Richard stopped her with a hand on her arm. Her heart jumped in her chest at the contact, but she schooled her features into a neutral expression the way the Hawk had taught her. A lady knew when to hide how she really felt, *especially* in the presence of a gentleman.

"Forgive me for being so direct." Richard clasped his hands behind his back. "I must say how much I admired your response. Your father is justified in his praise."

Poppy concealed her satisfied smirk with a demure glance down at her feet. "I'm flattered you think so, Captain."

"Do you envision yourself as an advisor to your future husband, when he is viceroy?" he inquired. "Most women don't pay much mind to politics."

Poppy considered this, unsure what response would please him. She settled for a coy reply. "I am not most women, Captain Montrose."

He winked. "I can see that." He drew himself to his full height, pushing his chest out. "Well, it was a pleasure meeting you again, Miss Sutherland. I won't keep you from the ladies any longer. Have a lovely evening."

"You as well," she said, smiling sweetly. As soon as he left the room, she let her face drop into a scowl. *That* certainly wasn't the desired outcome. Dinnertime niceties were an obligation, not the sign of an interested gentleman. Poppy would have to orchestrate another encounter with Richard—and when they met again, she'd ensure he walked away wanting more.

Chapter Six

To Hook a Husband

The morning after the dinner, Poppy set out to visit the one person she had yet to see: Catherine. Despite having once been a Montrose, she'd not been invited to last night's dinner on account of her husband's status as one of the Second Families of society. This kind of social demotion was akin to Poppy's worst nightmare, but Catherine had insisted on Theodore, much to the disapproval of her parents, who had been determined she accept James Alderfort's suit.

But Catherine loved Theodore, as she'd repeatedly told Poppy in her letters, and he was worth more to her than the rights accorded to a daughter of a First Family. According to her, he worked twice as hard as any heir, even those in the First Families. The Oakburys had made their living as shipbuilders in Welkland, but in Viryana, they'd expanded to logging and lumber, acquiring land and wealth. Allegedly, the Oakbury family was now as wealthy as the Alderforts.

Poppy hadn't had the chance to form an opinion on Theodore herself, having never met him. Headmistress Thornhaven had refused to grant her leave to attend the wedding. However in the three years since, Catherine had never written anything but the highest praises of her husband in her letters.

As the driver helped Poppy out of the car, the front door flew open, and a blur of blue and blond shot down the driveway. She had barely stepped clear of the car when Catherine engulfed her in a hug.

"You're here!" she exclaimed. "I can't believe it."

Catherine drew back, allowing Poppy a better look at her. She'd changed, albeit so subtly that only someone who had been away for seven years would have noticed. As a girl, she refused to put her hair up, trying to conceal what she called the "obscenely spherical" shape of her head. Now she wore her blond hair in a high bun, unconcerned about anyone noticing how round her head was. Where before she'd avoided bright colors for fear that they would draw attention to her, today she wore a bold cerulean dress that fit her generous curves well.

There were a hundred tiny different changes about her, but they all pointed back to one major difference: For the first time since Poppy had known her, Catherine was truly comfortable in her own skin.

"You've blossomed," Poppy said. "I feel as though I am looking at the woman you were always meant to be."

Catherine laughed. "I could say the same about you!" she gushed, guiding Poppy inside. Her maid brought over a tea tray, complete with a small tower of sandwiches and savory pastries. Catherine prepared Poppy's cup for her, adding her preferred amounts of milk and sugar from memory, as though it had only been seven days since her last visit, not seven years.

"I trust that the weather has been pleasant?" Poppy asked as she accepted her teacup.

"Asking about the weather?" Catherine let her jaw drop in mock horror. "I thought Thornhaven was meant to make you an educated lady, not a bore! Did you perhaps forget your personality on the boat?"

The pair burst into laughter at the same time. "Founder above, how I've missed you." Poppy sighed. "You must tell me everything. How have you been? How's married life?"

"Oh, what kind of hostess would I be if I talked about myself?" Catherine waved her hand. "Tell me about Thornhaven. You must have so many stories. In your letters, it seemed positively picturesque!"

Poppy winced. Her time at Thornhaven had not been *picturesque*, but Catherine had been such a gentle soul at sixteen, and Poppy's departure had broken her heart. She had been determined to put on a brave face for Catherine, unwilling to taint their limited communications with misery, knowing that she would be positively sick with worry if she'd known how horrid things really were.

But Catherine was no longer the teary, tenderhearted girl she'd once been. Even now, as the silence stretched, realization crept across her face. Slowly, Poppy said, "It was not quite as idyllic as I made it out to be. The headmistress had certain . . . ideas. About Virians."

Understanding dawned in Catherine's eyes. "Oh, Poppy," she breathed, coming to sit on the settee beside her. "You didn't have to pretend on my account."

"I could hardly burden you," Poppy protested. "I did want to tell you, eventually, but I couldn't. I'd pretended for years, and I didn't want you to think I was lying about the truth."

Catherine wrapped Poppy in a hug, one that was somehow more fierce than the one they'd shared on the driveway. "Never worry about that," she said. "You are my closest friend. I'll always believe you. You can tell me anything, no matter how unpleasant."

Poppy cracked a smile, trying to lighten the mood. "Well, if we're sharing unpleasantries, Headmistress Thornhaven was a *tyrant*. She had more rules than the Virian criminal code!"

Catherine smirked. "I suspect she was overcompensating for some dark sin of hers. It's often the prissiest of ladies with the worst habits. Why, I don't think I told you this, but you know Mrs. Ravenshaw?"

Poppy's eyebrows knit as she tried to recall. "The one who used to insist that unwed girls should not wear dresses with short sleeves at parties?"

"The very same. She was widowed just a few months ago. Her husband had a fondness for hunting tigers up north close to Jahnapur, a habit that got the best of him. She still wears the mourning black, but it's no secret that she's carrying on with her stable master."

Poppy choked on her tea. "You jest!"

Catherine shook her head. "No, I'm serious!" Her smirk grew more pronounced, and she added, "I heard that he's taught her to ride more than a horse."

Poppy's face burned at the lewd joke. "You're horrid." She sniffed, but she couldn't restrain a snicker, which gave way to an avalanche of giggles.

The two women laughed, sides aching with merriment. The noise echoed through the space, drowning out the sound of the door opening.

"What are you two giggling about?"

Poppy sat up straight. She recognized the newcomer instantly, his face unchanged from the wedding picture Catherine had mailed her three years ago.

That black-and-white photograph had done Theodore Oakbury no justice. Now that Poppy sat before him, she had to admit he was quite possibly one of the most handsome men in society. His hair was the same sandy brown as the beaches at Cloudcliff; his eyes were the frothy green of the sea. He wore thin wire-frame glasses, which were presently perched on his freckle-dusted nose. His lips, fuller than those of most Welkish men, twisted into a boyish smile when he saw Catherine. She had also gone starry-eyed, her gaze softening on him.

"Hello, lovely," he greeted her, then turned to Poppy. "This must be Miss Sutherland."

"Oh, where are my manners?" Catherine fussed, remembering herself. "Poppy, may I introduce my husband, Theodore Oakbury?"

"Pleasure to meet you at last, Mr. Oakbury," Poppy said. "I've heard a great deal about you."

"Please, Theodore is fine." He waved his hand, plucking a sandwich from the tray before taking a seat. "How are you spending your time now that you're back, Miss Sutherland?"

"Call me Poppy," she insisted. "I'm devoting my time to getting reacquainted with the city. You know, making the rounds, slowly working my way back into society. I'm sure you heard about my father's stroke?"

"It caused quite the stir," Theodore said. "Thank the Founder, His Grace seems to be doing much better now."

"Thank the Founder," she agreed. "But the doctor has recommended he begin to wind down. Given the state of the colony, particularly this city, I know he won't relax. It's imperative to me that I lighten some of his burden. I intend to find a husband who can support my father, aid him in his official duties."

"Well, I wish you luck in your search. Any gentleman would be lucky to have you."

"Do you have anyone in mind?" Catherine's blue eyes sparkled with curiosity. "I could make introductions if you'd like."

Poppy recalled the way Richard had turned his back on her at dinner. "Actually . . ." She paused to take a breath. "Do you know if your brother is courting anyone?"

Theodore and Catherine stiffened simultaneously, exchanging a look. "Oh, Poppy," Catherine breathed. "Surely, you don't wish to pursue *Richard*?"

The dismay in her tone did not surprise Poppy. Richard had not been a gentle elder brother to Catherine—he always had some critique about her body, her dress, her posture, her speech. Even as they'd grown into adults, Catherine had continued to write about Richard's incessant interference with her life and her marriage, which he had vehemently opposed on the grounds that the Oakburys were one of the Second Families—a group of untitled merchants within society who had managed to accumulate wealth equivalent to that of the nobility.

All this to say, she had not expected Catherine to endorse her brother as a life partner so easily. But she had seen the way the others had interacted with Richard last night, how they all naturally deferred to him, respecting his authority. That's what she needed: the social immunity of the Montrose name and title. These were the tools with which she would carve her place in society. Catherine wouldn't understand, not when she had traded privilege for love.

Poppy tried a different approach, drawing her face into a picture of hurt. "Whyever not? I thought you'd be enthusiastic at the idea of us becoming sisters."

Catherine flushed, stung. "We are already sisters." She took Poppy's hand. "We don't need to be connected by a man for this to be true."

"Catherine, it must be Richard." Poppy drew her hand back

to count on her fingers. "He's the heir of a First Family, which means that he will come into the title. He's well regarded in society. And he has the skills and experience necessary to assist Father."

"He's a beast of a man," Theodore said, his contempt surprising Poppy. "Oh, he's charming when he needs to be, but a bully to those he deems beneath him. Prideful and arrogant, utterly backward. You could not do any worse than that preening peacock, I assure you."

"Theo is right, Poppy," Catherine said. "You deserve a man who will cherish you, and I am not confident that my brother is that man."

Poppy shook her head. "I am not like you, Catherine, and you know it. I cannot afford to marry a man for love. I have no title, no male next of kin beyond my ailing father. My husband's name will become my sole power in this society that barely tolerates me. You did not see, last night, how they hardly spoke to me, except to cross-question me and ply me with backhanded compliments. There are many who would be pleased if, when my father passes away, I fade away for good. Only the best match will keep me anchored here beyond a doubt."

"I would keep you," Catherine said. "I will not let them discard you."

"Without a title, I will only be fit to be kept as a maid." Poppy spread her arms, gesturing at her skin. "Look at me, Catherine. It is no secret why the Imperial Family has denied me a courtesy title, even though my father is the emperor's cousin. The Colwick girls used to remind me every time I went to their house. My place is at the bottom of the social hierarchy—unless I can climb to the top of the highest possible family tree."

Catherine's mouth thinned.

Poppy saw the opening and pressed harder. “Please, won't you support me?”

“He's not a good man, Poppy.” Catherine put her face in her hands. “How can you ask me to send you in harm's way?”

“He will not harm me.” Poppy pulled her friend's wrist down into her lap, forcing the other woman to look at her. “If I ever feel unsafe with him, even for a *second*, I will drop this pursuit. I swear it.”

Theodore and Catherine exchanged a long, loaded look. Theodore's face was hard and unrelenting, but Catherine's shoulders softened, her resolve crumbling.

Finally, she said, “I won't be the one to introduce you, but . . . Richard always attends the dawn service at the Marnapur Cathedral at the beginning of every month.”

“Why, that's tomorrow.” Poppy clapped her hands together. “Excellent.”

Catherine pursed her lips. “I know I can't change your mind, Poppy, but be careful.” She hesitated, then added, “Richard and I aren't close for a reason. Every rose has thorns, no matter how soft its petals.”

• • •

“Miss Sutherland? Is that you?”

Poppy swallowed her smug grin and donned a look of surprise before turning around. Richard Montrose stood at the top of the stairs leading to the Marnapur Cathedral. She'd made sure to sit in the first row during the service, giving him ample time to notice her. Now, she studied him back, taking in his perfectly coiffed gold locks and neatly pressed suit.

“Why, it is you,” Richard said. “What are you doing here?”

"It's the first of the month," she replied, as though it were obvious. "I wanted to attend the service."

He lifted a brow. "At dawn?"

Poppy brushed a lock of hair over her ear. "The purpose of the service is to focus our intentions for the month. I find that coming first thing in the morning is most effective. Start as you mean to go on, as they say."

"That's a personal philosophy of mine." Richard's eyes widened in approval. He came down to stand on the steps beside her. "What did you think of Founderson Harold's reading?"

Founderson Harold had been a dead bore. Between the dawn hour and his droning, Poppy's jaw ached from the yawn she'd repressed the entire service. Today's reading, a transcript of the Founder's diary detailing his reflections on his voyage to discover new nations, had been particularly dull. The founderson then proceeded to opine for thirty minutes straight on how each person could go on a voyage inside their own souls, and search for the spirit of giving to donate to the work that the fellowship was doing. By the time the founderson had recited the dismissal—*Go and make civilized men of all nations, just as I have made of you*—she was nearly weeping for joy.

Still, Poppy enthused, "It was quite poignant. He has a certain gravitas that gives life to the Founder's writings, wouldn't you say?"

"I couldn't agree more." Richard gave Poppy a slow once-over, taking in the slim fit of her pastel-yellow dress, the shadow-spill of her long, shiny tresses over her shoulders and back. "Forgive me for being so forward, but would you be available for dinner? Perhaps tomorrow evening? I will secure the consent of His Grace, naturally."

Poppy dipped her head, satisfaction hidden under her show

of shyness. "Of course," she murmured. "I'd be honored."

"Excellent." He straightened up, swelling with gratification. "I will have an invitation sent to your house. I look forward to it, Miss Sutherland."

"As do I, Captain," Poppy replied, her first truth in this conversation. "Until then."

• • •

The following evening, Richard picked Poppy up in a silver Peregrine sedan. He took her for a drive around the scenic parts of the city, going up into the hills. The purple peak of the volcano, Mount Rukmini, shimmered through the haze, visible even all the way on the opposite side of the island. Below, the cars moved like ants in the downtown core. Even more gorgeous was the ocean, shimmering like a jewel. From this vantage point, the boats looked like toys floating in a bath.

Richard had made reservations at Willington's, a high-end restaurant that offered seating only to the city's elite. He spared no expense, ordering a tray full of tiny cheese and spinach quiches to start, followed by an entrée of tender steak, buttery green beans, and fragrant mashed potatoes that melted on the tongue.

While they dined, Richard told stories of the city from when Poppy had been absent. Occasionally, he'd ask her a question or two, but she kept the conversation on him, digging for details that she could use in her pursuit. Despite his earlier hesitation to speak about his work, she quickly found that it was one of his biggest sources of pride, just as much as his heritage. He spoke at length about different raids and investigations he had led, emphasizing his refusal to take bribes the way many of his colleagues did.

"They disgust me," he said, leaning forward. "To prioritize personal gain over one's duty to the state? It's corruption of the soul. There's a reason I'm the best at what I do: Once I set my sights on something, I never compromise."

"Never?"

"Never," he affirmed. He let his eyes linger on her face, his gaze dropping to her mouth. In a low voice, he added, "I always get what I want."

Poppy didn't have to feign the goose bumps that rose on her arms.

When the main course concluded, Richard turned the conversation to her. "More wine?" he asked, extending the bottle toward her.

She shook her head, drawing her glass back an inch. If she wanted to catch a man as sharp as this one, she would need all her wits about her. "No, I'm quite all right, thank you, Captain."

He didn't withdraw his arm. "You don't enjoy wine?"

"I find I enjoy the company of others more."

Richard laughed, setting the bottle down. "You're refreshing, Miss Sutherland. Most women would have seized the chance to drink their fill on another man's tab."

"Didn't I tell you I wasn't like most women?" Poppy lifted a brow flirtatiously.

"You didn't have to tell me for me to know that," Richard said. "Not many women have studied the Founder the way you have. Oh, they all attend the monthly services, but your comprehension of his texts is far more advanced. Tell me, Miss Sutherland, what is it about the Founder's texts that fascinates you?"

Fascination was an apt descriptor for Poppy's feelings about the texts, though likely not for the reason Richard thought. Her dilemma was this: If they were a guide to replicating the Welkish utopia in Welkland's colonies, why was Viryana suffering? If every man had an equal right to a role in society, why had her people been forgotten in the slums—or, worse, the morgues? Where was their place? Where were their rights?

But she couldn't criticize her father or his ancestors on the first date, so instead, she chose a half truth: "I find myself drawn to the Founder's conviction that all other nations of men can become equal to Welkland," she hedged. "I am, of course, an example of this. But so many of my brethren resist the teachings of the Founder. I took it upon myself to learn his works better so that I could enlighten other Virians, just as the Founder commanded."

"A noble cause," Richard said, "especially given the example you'll set once you're wife to the viceroy. Do you see yourself ruling by the side of your husband, then?"

It didn't escape Poppy that this was the second time he'd asked how she intended to work with her husband. Hopefully, he was envisioning himself in the role.

She tilted her chin down, glancing up at Richard demurely. "Well, it would depend on whether he wanted me there. But I wish to be more involved than previous wives."

Richard winked. "I don't think there's any man on the island who wouldn't want you beside him, Miss Sutherland."

Though Poppy assured him she was full, Richard insisted on ordering a three-tier stand of pastries. They couldn't bring themselves to finish even two tiers and had to send the rest back to the kitchen. Richard handed the waiter a wad of bills without counting them and rose to his feet.

As promised, he returned Poppy to the Sutherland estate by sunset. As he helped her out of the car, she gazed up at him through her lashes. "I had a lovely time, Captain Montrose."

He flashed her a charming grin. "It was my pleasure, truly."

He offered her his arm, and she threaded her own through his, resting her hand against his bicep. Interlocked, they made their way up the staircase. Just as Poppy was about to knock, Richard laid his hand over the knocker, stopping her.

His blue eyes met hers. “Forgive me if my directness offends you, but would you be agreeable to meeting again, sometime soon? Perhaps in two days, for luncheon?”

Poppy had to bite the insides of her cheeks to keep the satisfied smirk from blooming across her face. “The idea would be *most* welcome. I look forward to it.”

Chapter Seven

Unbalanced

Hasan summoned his crew leaders back to the shipping office to compile their notes so far. He'd been in touch with Samina and Vinay as they'd conducted their stakeout of the police precinct, and what they had reported back had been less than promising. A week ago, he would have secretly hoped that Zeyar's plan had crumbled as well, just so he wouldn't have to hear his brother gloat until the end of time. But now, two weeks into Paranjay's arrest, he would have gladly traded a lifetime of *I told you so*'s from Zeyar to have his brother back.

Once the eight had convened, Hasan tilted his head to Samina and Vinay. "You two go first," he said. "Get the rest of the room up to speed."

Vinay cut to the chase. "Attacking the police precinct is not a viable option."

Hasan snuck a glance at Zeyar, expecting to see a smug grin. But Zeyar's mouth was pressed into a flat line, which could only mean one thing: He didn't have good news, either.

"Long story short," Vinay continued, "Paranjay and his men are not being kept in the standard cells. They're being held below ground, in isolation cells reserved usually for the most violent of criminals. At least one of Montrose's men is scheduled on every shift."

"Poppy Sutherland's return has complicated things immensely, as well." Samina's lips puckered slightly, as though she'd bitten something sour. "The security measures have tightened, and there are more police per shift than usual."

"Thank you," Hasan said, permitting them to sit with a nod. "Jayendhra, Kaushal, Zeyar—any luck on your front?"

"None," Kaushal said, confirming Hasan's earlier intuition. His heart sank.

Jayendhra lay out tables of calculations. "We were able to collect on the debts owed from two men, and two more indicated they could repay us this week. Even so, if we set the cost at a hundred thousand crowns per prisoner, we could only realistically afford to spring five."

"This, of course, doesn't factor in what you learned, which is that Montrose has handpicked a guard on every shift," Kaushal added. "With that in mind, our odds go from low to nonexistent."

"So we're back to square one," Harithi said. "I told you from the start—we need to think out of the box on this one."

Hasan had run out of patience. Nothing was going right. Despite his prayers and hard work, their position hadn't changed in the last fourteen days. The gods mocked Hasan—he didn't need Harithi to deride him too. "Do you have any suggestions?" he snapped at her. "No? Didn't think so."

Harithi pursed her lips. "I understand you're frustrated, but that doesn't mean you can lash out at the rest of us."

"Frustrated?" He barked out a humorless laugh, crossing arms over his chest. "Harithi, my brother has been in the clutches of the police for fourteen days, and we still don't have a plan to rescue him. *Frustrated* doesn't cover it. What if it were one of your brothers arrested? Would you like it if all I had to bring to the table was *I told you so*?"

Harithi bared her teeth at him. "My brothers will never be part of this world. You leave them out of this."

"Okay," Zeyar cut in, putting a hand on Harithi's shoulder. "We're not going to make any headway when emotions are running high."

Harithi rolled her shoulder sharply, dislodging Zeyar's hand. Her chair screeched back. Tossing her thick mane of curls over one shoulder, she stalked out of the office.

Hasan sighed, pushing his hand into his hair. His temper cooled, but the flash fire of his anger had burned up the rest of his patience. This meeting was pointless when none of them had anything worthwhile to share. "Unless someone here has an *out-of-the-box* idea, I suggest you leave too."

The others exchanged glances, but eventually, they got up and left, one by one. Vinay patted Hasan's back gently. "You'll find a way," he said, then disappeared into the night.

When it was just the two of them, Zeyar said, "That was unwise. We can't be divided now, else we'll never get Paranjay back."

"We've been divided in our approach from the beginning," Hasan pointed out. "Splitting into two groups, investigating two different plans."

"And look how far that got us," Zeyar said, gesturing outwardly. "Look. I know we don't see eye to eye. But we challenge each other, and that's the only way either of us is going to come up with a solution outside of our usual methodology. We can't waste any more time or energy fighting each other."

Hasan sighed. Though he wanted to hit something, his brother was right—all their effort had to go into rescuing Paranjay. "We wouldn't fight so much if you tried to see things my way."

"I *have* tried to see things your way," Zeyar said. "The issue is, your world is one of absolutes. Black and white. Enemy and ally. Right and wrong. You push your own ideals on everything. You can't divide the world into fixed categories."

Hasan's brows knit as he tried to come up with a rebuttal. The best he could do was "And you don't?"

"The only categories in my world are useful and useless, and I reevaluate them constantly." Zeyar shrugged. "Whenever something fails to serve my objectives, it falls into the second category."

Hasan paused, fiddling with a pen as he considered that. He liked having a firm platform to stand on, a fixed set of rules that made the world make sense. Zeyar's method of living—where enemy could become ally on a whim—made him uneasy, like the ground beneath his feet was constantly shifting, throwing off his balance. Maybe Zeyar was right about him and the way he viewed the world.

"Very well," he said. "I see your point. I will be more open-minded—as long as you do the same. I want my ideas heard."

"Fine," Zeyar said, "as long as you bring your ideas to me *before* you enact them, instead of *after.* We need to make decisions together—not based on your personal moral code."

"Deal." Hasan took Zeyar's outstretched hand, shaking it once firmly. Though they were objectively no closer to saving Paranjay than they'd been that morning, Hasan couldn't help but feel like they had made a little progress, after all.

Chapter Eight

A Famished Nation

Though the viceroy's doctors had ordered him to ease his workload, Poppy caught her father in his office early one morning, half hidden behind a mountain of paperwork.

"You're not meant to be overworking yourself," she chided, stepping into the office. The space had not changed much while she'd been gone. The magnificent desk sat on the same carpet, the same curios and leather-bound books lined the glossy wooden shelves, and the tiger pelt hanging on the wall remained bright and glossy. Still, the room felt different, inexplicably smaller. She took a slow turn about the room, stopping in front of the framed map of the empire on the wall. It had changed marginally since her girlhood—primarily, the shift in borders as the empire inexorably expanded its reach.

Her father glanced up over his spectacles. "The colony won't run itself, Poppy."

"Let me help you, at least," she said. She sat in front of his desk, turning a stack of the papers to face her. She half expected him to shoo her off, insisting this was no work for a woman, but he let her stay, so she sorted his correspondence and skimmed reports.

As she examined the bookkeeping, something about one of the tables gave her pause. It was a summary of agricultural exports from the previous month, but the figures seemed too high for one month. She read the list again: *Cotton, pulses, rice, sugar, tea leaves . . .*

The list cataloged the number of pounds that had been exported, as well as the companies that had exported them. She was no expert in trade, but these numbers were double what she would have expected for an island of their size, even if they'd had an unusually bountiful season. If so much raw material had left the island, then what on earth had been left for the local population? There had to be a mistake.

She cleared her throat. "Father."

"Hm?" He looked up from his paper. "What is it?"

"This report." She flipped it around so he could see. "There must be some mistake. The figures are too high."

He took the paper from her, peering down his nose at the numbers. After a minute or two, he grunted, shoving the sheet back. "It's correct."

She stared at him. "But how? The agricultural amounts are too large, given the amount of farmland and the size of our population. How do we have space to grow enough crops for domestic consumption *and* support this volume of commercial exports?"

Her father smiled, derailing Poppy momentarily. "Look at you," he said affectionately. "Analyzing the figures, thinking critically and holistically about how they fit into the bigger picture. You remind me of myself, at your age."

Despite herself, she brightened at his praise, sitting up straighter. "Thank you, Father. But that still doesn't answer my question. Why is there such a high volume of raw agricultural exports?"

Her father readjusted his glasses with a sigh. "In recent years, the cost of maintaining farms has increased. Many farmers are unable to finance improvements to their land alone, so they take loans or sell their land. The best offers tend to come from the companies on this list, who buy the land to grow the crops you see here. These companies then sell the raw materials to other companies in Welkland or other territories." Her father flipped several pages ahead, then turned one around for Poppy to see. "See? These external companies refine and package the goods, and then we re-import those outputs. So, eventually, the crops *do* return to Viryana for consumption, but only after being processed."

"That sounds . . . inconvenient." Not to mention illogical. "Each time we ship cotton and grain across the sea, we add an extra layer of cost to these essentials, which makes it less affordable for common people. Why not establish refineries here, and establish a more domestic supply chain? We have an existing industrial sector. Why not expand it?"

"We already have some factories," her father allowed, "but the issue is twofold: First, we simply do not have the necessary real estate to build enough refineries to support the kind of demand we face. The existing factories are configured to process other finished goods—textiles, lumber, automobiles, and so on. The initial conversion would be incredibly expensive. It's easier to ship the raw agricultural produce overseas, where they already have established factories, and then import the finished goods."

She pressed her mouth into a flat line. Most of the factories in Viryana produced goods that regular Virians couldn't afford, especially given how cheap labor was on the island. It seemed like a mockery—to force a man to build something he could never own, even if he saved every crown he earned over his entire lifetime.

"What's the second reason?" she asked.

"The companies exporting the goods have established relations with the manufacturing companies." He took off his glasses, polishing them with a cloth. "Even if we did have refineries here, these companies would require a decent incentive to sever ties with their old partners just for the sake of giving the contract to local companies."

Poppy tapped on the sheet again as she thought about the unemployed men she'd seen by the docks, defeated and desperate. She recalled the bony children along the sides of the roads, lurking near food stalls, waiting with the gulls to swipe their next meal.

"What if we legally required a certain percentage of raw agricultural inputs be processed domestically?" she suggested. "Refining these items domestically would make food more affordable and create jobs for the lower class."

"We can't force companies to convert their factories into refineries." He shook his head. "We'd lose business like that, and then people would lose jobs. Besides, many of the companies that are exporting agricultural goods are owned either partly or fully by members of First Families."

And there it was. Her father would not change the rules if it meant inconveniencing his inner circle. She bit the inside of her cheek, sifting for an appropriately diplomatic response. Push too hard and she risked his ire—or, worse, his doubt in her complete transformation.

"Surely, it's in everyone's best interest, First Families included, to bolster the employment rate?" She tried to lead him along her thought path. "If people had a reliable source of income, they would not be so desperate as to turn to crime."

"Lack of income doesn't lead to crime," he said. "There is a natural defiance in those people that leads to deviant behavior. The only way to manage them is to take them in hand firmly. I've increased fines, jail time, and compulsory labor measures in response to the crime rate. If their moral compass cannot point them on the correct path, then fear of punishment will keep them from going astray."

"But, Father," she pushed, "punishment is a reactive response to crime. We should be addressing the source. The rise in crime has grown steadily along with the unemployment and starvation rates. There's a correlation. If we could give people jobs, lift them out of poverty—"

"Enough!" Her father slammed a hand down on the desk, causing her to jump. "It's their own responsibility to lift themselves out of poverty," he said, his eyes burning. "These people have already proven their deviant tendencies. Did I not tell you, seven years ago, that enabling their behavior with handouts will only aggravate it?"

Poppy shrank both at his reproach and at the reminder of what had happened seven years ago. "I apologize if I've displeased you. I was only trying to help."

The old man softened a touch as he reached across the table and laid a hand on hers. "I understand," he said. "But governing the colony is my responsibility, not yours. I have seen things that you have not, Poppy. Wisdom comes with experience."

An awkwardness filled the space, the easy silence vaporized in the heat of their tense exchange. Her father cleared his throat. "Besides, you have pleased me immensely, Poppy. You have become a graceful, sensible young woman. Richard Montrose is a very lucky man."

Her cheeks warmed. She and Richard had been seeing each other for nearly two weeks, going out every evening to dinner, the theater, the opera, even once sailing on his boat. Richard was the consummate gentleman. While most men would have tried to steal a kiss or other favors, he was traditional, firmly believing that physical affection should be reserved for engaged couples. Most women would have been discouraged, but she didn't mind. Yes, Richard's looks were desirable, but she had never been attracted to him for physical reasons.

"I am fortunate to have his attentions," Poppy said. "We are well suited."

He lifted one brow. "So, if Richard were to ask for your hand, you would be unopposed?"

She started. "No, but it's quite early for that, isn't it? Why, it's only been two weeks."

"In my day, short courtships were the norm." Her father shrugged. "All that mattered was the consent of the families. Your mother and I only had the opportunity to meet a few times before I made my offer."

Now, this was a story Poppy had never heard. She knew the facts of it—Demetria had been from one of the Welkish noble families, on a tour of the colonies with several other noble daughters when she had stopped in Viryana and met the young viceroy, Clarence Sutherland. But Poppy had never heard either parent tell it, and so she leaned in and asked, "How did you court Mother?"

Her father leaned back, the creases in his face easing, as if sinking into a memory. "Your mother was on that tour," he said, "with several other young ladies and their chaperones. I had taken the office eight years prior, after my father passed away from fever when I was only twenty, three years younger than you are now. He had barely prepared me for the office I had inherited, and so my first few years were dedicated to mastering the role.

By the time I turned twenty-eight, my council had been pushing me for several years to search for a suitable bride. At the time, I'll confess, I thought I had no need for a wife. My plan was to merely host the ladies at the estate for an evening, then send them on their way. But one dance with your mother, and I knew that she was the lady I wanted to spend the rest of my life with.

"Your mother took more convincing, admittedly—her tour had allocated only a fortnight for Viryana, and I spent the vast majority of it trying to convince her to stay behind and marry me. Though the point of the tour was to get away from the mainland and see the colonies, she was reluctant to leave Welkland behind for good. But I was nothing if not persistent. When she finally agreed, I fired off a telegram to both her parents and to the Imperial Family, and the rest is history."

Poppy blinked, surprised. She hadn't known that about her mother before. She opened her mouth to ask a follow-up question, but a knock on the door interrupted them.

"Forgive me, Your Grace," the butler said, "but Lord William Montrose and Captain Richard Montrose seek an audience with you."

Her father chuckled. "What a coincidence." To the butler, he ordered, "Let them in."

William Montrose entered first, Richard behind him. Surprise rippled across Richard's face when he noticed her sitting at her father's desk, pen in hand. The expression dissolved in a second, replaced by a dazzling grin. She returned it with a shy smile of her own.

"Your Grace," William Montrose said. "We seek a private audience with you." Poppy noticed that he hadn't said what for.

"Poppy," her father said, "you're dismissed. Thank you for your help."

She ducked her head, rising from her chair. “Lord Montrose, Captain Montrose,” she said, bobbing her head to each of them before hurrying from the room.

She cast one last glance back at the three men. Richard was still watching her, his gaze broken only by the closing door. While Lord Montrose often visited her father on government business, Richard had less cause to come by—in fact, she could think of only one reason for his visit. Despite her earlier objection that it was too soon for a proposal, it seemed to her that one was on the horizon nonetheless, perhaps within another month or so. Good, she told herself. This was what she wanted, after all. The sooner his name was bound to hers, the better.

Chapter Nine

A Perilous Proposal

On Saturday morning, a week after he'd come to speak to her father, Richard took Poppy to watch a game of polo in his family's box at the local club. He had taken her out almost every day since that first dinner together, a fact that had not gone unnoticed by others. The couple had been featured in *Miss Marnapur*'s gossip column at least twice, and other eligible society ladies shot Poppy frigid stares when she was out with Richard. She basked in their glares as she sat in the Montrose family box, savoring fragrant black tea and scones with jam and clotted cream.

After the match had ended, Richard rose and offered Poppy his hand. "Shall we leave? There's one more thing I would like to show you."

Intrigued, Poppy followed him back to the Peregrine. He drove them over Morning Bridge, out of the Welkish sector.

Poppy sat up straighter as they entered the Virian side of the city. Marnapur was divided by a river that flowed out to the sea. The Welkish families had taken residence on the west side, in green estates backing onto fine, sandy beaches. The east side was smaller, its shores rockier and less attractive, the ramshackle buildings crammed tight together, barely wide enough for the trucks that bore industrial supplies to scrape through. On occasion, their drivers struck people, often children too small to be seen over the wheel.

Richard slowed as he drove them deeper into the east side, carefully navigating past the marketplace and shabby shops, taking them away from the tall, smoking factories and toward the tin-topped homes of the slums. Despite herself, Poppy clenched her fists, unsettled by the proximity of pedestrians to the car, keeping a special eye out for any children.

Richard noticed her discomfort. "Don't fret, Miss Sutherland. The doors to the vehicle are locked. These people cannot harm you, I assure you."

Poppy sat back, too surprised to respond—she didn't fear the people; she feared *for* them. Yet it was sweet of Richard to think of her well-being. He would make an attentive husband, at least.

After twenty minutes, he pulled over across from a rundown building around three stories tall, the windows boarded up with plywood, the cement walls gray with dirt and age.

"Come on." He beckoned, blue eyes sparking like the ocean. "Let's go."

He took Poppy's hand. She glowed at his familiarity, a sure sign of his attachment. She followed Richard across the road until the two stood in front of the decrepit building. A small crowd of journalists had gathered there, carrying their bulky, heavy cameras. While the couple had been photographed at society events before, Poppy's palms began to sweat.

"Richard," she whispered, "the papers are here."

"I invited them," he replied, giving her hand a light squeeze. "You'll see. Don't worry."

She bit the inside of her lip, fighting to remain composed.

One bad picture, and those men could shatter her image in the flash of a second.

Once they were in front of the building, Richard turned to look at her. "You mentioned at our first dinner that you would like to be more involved in the viceroy's office than the ladies of the past."

Poppy swallowed a smug grin. Holding her hand, remembering small details—she had him eating out of her palm.

"I would." She beamed. "I have a mind for it, if you don't mind my saying so. I would be an asset."

"I have no doubt." He nodded. "I hope you'll forgive me for moving ahead without asking you, but I wanted this to be a surprise."

He turned and beckoned to the crowd of waiting men, and one of them—his footman—came forward with a cream-colored folder.

Richard flipped the folder open and angled his body so Poppy could see the first page inside it. "This is the deed to the building we stand in front of," he announced.

Her eyes widened. On the deed was her full name—Poppy Demetria Sutherland. She stared at it in disbelief. Women had gained the legal ability to own property relatively recently—her mother had been only a few years younger than Poppy when it happened—but it was still rare for a woman to own a property not in her husband's name. This was a break in tradition, a sign that Richard was willing to be more unconventional than generations past.

"I love it," Poppy gushed, and this time she didn't have to feign it. Hope—warm, genuine hope—bubbled in her chest like a rush of champagne. "Thank you."

Richard laughed. "I appreciate your enthusiasm, but you don't even know what I've bought this for."

He turned to the next page, handing Poppy the folder. This new page had a sketch of the building in front of them beside a second sketch, which appeared to be the same building after renovations. The windows had been restored, a fence surrounded the yard, and a porch had been added to the front of the building. The new building was beautiful, but the name printed above the doorway seized Poppy's attention: *The Poppy Sutherland-Montrose Home for Children.*

Poppy Sutherland-*Montrose.* His name, attached to hers, as though it were the most natural thing in the world. It could only mean one thing—but it couldn't be. It hadn't even been a month. Poppy's head snapped up, searching for Richard, but he wasn't standing beside her anymore. He had taken a step back, making room to sink onto one knee as he revealed a velvet box with a flourish.

"Poppy Demetria Sutherland," he began, his regal tone echoing, "though our courtship has been brief, I have seen many admirable traits in you: modesty, grace, and, most importantly, reverence for the Founder and his works. I do not need to go another day courting you to know that you are the woman I want by my side for the rest of my life. Marry me."

Poppy's chest and throat constricted, rendering her unable to speak. She nodded mutely, head still reeling in disbelief. The photographers rushed forward to capture the moment, their flashes bright, shutters snapping in rapid metallic beats. It took all of Poppy's effort to keep her arm from trembling as she extended it to Richard, her fingers so numb that she barely felt it as he took her hand. The camera shutters chorused again as Richard slid the ring, a pink diamond set in a platinum band, onto Poppy's finger. He stood, taking Poppy by the hand and turning her to face the blinding lights of the camera flashes.

"Let's give them a good shot, hm?" he whispered. "We can frame the articles in our home when we're married."

The words *our home* filled Poppy with a surprising warmth. Though she hadn't pursued Richard for love, the possibility of it was as exciting and delicate as a spring bud. Who knew what this would grow into, given time.

The journalists clamored for their attention. "Miss Sutherland," one shouted, "how does it feel to be back home?"

"Amazing." Poppy beamed. "While Welkland was gorgeous in every respect, Viryana is my home, and I am happy to be back."

"Did the two of you keep in touch while Miss Sutherland was overseas?"

Poppy tensed. There had been no keeping in touch nor letters; they hadn't even known each other. She could only imagine the way the press would use their lack of history to undermine this moment.

"Distance makes the heart grow fonder, and both Miss Sutherland and I were occupied with our respective duties," Richard answered smoothly. "Now that we have come to an age where it is appropriate, we will be devoting ample time to each other."

He winked at her, and the shutters took off, trying to capture the moment. She relaxed, relieved by his tact.

"Captain Montrose," another journalist called. Richard stiffened. Poppy peeked at his face quizzically as the reporter asked, "Statistics show that crime rates in Marnapur have doubled in recent years. Do you think this is a result of the poverty caused by the famine? If so, how do you justify lobbying the Council to spend its budget on police equipment instead of relief?"

She kept her face blank. Either the reporter was overstating the issue, or her father had downplayed the recent rise in crime.

She wondered at the use of the word *famine*—she'd imagined people were hungry, given the rise in poverty and the food shortage caused by the volume of exports, but had the situation truly grown so dire that it could be called a famine? Or was the reporter exaggerating?

"The equipment is to fight the crime," Richard said, a sarcastic edge to his tone. "I should think it's obvious to anyone that if you have more crime, you'll need more police, which means you'll need more resources for those police."

The journalist wasn't done. "But if the source of the crime is hunger, wouldn't those funds be better spent giving resources to the people? Stopping the problem at the heart?"

"You want to know what the heart of the problem is?" Richard said. His voice hardened, all traces of romantic tenderness gone. "It's not hunger. It's a thirst for power—*unnatural* power. The increase in crime has been directly attributed to a gang led by the Jackal. We know that there are unnaturals in their midst, that the Jackal himself likely has unnatural powers of his own. Their goal is to destabilize the order we have built, to regress from the Founder's civility and return to the savage era of self-governance, when they were once despotic kings. Though there are not as many as there once were, and though their power is diminished, I believe the unnaturals will not stop until we have eradicated them."

Poppy froze, veins turning to ice. Eradicated? Surely, Richard didn't mean—she didn't let herself even think of it, lest her expression betray her. Her cheeks ached, but she kept her smile airtight.

"Do you fear their power?" another reporter asked.

"Their power is no match for a bullet," Richard said, "and thanks to the Council, I have plenty of bullets."

He laughed, as though the thought of killing an entire group of people was *amusing.* The sound struck Poppy like a shovel full of grave dirt—not least of all because *she* was one of those people whose hypothetical deaths he found so amusing.

Richard didn't know her secret. No one did, not even Catherine. Poppy had discovered it accidentally, at age thirteen, while waiting for the bathtub to fill. In a fit of impatience, she'd wished the water would come out of the tap faster—and for a split second, it did, surging with such intensity, the tap snapped clean off. Immediately, a wave of dizziness had struck Poppy. She'd staggered, her limbs weak and heavy, and the flow had returned to normal. The plumber claimed the tap was old and faulty, and no one was the wiser.

It hadn't taken a genius to connect the freak accident with the stories Nanny had told. But none of Nanny's bedtime stories had mentioned such a drastic physical toll, and Poppy had no one to ask about it, either. This was the only thing she'd inherited from her birth parents, and they were no longer around to explain how it worked. Her adoptive mother could help her get fitted for a brassiere and explain her first blood to her, but this? Poppy was on her own.

No one could ever know Poppy was an unnatural, supposedly blessed by the same false gods that the Founder had replaced. Especially not Richard. Poppy repressed a shudder as his laugh echoed around her, grating against her skin. *Breathe,* she reminded herself. The cameras were still trained on her, one shot away from scandal at any point in time.

Besides, he wouldn't find out, she reasoned. The only way to prove such an allegation was for someone to catch her using her power, and she never would. But still, Poppy wondered: If Richard found out about her powers, would he truly harm her?

He was such a tender and sensitive suitor. Could he turn his gun on her? Would he really fire?

"No more questions," Richard announced with a clap of his hands, pulling her out of her reverie. "We'll take some last photographs, and then my fiancée and I would like some privacy."

After the photographers had gotten their fill of photos, Poppy turned to stare at the building—*her* building—once more. She let herself imagine what it would look like when the renovations were done and it was full of children. Orphans. Orphans like her. Orphans whose blood might harbor a power no one could ever—*no.* Poppy yanked her thoughts back.

Richard took her hand and pulled her to face him instead of the building. "This is only the beginning of what we can achieve together, Poppy," he said, his words low and private. "When we're married, you can open more homes. I want you to be a part of my office, as part of a new philanthropic effort I wish to bring to the viceroy's role, and help me take care of the vulnerable. I knew homeless orphans must be a cause close to your heart, so I started with this. I thought it would be a fitting testament to your roots."

Poppy's heart tightened to hear Richard's words, an echo of the thoughts that had just been running through her mind. Perhaps it had only been a few weeks, but he already seemed to know the essence of her. She gazed at the orphanage in the drawing again, recalling the child beggars she'd seen around Marnapur since her return. Her father had given her a home when he had taken her off the streets, and now, with the tools Richard was giving her, she could give that same opportunity to others.

"Thank you," Poppy whispered. "It's perfect."

Richard took the folder back and closed it. "We can talk more about it once we're married," he promised. "For now, though, I would have you turn your attention to our engagement party."

"Of course." Event planning had been a part of the curriculum at Thornhaven. Though she'd been uncomfortable with having the spotlight on her as hostess, she'd had to learn. A lady was judged by the quality of events that she hosted, from the splendor of the decorations to the taste of the food to the caliber of the entertainment. This would be Poppy's chance to prove to the nobility that she was not only one of them but *better* than most of them. Determination filled her, overshadowing her unease. "I'll plan everything. It will be a perfect evening, I promise."

"I know it will," he said, squeezing her hand, "because you'll be there."

Poppy looked away, falling easily into the act of blushing fiancée. "I fear you are too kind."

"Every man should aspire to kindness where his future wife is concerned," Richard said. "Shall we head off? I told your parents you'd be home for dinner, and a promise is a promise."

With one last glance at the orphanage, Poppy let Richard lead her back to his car. She didn't let herself think about what would happen if Richard learned about her unnatural power. Instead, she forced herself to focus on all the ways the future would be better.

Chapter Ten

A Brother for a Bride

The sun rose on the twenty-second day of Paranjay's arrest. Dawn trickled in through the slats covering the window of the Devar Brothers office, bars of gold light striping the newspapers and spreadsheets and intel reports scattered on every surface.

Despite their earlier truce, Hasan and Zeyar continued to butt heads. They'd tried to come up with alternate solutions. But every road they explored took them back to the exact same fork: bribery or battle. To Hasan, attacking the precinct was the only viable option. Zeyar was just being stubborn.

"If we attack the precinct, then we have no room for failure," Zeyar said. "If we don't get Paranjay out, they'll harm him in retribution."

"I'll rally my strongest men," Hasan reasoned. "Plus, we have the element of surprise."

"And they have military-grade rifles." Zeyar paced the room, a tail of cigarette smoke following him. "Our daivyakhi is limited as it is. Making offerings to household idols can only get us so much power, and our handguns are no match for their weapons. Plus, they're trained in combat. We don't have that same advantage, nor do we have months to train. We need to get Paranjay out before this moves to the courts and they sentence him to a high-security prison."

If they don't sentence him to the gallows instead. The unspoken alternative hung heavy in the air between them.

"There must be a price," Zeyar said, almost to himself.

"Oh my gods," Hasan groaned. "Will you fucking *drop* the bribery idea?"

"No"—Zeyar shook his head—"not bribery. I mean there must be something that Montrose cares about, something that we can leverage to at least gain an audience with him."

"Like blackmail?"

"Maybe." Zeyar sat at the desk in front of Hasan, shuffling a stack of newspapers to the side. "What have your spies learned of him?"

Hasan sighed, flipping pages in his notebook. "Not much that we don't already know," he admitted. "He graduated from the police academy after a year's worth of training and has been promoted thrice, most recently a few months ago, when he made captain and started to make our lives hell. His promotion is likely nepotism, given he's from one of the original five colonizing families, but he's clearly not an empty head."

"What else? Family? Siblings?"

"He has a younger sister. But she married a man from a lesser family, and if the rumors are true, he's been distant from her ever since."

"Surely he has *someone* he cares about." Zeyar waved his cigarette in the air. "A close friend, a mistress. He must have a woman—he's *Miss Marnapur*'s most eligible bachelor, for gods' sake."

Hasan paused. "Since when do you read *Miss Marnapur*?"

"I don't," Zeyar said. "Harithi enjoys reading it. Says it's funny."

Hasan's brow creased. "I don't think I've ever seen her with it."

Zeyar stiffened. "I must be mistaken," he huffed, stabbing his half-smoked cigarette in the ashtray. "Maybe it was Samina. I don't know. Fuck, I need a cup of chai. I saw Kishan opening his stall. Let's go. A break will do us some good."

Hasan didn't want to get up until they'd found a solution, but they'd been awake all night, and a cup of chai sounded exactly like what he needed to take the edge off.

As the two of them stood waiting for their chai, a paperboy drew near, carrying a heavy bag of newspapers over his shoulder.

"*Viryana Post*!" he shouted. "Just five copper crowns!"

"Boy," Hasan called, taking a silver crown out of his pocket. "I'll take one."

The boy scampered forward, collecting the coin eagerly and thrusting the paper into Hasan's hand. Hasan blanched, too startled by the headline to ask the boy for change before he scurried off.

"There you go again with your charity," Zeyar said. "How many urch—"

Hasan shook his head, cutting his brother off. "Montrose is engaged." He flipped the paper so the headline was facing Zeyar: "Montrose Heir Proposes to Viceroy's Daughter." Below, Poppy Sutherland was pictured, her expression one of shock and delight. When Hasan was growing up, it was not uncommon to see the viceroy's daughter in photographs beside him, but in the past few weeks since her return from Welkland, the papers had printed so many pictures of her that Hasan felt like he knew her face better than his own. She hadn't been featured this much since the scandal of her adoption twenty-one years ago. Hasan shook out the newspaper, revealing the rest of the photograph. Richard Montrose occupied the bottom half, down on one knee as he beamed up at Poppy confidently, her hand in his. The pair of them looked absurd against the backdrop, a shitty old building that hadn't been occupied in years.

"Give me that." Zeyar grabbed the newspaper from Hasan. He flipped past the front page, heading to the page with the rest of the article. His eyes widened. "He bought her that run-down house they're standing in front of," he said. "And he put *her* name on the deed."

"Seems like a big investment for a man who isn't besotted," Hasan observed.

"Besotted is strong," Zeyar disagreed. "The paper says they've only been courting three weeks. What's more likely is he needed her to say yes. Between the giant purchase and the public proposal, he all but guaranteed she couldn't turn him down. Very clever. So, the girl *is* important to him, though the *why* of the matter is not so simple as love."

"Should we threaten her?"

Zeyar shook his head. "She's Sutherland's daughter. He likely has a guard with her at all times. Threatening her will only increase the security around her and decrease the likelihood that we'll be able to make good on our words. An empty threat carries no weight."

Hasan crossed his arms. "Then what do you propose?"

"Act first; make threats later." Zeyar's lips curled into a wicked grin. "We're going to kidnap her."

Hasan understood immediately. "You want to do a prisoner trade. Paranjay for Poppy."

"Exactly." Zeyar tapped the newspaper. "Her engagement party is in three days, hosted at Montrose Manor. Everyone who's anyone will be invited, which means the house will be full of guests. Getting in and out unnoticed will be easy. It's the perfect opportunity."

"I'll send Samina to scope out the property." Hasan's mind raced. "We'll need a map of the house and the grounds. Given the size of the party, they'll need to hire Virian waitstaff. I'm sure Harithi can find out which catering company is getting the contract. We'll need a few men to infiltrate them. Perhaps Vinay and Kaushal—"

"No," Zeyar said. "This will be our biggest stunt to date. We aren't collecting a debt; we're seizing the viceroy's daughter. Send your team to make the necessary preparations. But only you and I are qualified enough to do the deed."

Hasan's lips curved up in a half smile. He and Zeyar had not worked a job together since their mother had handed them the reins of the family business. Though it seemed unimaginable now, they had made quite the team back then, with Zeyar's precisely crafted strategies backed by Hasan's brute strength and physical prowess. Oh, they'd argued back then, too, tussling like a pair of wolf pups—but they'd always made it out of a job laughing. Scuffed up, a trail of destruction in their wake, but laughing.

Hasan wanted to laugh with his brother again. "Let's do it, then. Let's get Paranjay back."

Chapter Eleven

Every Rose Has Thorns

Hasan tugged at the collar of his catering uniform, scowling at his reflection. "Remind me again why *I* have to be the one to infiltrate the party?"

"Because I've bribed several of the partygoers," Zeyar said, examining his cuff links as he lounged on Hasan's bed. Though tonight he was playing the role of getaway driver, he was dressed just as formally as Hasan, in a black-tie valet's uniform. "They'd recognize me, and then our cover would be blown. Also, I'm the better driver."

"That's debatable," Hasan said, but he couldn't refute his brother's first point. "Come on, then. Let's make a quick offering and go."

Zeyar jumped up, smoothing his slacks. The two of them walked down to the cellar. Hasan grunted as he pushed aside a crate of mango pickle, revealing a black tunnel with a ladder bolted to one side. He descended the ladder, Zeyar following. When they reached the bottom, Hasan's fingers grazed the stone walls as he pressed the light switch. The amber bulbs flickered to life, humming quietly as they bathed the room in golden light, illuminating the small pantheon of Virian deities on the other end of the room.

This was the Devar brothers' most closely guarded secret, the source of their power: the true gods of the island. After the empire had annexed Viryana, they'd desecrated the last of the old Virian temples and destroyed whatever shrines they could find, building cathedrals to the Founder on top of the wreckage, declaring him the one and only god of Viryana. But the temples had been more than just places of worship—for the daivyakt, who had been blessed by the gods, that was where they went to renew their power by making naumya, sacrificial offerings.

Hasan took his offering, his untouched dinner plate, and laid it at the feet of Nathria, the glittering goddess of victory.

"You'll need more than that," Zeyar said. "If you're caught inside the mansion, you'll need a lot of fire. Make a bigger offering."

Hasan bit his lip. He undid the clasp on his watch, a gift from Paranjay with a mother-of-pearl face, and set it beside his plate of food.

"My veins are a vessel for the divine power of the gods," he intoned. "If Nathria finds my sacrifice worthy, may I be filled with her cosmic energy." Though the goddess was earth-aligned and Hasan's gift was fire, a warmth spread through Hasan as his prayer was heard.

Hasan stepped back, allowing Zeyar to go next. He withdrew two packs of expensive cigars, laying them at Nathria's feet as well as at those of Dhilip, the god of speed. Zeyar repeated the prayer, then stepped back.

"Let's go." Hasan glanced at the watch, which ticked at Nathria's feet. "The party will be getting started any minute now."

• • •

No one who walked in the front door of Montrose Manor could

tell that Poppy had had only three days to plan this party, of that she was certain. She had selected scarlet and gold party decorations, intentionally matching the families' crests: the Sutherland crossed scepters, and the blooming Montrose rose. She had personally taste tested the drinks and appetizers circulating on gold platters, and she'd hand chosen every item in the six-course meal, which would be served once the dancing was over.

She had even made time to get fitted for a new dress for the occasion, with lace sleeves and a bodice with a built-in corset. The skirt bloomed outward in layers of tulle and blush-colored silk that matched the pink of her diamond ring. Her lady's maids had pulled half of her thick hair into a braided crown at the top of her head, leaving the rest of it to flow to her waist. Gold pins with heads of diamond and pearl kept the style in place. Poppy couldn't stop tilting her head, admiring the way they caught the light.

In other words, the evening was perfect. The seven years of education in Welkland had paid off. Not a single person in the room could deny it.

The party was in full swing, having started with the Montrose majordomo announcing Poppy's parents, Richard's parents, and then, finally, Poppy and Richard. She had glided down the staircase, nose held high, gloating at the dismay and envy on the faces of the ladies.

Poppy and Richard stood side by side at the front of the room, greeting every guest, fielding their well-wishes, and occasionally posing for a photograph with them.

After what seemed like an eternity, Richard released her arm. "I need to freshen up, but please, stay here and enjoy yourself. I'll return as soon as I can."

After he left, Poppy went to check the dining hall. Once

she'd ensured that the placeholders had been laid out exactly per the seating schematic she'd created, she made her way back to the ballroom. As she passed a gaggle of Welkish women, her name caught her ear. She paused, pretending to flag down one of the caterers as she eavesdropped.

"The Sutherland girl. He's only marrying her because her father is the viceroy," one of them said, derision dripping from her voice.

Poppy frowned. She'd known that her engagement would provoke envious slander, but she'd assumed that the jealousy would stem from the fact that Richard had chosen her over one of them. This rumor, however, seemed to imply that the person she was, the person she had become, was unworthy of his choice. Nothing could be attractive or desirable about *her*, because she was Virian.

One of the Virian caterers had seen her raise her hand and had swiftly reacted. She wanted to wave him off, but it was too late—he'd already reached her.

"She obviously doesn't realize it," another woman tittered. "Did you see how she was holding herself? Like she's some *lady* just because she got exiled to Welkland for a few years."

Poppy cringed at the derision toward her lack of a title.

A third voice piped up. "I heard His Grace thinks she's changed. That she's civilized now."

"Of course he thinks that," the second woman said. "He's too proud to admit that he made an error by adopting her, so he insists on carrying on this charade. Personally, I'm shocked that Captain Montrose is willing to play along with it. I always thought the Montroses to be honorable."

"Captain Montrose is a man of solid judgment," the third woman said. "Perhaps she truly has changed, if he's chosen her to be his wife when he could have had his pick of any other woman."

Her statement was met by a round of snickering. "I hardly believe it," the second woman said. "You can put a saddle on a camel, but you can't make it a thoroughbred."

Poppy found herself paralyzed. Her hand, half outstretched to take the drink from the caterer's tray, refused to obey her. Her gaze flickered up to his face. She hoped he hadn't heard—or at least had the tact to pretend he hadn't—but instead, he looked disgusted. When his eyes met Poppy's, his expression shifted, but it wasn't pity on his face. It was disdain, as though he couldn't believe she was willingly subjecting herself to this.

Her face burned—who was this man to judge her?

"Never mind," she said. "I'm fine."

He hesitated. "Are you sure?" he pressed. He picked up one of the drinks from the tray and offered it to her. "You might feel better—"

Poppy pushed his hand away. "Thank you, but I shouldn't be drinking right now. What I need is to find my fiancé."

As soon as she said it, she knew it was true. Yes, she had to find Richard. She needed to hear him say that he was marrying her because he dreamed of changing Viryana together, because he wanted her by his side as he ruled the island, because she was dignified and ladylike and deserving of a place in the nobility. Not because her father was viceroy.

Poppy spun on her heel and left the ballroom, holding back tears.

• • •

Richard wasn't in the restroom. Poppy pressed her lips together, fighting the urge to bury her face in her hands. The least he could do was be present when she needed him. She caught the arm of a serving girl. "Excuse me, do you know where Captain Montrose has gone?"

"I saw him in the west wing, Miss Sutherland," the girl answered.

"Thank you," she said, but the information did nothing to alleviate her agitation. The west wing didn't have a bathroom—only the Montrose library, and the personal offices of the men.

She released the girl and headed past the ballroom, cutting through the center of the house, past the twin staircases, until she reached the west wing. *Perhaps there's some work that Richard had to attend to,* she theorized. *He must have met a colleague and gotten distracted.*

She entered the library, heading for Richard's office at the back, weaving through the shelves until she reached her destination. The study door was closed, but an outline of light around the edges indicated that it was occupied. She lifted her knuckles to knock, but as she drew closer, a snippet of conversation hooked her.

"Sutherland woman?"

She froze. The voice was male, though she didn't recognize the speaker. But when the second voice spoke, she recognized it immediately.

"It was obvious," Richard said. "I first got the idea when the old man had his stroke. The viceroy has no male heir, see. But as his son-in-law . . ."

"Sounds to me like you have the office all lined up for you, then. Congratulations. But why smear the name of your future wife?"

"Plans change," Richard said. "The girl came back different—she's no longer the meek creature that used to blend in with the wallpaper at social functions. She holds herself like a lady and quotes the scripture of the Founder. Old Sutherland is convinced she's 'one of us' now. He even lets her sit in his office and help him; would you believe it?"

Her heart plummeted. This hard, angry voice couldn't be Richard. It might have sounded like him, but there was no way that the same man who had taken her out to the finest places in town and bought an orphanage in her name could speak about her with such derision. She was not so foolish to fancy them in love, but she had thought that he at least respected her.

"You disagree?" The first voice was neutral.

"Of *course*, I fucking disagree," Richard snapped. "I've worked with enough Virians to know that they're a race of crude creatures who will eat their own to survive. The Founder's manifesto doesn't call us to make other races our equals. He calls us to take them firmly in hand, to guide them the same way a shepherd guides its flock. We don't dress our sheep in silks and satins and then breed with them, do we?"

Heat seared her cheeks. Her head spun. Surely this must be a nightmare, a stress dream from having a limited amount of time to plan such an important party. She staggered backward, searching for support. Her hand met the bookshelf, and she braced herself against it, grateful for something solid as the world dissolved beneath her feet. But it still wasn't far enough from the door, wasn't far enough to protect her from Richard's next words:

"Sutherland thinks his daughter deserves more power. And while he's still alive, he may legally redefine the role of the viceroy's wife entirely, just for her. What the fuck do I look like, sharing power with a Virian? She ought to be shining my shoes, not sitting and debating legislation with me."

"If it came to it, we could try to vote him down in the House," the first voice said. "I doubt he would go so far as to try to change succession laws, either. Why go to such extremes?"

"Because as the old man grows more addled, he becomes less predictable," Richard said, his words audibly twisted by the scowl that must have equally marred his features. "Women's rights have advanced in the last half a century, particularly when the law changed to allow them to own land. If Sutherland brings this to a vote, I cannot confidently say that it will die in the House. And while he might be old, he still holds a lot of sway among the Council of Lords. No, framing Poppy is the only way."

At this, she straightened. Her cold, numb body flushed hot with indignation. *Framing* who *now?* She took another step toward the door.

"The smuggler we captured has been taking opium to Welkland for years," Richard explained. "I forced him to surrender a list of his clients and accomplices on foreign shores. It won't be difficult to add Poppy to the list, especially since he *has* stopped in Cloudcliff, the closest port to Thornhaven, several times. Once Sutherland sees that his daughter will always be a Virian sympathizer, he'll send her back to Welkland. Since we'll be wed by then, I'll be free to rule on my own. Once the whole scandal has passed, I'll seek out a proper wife."

"How can you remarry when your legal right to the office is through your marriage to Poppy?"

"Laws change," Richard said flippantly.

"So, what's the next step?"

"I'm going to return to the party soon, before people start looking for me. But I need you to write to your cousin in Welkland, the one who also attended Thornhaven, and get her to agree to sign a statement testifying that she saw Poppy Sutherland leave school grounds multiple times, especially on these two dates. This, plus the smuggler's records, should be enough to damn her. I'm sure deep down, her father doubts her, too, so it shouldn't be too hard to convince him."

The words struck her like a kick to the ribs. Her father didn't doubt her, did he? Poppy thought he had believed in her change. Believed in *her*.

But then again, she had also been foolish enough to believe that Richard cared for her as an equal. If she had been wrong about him, what else had she been wrong about? Was there anyone in this society who believed that she could be civilized, or were they all like those vicious gossips out there, racist and cruel?

She didn't care to find out. She turned and ran from the library, sprinting into the hall. *Fuck society,* she thought, and a thrill ran up her spine at the foul language. What a relief, to break free of the mold—to cast off the act. If an uncouth, uncivilized girl was all they would ever see, then she saw no reason to try to become anything else.

She skidded to a halt in the foyer. On her left, music drifted from the ballroom, an obscenely cheerful song given what a farce this whole engagement was. To her right, a warm breeze blew in from the front doors, propped open so guests could come and go with ease. Her heart slammed in her chest like a bird's wings against cage bars.

She needed to get out. Party be damned, she couldn't spend one more minute in this mansion.

She spun, turning her back on the ballroom, and hurried toward the front doors. The two valets outside started at the sight of her, but wisely held their tongues. She took off her earrings: genuine Welkish pearls, worth a hundred gold crowns each.

"You never saw me," she said, pressing one into each of their hands.

"Of course, Miss Sutherland," they said.

With that, she turned and started down the drive on foot. She didn't know where she would go, not yet—but it had to be anywhere but here.

• • •

Hasan had burgled homes and assassinated men twice his size, but somehow, his skill set seemed to have ended at kidnapping pampered noble daughters. Finding her had been the easy part—even if she hadn't been surrounded by a swarm of brownnosers and bootlickers wishing her well over her engagement, she looked just like every photograph of her he'd seen in the news. But it had taken him ages to get close to her, especially when she'd hung around her fiancé as though he'd had the same gravitational force that kept the moon trapped in the earth's orbit. The whole time, he'd had to play a skillful game of dodging the summons of entitled Welks, hoping to avoid one of them taking the spiked drink on his tray before he could give it to Poppy.

Then that bastard Montrose had finally left the room, and he'd closed in on her like an arrow to a bull's-eye. She'd spotted him, flagging him down, and he'd been too happy to oblige her. He'd all but put the drink in Poppy's hand when the two of them had overheard a group of women making disparaging remarks about her.

It hadn't shocked Hasan at all—the comments had been tame compared to things he had heard in the past—but Poppy had acted like she had been sucker punched. It became painfully obvious to Hasan that she had come into this party with her guard down, which was about as smart as coming to a gunfight with a butter knife.

That wasn't what had pissed him off, though. What had really infuriated him was the way she had brushed him off, spinning on her heel and running away, leaving him standing with the spiked drink. And *then*, because things had obviously been too easy for him earlier, the woman who had made the disparaging remark had come over and snatched the drink from him. Hasan couldn't say a word as she'd downed the whole thing in front of him.

Fuck it, he thought as the woman pressed the empty glass back into his hand. *We'll just have to do this the old-fashioned way.* An involuntary pang of guilt sprang up in response to the idea of hitting a woman, but Hasan shoved it down. This was for Paranjay.

He tossed the empty glass aside, ignoring the sound of it shattering in the corner. Then he stepped out into the hall, stopping another one of the caterers who was coming in from the kitchen with a tray of appetizers.

"Pardon me," Hasan said in lightly accented Welkish, "but did you see where Miss Sutherland has gone? Her fiancé is looking for her."

The other caterer shook his head. Hasan scowled. He rounded the corridor, opening the doors to parlors and sitting rooms one by one, but they were empty. When he looped back to the ballroom, Poppy still hadn't returned. He'd have to check the west wing. It had been closed off to guests and the hired help, but he tried to look purposeful as he strode toward it.

He heard her before he saw her: the swishing of skirts, the slap of slippers against the marble floor, the dry sobs of someone in the throes of panic. Hasan turned and bolted halfway up the staircase, crouching behind the banister.

Poppy Sutherland swept into the foyer, her cheeks flushed and her eyes bright—but she was not the joyful, bashful future bride of the Montrose heir anymore. He had stalked enough men to know the wild, hunted look in her eyes. For a moment, Poppy tilted her head toward the ballroom, evidently considering.

No! If she went back into the ballroom, he *definitely* wouldn't be able to knock her out there. The appetizers were nearly over. If this event got to dinner and he still didn't have her, he wouldn't get another chance. It had to be now. Noiselessly, he rose from his crouch, lifting the gold platter in his hands in preparation.

But before he could reach her, she sprinted past him, not even registering his presence, and burst out of the front doors. He hastened after her, keeping enough space between them so she wouldn't notice him tracking her.

His brows furrowed in confusion as Poppy took off her earrings and gave one to each valet. Then she turned and started to walk away, moving quickly, as though she were walking a fine line between speed and drawing attention to herself.

This was his chance. He nodded at the valets, then pursued Poppy down the driveway. To his amazement, she was headed in the exact direction where Zeyar was parked. Hasan closed in, invisible as a shadow in the night. When they were out of the valets' eyesight, he lifted the tray.

Then, because the gods clearly hadn't derived enough entertainment at his expense, Poppy stopped, so abruptly that Hasan nearly crashed into her.

"I can't do this," she gasped, her back to him. "What am I thinking?"

Before he could hide, she turned around. Her round nose wrinkled as she blinked up at him. "What—"

He swung the platter. It caught her on the side of the head

with a resounding clang. He tossed the weapon into the grass and caught her easily as her knees buckled.

Though his instincts were screaming at him to get running, he needed to see her injury. He brushed away some of the hair that had fallen into her heart-shaped face from the force of his blow. Her right temple was swelling rapidly, the shadow of what promised to be a nasty bruise blooming under her skin. He winced—he was supposed to *avoid* leaving a mark, lest Montrose demand they give her back unharmed. He looked away from the bruise, taking in the rest of his captive's face.

When he'd seen Poppy in the ballroom earlier, she'd carried herself with the haughty dignity of an experienced lady. Now, unconscious and vulnerable, Poppy looked like the young woman she *really* was—small and naive. Despite the lump swelling on her head, he had to admit that Poppy was undeniably beautiful—but not in the way the Welkish prized. Her skin was darker than theirs, her nose too big, her lips too full. He wondered if Poppy considered herself pretty, or if she felt disappointed every time she looked in the mirror and found she was not yet white.

The trees above rustled as a large owl swooped into its branches. Hasan started, suddenly remembering where he was. He slid his arm under Poppy's legs and tightened his grip around her back, lifting her off the ground. He ran down to the tree line, where Zeyar had parked.

He shifted Poppy over his shoulder like a sack of rice, then used his free hand to open the door to the back seat—or, at least, he tried to. He went around the car, where Zeyar was smoking out the driver's side window. "Unlock the door, idiot," he snarled.

Zeyar started, nearly dropping the cigarette. "Damn, you move quietly," he said, grudging admiration in his tone. "You got her?"

"No"—Hasan rolled his eyes—"I got the queen of Welkland instead. Of course, I got her! Open the fucking door."

Zeyar unlocked the doors with a metallic click, then got out of the car to open the door for Hasan so he could lay Poppy inside. It was harder than it looked—her dress was puffier than anything they had anticipated, and Hasan half feared that it would suffocate her before they reached their destination. Finally, they were able to get her into an upright position. By the time Hasan slid into the passenger seat, sweat dotted his forehead.

They didn't speak until they had crossed Morning Bridge.

"We did it!" Zeyar whooped. "We pulled it off, Hasan."

"We did it," Hasan echoed, amazed. For the first time in years, they had done something *together.*

Paranjay would have been proud.

Chapter Twelve

In the Den of the Jackal

Poppy's head pounded viciously. It started as a soft ache, but as she came to, it swelled into a pulsing pain concentrated in her right temple. She squeezed her eyelids together, trying to make it go away, but that only caused another sharp flare of pain.

Founder above. How much had she had to drink? She tried to recall the previous night, praying she hadn't made a fool of herself. How had it ended? She couldn't even remember what she'd eaten for dinner.

Slowly, her memories returned in fractured slivers. First, the beginning: the fizz of champagne, the flash of the cameras, the floorboards thrumming with music and dancing. Another shard: Richard, going to the restroom. She winced, recalling the ugly comments those women had made while she was alone, more hurtful than her hangover. She'd gone to the library for comfort, where she'd stumbled on—

Her eyes flew open.

Betrayal. She remembered Richard's betrayal.

She jerked up, but something cold and hard dug into her wrists, rending an involuntary gasp from her as her bones jolted in their sockets. She looked down and found that she was chained upright, in a wooden chair. Her wrists had been cuffed behind the backrest, the hem of her engagement dress rucked up from where someone had tied her ankles to each chair leg.

She swiveled her neck. The shackles dug into her flesh, limiting her range of motion, but she ignored the pain, straining her eyes to take in every detail. The narrow room was windowless, furnished only with a low cot in one corner and the chair she was currently chained to. Dim light came from a single, naked incandescent bulb hanging from the ceiling. Grills covered a small window cut into the door, much like the door of a jail cell.

Was that where she was? Jail?

Panic rose in her throat. Had she been arrested? Had Richard managed to convince her father of her supposed guilt after all? Surely he couldn't have. But underestimating Richard was what had landed her here in the first place. Not even Catherine's warning could have prepared her for this. *Some damned thorns,* she thought, recalling her best friend's words.

She closed her eyes, dragging through the rest of the scattered pieces of her memories, but the pain in her head and the desperation swelling in her chest dashed her focus.

She needed to get out of here. She needed to talk to her father. He couldn't send her away, not again. But if he believed the tale Richard had fabricated, she knew what he would say: *You are better off returning to where you came from.*

The chains rattled as Poppy wrenched her arms forward, trying to pull out of the cuffs, but her efforts were futile. "Damn it," she ground through her teeth. "I don't *deserve* this!"

Then she heard it: a man's voice shouting, the words coarse and unfamiliar. It took her a minute to realize he was speaking Virian. It had been a long time since she'd heard the language, and he was speaking too quickly for her to pick apart the individual words, but his voice jostled something in her head. Her last memory came back to her, snapping into place: Turning around on the driveway. The caterer with the golden tray. A starburst of pain.

She hadn't been arrested. She'd been abducted by one of the hired help. *But why?* What could they possibly want from her?

Footsteps echoed outside, drawing closer by the second. She stiffened, drawing herself upright. Her crown of braids had become loose and skewed to one side, and her dress was a crumpled mess, but she was determined to hold herself with dignity, chains or not.

A figure stopped in front of the cell door, their face blocked by the bars on the window. The grinding of a key turning in the lock echoed in the silence. Then the door swung open. The man entered, his head down as he clipped a key ring onto his belt. Her eyes latched onto it. Was the key to her shackles on there too? As he came to stand in front of her, she lifted her gaze to glare at him directly.

She locked eyes with the caterer, the one who had followed her onto the driveway. She hadn't spared him a second glance at the party, but now she looked—*really* looked. In the dimly lit cell, his facial structure was all harsh angles and shadows, like a sculpture whose edges had never been sanded down. Full, soft lips, twisted into a smirk, offset the sharpness of his stubbled cheeks and jawbone. His eyes, framed by thick lashes, gleamed with an intensity that was almost predatory. He reminded her of the tigers that noblemen were fond of hunting: handsome at a distance, but lethal in close quarters. Fear knotted itself just below her stomach.

"Who are you?" she demanded, choking back her sour unease. "How dare you chain me? Release me at once."

The caterer didn't react. "Good to see you awake. You suffered quite a blow to the head."

Her cuffed hands curled into fists. He had *struck* her, kidnapped her, chained her like a common criminal, and now he had the nerve to ignore her question? She drew herself up even straighter, turning up her nose, channeling the imperious manner of the Hawk. "I asked you a question. Who are you?"

He was silent. Just as she began to think he wouldn't answer, he said, "While I go by many names, you may know of me as the Jackal."

She rifled through her memories, trying to place where she'd heard the name before. Then she recalled Richard's words at that first dinner: *He's responsible for various grifts, extorting the poor, dealing in contraband, committing murder and arson.* She repressed a shiver as she realized she was now in the presence of an infamous criminal. "What do you want from me?"

The Jackal lifted a hand loosely. "Nothing—not from you, anyway. Your fiancé has something important to me, but he won't give it back. So I've taken something important to him."

"I'm not a *thing*," she said. "You can't keep me here, in this—where am I?"

His smile flashed like a dagger. "In the den of the Jackal. Consider yourself a guest of honor."

"Prisoner, you mean," she spat at him. "This is madness. How long will you keep me here?"

"Until your fiancé agrees to what I want," he said, spreading his hands. "It's up to him. Let's hope he wants you back as badly as we want you out of here, hm?"

But Richard doesn't want me back. She bit her tongue. Lord Montrose had an abundance of wealth, but if Richard's endgame was to push her out of the way, would he refuse to pay the ransom?

A knock on the door broke the silence. The Jackal opened it, conferring with the other person in low Virian. The language was a dance between harsh consonants and dramatic vowels, and just as before, he spoke too quickly for her to understand what he was saying. She could catch a few words—*girl, awake, ring*—but not enough to make out the meaning of the conversation. *Damn it.* Why hadn't she made a stronger effort to stay in touch with the language?

Finally, he finished with the person outside, coming back to stand in front of her. "I'm going to go let your fiancé know you're here," he explained, as though she were a child who had gotten lost in his office. "But first, I need to borrow something of yours."

He slipped around her, his movements liquid. She twisted, trying to keep him in her line of sight, ignoring the bite of the restraints against her skin. His rough fingers pressed against hers, and she jolted at the sudden contact. Her pulse hammered at the surface of her skin, hitting the unrelenting metal of the cuffs. What was he doing back there? Her mind immediately jumped to the worst-case scenario.

"Are you going to cut my fingers off?"

"What?" The Jackal sounded genuinely surprised. Then he chuckled, his amusement grating on her raw nerves.

Glad my terror is so amusing to you, she thought blackly.

"All I need is this." He stepped in front of her again, holding up a platinum ring set with a pink diamond.

"That's my engagement ring," she said. "You can't have that." Richard might have been a bastard, but that didn't mean the Jackal was entitled to her belongings.

"I'm not taking it; I'm borrowing it," he said, slipping it into his pocket. "I'm sending it to your fiancé, to verify my claim that you're in my possession."

"I'm not anyone's possession!" She jerked at the chains in futile frustration. "I order you to let me go, right now!" Then she took a deep breath, recalculating. *You catch more flies with honey,* Headmistress Thornhaven had admonished whenever girls were arrogant enough to demand things from her. Poppy bit her lip and shrank, folding her temper away. "Can't you at least take me out of these cuffs? My wrists hurt."

The Jackal didn't even look at her as he headed for the cell door. "Someone will be by to help you shortly," he said. "I know it must be so hard for you, not having a servant on demand, but rest assured, Miss Sutherland, you will survive."

With that, he locked the door, stalking out of the window's limited view.

"You're a brute!" she shouted, hoping that he was still in earshot. If he was, he didn't respond.

She wanted to slouch back in despair, but she had to be strong, just in case he came back. Only once she felt confident that he was truly not returning did the silent tears come, leaving wet tracks on her face that her chained hands couldn't wipe away.

Chapter Thirteen

Radio Silence

As the Jackal had promised, a woman came by after he left. She carried a faded canvas bag in one hand and a steaming bucket of water in the other. Looped around one finger was her own key ring, although it was not nearly as heavily decorated as his. Poppy measured the maid, trying to judge if she could knock her out long enough to take her keys and run.

"Save your time," the woman said in accented Welkish. "It won't work."

Poppy started, unsettled at how easily the woman had read her mind.

"I would try too," the maid continued, grudging respect in her tone, "but in this case, your efforts would be futile. I'm grossly overqualified compared to whoever normally assists you."

"What's your name?" Poppy asked.

The other woman tilted her head, sizing Poppy up with hazel eyes that stood in sharp contrast to her deep-brown skin. Poppy's cheeks flushed—though she'd pulled herself together long before the maid had arrived, her tears had dried in two stiff tracks, a white salty trail on each cheek. Still, she drew herself up higher, trying to match the other woman's confident stance. It bothered

Poppy how this maid carried herself with the same arrogance that only the most powerful matrons in Welkish society had. How did she maintain her pride and self-assurance, she wondered, especially with her thick, coarse black hair and nut-brown skin? If Poppy looked so common, she'd constantly be self-aware. Was the maid faking her poise? Or was she simply ignorant?

"Harithi," the maid said.

"Pardon me?"

"You asked for my name. It's Harithi."

"Oh," Poppy said. "My name—"

"I know who you are." Harithi waved her hand.

Poppy's jaw dropped—had the maid just cut her off?

Harithi continued. "You're Poppy."

"That's *Miss Sutherland* to you."

"Oh, right," Harithi laughed. "I'd forgotten you were raised to have a stick up your ass."

Poppy pressed her lips together in reproach. "Are you always so coarse?"

"Usually, I'm worse," Harithi said. "You'll just have to tolerate it. Unless you wish to remain in your chains?"

Poppy glowered at her but remained silent. Triumphant, the insolent maid sauntered forward and crouched behind her chair, unlocking Poppy's manacles with a click. Poppy brought her wrists forward, rubbing them gingerly to get the blood flowing again. The skin underneath the metal was mottled with purple and blue bruises, the only fruits of her attempts to pull free. With Harithi's assistance, she removed her engagement dress, resisting the urge to kick it aside. Most noblewomen repurposed their gowns to save the time and expense of having an entirely new one made, but this was one dress Poppy swore she'd never wear again.

Harithi came forward with the bucket and a towel.

Poppy eyed them with mistrust. "What's that for?"

"Basic hygiene," Harithi deadpanned. "We may not have state-of-the-art plumbing, and there may be a water shortage, but something is better than nothing."

How low Poppy had sunk, to be cleaning her body with a wet rag. But the warmth radiating from the bucket won her over, as did the promise of clean skin.

"Fine," she said. "Turn around."

It was objectively the worst bath of her entire life. Just yesterday, Poppy had sat in a porcelain tub full of steaming, scented water while maids massaged her scalp and detangled her hair. Now she shivered, naked and vulnerable in a cell, dragging an abrasive, worn-out towel over her skin.

When it was over, Harithi removed a clean set of clothes from her bag: a long blouse and a loose pair of pants like a man would wear. "This is a salwar kameez," she said, enunciating the words slowly, as though speaking to a child. "It may not be a pretty gown, but it's what we have, so it's what you'll get."

Poppy prickled. She might not have been raised by Virians, but even *she* knew what the basic fashions were called.

Harithi helped her into the salwar first. Though Poppy had expected them to feel foreign, they were baggy enough that it wasn't uncomfortable. The kameez fell past her knees, and though Poppy had to roll the sleeves a couple of times, it was a decent fit.

She sat back in the chair, looking at Harithi expectantly. Harithi caught her look, lifting a brow. "Something I can do for you?"

"Aren't you going to help braid my hair?"

Harithi scoffed, crossing her arms over her chest. "What, you can't do it yourself?"

Poppy bristled at the criticism. She *could* do it herself. She had done it alone for years in Welkland, and could have very well done it now if not for her stiff limbs and aching wrists, courtesy of the Jackal's hospitality. But she refused to respond to Harithi's dismissiveness with vulnerability. Instead, she drew her armor tight, sneering. "Why would I need to? I belong to a First Family."

Harithi's expression grew cold. "Ah, right. The lords and ladies of the upper class would *never* have reason to groom themselves independently, unlike the denizens of the slums. You know, for a culture that gave us shit about the castes, the Welks certainly put a lot of emphasis on their social groups, hm?"

With that, she lifted the bucket and marched out of the room, leaving Poppy alone again, her wrists and pride smarting.

• • •

After he sent Montrose a ransom letter with Poppy's engagement ring enclosed, Hasan waited eagerly to hear back. In a few days, they'd trade Poppy for Paranjay, and this nightmare chapter of their lives could end. Just yesterday, Zeyar had received a coded telegram from one of their contacts on Welkish shores. The news had been grim: The identity of their opium customers had leaked to Welkish authorities; only one other person besides the two of them would have had access to that information: Paranjay. Hasan knew his brother was not a coward and could weather more than his fair share of pain. If they had extracted such precious information from Paranjay, then Hasan did not want to imagine the things they were doing to his brother in captivity—if he was even still alive. He didn't dare voice the thought aloud.

Zeyar firmly believed Paranjay had not been killed. "They'll want to make an example of him," he kept insisting. "A public trial, to discourage any copycat criminals."

But as the days went on with no response from Montrose, Hasan's faith weakened. The impossible question had swollen inside his chest, and on the third day, it burst free, tearing a ragged hole through him as he asked, "What if he's dead?"

Zeyar's head snapped up from the newspaper he was poring over. "What makes you say that?"

"Montrose should have jumped at the chance to get his fiancée back," Hasan said. He'd never had a serious partner, but in theory, if he esteemed a woman highly enough to make her part of his family, then there would be no price he wouldn't pay to keep her safe. "The only thing that would stop him from trading for her is no longer having something to trade."

Zeyar shook his head. "Montrose is more strategic than that," he reminded Hasan. "Remember, we're dealing with the youngest police captain in Viryana's history. He's probably looking for any other option to get her back, to avoid negotiating with us. He'll see reason eventually, especially if the press keeps up the way it has." Zeyar folded his newspaper and tossed it to Hasan.

Hasan caught it deftly, flipping it to the page Zeyar had been reading. Above a photograph from Richard and Poppy's engagement party, the headline read, "Clueless: Montrose Allegedly Stumped over Missing Fiancée."

"The longer it takes him to come to his senses, the more incompetent he'll look." Zeyar leaned back in his chair, crossing his arms over his chest. "They're already writing pieces questioning his quick promotion. He'll come to heel eventually."

"And if he doesn't?" Despair roughened Hasan's voice. "Paranjay is at his mercy—has been at his mercy, for the past *month*. You said we shouldn't raid the police station because if we failed, Richard would retaliate against Paranjay. What's stopping him from retaliating now?"

"He cannot retaliate in any way that counts," Zeyar said. "The public doesn't know that the two cases are related—in fact, many of them don't know who Paranjay is at all. But if we reveal ourselves by attacking the precinct, Richard can use it against us and move Paranjay to a high-security prison on a completely different part of the island. He can claim that Paranjay is a threat to civil safety and push for a more severe sentence. *This* is the best way, Hasan. Violence won't solve this."

"You said you would listen to me," Hasan objected. "That was the deal."

"I do listen. It doesn't mean I have to agree."

"This is a shit bargain." Hasan threw the paper to the floor. The crease in Zeyar's forehead deepened at the action. "You get all the veto power, and we end up doing whatever you want. This is supposed to be a family business, but you call every shot."

"I can't help it if your ideas are stupid and reckless," Zeyar said. "If you came up with some good ones, maybe I wouldn't have to veto them all."

Hasan couldn't stop himself. "If *you'd* been captured, Paranjay would have gotten you back by now."

Zeyar flinched, the low blow landing exactly as Hasan knew it would. What he hadn't expected was the way the crack in his elder brother's demeanor rippled through him, an aftershock of regret that rumbled right down to his bones. Before Hasan could retract his statement, Zeyar's expression cleared, his stare becoming cool and indifferent. He rose to his feet, gathering his stack of newspapers.

"It might take me a little longer than it would have taken him, but I'll get Paranjay back," Zeyar said. He stepped over to where Hasan had thrown the final newspaper, bending to pick it up. "But you, Hasan?" Zeyar righted himself, turning his hard, accusatory stare onto Hasan's face. "If you had your way, you'd only get him killed."

With that, Zeyar left the room.

• • •

The most torturous part of Poppy's captivity was the silence. After Harithi left, Poppy had been alone for an interminable amount of time. It drove her mad, not knowing what was happening back at home. Were they searching for her? Were they celebrating her disappearance? The Jackal must have known exactly what was going on, but she only ever saw him when he came by with food, and he never stuck around to answer the questions she flung at him.

It had become a routine of sorts, though the intervals between his visits were odd and seemingly random. The jingling of the Jackal's key ring would announce his arrival before he came into view, giving her enough time to put herself together. The first time he'd unlocked the door, she'd considered trying to rush him directly. She could knock the tray from his hands, launch the watery tea and thin sandwiches into his face, and make a break for it. But the idea was meritless, and she knew it. He was a head taller than her, his lean, muscular frame at the epicenter of speed, strength, and agility. Even if she could push past him, he'd catch up to her in seconds.

So instead, she attempted to make conversation with him, hoping to glean something useful. She wanted to know if Richard had responded to his demands. She wanted to know what the Jackal's demands were in the first place. She wanted to know his name, if not to have him arrested, then at least so that she wouldn't have to keep calling him *Mr. Jackal* every time he came by.

"*Mr.* Jackal?" The right corner of his mouth had twitched the first time she'd addressed him as such. "That's new."

"What else should I call you?" she asked. "Surely you have a given name?"

"Nice try," he said. "If only you weren't as transparent as a sheet of glass."

He hadn't spoken to her again, no matter how much she chattered at him.

Being alone gave her plenty of time to think about her engagement evening. Now that she had recovered from the shock, a new question plagued her: Whom had Richard been speaking to? Clearly, whoever the other man had been, his loyalties were to Richard, not to the office of the viceroy. Otherwise, he'd have never dared to conspire so openly against the daughter of the duke. His voice had sounded vaguely familiar, though she had not been back in Viryana long enough to associate voices with faces.

It had to be someone Richard trusted immensely, which meant that it was either a friend or an underling of his who could not go against him. From the way the other man had questioned Richard, she believed it was a friend. Unfortunately, this deduction didn't help with her short list. Everyone was friends with Richard. He was magnetic. She had no idea whom he trusted, whom he valued above the others.

It was a hazard, she supposed, of getting engaged to a man after a three-week courtship. She really didn't know much about Richard at all. She had been taken in, just like everyone else, and if she hadn't heard him confess his plot herself, she would have never believed it.

This, of course, begged the question—would anyone believe *her*? The thought provoked a humorless laugh. If it was between the golden boy of Marnapur, high society, morally unassailable Richard Montrose, and the lowborn, brown-skinned girl who was exiled over a necklace, Poppy knew exactly where everyone stood.

Everyone, save for one man—the most important man: her father. She didn't know if he would believe her, a doubt that weighed on her heart, but Clarence Sutherland was a fair man. At the least, he would hear her side before passing judgment. But she had been denied even that small dignity, her body and her voice locked in this accursed cell. The longer she rotted here, the more opportunity Richard had to poison her father against her. Her nails dug into her palms as she pictured Richard whispering in her father's ear, smearing her image into a portrait of duplicity.

"Damn it, Jackal!" she shouted into the empty room. She kicked the chair, toppling it, but it didn't ease the pressure on her chest. Sighing, she bent to right it, then froze: The square of light that spilled in through the window in the door was half blocked, creating a shadow in the shape of someone's head.

"Who's there?" She whipped upright, just in time to see the other person duck. Heart racing, she called, "I know you're there. I saw you."

For a moment, she didn't think they would come back. Then, soundlessly, they stepped back into view. Poppy gasped. It had been years, but she'd know that face anywhere.

"Samina?"

Chapter Fourteen

On the Other Side of the Bars

Samina was a fool. After the abduction, Hasan had explicitly forbidden any of the gang members from interacting with Poppy Sutherland.

"She asks far too many questions," he'd said, "and while they may seem harmless or even innocent, she is not to have any answers. Nothing she can report back to her fiancé after this is over. Understood?"

Samina had nodded with everyone else, but in the end, her morbid curiosity and a seven-year-long grudge had led her down here. At first, she'd told herself she just wanted a look. She'd stood off to the side of the cell door, studying the other woman in silence. Peeking through the bars, Samina was unwantedly taken back to the last time that she'd seen Poppy, through the wrought-iron gate of the Sutherland estate.

Oh, she hated how every reminder of that day evoked the same, raw animal feeling of desperation that had driven her back to the Sutherlands a decade after they'd fired her mother. The grief, the hunger, the rage that twisted her insides every time she looked at her little brother and counted his ribs. She had gone there because she was at her lowest—but she hadn't yet known that there were far deeper places to sink to. Now, almost a decade later, everything had changed. Perhaps that was what had driven Samina to move without thought, revealing herself to Poppy—to show her just how different things were. But standing across from Poppy Sutherland, divided only by metal bars, Samina couldn't help but feel as though everything were exactly the same. Though Poppy now wore cotton clothes instead of silk, she still held herself carefully, as though she were a doll and someone else had positioned her limbs for her.

"Samina?" Poppy asked. "That is you, isn't it? What are you doing here?"

Her question almost made Samina laugh out loud. In a way, Poppy's actions were the very reason that Samina stood in this hallway.

"I work here now. For the Jackal."

"As a maid?" Poppy asked, her voice curling up with uncertainty.

"No," Samina said. "I'm part of his gang."

"How did you become a—a criminal?" Poppy's eyes were wide with dismay.

This made Samina laugh humorlessly. "Don't you remember? My first criminal charge was 'stealing' a necklace from the Sutherlands—a family heirloom, so I'm told."

Samina watched the blood drain from Poppy's face. It was the admission of guilt that she had been looking for. For seven years, she'd wondered if Poppy had truly betrayed her, and now, she supposed she had her answer. "I hope you like your cell," she said, injecting as much contempt into her tone as possible. "It's nicer than the ones I've been in."

"Wait." Poppy stepped forward. "If you work for the Jackal, then surely you must know why I'm here. What does he want from Richard? When will I be freed? How many days have I been here? Do you know if anyone's looking for me?"

Belatedly, Samina remembered what Hasan had said—*she asks far too many questions, and she is not to have any answers.* Samina had already erred by coming here, and she could not afford to make any more mistakes because of Poppy Sutherland.

"Why should I tell you anything?"

"I won't tell anyone you told me, I swear," Poppy said.

"Just like you didn't tell anyone about the necklace?" Samina shot back. "I owe you nothing. *Nothing.*"

With that, Samina turned and raced away, ignoring her name as it echoed down the hallway after her.

• • •

Seeing Samina had rattled Poppy to the core, and her parting words now shook her severely again. What had she meant, about the necklace? Poppy knew the incident she was referring to—after all, it was her ultimate shame, the reason her father had decided to send her away. Poppy remembered it all too well, but she had never told another soul about it.

Samina had caught Poppy alone, near the gates of the estate. She hadn't recognized her at first—it had been a decade since she and Nanny were exiled, and Samina had changed. Her frame was thin and bony, and her haunted eyes, shadowed by dark circles, were too big for her angular face. But when Poppy looked at her properly, there was no doubt: This was the girl she had spent her early childhood with.

Of course, Poppy had asked about Nanny. "How is she?"

"Dead," Samina said bluntly. "My mother is dead."

Poppy reeled back as if Samina had physically struck her.

In short, sharp sentences, Samina laid out the events of the last decade: how her mother had been unable to find respectable employment after being fired by the Sutherlands, how she had worked as a maid in a merchant's household until she became pregnant and her belly was too big to hide, how after Samina's half brother was born, Nanny had been forced to work in various factories to make ends meet.

"She got injured in a machine accident at the auto parts factory," Samina said. "It got infected. We spent all our savings on her medicine, but she passed away three months ago."

Samina's mother wasn't the first factory casualty that Poppy had heard of. Her father had told her the story of her own biological parents' demise, lost to a fire in a textile factory in Andhra, a city south of Marnapur. Just like Poppy, just like thousands of kids on the island, Samina had become an orphan born of an industrial accident.

"I know we're not really friends anymore," Samina said, twisting her hands together, "but I want, just once, to take something back to my brother that I didn't find in a trash can. It's hard, finding work. The only places that will hire me are the factories, but after what happened to Ma . . ."

Poppy knew what her father would say: Handouts enabled laziness. The Founder decreed that everyone had a part to play, and those who did not play their part should not be encouraged by blind charity. She had promised to accept the Founder and his teachings, hadn't she?

"I can't get you food, Samina."

Samina deflated, becoming impossibly smaller. "That's okay. I shouldn't have asked. You probably have other things to worry about anyway." She offered Poppy a weak smile. "You look really pretty, Poppy. So grown up."

Though Samina's words had a genuine air, Poppy cringed. She could only imagine how she must have looked to Samina, wearing the latest fashions, living in the largest house—the house that Poppy had inadvertently gotten her banished from when she'd exposed Nanny. And now, Nanny was dead, and Samina and her brother were starving, scavenging for scraps, while Poppy ate three meals a day. The guilt burrowed into her resolve, eating it away. What her father didn't know couldn't hurt him.

"I can't give you food," she repeated, lifting her fingers to the back of her neck, "but I can give you this, if you think it will help?"

Samina's eyes grew wide as saucers as Poppy unclasped her gold chain and held it through the gate, the emerald pendant swinging back and forth. Samina had refused at first, but Poppy had insisted she pawn it and use the money for food.

She thought she'd done the right thing. Her chest felt lighter, and she slept easier knowing that she had atoned for what she had done to Nanny ten years ago.

That feeling of relief had evaporated like dew in the morning sun the moment her father had summoned her to his office, the emerald pendant dangling from his fingertips. The pawnshop owner Samina had sold the chain to had reported her to police, who had traced the owner back to Clarence.

"Will Samina go to jail?" Poppy asked.

"Damn it, Poppy," her father said. "Even in your questions, you show a blatant disregard for our property. No, the girl will not go to jail—since she's under sixteen, she'll be sent to an orphanage instead. What is it to you?"

Poppy had tried to explain, then, about Samina, and who she was, but the revelation only made him even angrier. "That woman was a traitor. She taught you heresy, Poppy. Do you still feel for her, even now? I thought you were changed. But perhaps not enough distance has been put between yourself and those wretched tales."

Her father had written Headmistress Thornhaven that very night, and within a fortnight, they were on the docks, her trunks packed and loaded on the ship behind her. Though her father's anger had cooled by then, the intensity in his eyes remained just as bright as he clasped that same emerald-and-gold necklace around her neck. The metal was cold as ice against her skin. "Make me proud," he'd said, and then it had been time to board.

She'd worked every day to make him proud—to prove that she had learned her lesson, would not repeat the same mistakes. But she had made mistakes regardless, planted seeds of doubt that Richard now sought to water. He was likely dragging her name through the mud this very second, so that even if she escaped, it would be impossible to show her face. Without anyone to advocate for her, what would her father decide? They had been separated seven years. Her term reports had always been excellent, but the headmistress had never missed an opportunity to write home for every infraction. Was three weeks long enough for her father to see the change in her? To know that she could never commit the crimes Richard had charged her with? Her lungs constricted. She flung herself down on the hard cot.

Poppy couldn't go back to Welkland. She had lost seven years of her home and family to exile, and she would not allow it to happen again. She had not pushed herself so hard at Thornhaven, swallowing racist vitriol—

Thornhaven! Poppy scrambled upright. Richard had instructed his accomplice to write to a cousin in Welkland, who had *attended Thornhaven at the same time as she had.*

Only one woman at Thornhaven fit that description:

Geraldine Alderfort. Poppy's heart sank. Richard had allied himself with the Alderforts. If he was forging alliances with the other First Families, then he'd been gearing up to take the viceroy's office for a while now—*much* longer than their brief courtship.

Poppy wouldn't let him have it. She would die before she let Richard inherit her father's office. He was untrustworthy, manipulative, vile—the least worthy successor she could possibly imagine.

I would have made a better successor.

The rogue thought rushed through Poppy's mind with a vicious edge that shocked her. She tried to shove the idea back down. It was preposterous—there had never been a female viceroy, and certainly not a Virian one.

But why should that stop her? She had all the trappings of a proper heir: She was her father's eldest child, she had an education just as extensive as most of her peers, if not more, and she cared deeply about the future of her island. Had her father not said something similar at dinner the day she had returned? The possibility had certainly threatened Richard, so much that he had mentioned succession laws to his accomplice the night of the party. If he had taken her father's words seriously, perhaps she should too.

The more Poppy thought about it, the harder it was to silence the idea. The role of viceroy would bring her more stability than any husband. She'd hold the highest-ranked office in the land, answerable to none but the Welkish emperor. No one could exile her. She would be in charge, free to roll back the brutal, ineffectual laws that held the colony back. The export crisis, the famine—she could pass new laws, increase the food supply, distribute resources to those who actually needed them, not just the police. She could do so much more than build orphanages.

She could send *Richard* off to Welkland, where he could never threaten her again.

But for any of this to happen, she had to get out of this cell. And if it meant using the last tool she had available to her, the one she had sworn to never use again, well, so be it.

Poppy closed her eyes and reached for her unnatural powers. Holding her breath, she tentatively explored the walls of her cell with her mind. Her stomach turned in response, but she ignored the discomfort, pushing harder. Her senses found moisture, cool and smooth, in the ceiling. It flowed in a cylindrical shape—a pipe. If she could stop it from moving, and create enough pressure, she could blow a hole in the ceiling and escape.

She pushed on the water with all her might, forcing the flow to halt. Pressure built as the water accumulated behind her block, but she held firm, even as spots danced in her vision. *Come on.* The water tested her, seeking a way out. She gagged, the nausea disrupting her concentration. As she slumped back onto the cot, something gave way in her mind. The pipe burst—but not with the satisfying, room-destroying explosion she'd been aiming for.

Water trickled from a small fissure in the pipe, pooling in the space between the upstairs flooring and the cell's ceiling. It was trapped.

Just like Poppy.

She turned and retched over the side of her cot, then promptly passed out.

Chapter Fifteen

Stalemate

Zeyar had stopped speaking to Hasan.

Which was fine, because Hasan had nothing to say to him anyway. That was what he told himself as he stood in the Devar Brothers Shipping Co. office, angrily preparing Poppy's lunch: a cup of chai, a cucumber-and-chutney sandwich, and four digestive biscuits. It wasn't much, but it was more than what many had. He put the dishes on a tray and headed down to the basement.

Normally, when Hasan arrived, Poppy would already be standing by the door, looking down her nose at him as though she were one of the maharanis of old as she fired questions at him like bullets. Her ability to remain haughty and imperious, dressed in an oversized, threadbare salwar kameez, was impressive; he'd give her that.

But this time, she wasn't there. He frowned, balancing the tray against his hip as he turned the key in the lock. "Miss Sutherland?"

The door swung open. Poppy was inside, lying on her bed. He took a step forward—right into the middle of a small puddle.

He jerked back as water seeped into his sock. "Where the fuck did this water come from?" Something wet struck his forehead with a splat. He tilted his face up. A dark shadow stained the ceiling. *A pipe must have burst.* As he stared, another droplet fell, catching him right below the eye.

He cursed. In this drought, the burst pipe might as well have been a severed artery, the room soaked with blood. *Focus on the problems you can solve.* He turned his attention back to Poppy. "Get up, Miss Sutherland," he ordered. "I'll transfer you to a dry cell."

She didn't move. He glared at her. Of course, after consistently bombarding him with questions nonstop, the obstinate woman had chosen *today* to give him the cold shoulder. "If you want to molder away in a wet cell, be my guest! I'm leaving."

She still didn't stir. Hasan narrowed his eyes, sensing something amiss. He put her food tray down in a dry corner and approached the cot.

Then he noticed the bile spattered at the side.

"Are you ill?" he demanded, his frustration forgotten. How had she gotten sick? Had it been something in the food? Anxiety drove his voice up in pitch as he called her name, trying to rouse her. "Miss Sutherland. Miss Sutherland?"

She remained limp. He leaned over her, gently rolling her body face up. "Poppy?" She was boneless in his arms, just as she'd been that first night on the Montrose driveway. The green-and-violet bruise on her temple stood in lurid contrast to her ashen, bloodless face. The sight sent his heart plummeting.

He kneeled on the bed beside her, searching for a pulse. "Please, please don't be dead," he whispered, the sound barely audible over the blood roaring in his ears. The only heartbeat he could feel was his own, racing at an alarming speed. If she was dead, this would ruin everything. Montrose would kill Paranjay for sure. Zeyar would *never* speak to Hasan again.

Zeyar—Hasan swore. His brother had been right: Somehow, even without storming the precinct, Hasan had managed to fuck this up. He should have checked on Poppy more, should have kept a guard to watch the door. He hadn't wanted to station men down here, especially given how nosy she was—what if someone spoke to her and gave the game away? Now he was paying for his mistrust.

He pressed his fingers harder against her throat, bringing his ear to her nose, listening for her breathing. Nothing. Then—*there.* A faint flutter. Her stubborn heart, still beating. Her breath warmed his ear a touch. He sighed raggedly. "Damn, you scared me."

She stirred slightly, her weight shifting as consciousness returned to her body. Her warm-brown eyes cracked open, moving sluggishly over his face. They sharpened, recognition flooding her gaze. Her eyes flew open fully, and her hands slammed against his chest, shoving him away.

"What are you doing on my bed?"

Though her push had been weak, her cry made him jump. He scrambled backward, slipping on the slick tiles. He caught himself against the wall, chest heaving.

Poppy pushed herself upright. Though she still looked pale, her eyes were alight with ferocity as she said, "My fiancé won't have me back if you touch me."

The idea was so absurd, it took Hasan a moment to figure out what she was implying. He barked out an involuntary laugh. "Is that what you thought I was doing?"

"Don't act innocent." She crossed her arms over her chest. "I know what men like you want. You thought you could try and feel my—" She stopped, the expression on her face so mortified that he would have laughed had he not just had the fright of his life.

"The only thing I was trying to feel was your *pulse*," he bit at her. "You looked like a corpse when I walked in here, surrounded by your own vomit, in a room that's starting to flood. Forgive me for demonstrating a little concern for your basic well-being."

The intensity in his tone took them both aback. He needed to calm down. She was alive. The plan was still on.

"So you didn't want to ruin me?" Poppy quavered.

He would have never touched a woman without her consent—unlike many of the officers in her beloved fiancé's force, he didn't get off on brutalizing the powerless. It stung that she thought he was capable of such an act—but then again, who would believe that even monsters had morals? He forced himself to adopt an air of indifference. "Don't take it personally, Miss Sutherland, but overrighteous noblewomen are hardly my type."

"As if I'd want a brute like you," she said, glaring.

He didn't dignify that with a response. "Give me your hands."

"What?"

"I'm moving you into a dry cell, but I don't trust you to not make a break for it. Give me your hands." He put his right hand over his heart mockingly. "I promise I'm not going to make a pass at you."

She scowled at him.

"Unless you'd prefer to stay here?" He eyed the water stain on the ceiling and the vomit on the tiles pointedly.

After a beat, she extended her hands reluctantly. Hasan reached over and took both her delicate wrists in one hand, helping her off the cot. As they walked across the hallway to the other vacant cell, he studied her, wondering how much she knew about the man who had his brother. While he doubted she knew anything about how the police operated, she might know more about Richard and the way he thought.

He waited until they'd entered the new cell together before asking, "Where is your fiancé, anyway, Miss Sutherland?"

She stiffened in his grip. "I'm sure you'd know better than I," she quipped, "given that I last saw him at our engagement party, however many days ago that was." A new edge had entered her voice, one he didn't understand.

"Four," Hasan supplied. "It's been four days. Today is the fourth. And do you know how he responded to my ransom letter?"

She sucked in a breath, as though she couldn't bear to hear the answer. He frowned. Why did the girl have so little faith in her fiancé?

"He didn't," he answered, when it became apparent she wouldn't speak. "He hasn't responded to our ransom note. One might think he intends to leave you in my care."

"He has the money," she said, her voice steady. "He wants me back, I assure you."

"Then why hasn't he responded?" He raised a brow. "It's not a question of money. We didn't ask him for that."

"I don't know," she snapped, but her voice wavered.

He stopped, narrowing his eyes at her. "You *do* know." She averted her gaze, but he grabbed her chin and turned her face back toward him. "You know something, don't you? Answer me. Tell me why Montrose hasn't responded to our letter."

She jerked her head back, pulling her face free of his grasp. "I am not answerable to *you*."

Hasan had had enough. First, he had found Poppy lifeless and immobile. Then, after he'd tried to check on her, she'd accused him of assault. Now she had the nerve to be smart with him? He would show her who was in charge here.

"Not this hoity-toity shit again." He used his hold on her

wrists to pull her closer. She wriggled, but he held firm, bending so that she had no choice but to look him in the eyes. He ignored the loathing reflected in her gaze as he said, "If you want your meal, you'll tell me what you know."

Poppy launched herself at him, swifter than a snake. Hasan swore as her skull smashed into his face with a resounding crack. He released her, bringing his hand to his nose in disbelief. It came away wet. He stared at the blood on his fingers, then shifted his gaze to her. Clearly, he'd underestimated her, and she knew it.

She met his gaze, unrepentant. "Starve me, then," she spat. "The food is subpar, anyway."

"Only someone as spoiled and entitled as you would complain about the quality of food in a famine," he retorted.

That wiped the scowl clean off her face. "You're right," she said, dropping her gaze to her toes. "I shouldn't have said that. I just . . ." Poppy squeezed her eyes shut. The skin between her brows wrinkled as she sniffed. "I'm tired of being here."

The threat of her tears alarmed him more than her display of violence. "*I* don't want you here any more than *you* want to be here. That's why I need to know why your fiancé won't respond to our ransom note."

She tilted her head up at him, her silence calculating. Hasan held his breath.

"I'll tell you," she said, "but first you have to tell me what you want from him so badly." She twisted her fingers together, but her gaze held firm as she suggested, "Maybe . . . maybe we can help each other."

Help each other? Though it seemed like a bluff, the offer had certainly sparked his curiosity. What kind of arrangement did she imagine between a noblewoman and a brute? For a moment, he was tempted to ask.

Then he glanced at the blood on his fingers, proof of how he'd underestimated her. He would not make the same mistake again. "It's not worth the risk."

With that, he locked her in the room, taking the tray of food back to the kitchen.

Chapter Sixteen

Zero Leads

"Tell me how it's been seven days, and yet you have zero leads."

Richard clenched his jaw to keep from flinching at the viceroy's scorn. Once, he had considered the two of them alike, fancying himself an echo of a younger Clarence Sutherland, the one who had assumed control of the island at only twenty years of age and guided it into an age of economic prosperity that none had seen before.

How things had changed—both within the colony, now plagued by poverty and crime, and with the duke himself. All Richard saw now was the way Sutherland's suit sagged at the shoulders where muscle had once filled it in, the way his wispy white hair could no longer hide the patchy pink skin of his scalp.

Richard was nothing like Clarence—he was not weak, nor did he possess the elder man's grotesque fascination with Virians. Clarence was obsessed with them, determined to make them civilized, refusing to see them for the inferior species they were. Richard would have ended his bloodline before he tainted it with a Virian child, and therein was their greatest difference.

"It's a complicated case, Your Grace," Richard said. "Rest assured, we are working hard—"

"Working hard?" Sutherland repeated, glaring at Richard. "Working hard? You ought to be running yourself *ragged*." He slammed his hand on the table. The sound reverberated against the walls of the room. "That's my daughter, boy! The woman you publicly vowed to make your wife. As her husband, your only job will be to protect and provide for her, and you're failing already."

Richard bowed his head, wisely recognizing nothing he said could soothe Sutherland until Poppy was returned to him. He itched to reveal his plot right there, to show the duke the forged smuggler's records with her name on it just to see the old man's face fall. But Richard still needed to marry her for his claim to be legitimate. Until then, he could not ruin her reputation. If Sutherland disowned her now and put the succession to a vote, then the viceroy's office would become a free-for-all. The nobility was nothing if not self-serving.

"I'll get her back," he said. "I swear it."

Sutherland muttered something under his breath. Then, he said, "Let one thing be clear: The only reason you're still the lead investigator is because when Poppy is found, I don't want her to be humiliated marrying the man who failed to bring her home. But if you cannot produce a lead in forty-eight hours, I *will* have you taken off the case."

Humiliated? Richard's vision flared red. *It is* I *who will be humiliated, reduced to marrying a lowborn Virian in front of society and the Founder.* Richard bit back one last urge to put the old man in his place.

He bowed, uttered a flat "Your Grace," then left. As the door swung shut behind him, he turned back. Sutherland had folded, his face in his hands as his shoulders shook silently. Richard filed away the image of the old man's misery to recall later, when he needed a boost of strength.

At first, when Poppy had gone missing, there'd been theories—cold feet, perhaps, or another man. It couldn't have been either of those things, not when Richard had spared no expense in winning her heart. She thought he was a perfect prince, traditional enough to provide for her, but liberal enough to treat her like an equal. Abduction was the only plausible answer. When the ransom letter arrived at his house, his suspicions had been confirmed.

He hadn't told anyone about the letter yet, save for Ernest Alderfort. Ernest was the second son of Gerald Alderfort's fourth brother, which meant that his inheritance would be chump change compared to what the other children of the nobility would receive—especially Poppy. It hadn't taken much to convince Ernest that he deserved far more than that, and that Richard was willing to give it to him, for a price.

"Why don't you just tell Sutherland about the letter?" Ernest had suggested.

"Because," Richard had said, drawing out the second syllable, "if Poppy is supposedly working *with* the Jackal and his smuggler, then why would they kidnap her? If I admit to Sutherland where she really is, I'll have to scrap the whole plot. Who knows when I'll get another chance to get rid of her?"

Richard was trapped. If he was taken off the case, the new lead investigator would almost certainly discover his cover-up. While Richard's own squadron were handpicked and loyal to him, there were other men—older men—who resented his quick promotion and would seize any opportunity to tear him down. But if he revealed his lead, the letter, then he would lose the chance to incriminate Poppy, extending their marriage for an interminable amount of time.

Either way, he was screwed, and he knew it. He got into his

car and pressed his forehead to the steering wheel. *Founder, grant me a miracle.* With a deep breath, he peeled out of the lot, driving back to the precinct.

• • •

When Richard walked into the police station, two of his men jumped up.

"Sir," one said, "we need to talk."

Richard tensed. Had his duplicity been discovered? He kept his voice level as he asked, "What is it, Officer Edwards?"

Edwards and the other man—Underwood—led him past the bullpen, toward the individual holding cells. "We've been tracking down the staff who served the party," Edwards explained. "We found this in one of the valet's homes. He hadn't had the chance to pawn it yet."

Richard squinted at the small item Underwood held up: a pearl earring, set in white gold. He didn't recognize the jewelry, but given the context, he concluded, "This belongs to Poppy."

Underwood nodded. "When we asked him how he got the earring, he said she gave one to him and the other to his fellow valet, if they promised to tell no one that they'd seen her. We've tried beating him, sir, but he won't change his story."

Richard was silent as he shuffled through the pieces of the story to accommodate this latest development. A revelation dawned on him, one so powerful he had to fight back a smile. He had pleaded to the Founder, and the Founder had granted him a boon.

"Find the other valet," Richard ordered. "If he can corroborate the first man's story, then we'll know they aren't lying."

"But what if they're working together?"

"I have reason to believe they aren't." Richard hardened his voice. "If you cannot do the task, Officer Edwards, I will see to it myself."

The other man paled. "No, sir, I didn't mean to—I'll find the other valet, Captain."

"Good. One more thing. Did the valet say she was with anyone when she left?"

"She left the party alone," Underwood answered, "but the valet said one of the caterers exited right after, in the same direction as her. If he returned to the party, they didn't see it."

"Officer Underwood, have a sketch artist sit with both the valets and have them describe the man—separately, mind you," Richard instructed. "Come to me when it's been done."

"Will you share your theory with us, sir?" Underwood inquired.

Normally, Richard would have lambasted the man for his presumptuousness. But in this case, it would be to his advantage if word spread. He inhaled deeply, twisting his lips into a grimace, as though it physically pained him to speak. "I believe Miss Sutherland has fallen in with the wrong crowd," he whispered. "She has a generous nature. I have cause to believe that she has grown sympathetic to the cause of a particular criminal in the city."

Edwards's eyes widened. "You don't mean the Jackal?"

Richard nodded, pleased that the other man had caught on. "The very same. I believe that it was he who followed her from the party. They must have arranged to leave separately, to avoid suspicion. She is likely with him as we speak."

"But, sir, why would she go with him?"

"To extort her father." Richard shuddered. "The Jackal is notorious for manipulating others. Usually, he bullies the poor, but he must have seen Poppy as bait to hook a much larger fish. Sheltered as she is, she likely does not even realize she's being used."

Richard let silence fill the hall for dramatic effect. Then, he said, "You must tell no one. It's only a theory, and I would not have my fiancée's reputation tarnished without proof."

"I swear it," Underwood said. Edwards echoed the affirmation, which all but guaranteed that by tomorrow, the entire precinct—and soon the nobility—would doubt Poppy Sutherland.

The only thing he had left to do was to prove there was a connection between her and the criminals, something public and irrefutable.

And if there wasn't proof, he would create it.

Chapter Seventeen

The Eighth Day

On the eighth day of Poppy Sutherland's kidnapping, Richard Montrose responded to their ransom letter.

Zeyar burst into Hasan's room for the first time since their argument, dress shirt untucked, hair askew. He came up short, taken aback by Hasan's bruised, slightly crooked nose. Hasan prepared to concoct a lie—he'd never admit that a cosseted noblewoman had gotten the better of him—but Zeyar didn't comment on it.

He waved the letter in his hand. "Montrose wants us to meet at the Marnapur Museum of Modern History tomorrow night," he said. "We'll go just before closing and trade hostages."

A weight lifted off Hasan, the sudden relief leaving him breathless and dizzy. If he'd been standing, he might have fallen to his knees. As it was, he gripped his bedpost hard, the wood creaking from the pressure as he rose on unsteady legs. "Is this real?"

He was aware of how stupid the question sounded when the letter was literally in Zeyar's grasp, but it was the only thing he could manage. He had lived in the nightmare for so long, he couldn't believe that there was a way out. Paranjay was still alive.

Montrose was willing to return him. By tomorrow, their family would be whole once more.

"It's real," Zeyar said.

For a moment, the two of them stared at each other. There was no scorn or irritation on Zeyar's face, only a deep happiness, one that reflected in Hasan's heart. He couldn't remember the last time they'd looked at each other with this kind of vulnerability. With hope.

Hasan rushed forward. Zeyar opened his arms, his steady weight absorbing the impact of Hasan's embrace. His elder brother closed his arms around him, thumping him on the back triumphantly. It didn't matter, all those things they'd said before. They might have been brothers at war, but Montrose's letter had been a reminder of whom they were fighting—and whom they were fighting *for.*

Whatever they did, they did for each other.

• • •

Poppy didn't try to jailbreak herself again after her first disastrous attempt. For one, she didn't think she had the energy to summon her unnatural power again. Her entire body had ached from head to toe afterward, each beat of her pulse sending a spike of pain to her brain, reminding her of the way the Jackal claimed to have found her—looking like a corpse.

She spent a lot of time thinking about their last interaction. Once she'd calmed down, she'd been stunned at the way she'd behaved. What kind of lady resorted to violence? She stared at the bloodstains on the tile, unable to believe that she had been the one who spilled it. The woman who had attacked a beast—who was she? Even if he had deserved it, it had been incredibly foolish to rush him. At worst, he could have retaliated in kind. As it was, she had all but guaranteed he wouldn't work with her.

She resolved to apologize, but the Jackal hadn't come back since, sending Harithi to deliver meals instead. Though she would never admit it out loud, she wished he would. She hadn't forgotten the last thing she'd said to him: *Maybe we can help each other.* Admittedly, she had been grasping at straws, trying to get him to talk. But the more she thought about it, the more the idea made sense. If she wanted to overthrow Richard, she would need manpower to match his. As long as Richard was backed by the police, he would always outnumber her. Richard himself had said the Jackal had at *least* two hundred people in his network. If she allied with the Jackal and his gang, then she would have a force of her own.

The Jackal stood to benefit as well. Once she was viceroy—vicereine—of Viryana, they could come to some sort of arrangement. She couldn't give him free rein to terrorize her citizens, obviously, but it would be in his best interest to ally with her, someone from the upper echelon of Welkish society. He'd be foolish to pass it up, at least without consideration. But for her proposal to be most effective, she needed to know *what* the Jackal wanted. He had refused to share what it was he was trying to get from Richard. The only thing he had confirmed was that it wasn't money, which was a damned shame, given that it was the one thing she had a surplus of.

Footsteps echoed in the hallway. Her head swiveled toward the door—could it be Samina again? She hadn't shared the interaction with Harithi, half afraid that Harithi would tell her there was no such woman here and that she had imagined the whole encounter, isolation driving her mad. She held her breath, but when the cell door swung open, it was the Jackal on the other side. For a moment, she didn't recognize him. He was outfitted in Welkish formal wear, with a white button-down dress shirt and a dark suit jacket that accentuated his trim waist and broad shoulders. His hair was still wild, falling over his face as he looked down, slipping his key ring into his pocket.

Then he tilted his chin up to look at her. She stifled a gasp. Blue and green half-healed bruises mottled the skin around his nose. It looked far too serious to be her handiwork, and yet it was. The Jackal raised one eyebrow at her, daring her to look away. For a moment, she considered staying silent, but it seemed cowardly.

She steeled herself. "I'm sorry about your nose."

"Oh." The Jackal opened his mouth, then closed it. Finally, he said, "It'll heal. I've had worse."

An awkward silence filled the room. She dropped her gaze to his hands. Instead of a tray of food, he carried an unmarked shopping bag. "What's in there?"

"A new dress," he said. "You're going back home."

His words took a moment to register. "What?" Poppy spluttered.

"Your fiancé finally took the time to write back," the Jackal said, smirking. "The trade will happen tonight." His smirk faded. "You don't look nearly as excited as I thought you'd be. What's the matter?"

All the blood had drained from her face. She couldn't go back, not yet. She hadn't struck her deal with the Jackal yet, nor did she know what Richard's plans were. She would be walking back into the lion's den blindfolded, with no weapon or armor of her own.

"Nothing." She forced herself to put on a smile. "Nothing's the matter. I'm just relieved."

"You have an odd way of showing it," he remarked, dark eyes

narrowed. "You know what I think? I think you look scared."

"Forgive me if I ascribe no importance to your thoughts," she said, trying to snatch the bag from him.

He didn't release it, holding it firmly between them as he gave her a long, lingering look, searching for something in her face. She closed it off, hardening the set of her jaw. The Jackal already held all the power by virtue of being her kidnapper—she would not give him the last card she held, not unless he started laying down some of his.

Finally, he released the bag, seemingly finished with his inspection. She hoped it had been inconclusive. "I'll wait outside while you change. We'll leave once you're dressed."

After the door had closed behind him, she lifted the dress out of the shopping bag. It was an off-the-rack piece, but after her days spent in the borrowed salwar kameez, it seemed the most luxurious thing she had owned in her life. The dress was pure white, cut at calf length, with a fit-flare form and elbow-length sleeves. Small seed-pearl buttons trailed from the collar to the belted waist. The Jackal had also acquired white lace wrist-length gloves, matching patent-leather kitten heels, and a lacy white parasol. It was two seasons out of fashion, but Poppy gave it a content twirl anyway.

When she announced that she was dressed, the Jackal returned to blindfold her. His touch was surprisingly gentle, but he tied a firm knot, preventing her from squinting down at her feet while they walked. His palm burned against her back as he guided her out of the basement. The sun kissed her cheeks like an old friend. Even though she couldn't see it, she tilted her face up instinctively, gulping down fresh air like she'd been trapped underwater for the past week. The scent of sea brine flooded her nose—were they near the docks? The Jackal continued to lead her for another minute or so. Then they stopped, and he removed his hand from her back.

He tugged on the knot at the back of her head, and the fabric fell away. Poppy exhaled in relief. She glanced around, surveying her surroundings. He had taken her to a garage behind a stretch of buildings. Above the tin roofs, thick gray clouds marred the blue sky, spiraling from smokestacks. From here, she had no way of telling which way they had come from, preventing her from returning to the Jackal's den again.

The Jackal unlocked a dark sedan with tinted windows. "Ladies first," he said, opening the passenger door.

"Where are we going?" she asked, sliding inside.

He didn't look at her, but his lips twitched, amused. "You'll find out soon."

She bit her tongue. She hated being ignorant, but she'd learned by now that pushing the Jackal was a waste of time and effort. She needed to unlock the final piece of her proposal, the worm with which to bait her hook: She needed to know what the Jackal wanted from Richard.

"Is Richard going to bring the goods wherever we're headed?" she pried, trying to keep her tone casual.

"Yes," he said unhelpfully.

"What is it that he has, again? You said it wasn't money. Is it weaponry? Guns?"

He snorted. "No."

She'd have better luck conversing with a brick wall. "What is it, then?"

"None of your business, that's what," he retorted.

She turned to look out the window, her scowl reflected in the glass. The crush of brown-skinned people outside confirmed her suspicions that they were deep in the Virian quarter of the city.

The car crawled at a snail's pace, bumper to bumper with the one in front of it. Still, people ran between vehicles carelessly, criss-crossing their way through the road as though it were empty. Most of the buildings on this street were ramshackle shops, cubical, concrete structures with rusty corrugated roofs. Half of their wares were out on the street itself, mannequins and battered crates of coconuts sheltered under sagging canvas awnings faded by years in the sun. Groups of beggars sat in the shadows between buildings, their yellow eyes searching as others walked past as though they were invisible.

As the Jackal drove westward, conditions improved gradually, the buildings becoming more modern and clean, the roads becoming wider and emptier. They crossed Morning Bridge into the Welkish side, then turned toward the arts and entertainment district. Gradually, the buildings began to space themselves out. Instead of market stalls, lawns with lush topiaries lined the road. The smell of petrol and street food faded, replaced by the faint perfume of jasmine flowers from the nearby shrubs. Compared to the riot of potholes in the Virian quarter, the newly paved roads here were practically silent.

Though Richard had brought Poppy here a handful of times already, this was the first time she recognized it for what it was: wasteful. A sour taste coated her tongue. How much money had been spent on the upkeep of the Welkish neighborhoods while Virians begged for scraps? How many Virians had died of thirst while the Welks showered their shrubs with water? Her lips pressed into a grim line as she recalled what the reporter had said about Richard lobbying for police funding. If he became viceroy, the suffering would double.

Poppy had to become vicereine. She had to strike her deal with the Jackal now, bait or no bait.

"Jackal," she began, "do you remember what I said to you, the day the pipe burst?"

"Was it before or after you broke my nose?" he asked. A ghost of a grin touched the corners of his mouth.

Her brows stitched together. "I apologized for that! Besides, *you* hit *me* with a tray," she sniffed.

His smile grew a little more solid. "So I did. We'll call it even, then."

The Jackal slowed the car. Poppy turned, distracted from the subject, craning her neck to see out of the windshield as he parked.

"The museum?" She stared at the grand white building, bewildered. "This is where you're trading me?"

The Jackal checked his watch. "In approximately fifteen minutes, yes."

Fifteen minutes? Her heart plummeted. When he opened his door and extended his hand to her, she stalled. "I said we could help each other. The day the pipe burst."

He frowned. "Why are you talking about this now?"

"If there was a way to get what you wanted from Richard, without working with him, would you take it?"

He scoffed. "In a heartbeat. But there's no alternative. Trust me. I've thought about it extensively." He glanced at his watch a second time. "We can talk more once we're inside," he decided, shoving his hand at her again. "We're late."

Reluctantly, Poppy placed her hand in his outstretched one. The rough skin of his palms was warm, even through the gloves. This touch felt different from the way he'd handled her on previous occasions. Instead of the viselike grip he'd used on the day the pipe had burst, he held her hand gently, almost delicately. This time, it was her turn to clutch his hand firmly, determined not to release it until she got what she needed.

Chapter Eighteen

Set Up

Hasan put Poppy's odd behavior out of his mind as they ascended the steps to the museum. His gang had only had twenty-four hours to plan this. His focus had to be entirely on the mission—inarguably the most important mission he had ever carried out.

When they got to the ticket booth, he swallowed a sigh of relief. The first step in the plan had gone correctly: On the other side of the booth was Arvind, a vasudhakt member of his gang. Keeping his expression indifferent, he opened his wallet.

"How many crowns?" Hasan asked Arvind, keeping his voice low. This was the predetermined code for *How many of our men are inside?*

"Thirty," Arvind answered. "The price does not include roof access, sir." *Thirty daivyakt inside, plus Samina and her crew on the roof.*

"And the special exhibit?" He lowered his voice as he slid the money across the counter. "How many crowns?"

Arvind couldn't hide the way his forehead creased as he replied, "None, sir."

Hasan's frown mirrored Arvind's. *None of the officers are*

here? "Are you sure?" he pressed. "I was informed it would cost me twelve extra."

Arvind shook his head insistently, ripping two tickets from the roll. "It's only the thirty for entry."

"Thank you." Hasan accepted the tickets, unsettled. To Poppy, he said, "Let's go."

Poppy's heels clicked rapidly, echoes of his own hurried footsteps, as the two of them pushed into the foyer of the museum. He could hear her voice, stammering away, but he tuned her out, orienting himself in his new environment. He had never been to the museum. What was the need? It wasn't so much educational as it was egotistical, a narrative built by the Welks to sanitize the tale of their colonization of the Virians. For one thing, there were no exhibits or artifacts from the eras before the first Welkish settlers arrived—and not for a lack of recordkeeping.

Hasan and Poppy walked deeper into the museum, directly into the shadow of a two-story statue of a broad-shouldered man, made entirely of marble save for a thick velvet cape that tumbled down his back. Hasan knew who it was, even without the placard at the bottom: Charles Sutherland, Duke of Cloudcliff, and the leader of the Welkish expedition that had first landed on Viryana's shores. In his hands, he held a pair of crossed gold scepters. A circular chandelier hung just above his head, illuminating his serene expression, bathing him in a heroic light. The sight made Hasan's stomach turn.

He forced himself to look away, scanning the corners and shadows of the room, holding his breath. *There*—the security guard by the potted plant. Though his cap was pulled low over his face, Hasan recognized Raman. He tilted his gaze up, searching the second-floor balcony that overlooked the foyer. *There* and *there*, two more daivyakt gang members, dressed as a custodian and a repairman, respectively. His crew was here.

So why weren't the police?

"Excuse me."

Hasan and Poppy both jumped as a stout old man appeared in front of them, peering up at their faces through wire-rimmed glasses. "Are you Mr. . . . ?"

"Jackal," Hasan informed him brusquely, aware of the way Poppy's grip flexed around his hand, her curiosity piqued. "You can drop the *Mr.*"

"Very well," the old man sniffed. "Are you interested in the special exhibit?"

Hasan relaxed a fraction. Richard indicated in his letter that he would arrange for a curator to take them somewhere private. "The new exhibit," Hasan said, parroting Richard's instructions. "A History of Rose Gardening in Viryana."

Satisfied, the curator inclined his head. "If you'd both follow me."

He led them through the foyer into the west wing, which contained two exhibits about life in early colonial Viryana, detailing the work that the settlers had done to put down roots in their new home. In one of the display cases, the museum had installed a life-sized recreation of one of the first deep-water wells, built by the Welkish people to draw water from the island's natural aquifers. Hasan knew from his grandfather's lessons that the Welkish settlers hadn't been the first foreigners to stop on the island, but they had been the first to draw water independently. They'd used that water like bait in a trap during dry seasons, manipulating vasudhakt peoples into coming to drink for free if they renounced the gods of Viryana and embraced the Founder.

Of course, that was not how the museum curators had framed it—they made it seem like they were rescuing the vasudhakt, or, as the placards said, "uplifting the island's natural population, who had long been suppressed by the tyrannical regime of magic-wielders." Hasan wasn't surprised to see that the rest of the exhibit only detailed what life was like for the colonizers, either skirting around the dark realities that the native residents had endured or blaming the suffering on the royal daivyakt families of old. Though any artifact that testified to the crimes of the Welks had been destroyed, the atrocities committed had been passed on in an oral tradition, parent to child.

It occurred to Hasan that Poppy had likely never heard the true history. Did she believe what she was seeing, then, or did she have her doubts? He glanced down at her, but she wasn't looking at the exhibits. She was staring straight ahead, eyes unseeing, her cheeks pinched as though she were biting their insides.

He squeezed her hand, getting her attention. "What were you trying to tell me, earlier?" he asked. "Outside the museum."

Her gaze zigzagged to the curator, then to his face, then forward again. "I don't recall."

He understood immediately. What could she possibly have to say that she wouldn't want overheard by the curator? He shifted through his memories of the day the pipe had burst. *You know something, don't you?* he'd asked. She'd never answered him. Ice collected in his stomach. She knew something. She knew why the police weren't here when they said they'd be—she must. He cursed silently, wishing he'd pushed her that day in the cell.

The two of them followed the curator up the stairs to the third floor, where he then led them down another hallway of exhibits. They passed a cleaning woman pushing a bucket and a mop. Her dark curls were tucked under her uniform cap, but when she turned to see who was coming, her hazel eyes flashed in recognition.

Harithi ducked her head, but it was too late. "*You,*" Poppy gasped. "What are—"

Hasan squeezed her hand sharply, silencing her before she drew the curator's attention.

Finally, he showed them to a cordoned-off room, instructing them to wait there. Once he'd left, Hasan rounded on Poppy, his eyes narrowed.

"You know why your fiancé hasn't come, don't you?" he demanded, his heart racing. She dropped her gaze, and it was all the confirmation he needed. He closed the door, blocking the exit. "If you want to go home, you'll tell me what you know, right here, right now."

Poppy lifted her gaze back up. "I do know. But I'll tell you only if you give me something in return."

• • •

Samina and her team stood on the roof, out of sight of any passerby, but close enough to the edge that she could watch the roads. Up here, the air was insufferably still, no breeze to relieve her from the heat. She traced her left thumb over the brass knuckles on her right hand, a nervous tic she hadn't been able to beat. A trickle of sweat traveled down the nape of her neck, one that the heat was only half accountable for. The Marnapur police should have arrived twenty minutes ago to complete the deal, and yet there was not a single cop car in sight.

Hasan had already arrived, five minutes prior, with Poppy in tow. Samina's chest tightened when she'd seen the woman she had once called *friend* headed up the stairs, pristine and untouchable in a secondhand white dress. Poppy hadn't told anyone about her visit to her cell—of that Samina was certain. If

Hasan or Harithi had known, she would have already been reprimanded. But why not? Perhaps Poppy felt guilty for what she'd done, both to Samina's mother and to Samina herself. It didn't matter what Poppy felt. Samina would never forgive her for any of it—for the orphanage she'd been sent to after her arrest, for the years of abuse she had endured there, for dangling false hope in front of her on a gold chain.

She pushed the memories from her mind roughly, turning to one of the men on the roof. "See anything on your side?"

"Nothing," he confirmed.

She scoured the roads again. *Richard Montrose, where are you?*

Then one of the girls gave a shout. Samina hurried over to see where she was pointing. Sure enough, a trail of police cars was coming their way, their lights off and sirens silent. In the middle of the convoy was a large armored paddy wagon, which presumably contained Paranjay and his men.

The crew watched as the police cars slowed in front of the museum. Twelve men exited the first two vehicles, which matched what Hasan had said. The extra forty-eight men who got out of the next eight vehicles did not. Something hard and sharp weighed on Samina's chest.

She held her hand out to the girl. "Give me your binoculars."

Pressing them to her eyes, she focused the lenses on the two men who had gotten out of the very last car: Captain Richard Montrose, his gold locks gleaming in the Marnapur sunset, and Paranjay, wearing a bag over his head.

Samina squinted. *If they brought the prisoner transport vehicle, why did Paranjay ride with Montrose?* She focused the lens again, zooming in on Paranjay as Montrose gave him a shove forward.

Something was off about Paranjay. His clothing matched

what Hasan had described, though it hung loosely on his body, his denim slacks pooling around his ankles. A pang went through her at the sight. *They must have starved him for a month, for him to have lost so much weight.* But she couldn't shake the sense that there was some key detail that she was missing. As Paranjay disappeared into the museum, Samina squeezed her eyes shut.

"Think," she hissed. "Come on, come on."

She drew up the image in her mind: Paranjay, head bent, face covered, bare arms pulled back into cuffs as he—*oh, fuck.* Her eyes snapped open, heart pounding. She thrust the binoculars back at the girl with a curse.

Turning her attention to the other crew members on the roof, she whistled loudly. "One of you, fetch Zeyar!" she shouted. "Tell him that we're going to need backup *now.* The rest of you, get inside the building! There's going to be a fight, and we're already outnumbered."

The group hustled to the door on the roof. The girl with the binoculars paused, turning back to Samina, who hadn't moved. "What about you?" the girl asked. "Aren't you coming?"

Samina shook her head, her short hair falling into her face as she crouched on the edge of the roof, staring down at the street below. "I'm taking the fast way."

Gripping the bricks, she launched herself over the edge. Samina scaled her way down to the room that the museum staff had cordoned off earlier, hoping that she wasn't too late.

She perched on the ledge of the window, peering into the room. Hasan stood with his back to her. Behind him, Poppy's white dress was barely visible, hem peeking out between the wide stance of his legs. Their bodies were nearly touching as he bent his head. Samina nearly lost her grip as she took in the scene. *Pantheon, save me. What is he doing?* Though she was clearly interrupting something, she needed to warn Hasan before Montrose arrived. Samina lifted her hand to pound on the window, but before she could, the door flew open.

Samina dropped immediately, clinging to the ledge with her fingers, her breath coming in short, ragged bursts that matched the sprint of her pulse. Her torn finger pads ached, but the threat of the fall only made her dig them in harder. By some miracle, Richard Montrose hadn't seen her.

But Samina would wait until the night was over before she offered the gods any thanks.

• • •

Poppy's offer hung in the air between them. Hasan recognized the look in her eyes now—it was the same expression she'd worn on her face minutes before she'd broken his nose: defiance. He didn't have time for this. His brother's life hung in the balance. Each second she didn't give him the information he needed was a second he could be spending getting Paranjay back. Seizing her wrist, he backed her up, pinning her against a glass display case. In his hand, her pulse thrummed like a hummingbird's wings.

"You," he growled, "are in no position to negotiate. You're the prisoner here, and you would do well to remember that."

"A prisoner with knowledge you want," she fired back.

He glared at her, the intensity so strong that she turned her face in an attempt to avoid it.

"Don't play coy with me, Miss Sutherland," he said, pulling her chin forward with two fingers. "Lives are at stake."

She closed her eyes, steadying herself. Then she opened them again, locking eyes with him. "R-Richard," she began, her voice trembling. "Richard doesn't—"

Footsteps marched down the hallway, fast approaching. Hasan spun away from Poppy, but he kept one hand firmly clamped around her wrist. The brass handle turned, and then the door swung open on silent hinges. The shadow entered before the man, but Hasan knew who it was by the voice alone.

"I see you've brought my fiancée," Richard Montrose said. He entered the room, flanked by two officers. More officers waited outside the closed door, preventing anyone else from coming—or going. Six more officers entered, surrounding a man with a burlap sack over his head from all sides.

Hasan's heart skipped a beat. *Paranjay.* He bit his tongue hard to keep from calling out to his brother. Though he was mostly concealed by the officers flanking him, Paranjay looked different—thinner, dimmer, his once-easy stance now curled away under the tense line of his hunched shoulders. Hasan couldn't see farther below his shoulders, and he didn't dare risk studying him much longer. If he showed too much interest in Paranjay, he had no doubt that Montrose would try and change the stakes of their bargain. *Stay focused,* he reminded himself, training his eyes on the biggest threat in the room. His gaze met a frigid blue stare.

"So," Montrose sneered, sizing him up. "*This* is the infamous Jackal. What a shame. You're not quite as big as your reputation."

Hasan ignored the transparent attempt to bait him. "Captain Montrose, I've brought your fiancée, unharmed, as you can see. Remove my sailor's hood, and then we can leave."

"I don't think so." Montrose clicked his tongue. "Release my fiancée first. Once I've got her, then you can have your man back."

"And give up my leverage?" Hasan shook his head. "Remove his hood, or the girl goes nowhere. I have all evening."

"I call the shots here, not you," Montrose spat.

"On the contrary," Hasan retorted. "You have one of my men, and I have your fiancée. Men are replaceable. Fiancées? Not so much."

"But he's not just one of your men." Montrose's expression was far too gleeful for Hasan's liking. "He's your brother. And while fiancées are hard to replace, brothers are even harder."

Poppy stiffened in Hasan's grasp, but he paid her no mind. "That's preposterous," he bluffed, even as his heart sank.

"Hardly," Richard countered. "I've been following you Devars for a long time, *Jackal*. All the evidence lines up. In fact, I myself thought there was quite a strong family resemblance. You two share very similar features—well, *shared*. He looks a little different, an unfortunate outcome of being uncooperative during our interrogation. Let's hope it isn't permanent."

A snarl ripped out of Hasan's chest before he could stop it, all but confirming Richard's hunch. "Take. The. Hood. Off."

Richard's eyes narrowed. "Let my fiancée go."

When Hasan didn't move, Richard snapped his fingers at one of his men. They struck Paranjay over the head. His brother grunted in pain. Despite this, Hasan held firm, but then they lashed out at Paranjay's knees, causing him to cry out and stumble.

"Stop!" Hasan shouted. "Okay, you want her back? Here."

He released Poppy's wrist. She didn't move. Both feet remained rooted to the floor, her expression blank save for her eyes, which burned with an emotion that Hasan didn't understand.

"Poppy, come here," Richard said.

Poppy remained beside Hasan. She glanced at him, then at Richard. He stared at her, bewildered. He opened his mouth to ask her what she was doing, but before he could speak, the window shattered with a crystalline crash.

Samina stood among the shards, a gun in her hands. Before he could move, she fired once. Her bullet cut between the guards, striking Paranjay squarely in the throat. Blood sprayed the officers behind him. They scattered, crying out in alarm as his body slumped to the floor.

For a moment, his heart stopped, his ears ringing in the aftermath of the shot. His vision flickered black, then red. Nausea rolled in his stomach; he swallowed back the taste of bile. "What the fuck?" he roared. "You killed him!"

Samina shook her head, firing at two more officers while the others fumbled for their weapons. "It's not Paranjay!" she shouted. "He's a plant. None of the prisoners are here."

Now that the body was on the ground, no longer blocked by the other officers, Hasan could see that Samina was right—this man's arms were bare, whereas Paranjay's had accumulated a plethora of tattoos and scars over the years.

Paranjay was not here. He had never been here.

They had been set up.

Chapter Nineteen

Over the Bridge

Everyone moved at once. The officers drew their weapons, pointing them at Hasan and Samina. Montrose sprang for Poppy. Poppy jumped back, crashing into Hasan. He grabbed her, pulling her into his chest. Keeping one arm around her front, he pulled a dagger from his belt, pressing it against her throat. Poppy squeaked, but he held firm. Montrose came up short.

"Let us go," Hasan growled, "or the future Lady Montrose won't leave this room alive."

"You wouldn't harm her," Montrose said, but Hasan had seen him waver. The man might have taken his own sweet time getting his fiancée back, but it was clear that even if he didn't care for her well-being, he still needed her alive. "If you kill her, I'll kill your brother," Montrose threatened. "Don't forget—he's still in my custody."

The reminder wrapped itself around Hasan's neck like a noose, but if he faltered now, he'd never recover the higher ground. Montrose thought him a soulless criminal, loyal only to greed. Though his pulse was roaring louder than his thoughts, he forced himself to sneer, leaning into the other man's prejudice.

"You're already planning to kill him—if you haven't already."

He shifted the angle of the blade, allowing it to bite a fraction into Poppy's throat. Hot blood kissed his fingers, trailing down her neck until it seeped into the neckline of her white gown. "If I can't have my brother, then I'll have my revenge."

"Get down!" From the doorway, Harithi's order swept through the room. He dropped the dagger and wrenched Poppy to the floor, covering her body with his as Harithi opened fire. Richard dove, crawling toward them at lightning speed, but Samina pounced on him, her brass knuckles flashing as she pounded him in the back of the head. He roared, trying to buck her off.

"Let's go!" Harithi shouted. "It's a bloodbath downstairs."

"Leave me!" Samina said, choking Montrose with his own collar. "I'll hold him."

Hasan yanked Poppy to her feet, running out into the hallway with her. Harithi led their group, their blood-soaked shoes leaving tracks on the pale green runner. "You knew, didn't you?" Hasan hissed at Poppy. "You *knew* Montrose was up to something."

"No," she cried, shaking her head. The gesture made her neck bleed even more. "I didn't!"

"Then what were you going to tell me?"

Rat-a-tat-tat. Gunfire interrupted their conversation. The three of them ducked behind a statue of the five founding lords for shelter. Hasan peered down into the foyer, where a full battle raged. Things did not look good for their crew of daivyakt. Though most of them were equipped with both daivyakhi and pistols, Montrose's men had come in full-body armor, with the most advanced weaponry he had ever seen. Though his men fought valiantly, their blood painted the walls of the museum.

Hasan lifted his gaze to Harithi, who nodded at him in silent agreement. He positioned his pistol between the stone shoulders of the first Lords Alderfort and Whitecliff, firing into the fray. He and Harithi took down two, five, six officers, until one of them looked up and saw them.

He ducked back behind the statue as a bullet blew off Lord Alderfort's stony hand. Harithi fired once more, but her gun clicked uselessly.

"Empty," she cursed, crouching behind the statue. "How big was your naumya?"

"Decent." In addition to the sacrifice of Paranjay's watch that he'd made a week ago, he'd been regularly giving up meals, storing up power in anticipation of a potential assault on the precinct.

"Look," Harithi said. "If we go down there right now, we'll be shot so many times, our bodies will be more lead than flesh. We need to smoke the pigs out."

"And risk burning our own?" Hasan shook his head. "I can't."

"You must," Harithi insisted. "Our crew will manage. This is the only way."

"Watch out!" Poppy shouted, interrupting them. She yanked Hasan backward, pulling him out of the trajectory of a bullet. Hasan followed its path back to the man who had fired it: Montrose. The captain stood at the other end of the hallway, hat missing, golden hair rumpled, blood pouring over his rapidly swelling lip into the torn collar of his shirt.

His heart sank. *What had happened to Samina?* His vision clouded over, and he lifted his gun and fired back at Richard. Once, twice, click. His gun was out of bullets.

"You'll regret killing my men, Jackal!" Richard bared bloody teeth as he advanced on them. Hasan stepped out into the hallway, flinging both his arms forward. A wave of flame burst from his fingertips, catching on the runner, forcing Richard to stop short.

Behind him, Poppy sucked in a breath. "You're like me."

He turned, narrowing his eyes at her. "What does that mean?"

Then Montrose fired through the flames. Searing pain pierced Hasan's back, and he bellowed, his vision flickering as he dropped to one knee. The bastard had shot him, he realized, the thought hazy and disjointed by his initial shock. Indignation followed. *How the fuck had he let Richard Montrose draw first blood?* He'd hit him back twofold—once he found a way to get off the ground. Harithi seized his arm, hauling him back to his feet.

"Move!" she commanded. The three of them ran around the curved balcony, ducking behind the railing on the other side. Every movement tore through Hasan's body like he was being shot anew. When they stopped, he slouched, blood staining the marble. His breaths came in uneven, ragged gasps, like those of the fish his father used to catch right before they were clubbed and tossed in the bottom of the boat. Faintly, he registered Poppy and Harithi conferring over his body, but the blood rushing in his ears drowned out their words.

Harithi slapped his face once, twice. Hasan's eyes flew open—he hadn't realized they'd drifted shut.

"Get up," she said, her face drawn with worry. "We have a plan."

Harithi hefted him to his feet. "The statue." She pointed down at Charles Sutherland. "You get his cape, and I'll do the rest."

Hasan understood in a second. Putting out both his hands, he poured the last of his energy into two jets of flame. They caught the dark velvet easily, devouring the rich fabric. Harithi took over, stretching out her hands. As she curled her fingers into fists, the ground rumbled beneath the statue. An earsplitting crack filled the museum foyer, the only warning before the first viceroy of Viryana toppled, falling to the right. He crashed to the floor, crushing several of the officers hiding behind him. His shoulders and head shattered the window, tearing through the wall. Dust and smoke filled the air as men of both camps fled from the flaming statue. The fire leaped from the cape, catching on to the drapes nearby.

"Now!" Harithi said. Poppy laced one arm through Hasan's, Harithi taking the other. Together, the two women dragged him down the stairs, through the hole in the wall, and out into the street.

• • •

Poppy was having a nightmare. That was the only explanation for what was happening. Never before had she seen so much carnage. A cacophony of violence roared in her ears, gunshots blasting and bones cracking and the wet slap of her once-white shoes as they ran through puddles of blood.

Blood. She had basic medical training, but no amount of preparation could have prepared her for this much blood. It soaked the back of the Jackal's jacket, an ominous shadow that spread with every passing second. As he leaned heavily against her, the wet warmth seeped into her dress, blooming in patches like the flower she'd been named for.

"We need to move faster," Harithi ordered. She had taken over completely, a natural battle commander, fearless and fierce. She'd nicked one of the police weapons from the ground as they'd made their escape, wielding it with one hand, hauling the Jackal with the other as they hustled through the back alleys of the art district.

"We have to stop," Poppy said, her voice shallow and breathless. "He's losing too much blood. We have to apply pressure to the wound."

"We can stop once we get in the car."

"He'll die if he doesn't get help!"

"He'll die if we get caught!" Harithi retorted. "Once the cops regroup and call for backup, our chance at escape narrows significantly."

They turned out of the alley onto a quiet street. Not a single car was in sight. Harithi said, "Where the fuck is—"

A charcoal sedan with heavily tinted windows swerved into view, squealing to a stop beside them. They ran to the car as the driver's side window rolled down, revealing a Virian man in his early thirties, with a close-shaven beard.

"You're late, asshole!" Harithi shouted, her shoulders sagging with relief.

"They've blockaded the roads," the newcomer explained. "We have to go quickly." Then he caught sight of the Jackal, and his jaw dropped. "What happened to Hasan?"

Hasan. So that was the Jackal's name, Poppy thought. Though the round syllables seemed incongruous with the bloodied man leaning on her, it suited him, the soft, unvoiced *s* like the hiss of a viper.

"Gunshot wound," she said, while Harithi simultaneously snarled, "Montrose."

She opened the back-seat door, and together, the two women managed to get the Jackal—Hasan—inside, streaking blood on the cream leather seats. "Sit with him," Harithi ordered, getting into the passenger seat. "Do not let him lose consciousness."

The second Poppy closed the door, the driver slammed on the gas. As he peeled away from the curb, the wail of sirens rose behind them, coming from the same direction as the column of smoke spiraling out of the museum. Poppy pressed on Hasan's back, trying to staunch the flow of blood, dyeing her gloves crimson.

"We have two options," the driver said as he made a hard right, sending her careening into the window. "They're sending men to secure Morning Bridge. We can either plow through them, or go up into the countryside, then around to Sanivali."

"Sanivali?" Harithi asked. "Can't we take him to Azha?"

"The cops are going to tear the city apart." The man shook his head. "We need to get to the safe house."

"Well, he won't make it that far if we take the long way," Harithi warned.

"Then we'll have to push." The driver set his jaw and met Poppy's eyes in the rearview mirror for the first time. His gaze felt familiar, though she couldn't say why. "You'll need more pressure than that to treat a gunshot wound. Take his jacket off. Ball it up and use it as a compress. Kneel on it. As much pressure as you can apply."

"Zeyar!" Harithi shouted. "Ahead!"

The driver—Zeyar—snapped his eyes back onto the road. Two police cars barreled toward them, one in the oncoming lane. "Get ready."

He swerved, the car hitting the curb, splintering the flimsy barrier designed to protect pedestrians. As they passed the police vehicles, Harithi pointed her stolen handgun at the closer of the two cars, firing at the driver. Red burst across the windshield as her bullets struck home. The car swerved away, crashing into the other police cruiser with a hefty metallic crunch. The mangled remains of both vehicles collided with the pedestrian barrier on the other side of the road and slid to a hard stop.

Zeyar pulled their car off the sidewalk back onto the road, making another hard turn. This time, Poppy stayed grounded, kneeling in the footwell of the back seat as she wrestled the suit jacket off Hasan. He was still conscious enough to carry his own weight, sitting up so she could slide the garment off.

"Thought you didn't want a brute like me?" he slurred, but she barely heard him. His dress shirt, once white, was now drenched red with blood.

"Founder, help us," she breathed, bunching up the ruined jacket and pressing it onto the wound.

"Pretty sure your Founder wants us dead," Harithi remarked. Up front, three more police cars were parked in a line, forming a blockade. Their drivers had gotten out, aiming rifles at them. Bang. Bang. Bang. Harithi fired at the officers, forcing them to duck behind the open doors of their vehicles for cover.

"I have this," Zeyar said, "but it's going to take all of my daivyakhi." He lifted one hand off the wheel, putting it out of the window and punching the air once, hard. The police vehicles flew as though struck by an invisible fist. Poppy gaped at the open display of unnatural power. The cops shouted in terror and dismay, but Zeyar tore past them.

Harithi leaned out of the window, the wind ripping her hair out of its bun. She fired at the few cops who pursued them on foot, striking each one with ease.

"I'm out!" Harithi swore, clicking the trigger pointlessly.

"There's a rifle under the seat and a handgun in the glove compartment," Zeyar barked. He glanced at Poppy in the mirror. "Not enough pressure, Miss Sutherland! Kneel harder. Put your full weight into it."

"Look out!" she shouted. Another police car had hidden between two buildings, headlights off, nearly invisible in the night.

Zeyar swore, swerving at the last moment as the police vehicle rushed forward, trying to T-bone them. The other car fishtailed, accelerating on their heels. Harithi shouldered the rifle, firing at the windshield. Cracks spiderwebbed across the glass, and the police car zigzagged as the driver attempted to prevent Harithi from shattering it.

"Hold tight," Zeyar said. "I'm going to take a little shortcut."

He wrenched the wheel into a hard right, driving up onto the sidewalk. Despite his warning, when the car hit the curb, Poppy flew backward into the window. The blazer fell from Hasan's back. Zeyar threw the car down a flight of pedestrian stairs. The sideview mirrors scraped the railing with a screech, sparks flying. Poppy couldn't help the shriek of alarm that escaped her lips.

"We're in the last stretch," Zeyar said.

True to his word, the turn for the bridge was up ahead on the left. But that wasn't the only thing in front of them: A cavalry of police vehicles hurtled toward them from the opposite direction.

"We have to get to the bridge first," Poppy said, pressing the blazer back onto Hasan. The hem of her dress bloomed red as she did what Zeyar had instructed, pressing her knee to the wound.

"Nathria, get me there," Zeyar muttered. He laid into the gas pedal, the engine roaring in response. Ahead, the police vehicles accelerated toward them, approaching dead on. There wasn't enough room to swerve around them. If Zeyar didn't make the turn, they would collide at a speed they wouldn't survive.

"Zeyar," Harithi said, her voice wavering, "you'd better know what the fuck you're doing."

"I got this." He brushed her off. "Trust me, Harithi."

Zeyar hit the brakes so suddenly that Poppy was nearly thrown for a third time. The smell of burned rubber filled the car. As he turned the wheel, he eased off the brakes. The car skidded onto the bridge with a hard bump, the trunk scraping one of the bridge posts. Zeyar straightened, slamming back onto the gas as the police cars behind them either sailed past the turning point or turned too soon, spinning out of control and through the guardrail, falling like boulders into the river below.

Then one of the police cars cleared the turn, getting onto the bridge. Poppy watched through the rear windshield as, slowly but surely, the rest of the cop cars made the turn, learning from the mistakes of those who had failed earlier.

"Zeyar," she said, "they're behind us."

"Harithi," Zeyar gritted out. "Your daivyakhi. Can you destroy the bridge?"

"Not in your wildest dreams," Harithi retorted, "but I can do my best."

She leaned out of the window again. This time, Poppy studied her, determined to see how she used her power—*daivyakhi*, Zeyar had called it.

Harithi inhaled deeply, splaying her fingers wide. She brought her hands together, interlacing them. A low, grating sound filled the air. Before Poppy's eyes, a deep, uneven crack shot through the bridge. As Harithi knotted her hands together, the pavement on the two sides of the division pressed together with a groan before rising up into a sharp, jagged ridge.

Now *that* was a true display of power, one that reminded Poppy vividly of the tales that Nanny used to tell, about kings and queens who could move the earth at their whim.

Bang. The first car hit the ridge, front tires exploding as the spikes punctured the rubber. The other cars slammed on the brakes, but it was too late—they struck Harithi's barrier first, then each other, piling into a glittering mass.

Harithi sighed, rolling the window back up as they zipped

through the Virian quarter unchallenged. She didn't look ill, though what she'd done had been far more complex than bursting a pipe. Poppy's heart sank. Was she broken? Why couldn't she do that?

Zeyar raced past the docks, turning out onto the highway to the countryside. They might have driven for an hour, it might have been the whole night. Later, Poppy would only be able to recall flashes: Her knee, pressed on the Jackal's wound. The copper scent of blood, sticky on her skin. Stiff red gloves, no longer white, discarded in the footwell. Finally, the car slowed to a stop underneath a streetlight in front of a nondescript country house, with a thatched roof and weather-beaten wooden shutters over the windows.

After killing the engine, Zeyar turned around fully, giving Poppy her first full look at his face. "How's he doing?" he asked, his brows knitted in concern. His right eyebrow was split, scarred in a way that mirrored Hasan's. That little detail jiggled something in her brain, and then all Poppy could see were similarities: the same dark eyes, serious and intelligent; the same proud nose, albeit unbroken; the same full lips, pressed tight with worry.

She sucked in a breath. "You're his brother."

Chapter Twenty

A Man Born of Flesh

Hasan woke to the sound of his mother shouting. He cracked one eyelid open slowly, staring at the white ceiling above him. *Where am I?*

"So stupid!" his mother railed. "You had one job. . . ."

His throat was tight, his tongue parched. "Water," he said—or tried to. It came out as an incoherent rasp, no louder than a wheeze. His mother's ranting overshadowed his voice.

"Bring your brother back, not lose the other . . ."

"Ma," he croaked, lifting his left hand feebly. A spasm of pain ran down into his shoulder blade.

"Ma," came Zeyar's voice, interrupting her tirade. "Ma, Hasan is awake."

The yelling stopped immediately. Rohini's face appeared over Hasan, the wrinkles in her skin creased deeply. "Zeyar, get your brother a glass of water."

To Hasan's right, he could hear water being poured from a pitcher. Together, Zeyar and their ma lifted him into an upright position. Hasan accepted the water. Little ripples formed in the surface as his hand trembled, but he managed to take a sip without spilling it. Once he had drunk his fill, he passed the glass back to his mother.

"How—" he began, but Zeyar spoke first.

"We were ambushed. Montrose and his men got the jump on us. We made it out—you, me, Harithi, Poppy. We're in the Sanivali safe house now."

Slowly, the memories returned to him. He stiffened, his grip tightening around the glass. "What about Samina? Vinay? Raman? Jay—"

"We don't know," Zeyar said. "I'm making calls, Hasan. We'll find out. You need to rest."

"Your brother speaks sense at last." Their ma scowled at Zeyar, then switched her gaze back to Hasan. "You were shot in the shoulder. The bone looks fine, and I've gotten the bullet out, but you lost a lot of blood."

He vaguely remembered Poppy, her face smeared with a streak of blood—his? hers?—leaning over him in the car, her knee jammed into his shoulder as she tried to stop him from bleeding out. She had surprised him yet again. First she had broken his nose, then she had refused to go to Richard—

The memory drew him up short. "Where's Poppy?"

Zeyar and their ma exchanged a look. "She's upstairs, resting," Rohini said. "We've locked her door from the outside. What do you want with her?"

"I need to talk to her," he said. "There's something wrong between her and Montrose. She resisted going back at the museum, and right before he walked in, she was going to tell me something."

"Tell you what?" Zeyar asked.

"I don't know!" Hasan threw his hands up, wincing as the gesture pulled on his stitches. "Montrose interrupted. He still has Paranjay. We need to attack the precinct, get him out *now.*"

"Hasan, we haven't heard anything from Marnapur," Zeyar said. "We have no idea if Paranjay has since been moved. Plus, Montrose has locked down the city. We'd be going in blind. Attacking the precinct is a suicide mission."

"But Poppy didn't want to go back to Montrose," Hasan repeated. The more he thought about it, the more her earlier behavior made sense—her touchiness whenever he mentioned Montrose, her lack of enthusiasm when he'd come to prepare her to return, the way she hadn't called out or run to her fiancé in the museum.

"He seemed to want her back just fine." Zeyar shrugged, unfeeling. "How she reacted to him has nothing to do with how willing Montrose is to work with us."

"He's. Not. Willing. To. Work. With. Us," Hasan bit out. "Paranjay wasn't even at the museum. Montrose set us up from the beginning. If we're depending on his response, then we'll never get Paranjay back."

Silence fell in the room.

"He will respond," their ma stated, calm and matter-of-fact. "Once we send him his fiancée's thumb in a box, he'll start taking the threat to her seriously. A finger for each day, we'll say. He won't waste any time. A bride without a ring finger will be an eternal reminder of his failure."

Hasan had grown up with his mother's violent ideas. She, along with their father and grandfather, had started their gang, decades ago. People had targeted Rohini Devar because she was a woman, because they thought they could press her and she would fold. She'd been underestimated at every turn, forced to be twice as bloodthirsty to earn the same amount of respect as the men.

But this plan turned Hasan's stomach. He'd tortured men in the past, left scars far worse than severed fingers, but this was different. Holding Poppy captive was one thing, but mutilation was another beast entirely, especially since she had not done anything to justify her involvement in this scheme, aside from having the misfortune of being engaged to Richard. Moreover, she had saved his life last night—twice. First, when she pulled him out of the way of Richard's first bullet, and second, when she had staunched his bleeding until they'd reached Sanivali. For him to harm her after that would be a violation of his debt to her.

It also didn't help that he could still recall the feeling of her hand in his perfectly, her fingers long and delicate in those white lace gloves.

"We can't—" Zeyar protested, at the same time Hasan began, "Ma, that's not fair to—"

"Is it fair that I am going to lose my second son because the other two are too soft to get him back?" she demanded, her gaze blistering.

Zeyar lowered his head. "No."

Hasan flinched, shame and righteousness warring in his chest. He couldn't argue with his ma's statement. Paranjay was still in police custody because he and Zeyar had failed him. *This is about family,* Paranjay had said. *We do this so we can take care of each other.* Hasan's duty was to his brother first, and Poppy second. He fought back his uneasiness as he said, "We'll do it, Ma."

"Do it now," she ordered. "If we send the first finger today, it will reach him before sunset."

• • •

The blood under Poppy's nails tethered her to reality. The Jackal's brother had allowed her a bath last night before locking her in a spare bedroom, but even half an hour of scrubbing couldn't purge those dark crescents trapped under her nails. In a way, they comforted her, proof that last night had been real. Pieces came back to her in flashes, out of order and at random: the thick smoke that had filled the air as the museum burned, the groans of dying men as they escaped from the building, the fountain of blood that had erupted from the hostage's throat when Samina had shot him.

Poppy recalled how Samina had thrown herself on Richard, a man who likely weighed twice as much as she did. A lump welled in her throat as she remembered that he had emerged from the room, bloodied and battered, but triumphant. She desperately hoped that her childhood friend was still alive, even though the odds were near zero.

She wondered how the Jackal was faring. She hadn't seen him since last night. When they'd arrived, a small group of women in white had rushed out to their car, headed by a loud, intimidating matron barking orders in Virian. Poppy hadn't understood half of the words she said, but when the woman looked at Zeyar, she recognized three:

My foolish son.

She was Zeyar's mother—*Hasan's* mother. Poppy didn't know what she had expected Hasan's mother to look like. If she was being entirely honest, she hadn't imagined him as the kind of man who had a mother at all. Men like him were born from the same shadows they haunted, reared by the same roads they prowled. They didn't have mothers, especially not mothers who berated them while checking for injuries.

But Hasan had a mother, and a brother, and a handful of sisters or cousins—Poppy wasn't sure what exactly his relation was to the women in white who had helped her bathe and lent her a spare set of white salwar kameez. *No.* She recalled Richard's words in the museum. *Not just one brother. Two.*

She had been asking the wrong question all this time—*what* the Jackal wanted, when she should have been asking *whom.* She had carelessly assumed that Hasan wanted money or weapons, never guessing for a second that he may have been negotiating on behalf of someone he loved—because she had never imagined him as capable of love.

She tried to picture what the third brother would be like. Was he as cool and collected as Zeyar? Or was he as intense and unpredictable as Hasan?

Hasan. Her fingers crawled to her throat, where her knife wound had scabbed over. Hasan's mother had given it a cursory check, deeming it too shallow for stitches, but the wound of her terror ran so much deeper. She'd been manhandled by Hasan before, but it was nothing like the way he had caged her in the museum, cutting her throat as though it were no harder than slicing through an envelope with a letter opener.

Poppy had only ever wielded blunt knives, meant for cutting through tender, cooked meats. She'd never thought about the butcher's knife, never imagined the animals' terror before the cold kiss of steel drained years of their lives away in seconds. She had been hunted by Richard, and trapped by Hasan, but she was not truly prey until the moment the Jackal's pointed claws rested at her throat. She knew without a doubt, if Richard had asked him to drive the blade into her artery in exchange for his brother, he would have done it, no hesitation.

That kind of devotion was terrifying. But it was terrifying because it was powerful, and if Poppy could harness that power, then she had a decent chance at fighting back against Richard.

Though Hasan had tried to work with him, Richard was still their common enemy. Hasan would be just as eager to see her fiancé fall as she.

She wondered where Hasan was now—if he had made it through the night. If someone had asked her yesterday, she'd have been certain that he'd bounce back immediately. Shadows couldn't die. But Hasan was made of flesh and blood, and his soul could be severed from his body just as easily as the soul of anyone else.

Chapter Twenty-One

Lady Fingers

Poppy was sitting at the window, watching a pair of hawks circle over the field, when the doorknob rattled on the other side of the room. She spun around and, when Hasan walked through, jumped to her feet.

"You lived!" she said, and for once, she didn't have to fake the emotion in her voice. "There's something I wanted to talk to you about."

Then her eyes fell to the knife in Hasan's hands. Her stomach knotted. She touched the scab on her throat involuntarily. "What's that for?" she asked, hating how her voice wavered.

He took a step toward her, then another. Poppy scuttled back, but her borrowed salwar was several inches too long. Her heel caught on the excess fabric, and she tripped backward, hitting the hardwood floor with a muffled thump. Hasan crouched beside her swiftly. He caught her wrist and squeezed hard on one of her pressure points, causing her fingers to splay. Her stomach churned.

"Stop," she begged, wrenching her arm back. His grip was too strong, and the bones of her wrist popped as she continued to struggle. "Please, Hasan."

The sound of his name—his *given* name—seemed to have some effect on him. He froze, staring down at her.

Zeyar appeared beside Hasan, helping him pin Poppy's arm to the floor. "Do it now," he ordered.

"Wait," she said. Her mind was racing faster than her pulse, searching for the right combination of words to stop the nightmare. "Wait, please. Richard won't want me back if I'm damaged—"

"Then he shouldn't have tried to pull a fast one on us at the museum," Hasan said. His voice was tense, stretched thin as though he were holding something back. "Now we have to do things the hard way."

He put the edge of the hunting knife to the base of her thumb.

"No," she gasped. All her eloquence and rationality crumbled into panicked pleas. "No, no, please—"

Hasan began to make the cut. Her soft skin parted easily, a line of red welling to the surface. She had to stop him, had to offer the men something they wanted more than her thumb.

"Paranjay!" Poppy yelped, remembering suddenly. "I can get him back for you. Just stop! Listen to me."

Hasan stiffened, but he didn't push the knife down any farther. He and Zeyar exchanged a glance, as if silently coming to an agreement. Hasan turned back to her, eyes narrowed, not removing the knife from her hand. "How?"

"Let me up, first," she said. "Can't we talk about this like civilized people?"

"No," Zeyar barked. "Talk. Now. Or Hasan will finish what he started."

She bit her bottom lip, staring at the blade. She had so few cards left to play, she was loath to flip them over. But if she held her silence, then she wouldn't even have fingers to hold those cards. Taking a deep, ragged breath, she said, "Okay. Fine. Do you remember how long it took Richard to respond to your letter?"

"I knew there was something wrong about that," Hasan said.

Poppy bobbed her head eagerly. "It might sound far-fetched to you, but Richard doesn't truly care for me. He has been plotting to marry me only to inherit my father's office as viceroy, and then dispose of me once he's gotten what he wants."

Her voice trembled as she spoke, all the rage and devastation from her engagement night rising to the surface. Hasan scrutinized her face, but she refused to look away. After a brief standoff, Hasan glanced at Zeyar, whose face was still blank.

"Continue," he said.

"I have a plan." Poppy rushed forward, tripping over her words. "Richard thinks he can oust me, but I won't give up so easily. I intend to outmaneuver him and become heir to my father's office."

Hasan and Zeyar shared another look. This time, they didn't bother to hide their expressions from her. They wore their disbelief in their raised eyebrows and closed mouths.

"And how," Zeyar drawled, "do you intend to manage that?"

Poppy lifted her chin slightly, doing her best to project confidence despite being pinned to the ground. "By allying myself with you."

Silence followed her proposition. For a moment, both men stared at her. She held their gazes, not letting her eyes wander down to the blade pressing against her stinging thumb.

Zeyar cracked first, his lips twitching. A small muffled noise escaped the back of his throat, and then he and Hasan were laughing, their shoulders shaking. She stared at them both in disbelief.

"You're laughing." Poppy glared. "The future vicereine of this colony has just offered to ally herself with you, and you're laughing."

This, for some reason, only made them laugh harder. Zeyar's grip on her arm loosened, and she wrenched it free, cradling her wounded thumb. Her face burned, but she sat upright and crossed her arms as she waited for them to stop conducting themselves like children.

Finally, they managed to rein themselves in. "Be reasonable," Zeyar said. "You are a woman. A Virian woman, besides. This colony has never had a female, non-Welkish viceroy in its history. Richard will be viceroy, and you will be his marchioness."

Defiance streaked through Poppy. *We'll see about that.* "Why should he be viceroy?" she demanded. "I am my father's child, not he."

"Isn't it enough to be his wife?" Zeyar smirked. "You were found on the streets, and now you wear silks and walk on the arm of the nobility's golden boy."

"It *was* enough for me," she said, "but then I found out what he was planning."

Hasan's sharp eyes gleamed with interest. "So this is about revenge, then? Tit for tat?"

She paused, considering that. "Yes," she said. "But it's also about so much more. This is *my* home. I have been exiled once, and it led me to lose everything." Poppy set her jaw. "I will not be forced out again. Not when I have worked so hard for this. What qualification do I lack?" She held up her fingers as she counted, "I am well educated, well read, well spoken. I can do arithmetic twice as fast as most of the sons of the First Families. The only skills I lack are physical prowess, but marksmanship and self-defense can be learned, and I am a quick study." She squared her shoulders and straightened her spine. "I would make a better ruler than most."

"Why ally with us?" Hasan pressed. "If you are so qualified, why not just ask your father to name you explicitly in the line of succession?"

"It will be contested," Poppy admitted. "A viceroy's word does not become law just because he says so. All legal motions must be voted upon in the House of Representatives. Even if the motion to make me the official heir passes there, the Council of Lords must vote on it, too, before my father can finalize it with royal assent. And it will certainly fail, because the lords and most of the representatives have the same old-fashioned mindset as your brother." She tossed a disapproving look in Zeyar's direction.

Zeyar tucked his hands into his pockets. "You can impugn my character all you wish, Miss Sutherland. It will not change the fact that, to society at large, you are not a suitable successor. And you have no manpower to force the issue, either, which is why you wish to ally with us, is it not?"

She nodded. Zeyar may have been obstinate, but at least he saw the plan clearly. "Richard has his police force. You and Hasan have your gang. We are evenly matched should this contest of wills turn violent, though I hope that it doesn't lead to that."

"What do we get in exchange?" Hasan pressed. His mouth curved in a half smile, as though recalling an inside joke. "This isn't a charity."

She couldn't tell if he was pulling her leg, but a spark of hope ignited in her chest. "I'll give you your brother back. And I would turn a blind eye to your future smuggling operations."

"That's not good enough," Zeyar said. "We could likely negotiate the same things from Montrose once he gets a couple of your fingers."

She clearly wouldn't get anywhere with him; his mind was set. She turned to Hasan.

He was silent, studying his reflection in the blade, deep in thought. Then, he spoke, still looking at his reflection, his expression neutral. "It's a family business," he said evasively. "I don't make the decisions alone."

"Take her thumb," Zeyar said. "Enough dallying."

In that moment, she made a crucial mistake: She thought Hasan would defy Zeyar's order, so she was entirely unguarded when he snatched her hand, unable to draw back before he pressed the knife back to the thin cut he'd made earlier. As he dug the blade in deeper, she shrieked. Her hand burned with pain on a level she had never experienced before.

"Stop!" Poppy played her last card, the one secret she'd thought she'd take to the grave. "I have powers, just like you!"

Hasan's hand stilled. Her blood trickled down her wrist and over his fingers, but he didn't seem to notice.

Before he could resume cutting, she spoke, the confession rushing out. "I can control water," she blurted, "but it causes me intense pain each time I do it."

Hasan's jaw dropped, then snapped shut just as quickly. She relished his shock. She could see his mind racing behind furrowed brows. "So that was what you meant in the museum, when you said I was like you." His eyes narrowed. "That day in the cell. *You* made the pipe burst. That was why you looked ill. You'd overextended."

"I don't know how you can use your powers without hurting yourselves, but if you showed me, then I could help you. We're in the midst of dry season, on the verge of a drought—surely you could benefit from having your own, *exclusive* water source. Richard may be a Welkish man, but even he can't give you *that*."

Hasan stared at her for a good second. She held his gaze evenly, until finally he turned to Zeyar. "We should—"

"No," Zeyar said, "the only thing we *should* do is go and talk about this privately." He looked intently at Hasan as he stressed, "As a family."

Zeyar's meaning was clear: He wanted to discuss it somewhere Poppy couldn't hear them. Relief flooded through her as Hasan lifted his knife away from her skin. She squeezed her eyes shut, the sight of her blood coating the blade making her ill. Between the hunger, the stress, and the smell of rust in the air, she thought she might faint. But she couldn't get woozy. She couldn't be weak.

Hasan pulled her to her feet by her good hand, eyeing the gash in her thumb. His expression was almost inscrutable, but the slight downturn of his lips betrayed his conflict. "I'll send someone to have that bound," he said. "Put pressure on it for now."

She wrapped her fingers around the wound, pressing it shut. Her flesh cried out in protest, nerves screaming at the touch, but she maintained a tight-lipped smile until they left, determined not to let them see how visibly shaken she was.

When the door had closed behind them, she slumped back down, trying to steady her breathing as she waited for them to return with their verdict. She tried not to think about all the ways that could have gone better. She had done her best with what she had, but the thought brought her no comfort. If Poppy had failed to persuade them, she stood to lose far more than just her thumb.

Chapter Twenty-Two

Two Paths

Needless to say, their ma was just as shocked as Hasan to learn that Poppy was daivyakt. At first, she'd been piqued to see the two of them downstairs without the thumb, but when Hasan revealed what Poppy had told them and recounted the story of the burst pipe, she'd been stunned into silence—a rare thing for someone as sharp as his mother.

"I thought the viceroy picked her off the street," she said. She was chopping behndi for lunch, her movements deft and quick. "What was a daivyakt girl doing in the gutters?"

"She was orphaned," Zeyar said. "They found her in the ashes after a fire in a textile factory in Andhra—"

"I'm familiar with the tale," Rohini snapped. "I was there when it happened. Gods, it was a scandal. I've never seen anything like it in my life. The Welks were all displeased—I don't think I saw any positive press coverage. Virians were divided; some felt that it was a sign that Welkish society was becoming more accepting of us, whereas others thought it was a new phase in eradicating our identity, by taking our children and implanting their values in them."

"What did you think?" Hasan asked.

His ma sighed. "It was one less child on the streets. Evidently, no Virian was planning to claim her if they found her in the wreckage of that factory. I suppose it makes sense, that this girl from Andhra has control over water. Narayan Sovan and his family spent years in that city before Jagat Rai finally executed them all at the end of the war. Perhaps he didn't do a thorough job, and whoever escaped had to start over with nothing. But still, daivyakt living like vasudhakt?" She shook her head. "What has this island come to?"

Hasan's mouth flattened into a straight line. "Vasudhakt don't belong on the streets either, Ma."

His mother waved his words off with her knife. "The gods place us where we need to be," she stated. "It's not for us to decide what roles we play in the destiny of the world."

Silently, Hasan wondered if it was power or the cold indifference toward the plight of the human condition that marked the difference between man and god.

"Anyway," Rohini said, bringing him back to the conversation at hand, "we cannot continue with our plan as it is."

"Why not?" Zeyar asked.

She shot him a dirty look. "She is beloved by the gods," she said. "Not only does she have the power to channel divine energy, but her domain is water. Since the slaughter of the Sovans, water daivyakt have been practically unheard of. The gods show us great favor by blessing her with such an ability. To cut her fingers off would be inviting their wrath. They might forsake us, and then we would be even worse off than the vasudhakt."

"So then we ought to back her, then," Hasan said, pouncing on the opening. "If she's daivyakt, likely descended from the royals of old, then she's born to rule. The gods would want us to support her, don't you think, Ma?"

Zeyar glared at Hasan. "If she's truly destined for the role, she'll come into it on her own. If the gods want her to have it, then it will come to be, with or without our interference."

Their ma blew out an exasperated breath. "What are you talking about?"

"Poppy and her fiancé are in a power struggle," Zeyar explained. "Montrose intends to marry her so he can be the next viceroy, but she wants the role herself."

"There's never been a vicereine," Rohini said.

Zeyar shot Hasan a triumphant look. "That's what *I* said."

"More's the pity," she continued. She lifted her bowl of chopped behndi, walking to the stove where the rest of her ingredients waited. Hasan and Zeyar followed, flanking her as she turned on the gas stove and poured oil into the pan. "In the age of maharajas, there were several, highly competent dowager maharanis, some of whom were even more blessed by the gods than their late husbands! This island could use a woman's touch—especially one of *our* women, with divine favor."

"She has no one to support her, Ma," Zeyar said. "She's been gone for seven years and has only just returned. She has no connections, no allies. By her own admission, even her lord father's influence isn't enough. She wants us to fight for her, but once she's in office, then what? Do you think white men will lie down and accept orders from *her*? A brown woman? They'll overthrow her, and then whoever succeeds her will stamp us out like cockroaches."

"But she would be sympathetic to us," Hasan countered. "Having her as vicereine could open the doors for real change. She could introduce all kinds of legislation to improve the quality of life for Virians in this country. Montrose has always persecuted us, has even chosen a career that gives him the license to do it without repercussion. Do you think that will stop if he gets even more power?"

"Her sympathy would be her downfall," Zeyar said. "The other nobles would see it as a weakness, and work even harder to overthrow her. What do you think she'll do then? If it comes to saving her own neck or fighting for your idealist notion of a better world, she'll pick herself. Then you'll have chained yourself to the losing side, with nothing to show for it."

Hasan turned on as much of his youngest-son charm as possible. "Ma, what do you think?"

Zeyar shot him a look: *Not fair.*

He gave him a wry smile in return. *I thought we weren't in the business of* fairness*?*

"Both of you are a disappointment," she said, dropping chopped onions into the pan with a loud sizzle. Hasan's smile fell off his face. "Your brother is imprisoned, and yet you sit in this kitchen, playing at being kingmakers."

Queenmaker, he thought, but said nothing, instead bowing his head. Zeyar lowered his gaze as well.

Their ma pointed her rolling pin at both of them. "Have you forgotten what the goal is?" she asked, her voice scathing. "We need to rescue your brother. Back either one of them—back both, if you must—but make the decision that will return Paranjay to us the fastest."

"Poppy would do it," he insisted vehemently. "We tried dealing with Montrose, and he proved that he's unreliable. Now, let's try Poppy."

"It would take a long time for her to even assume office," Zeyar said. "Remember, her father is still viceroy until he retires or dies, and he wouldn't agree to returning Paranjay. Are we just going to wait for the old man to bite it to get Paranjay back?"

"Ma." Hasan cast his eyes toward his mother, begging her to intercede for him. "What do you think we should do?"

"I told you." His ma scowled. "Get Paranjay back. Do what must be done. You are grown men, now. Don't tell me you cannot come up with a plan on your own?"

"The way forward is clear," Zeyar said loftily, "but Hasan can't see it because he's too busy envisioning a utopian future where all injustice is miraculously solved by a Virian leader."

"You have to admit that things would be better if we had a leader who was sympathetic to us," Hasan said. "One of our own."

"If we're going to be ruled by one of our own, it should be someone who has a fighting chance of *staying* in power!"

"Like who?" Hasan leaned over his mother's head, his lips curled into a leer. "You? Since you seem to think you know it all. Well, you don't know sh—"

"Enough!" their ma exploded, slamming her wooden ladle against the counter. "This kind of childish fighting is counterproductive and will not get your brother back. Get out. Cool off. When you can behave like grown men, then we'll discuss it."

Zeyar gave Hasan a cool, indifferent look over their mother's head. Then he spun on his heel and left the room.

"Okay, Ma," Hasan sighed. He bent to kiss his mother's cheek, but she swiped at him with the ladle, forcing him to jump back.

"No," she said. "I want my son back. If you loved me, you would do that for me."

He bowed his head, teeth clenched. With that, he left his mother to prepare lunch.

• • •

It was a blistering day for a walk. Hasan wiped his hand uselessly along his sweat-slick forehead as he slogged up the road. Though the exercise aggravated his gunshot wound, he had to blow off steam. After an hour, however, he couldn't ignore the throbbing in his shoulder any longer. He forced himself to turn around, cringing with every step.

By the time he returned to the house, his shoulder was on fire. He let himself in, the screen door slamming shut behind him. The large wooden ceiling fans wafted cool air over him in gentle greeting. He tilted his head up in relief, heading to the kitchen for a glass of water to soothe the harsh burn of his parched throat. There, he discovered a grim tableau: his mother, standing beside a tray of her medical implements, her features drawn, while Zeyar and Harithi flanked her, helping to hold down a slight woman with short hair.

His mother's patient lifted her head at the sound of Hasan's footsteps. It took Hasan a moment to recognize her, because in all his years of working with Samina, he had never seen her so badly injured.

Blue-and-purple bruises flowered around her eyes and the crooked bridge of her broken nose. Her lips were split and swollen; some of the scabs had cracked, silently weeping blood. A dark bruise peeked from the hairline close to her right temple. Her right arm had been set in a fresh cast.

"Lie back down," his mother told Samina. "You have at least one broken rib, if not more."

Samina didn't listen, wincing as she sat upright.

"Who did this to you?" Hasan demanded, but he already knew. He'd known since the moment Montrose had emerged alone from that room at the museum. "I'll kill him," Hasan seethed. "We won't let him get away with this."

"Sit down," Zeyar said gently.

Immediately, Hasan's guard went up. Zeyar did a lot of things in a lot of different ways, but none was ever *gentle*.

"What's going on?" He approached the table. "Someone tell me."

Zeyar opened his mouth, but Samina spoke first. "It's my news. He should hear it from me." Her dark, haunted eyes met Hasan's. "Vinay is dead."

Her words hit him like a kick to the ribs. The waver in her voice left no room for doubt. If Samina had said it, then it was true. But Vinay, dead? He was a formidable fighter, one of the most experienced. Yet this same prowess would have made him a target to the pigs, so it made sense that they would have focused all their efforts on bringing him down.

Vinay had been a part of the gang longer than Hasan, had been there when his father had passed away, had been there when his grandfather had neglected his two younger grandsons to train Zeyar. He'd helped him learn responsibility when Rohini had transferred her duties to him. Most men would have been unhappy to take orders from one as young as Hasan, but Vinay had always treated him with deference, advising him gently while respecting his authority. Even now that he had been in charge for a while, Vinay had never hesitated to support him. A lump rose in his throat as he remembered how Vinay had laid a hand on his shoulder the morning they'd learned of Paranjay's disappearance. No one would be able to bring that steady presence to the gang again.

"Were you able to recover a body?" Hasan asked finally.

Samina grimaced. "Raman found him. They'd shot him in both kneecaps. So when the building burned, he couldn't run."

He squeezed his eyes shut, trying—and failing—not to picture it: Vinay, lying in a pool of his own blood, unable to move as the fire—*Hasan's* fire—caught him, choking on the smell of his own burning flesh.

"Any other casualties?" he forced himself to ask.

"Eleven men, including Vinay."

Eleven. They had brought over thirty daivyakt fighters, and they had lost *eleven*. Hasan's head spun. Harithi stood and caught him as he staggered, easing him into a chair. He didn't struggle as his mother laid one hand against the warm red stain seeping through his shirt.

"You've pulled your stitches," Rohini scolded, but there were no teeth in her tone. She patched the wound up as Zeyar interrogated Samina about the gang and the state of the city.

"I have to return to Marnapur," Zeyar said. "Tonight. I'll see to Vinay's funeral rites and his family, as well as those of the other ten fighters."

"I agree," Hasan said. "We have to bury our dead."

"There's no *we*," Zeyar corrected. "*I* am going. *You* are staying here."

"The fuck I am," Hasan barked, slamming his fist on the table, ignoring the jolt of pain that echoed in his shoulder. Samina flinched. He winced, apologetic, but his tone remained firm as he demanded, "Give me one good reason why I have to stay behind."

"Weren't you listening? Marnapur is under extreme lockdown. The cops *know* what you look like now, and all of them are looking for you and Poppy." He shot a pointed look at Hasan's shoulder. "Besides, you're injured. It's too risky."

Hasan pressed his lips together, unable to refute those points. "I should be the one who goes," he insisted. "Vinay was one of *my* men. What kind of leader will I be if I hide in the countryside while my own men burn for me?"

He couldn't bring himself to say the unspoken part: *He died in* my *fire.* Vinay could have recovered from his gunshot wounds. Maybe he would have lost his mobility, but he would have been *alive.* But the same fire that had saved Hasan had killed Vinay, and for that, he didn't know if he could ever forgive himself.

Zeyar ran one hand over his hair, closing his eyes for a moment before he spoke. "Hasan, please. Hear me out. It makes more sense for me to go because I control our finances. I can establish a small fund for Vinay's family while they adjust to the loss." He softened his tone, pleading. "They'll understand, Hasan. While I'm sure they'd appreciate your presence, they need the money more."

"Zeyar is right," Samina said. "No one will think poorly of you if you stay, Hasan. But if you go and get caught, then people will be upset that you endangered yourself in their time of need. You can't be a leader if you're behind bars—or worse."

"Vinay would advise you to stay, and you know it." Zeyar rested his hand on Hasan's uninjured shoulder. Lowering his voice, he said, "He knew what he was signing up for. He would have traded his life for your freedom without question. Don't render his sacrifice meaningless by rushing into a trap."

Hasan couldn't argue with their logic. "Fine," he said, though it pained him to say it. "But don't linger. If you get caught, I won't forgive you."

Zeyar lifted the corner of his mouth in a smile. "Careful now. One might almost get the impression that you'll miss me."

• • •

Zeyar left after dinner. Their ma had tried to stop him from going, trying everything from ordering him (*You cannot go! I won't allow it!*) to threatening him (*If you leave, then don't come crawling back!*) to guilt-tripping him (*Haven't you thought about what losing another son would do to your poor mother?*), but Zeyar was an unmovable force when his mind had been made up.

"I'll be back," he'd said. "Shouldn't take me longer than two weeks to get everything in order."

Hasan, Rohini, Samina, and Harithi all stood side by side, watching the red taillights of Zeyar's car fade into the distance, two dying embers in the night. Afterward, Rohini went to their pantheon to ask the gods for Zeyar's safe passage through the city. Hasan, on the other hand, went outside with his mother's old chakrams, which she kept in a velvet-lined case in the dining room cabinet the way most women usually kept silverware or porcelain.

Vinay's face wouldn't leave his mind, even as he hurled each disc into the dead tree in their yard. Though he ought to honor Vinay's memory by remembering his best moments, all he could think of were those last minutes of his life. Had Vinay died choking on smoke? Or had the flames reached him first, devouring what it could before he blacked out from the pain, succumbing to the next life?

He had never feared fire—why would he when he wielded it as easily as the chakrams stuck in the tree stump? Some Virians thought fire was destructive, the tool of the war god Aganath. But there were some sects who believed that the fertility goddess Rukmini was fire-aligned, rather than earth-aligned. They pointed to the volcano, which had given birth to the island eons ago, her fiery cavern like the warm womb of a mother.

Hasan believed both—fire could forge, just as it could raze. For the most part, he'd tried to use it to do the former throughout his life, using violence judiciously as a channel to carve out a safe and stable world for himself and his brothers, especially after their father had died.

But Richard? Richard used violence to destroy, to crush others into subservience. The more power he had, the more destructive he became. If he were viceroy, he'd kill them all.

When Zeyar came back, Hasan would have to convince him that backing Poppy was the only viable option. But how could he do that when Zeyar was right? Poppy was the right person to inherit the office, but she was the weaker choice. She didn't have the support of the nobility, nor did the average Virian care much about her. She couldn't even use her daivyakhi. Hasan couldn't fix the former problem.

But maybe he could fix the latter.

If Poppy could wield her daivyakhi efficiently, then it might prove to Zeyar that she was a viable candidate. If anything, it would help her gain respect in the eyes of Virians if they knew she was gods-blessed like the rulers of old. The nobility only had power as long as the people obeyed, and the masses had been teeming on the edge of chaos for a while now. The crime rate had come to a hard boil, and the gutters overflowed with desperation. If Hasan gave the people a reason to resist, a leader to unite behind, they could intimidate the Council into accepting Poppy.

But he was getting ahead of himself. If this plan was going to work, he would have two weeks to teach Poppy everything she should have learned in her childhood. He stood, yanking the chakrams out of the tree, replacing them in his mother's cabinet before going upstairs.

He hesitated, his knuckles inches away from Poppy's door. He had promised Zeyar that he would consult him before doing anything drastic. His last vow to Paranjay had been to stop making rash decisions without conferring with his family. If he did this, he would be reneging on his word to both of them.

Hasan fought the urge to lower his hand and walk away even

as he yearned to knock on the door and let himself in. Then he thought of Vinay, and his resolve solidified. If he went behind his brothers' backs to train Poppy, then he would suffer their wrath at first, but they would come around given time. But if Richard became viceroy, then the whole country would bleed, and he could not live with that.

It was too late to ask for permission. Hasan would have to ask for forgiveness.

Before he could change his mind, he knocked twice on Poppy's door.

"Who's there?" Poppy's uncertain voice called back. "Harithi?"

"It's me." Hasan opened the door and stepped inside.

Poppy sat on the bed, her thumb wrapped in white gauze. Her hair had been braided into a thick, glossy braid, and a serving tray was positioned over her legs. She'd been served a small thali with dhal, behndi, rice, and chicken. To his amusement, she was eating each one separately, with a spoon.

Poppy narrowed her eyes. "Can I help you with something? Or are you back for my thumb?" She tilted her head, smiling sourly. "I hear third time's the charm."

He leaned against the doorframe, ignoring the way her words struck him like stones. "It wasn't my idea, if that makes things better."

Poppy turned back to her meal. "It doesn't."

"Okay," Hasan said. "Then this will: I've decided to back your bid for vicereine, provided you prove to me your ability to succeed in the role." He gestured to the door with his thumb. "Get up, Miss Sutherland. You have two weeks to show me what you're made of, and we don't have a second to waste."

Chapter Twenty-Three

Pantheon of Silent Gods

Buzzing with adrenaline, Poppy followed Hasan to an unremarkable door adjacent to the mudroom. Inside was a closet, full of raincoats and jackets. Hasan pushed inside, hunching his shoulders to fit through the narrow doorframe.

"What are you doing?" Poppy balked. "We'll never fit."

"Come on," Hasan said. "You'll see."

Poppy hesitated, but she needed this alliance. She pushed through the garments, stepping into the closet. Her foot plunged down, finding only empty air where she'd expected the floor to be. A strong hand wrapped around her upper arm. Hasan pulled her back, gripping her hip to steady her. Blood rushed through her cheeks. Even though his touch was purely practical, no man had ever touched her like that, not even Richard. His hand didn't linger, but the shadow of its weight remained.

"What you're going to see down here is Viryana's best-kept secret," Hasan said. "Once we go down this staircase, there's no going back. You *will* be one of us, even if it makes your life as vicereine harder. You will protect this secret with your life, the way the rest of us have since the Welkish settlers landed here. Understood?"

His tone was fierce, more serious than it had ever been, even at the museum. Poppy pulled back a touch. What was she consenting to? But the words *one of us* rang through her mind, alluring and foreign at once. Her foot hovered over the first step. Then she planted it down firmly. “Understood,” she said, solemn.

The pair descended the staircase. At the bottom of the stairs, he reached out into the darkness and tugged on a chain. With a click, electric lights flickered to life, illuminating the space in front of them.

“Wow,” she breathed.

In front of them stood a diorama of the island, with a collection of at least thirty idols arranged across the landscape. Most of them had brown skin, though there were some with inhuman features, extra arms and eyes, or skin tones of blue and red and green.

“These are our gods,” Hasan said, placing a slight emphasis on the word *our*. “Each of them has an affinity for one of the four divine elements of our land: earth, water, sky, and fire.” He pointed to an idol painted in indigo lacquer and speckled in stars. “For example, this is Swapnil, the god of dreams. His element is sky, though some also believe him to be water-aligned.”

“Why is there disagreement?” Poppy asked. “Wouldn’t their texts tell you what their alignments were?”

“Texts?” Hasan repeated. “What are you talking about?”

She waved her hand. “You know, like how the Founder left behind his manifesto. Didn’t your gods leave behind teachings for you to follow?”

He laughed. “The Founder was a historical figure,” he said. “These are *gods*, Poppy. True gods, not a man whose legacy has been used to justify colonization. They didn’t leave us a rule book with a carefully prescribed morality.”

"Then how do you know they exist?" Poppy asked, baffled. "How do you know anything about them at all?"

"That's faith—to believe in that which you can't see," Hasan said. "As for where our knowledge comes from, well, we tell each other stories. In the old days, you could hear the epic stories being told at the temples, with certain stories reserved for different days and seasons. But when the Welks desecrated our temples and banned the teachings of the true gods, we were forced to adapt. Now we tell our stories in the form of song and dance. There are troupes, performers that travel between villages for a living. When we were boys, whenever a troupe came to our village, our grandfather would take us to see them. He was insistent that we remember the traditions and legends of our ancestors."

His expression softened slightly as he reflected on the tender moment, a memory for which Poppy had no match. Something sharp and thorny wrapped itself around her heart. The Sutherlands had forced her to attend operas and plays, but those events had never been about the art or the story being told—*Poppy* had been the true performer at those outings, demonstrating her manners before the nobility, hoping desperately that civility would equate to humanity in their eyes. The only person who had ever told her stories was Nanny—and those stories had cost Nanny her life.

Poppy switched her gaze back to the table so that Hasan would not see the envy on her face. "There're so many gods," she said, skimming a hand over the edge of the table. While Nanny had told her plenty of stories, there had to be at least three times as many gods as she remembered.

Hasan chuckled. "And these aren't even all of them."

She tilted her head in question.

"These are only the gods that have been important to my

family," he explained. "They don't represent the full pantheon. If you travel to different parts of the island, you'll find different gods who are important to the people there." He walked around the diorama, trailing his finger up the slope of the hills. "For example, in the North, the communities who live at the foot of the volcano place more importance on the fire and earth deities than the seaside communities, who revere water and air deities."

"I see." Poppy shuffled closer, examining a small mound of dried fruit, coins, and flowers that had been left at the foot of the diorama. "So, how does this fit into the bigger picture?"

Hasan stayed silent. For a moment, she thought he'd changed his mind. She bit her tongue, fighting the urge to speak. The harder she pushed, the more he'd clam up. "The gods are our source of power," he said at last, his words tumbling out in a rush. "When the Welkish settlers came, they knew two things: one, that we worshipped the pantheon, and two, that some of us had immense power. They did not realize that the two were connected: We only have immense power *because* we worship the pantheon."

"So anyone who prays can use the power?" Was that why she had gotten ill when she had tried to use her power? Because she hadn't prayed first?

He shook his head. "That's not exactly it. Everyone is born with different abilities and into different circumstances dependent on their parentage. Virians believe that the circumstances of one's birth are an indication of what the gods have chosen for our lives."

"But not you?" When he stared at her, Poppy clarified. "You said *Virians*, not *we*. Do you believe differently?"

"What I believe isn't relevant," Hasan said. "Some of us are born with the ability to channel daivyakhi, which is control over one of the four divine elements. These people are gods-blessed, or daivyakt. Historically, they were considered the gods' chosen rulers, but the trait is passed through families. If two parents have the gift, then the child will inherit the ability to control one element from their parents. But if only one parent has the gift, then there is a chance that the child will be born without any powers at all. Therefore, in order to protect the gift and ensure it did not get diluted, daivyakt were not permitted to marry vasudhakt—a caste of people unable to harness daivyakhi, even if they pray."

"What about Jagat Rai?" she interjected, referencing the last maharaja of Viryana, infamous for being the country's only natural—or *vasudhakt,* as Hasan called them—king. His people had mutinied against him, and the Welkish people had offered their support in exchange for power.

"There are plenty of theories about Jagat, especially surrounding the legitimacy of his parentage." He shrugged. "Most likely, he was a bastard. Either way, it didn't matter. His father still recognized him as his lawful heir, but his failure to rally the support of the people cost him not only a throne, but Virian self-governance." Hasan locked eyes with Poppy, his expression serious. "If you take anything away from his story, let it be this: Neither gods nor blood decide who rules. The people do. Understood?"

She nodded, though she doubted if she agreed. If the people had so much power, why didn't they simply rise up? If kings and gods were so easily overruled, why had they prevailed for centuries? Power games took more than numbers. Hasan's words struck her as a complex truth boiled down to an idealistic sentiment.

"Where were we?" He turned back to the pantheon. "Right.

Daivyakt are nothing more than vessels. We have the ability to *channel* daivyakhi, but we only *have* mortal energy, or kanusakhi. That's why you were drained when you used your powers. Because the amount of kanusakhi it takes to control an element is far more than the amount of daivyakhi required."

Relief swept through her. *I'm not broken.* "So how do you get divine energy?"

"Sacrifice," Hasan answered. "Prayer. We can't just *demand* that the gods give us their energy. It's an exchange: a give and take. A bargain. We give up something of value to us, and in return, they bestow on us divine energy equal to the value of the sacrifice."

Poppy processed this. So she had the *ability* to control water, but not the *energy*. "That seems . . . fairly simple."

"Hardly," Hasan said. "There's nothing *simple* about bargaining with the gods. If they believe the sacrifice isn't genuine, or if the intent behind a person's request for divine power is unworthy, they'll deny you. For example, in the old days, the daivyakt would use their divine energy to care for the island: to temper tsunamis, soothe the volcano, regulate rains, and keep the earth fertile for planting. But if they prayed for power to usurp the king and seize the throne, the gods might deny their request."

"What stops the person from asking again?"

"Common sense, I'd hope." Hasan traced one of the rivers on the diorama. "You don't want to piss off a god. Especially because, in rare cases, the gods have been known to forsake men. If a person commits a sin so offensive in the eyes of the pantheon, the gods can refuse to bestow power on them for the rest of the person's life. It's considered a great shame, and often the ruling class would strip these people of their names and cast them out of their homes."

Her stomach turned. *What a horrible fate, to lose your name and your home.* "So how do you ask the gods for power, then?"

"We make sacrifices, or *naumya*," Hasan answered. "Usually, we dedicate the sacrifice to the god whose patron cause is similar to what we intend to use the power for, or a god who we think would be most sympathetic to us, so that there's a better chance of the prayer being heard."

"Is there a specific prayer?"

Hasan spoke, two lines in Virian. She could recognize the smaller words, but the meaning of the prayer was lost on her.

Poppy winced, averting her gaze. "I don't understand what you said."

"How much Virian do you know?"

"Some," she admitted, crossing her arms over her chest. "Basic words and phrases. I haven't needed to use it in seventeen years."

Hasan's brow creased. She braced herself for his judgment, but it didn't come. "We'll have to practice, then."

Silence filled the room. Poppy walked around the edge of the miniature island, careful not to step on the flowers and other offerings. She studied each god, taking in their lacquered faces, their whimsical designs. They stared back at her, their gazes hard and unyielding. She swallowed. When she looked up, Hasan was watching her, his face inscrutable.

She changed the topic. "What's the plan, then?"

"The plan is twofold," he said. "First, you're going to reacquaint yourself with Virian. You'll be allowed out of your room whenever you please from now on. Harithi and the widows will speak to you in Virian only, and you'll pick up the language from them."

"Widows?"

"Those women in white," Hasan clarified. "They help my mother around the house."

Poppy recalled the women who had aided her upon her arrival. She'd assumed they were Hasan's family. "But they're so young," she said. "How can they be widows?"

Hasan hesitated. "I'll explain another time," he said. "It's late, and that's a long story."

"Okay," she said reluctantly. "And the second part of the plan?"

"You'll learn to make naumya and wield daivyakhi."

Poppy's heart sank. She had to relearn an entire language? While seeking the blessings of gods who might or might not exist, so that she could use magic? If anyone from back home found out, she'd be branded a heretic in an instant. Nanny had been fired just for talking about magic—what would happen if anyone found out she practiced it?

"Seems like a very reasonable itinerary for two weeks," she deadpanned, trying to hide her discomfort.

"I don't expect mastery, Miss Sutherland, but you need exposure." Hasan sighed. "I wish we had more time, too, okay? But we have to make the best of what we've got. Do we have a deal?"

He extended his hand. Poppy's gaze flickered from his hand, to the pantheon, to his face. She doubted this would work. She didn't have the upbringing Hasan did, never had parents who could sit and show her how to use her budding powers instead of teaching her to revile and fear them. There was no guarantee that the gods would even hear her prayers, given that she had been raised to follow her adoptive culture's religion. But what choice did she have? She had already tied her fate to the most notorious criminal in Marnapur; she might as well put her trust in these unseen gods as well. She placed her hand in his. His bare skin was callused and warm, but his grip was soft.

"Deal." Under the watchful eyes of the island's gods, they shook once, firmly.

• • •

Poppy had already washed and dressed in her white widow's attire when Hasan fetched her for breakfast. He'd dressed casually, in a plain green cotton kurta with little white buttons. Though the sun had just begun to stretch into the sky, Rohini had already set the table with platters of parathas, fresh fruit, puffed puris, jam, and a rotund pot that no doubt was responsible for the aromatic scent of cardamom and black tea wafting through the air.

Poppy got in line in front of Hasan, reaching for a plate eagerly.

"Take some food," he said, speaking in slow, precise Virian, "but touch none of it."

Though her stomach rumbled in protest, she did as he instructed. She thought back toward the little motley mound of food and flowers and coins at the base of the pantheon. "Will this be my sacrifice?" she asked, wincing at her stilted Virian.

Hasan grinned, approval on his face. "Yes, you're going to make your first sacrifice today."

Her limbs went leaden as she followed him to the pantheon. Though Hasan had said he didn't expect mastery from her, she set her heart on it anyway. Throughout her life, people had only ever expected perfection from her. To strive for anything less would be to risk rejection.

But it wasn't human approval she'd need this morning—it was that of the divine. This entire deal hinged on one thing: if the gods accepted her sacrifice as worthy. If they deemed Poppy as worthy. As she stared at the pantheon, it seemed like all the idols had pulled rank, shutting her out as they glared with hostile eyes.

One thing Hasan had said yesterday had kept her up nearly half the night: *If a person commits a sin so offensive in the eyes of the pantheon, the gods can refuse to bestow power on them for the rest of the person's life.* It was likely incredibly rare, she reasoned, and probably for very dark sins, like murder. Nothing that she had to worry about.

Except she did worry, because what if, in all her years of ignorance, she had done something to turn the gods against her? What if she put her plate down, said her prayer, and still felt nothing? The royals of old had been stripped of name and family, but Poppy's name and family had been given to her by Clarence Sutherland.

And if he learns you've summoned this magic, he will *strip you of name and family,* a little voice in her head said. *Would it truly be so bad to fail?*

"Okay," Hasan said, completely unaware of her inner turmoil. "I'll go first, show you how it's done. I'm going to put my plate there, where the rest of the offerings are, and then say the prayer. Let's practice it a couple of times before we start." He recited a line in Virian.

She still didn't understand it. "What does it mean?"

"My veins are a vessel for the divine power of the gods. If they find my sacrifice worthy, may I be filled with their cosmic energy," Hasan translated. "Okay, now, repeat after me." He restated the lines in Virian.

Poppy echoed the words, concentrating hard to match his pronunciation.

"Better. Try one more time," he insisted. She obliged him, focused on navigating the sticky consonants and lilting vowels. He nodded. "Good enough."

She wrinkled her nose. *Good enough?* She made a mental note to recite the prayer to herself later, until it was just as good as his pronunciation.

"Now, take a minute to choose which god or goddess you want to direct your intention to. I would recommend Indara, god of knowledge, and Nathria, the goddess of victory." He brushed his fingers over the head of each idol. "You can direct your prayer to the gods at large, but I find it's always nice to name one close to the cause."

Before she could protest that she didn't know what a single one of these gods represented, Hasan stepped forward and placed his plate at the foot of the pantheon. Kneeling, he recited the prayer, then lingered a moment before rising.

"Nothing happened," she said. "How do we know that it worked?" *How will you know if I've failed?*

He chuckled dryly. "What, were you expecting something theatrical? The room to light up? A holy choir?"

Poppy glared at him.

"Sometimes, you feel your skin prickle." He turned his palms up casually. "There really *are* no theatrics involved."

She slackened a degree in relief. There would be no visible sign of her failure, no empty silence following her desperate plea.

Then he added, "Most of the time, the only way to tell if your prayer was answered is to summon your daivyakhi."

Of course. She would have to prove that the gods had answered her with a display of power, on which this entire deal hinged. Her stomach turned over again. For once, she was grateful that it was empty.

Then Hasan spoke the dreaded words. "Okay, your turn. Show me what you've got."

His eyes burned like a lit cigarette against Poppy's skin as she stepped forward, placing her plate beside his. Saying a mournful goodbye to the stuffed parathas, she stepped back, clearing her mind as she recalled the prayer. "My veins are a vessel for the divine power of the gods," she recited slowly, putting all her attention on enunciating the unfamiliar words. "If they find my sacrifice worthy, may I be filled with their cosmic energy."

She held her breath, waiting for something—skin tingling, hair rising, *something*—but nothing happened. No one had listened—or, worse, someone *had* listened, and then judged her unworthy. Instinctively, she knew it was the latter. Wasn't that the story of her life? Too foreign for the Imperial Family, too coarse for the Welkish nobility, and now, Poppy was too little for the Virian gods. It didn't matter what her sin had been—maybe it was something as simple as the stilted way she'd pronounced the prayer. The answer was still silence.

She exhaled slowly, curling her fingers into fists. Her throat grew tight, but she clenched her jaw in response. Deep down, she'd *known* that the gods wouldn't heed her plea. Half of her had even hoped for it, so that she wouldn't have to use the magic her father so despised. So why was she still blinking hot, disappointed tears away?

"Okay," Hasan said, oblivious to the fact that Poppy was clearly forsaken. "Let's go upstairs. Harithi should be ready—"

"No," she whispered. She didn't need the rest of the household to witness this. Having Hasan here was humiliating enough.

"What?" he asked. "Why not?"

"I can't," she croaked out, looking somewhere over his shoulder, too ashamed to look at his face. "I can't—"

Can't summon daivyakhi.

He misunderstood. "Yes, you can. It's exactly the same as whatever you did when you burst that pipe—"

"No," she said, shifting her eyes to meet his. "The gods didn't answer me."

She waited for his reaction. Poppy knew enough of Hasan's body language by now to know that he stilled whenever confronted with the unexpected, muscles tensed as his fight-or-flight instinct warred within him. But he didn't freeze, didn't even blink.

"You can't know that," he said. "I told you, there's no physical reaction when the naumya is made."

"I do know." She hated the way the tightness in her throat caused the words to come out creaky.

"How?"

She ground her teeth together. "I just do!"

"You can only know if you try—"

Poppy spun on her heel, jabbing her finger at cut flowers sitting in a vase of water left at the foot of the pantheon. Curling her fingers into a fist, she jerked her hand upward, flowers spilling out as she lifted the water. The aqueous blob made it three feet in the air before the first wave of nausea hit. Hasan caught her as she doubled over; water splashed over their feet.

"See?" she gasped as he hauled her back upright. "Nothing. Forsaken."

His fingers tightened imperceptibly around her forearms. There it was, finally: the stilling of his limbs as the gravity of the situation weighed over him. "You can't be forsaken," he said. "The gods *rarely* forsook the daivyakt of old, and only for things like patricide, or stealing from the temples. You've never done anything so severe—unless there's something you want to confess?"

He quirked one eyebrow gently, and Poppy softened involuntarily as she shook her head once, quickly. "But if I'm not forsaken, then w-why—"

"Why wasn't your prayer heard? Sometimes, individual prayers can be rejected if the gods don't think it was felt. Remember, they're divine beings. They can see if your intentions are genuine. Whom did you direct your prayer to?"

"The entire pantheon."

He frowned. "You didn't try to invoke one god specifically?"

"I didn't know whom to ask." *Because I don't know anything about any of the gods, so how could I know whom to ask?* She pulled her arms out of Hasan's, hugging them to her chest. "I don't have a connection to the gods the way you do." She trembled, shaking with the depth of this loss. "I've spent the last two decades unaware of their existence, following the teachings of the Founder. I was *raised* to shun the stories of the gods and their divine energy, to rebuke them as heresy. It may not be patricide, but I doubt the gods will ever listen to me."

Hasan listened intently, his face impassive. When she finished, he dropped his head down for a second, nodding to himself before he looked up and locked his gaze on hers.

"Tell me one thing, Miss Sutherland," he said. "How long are you going to let who you are hold you back?"

Poppy flinched at the sudden ice in his tone. "What are you talking about?"

He crossed his arms over his chest, mirroring her stance. "It sounds like you've decided—perhaps from the moment I introduced you to the gods and the concept of naumya—that you were too scared to be answered, and so you didn't even *try* to make yourself heard."

"How dare you?" she seethed. She wasn't sure what stung

more: his accusation that she was self-sabotaging, or the fact that he had accurately guessed the depths of her self-doubt.

"You heard me." He took a step forward. Coolly, he said, "If you're not even going to try, Miss Sutherland, then I might as well take you back to your fiancé today."

She stopped shaking. Sorrow and shame gave way to anger. *Who is he to threaten me?* She straightened up, taking another step forward instead of back. Surprise flared in his eyes.

"You're one to talk about not making any effort," she retorted. "You all but *dumped* these new concepts on me, didn't bother to tell me a single story about any of these gods, and now you're surprised that I don't have any personal connection with them."

Hasan's expression shifted, some of the heat leaving his eyes. "Poppy—"

"No." Something heavy had shaken loose in her chest, and Poppy couldn't stop talking until she was free of it. "I'm not like you, Hasan. I didn't have an heirloom pantheon passed down through generations of my family. I don't even know what gods were *important to* my birth family, because I was adopted by the Sutherlands as a toddler. All I know of the Virian gods is what the Welkish people taught me: that it's heresy to follow them, and that their magic is forbidden. You have no idea what kind of environment I was raised in. When I learned that I had powers, I vowed I would never use them, for my own safety. So for me to break that vow means that I *am* trying. What else can I do? I'm repeating what you're saying, copying your actions, and it's still not enough, because I'm a lifetime behind, and I'll never catch up. I'll never have what you have."

Poppy's speech drained out of her, chest heaving. Hasan stared at her, his expression blank, but his body loose and free of tension. He lifted his thumb to her face. Only when she felt his thumb smearing something wet across her cheek did she realize she was crying. Her skin went hot under his touch, and she shoved his hand away.

He opened his mouth, but she didn't want to—couldn't bear to—hear whatever he was going to say next. She shoved past him and rushed up the steep steps, roughly wiping her eyes with her dupatta, leaving him downstairs with the pantheon of silent gods.

Chapter Twenty-Four

Complicated History

Hasan realized Poppy was right about one thing: He didn't know how she'd been raised. He'd lived with the gods all his life, and though he knew the Welkish position that it was heresy to follow them, the people in his life hadn't taken it seriously. Poppy, however, hadn't had that option. He couldn't begin to guess at her upbringing, and she was unwilling to share it with him. But there was one other person in the safe house who could shed some light on her past for him. Hasan knew that before Samina had come to him seeking employment, before she burned down the orphanage she had spent two years in, she had lived on the Sutherland estate, where her mother had worked as a servant. She might be able to tell him more about Poppy as a child.

He found her inside, recovering in one of his mother's spare bedrooms. When he asked about Poppy's early years, her whole body tensed, like a bird ready to take flight.

"Yes. I knew Poppy as a girl," Samina answered tersely, twisting the bedsheets in her fists. "We were friends."

Hasan sensed a complicated history there, but he knew Samina too well to demand the story from her. He lifted a stool from the corner of the room and put it down beside her, settling in patiently.

"Things were different, when we were children." She sighed. "My mother was her nanny, but Poppy never treated us like we were beneath her, or tried to pull rank. When she was scared or hurt, I remember she would find my mother in the servants' quarters instead of going to the duchess. Most of the Welkish kids wouldn't play nice with her, so she sought me out instead. We were . . . close. She was the closest thing to a sister I've ever had."

How different this child Poppy was, he mused, comparing her to the lofty lady who had sneered down at him even as her own wrists had been chained together. Was her pride something she had learned at that Welkish college? Or was it a callus, something that she'd grown to protect her from the friction of being jammed into a world in which she had no place?

Samina continued her story, interrupting Hasan's thoughts. "My mother thought it was important for Poppy to know the stories of the gods. When Poppy came seeking comfort, she used to tell her the old epics. Poppy loved them, believe it or not. But when her father found out, he fired my mother. I will never forget how he came all the way to the servants' quarters to shout at her. He threatened to have her exposed as an unnatural, but it was an empty threat—he didn't actually know that she herself was daivyakt."

He frowned. "Poppy doesn't seem to remember any of those stories about the gods."

Samina shrugged. "She was six, and her father likely bulldozed right over those stories with some more rubbish about the Founder. Either way, life moved on. As you know, my mother never found comfortable employment in a household again. She passed away after a factory accident. I became desperate. My mother had moved to the city from her village years ago, and I didn't have the means to go back safely—especially with my half brother. I couldn't write home for help; my aunts and uncles were as illiterate as I was. I turned to the only person I thought could help me."

"Poppy," Hasan said.

Samina's face darkened. "I told you, she was the closest thing I'd ever had to a sister. I had no one else to reach out to. I waited outside the gates of her house, hoping for some scraps from her table, something to bring home to my brother that I hadn't fished out of the trash. She looked . . . different. Stiff, not the curious and adventurous person I remembered. But she still gave me the emerald necklace off her own neck, encouraged me to pawn it for money."

"That must have kept you well fed for some time." Even if it had been small, the pendant alone would have bought Samina and her brother enough rice for three weeks.

"In theory, it might have." Samina picked at the edge of her cast. "But the police came to arrest me just two days later. For stealing from the viceroy. My brother and I got sent to a state-run orphanage. You know how that ended."

Hasan did. Samina didn't often speak of her time in the orphanage, but she didn't need to. He had heard enough stories from survivors over the years. "So you think what? That Poppy turned you in?"

"What else am I supposed to think?" she demanded. "They found me so quickly. More than likely, her parents gave her hell for losing that necklace, and it would have been much easier to point the finger at me than to tell the truth."

"You didn't ask her?"

She turned away. "I don't need to ask. I already know."

He turned that new information over in his mind, adding it to what he already knew of the woman he'd agreed to champion. Poppy had been humble once, comfortable among the company of her own, sharing whatever she had with them. A promising sign that she had not always been so aloof among Virians. So what had changed? He wanted to know Poppy's side of the story—but she was too angry to speak to him. Samina had given him context, but whatever event had made Poppy who she was today had clearly happened after Samina had left the Sutherland estate.

"Why all the questions?" Samina asked. "This seems like an absurd amount of interest in a hostage."

Hasan ran a hand through his hair. "She's daivyakt," he said. "With an affinity for water. But she seems unable to summon any daivyakhi."

She sucked in a shocked breath, then winced, clutching her ribs. "Explain," she wheezed.

Quickly, he summarized the situation: Richard and Poppy's power struggle, the bargain he'd struck with Poppy, and the events of the morning. "She doesn't know the first thing about any of the gods," he said. "Something is holding her back, and I don't know what."

Samina scoffed. "She was raised by Welks, Hasan. The emperor is supposed to represent the Founder on earth, and her adoptive father is *literally* his cousin. Do you think they were taking her to see village performances of the epics? He had her shipped to Welkland to put as much distance as possible between her and this country. When I was in the orphanage, they beat us for speaking Virian. At night, we were forced to say our prayers to the Founder, else we weren't allowed to eat supper. They did everything in their power to make us forget who we were. I doubt

Poppy Sutherland's *education* looked any different from mine. The only thing they would have taught her at that fancy overseas college is prejudice and self-hatred. You cannot ask for blessings when you secretly fear being cursed."

An idea bloomed in Hasan's mind, blotting out the rest of his thoughts. "Fair enough," he said distantly. "Thank you, Samina." He stood to go.

"Hasan," Samina called. He paused, turning in the doorway. "Don't tell her I'm here, please."

He studied Samina's face, not understanding the rationale behind her request. Nonetheless, he inclined his head. "You have my word."

• • •

After the morning's humiliation, Poppy spent the rest of the day in her room with a chair wedged under the doorknob, refusing to open the door for anyone. This house was full of criminals; if one of them wanted to come in, they could break the door down themselves.

She lay on the bed, reflecting deeply. Catherine would have called it *sulking*, but Poppy felt she had earned the right to sulk. It wasn't every day that your ancestral gods rejected your prayers. She dwelled on a past that wasn't the past, imagining her life if she had grown up in a house like this one, raised by her birth parents. What future had they imagined, when they pressed their hands to her mother's swollen belly? She didn't even know the name they had given her. Who could she have been, if not Poppy Sutherland?

By the time the sun began to set, her mood had not improved from her hours of introspection. Her empty stomach did nothing to help. When Hasan came to announce that dinner was ready, she no longer had the willpower to shut him out.

She followed Hasan downstairs, but he walked straight past the kitchen, toward the rear doors. "What about dinner?" she protested.

"We're dining outside tonight." His lips curved up slightly. "Trust me. You'll see."

She sighed but trailed after him. When they stepped out onto the patio, she froze.

The backyard had been transformed. Two tents with mosquito-net walls had been set up in front of a low wooden stage. Instruments lay in the grass in front of the stage beside the firepit, which, despite the heat, had been lit. Its flames cast a warm glow on the stage, illuminating it.

"What's all this?" she asked.

"You'll see." Hasan smiled. "Eat first."

That was one instruction she was more than happy to obey. He led her into one of the tents. Harithi was already inside, sitting on a cushion in front of her thali, propped up on a serving tray. Poppy sat beside Hasan on a cushion of her own, mouth watering at the silver plate in front of her.

Dhal, mutton curry, mashed eggplant, potato bhaji, coconut chutney, and several other items filled the small metal bowls that ringed the rotis stacked in the center of the plate. Poppy paused; they had not provided a spoon with this thali. With the exception of tea sandwiches, the Hawk had declared eating without cutlery incredibly ill-mannered. She had whacked the backs of Poppy's fingers with her cane when she caught her picking up food with her bare hands, determined to beat "the savage" out of her. Instinctively, she flexed her fingers, recalling nights of knuckles so raw they bled.

"What's wrong?" Hasan asked, picking up on her hesitation.

"I don't have a spoon," she whispered.

Misunderstanding, he replied, "You don't need one. You can rip off a piece of the roti and use it to scoop your food. See?" He demonstrated for her, tearing a strip of roti and picking up some of his own potato bhaji. Instead of eating it himself, he offered it to her.

She reached for it, then curled her fingers back into her palm. "Isn't it rude?"

Hasan's expression shifted, some of the easiness melting away. "Miss Sutherland, I understand that you were raised among Welkish nobility, and so all you know of being Virian is what they taught you. But let me make one thing clear: Our culture and traditions are not *rude*. Our way of life is no less valid or civil just because it hasn't gotten the imperial stamp of approval."

Poppy blinked, stunned by his lecture. She hadn't meant to cause offense—though now she could see how her question had appeared demeaning. She opened her mouth to explain, then shut it with a snap. Why would he care about what she'd gone through at Thornhaven? It would probably sound like excuses to him anyway. She snatched the food from his fingertips wordlessly and put it in her mouth.

She finished the rest of her dinner without speaking. Harithi and Hasan exchanged a long, loaded glance, but otherwise remained silent. In stark contrast to the tension, Rohini and the widows chatted merrily in the other tent.

When dinner was finished, one of the widows went into the kitchen and brought out finger bowls of lemon-scented water. The sun had gone down fully, the lawn now illuminated by the bonfire at the foot of the stage.

A group of people emerged from a coarse curtain set up

behind the stage. Some walked around to collect the instruments; others, dressed in colorful costumes, assumed positions on the stage.

"Are we going to see a play?" Poppy asked, forgetting her pique. She hadn't seen a play in ages.

"Not just any play," Hasan said. "Remember how I said that when the Welks banned our gods, we found other ways to tell their stories? These performers are from the local village, Sanivali. They know dozens, if not a hundred, of the songs and dances that honor our gods. Normally, they perform at festivals or on auspicious dates, but I asked them to come here tonight for you."

"Me?" she asked. "Why?"

"Because," Hasan said, his mouth twitching into a small smile, "I'm a terrible teacher. You might not have had the same upbringing as me, but I want you to have a connection to our gods. A real one, not the lies that you were fed. Poppy, I realize that your only exposure to our culture and faith must have been negative. But it's not too late to build positive associations. The only way to lose is to give up. And I'm not giving up."

Her throat tightened. Though she knew he'd done it only because he needed her powers for their bargain, her chest warmed at the effort he must have gone to in order to organize this evening for her. She didn't know how to show him her gratitude without also revealing her vulnerability, so instead she said, "Who said anything about giving up?"

Harithi cleared her throat. "Play's starting."

Sure enough, the drummers in front began to strike their instruments, setting a slow pulse.

"What song did you choose?" Harithi asked Hasan.

"'Savana and Altan,'" he answered.

Chapter Twenty-Five

The Gift of a Story

A woman dressed in red and brown, with a green dupatta over her hair, entered the stage, her anklets chiming with each step. Her announcement was accompanied by the lilting harmony of the sitar and wooden flutes. Her kameez stretched tight over her belly, which had been padded to give the appearance of pregnancy.

Hasan leaned toward Poppy to whisper, "That's Rukmini. She's the goddess of fertility, motherhood, and the bountiful harvest."

A second woman entered the stage, dressed in a cropped aquamarine blouse and a skirt that flared when she spun. The music intensified, the pitch frenzied as the newcomer whirled around Rukmini.

"Neelam," Hasan supplied. "Goddess of the sea. She is Rukmini's sister. Their constant clashing created Viryana, with the lava from Rukmini's womb becoming solid ground when it touches Neelam's waves. In turn, the ocean throws itself on the land, eroding it. It is a constant battle between the two, but they love each other dearly."

The actress playing Rukmini opened her mouth and began to sing in high, clear Virian. As she sang, Hasan shifted closer to Poppy and began to interpret in a low voice: "Sister, be still for me. I seek a mirror to the stars."

Neelam fell still, tumbling gracefully to the stage. As she lay flat on her stomach, stagehands rushed forward, pulling a reflective black cloth studded with silver pieces over her.

Rukmini circled her sister, tracing her finger over the cloth. Suddenly, she gasped, holding her padded belly. "Daughter," she cried, "the stars have seen an auspicious match for you! Your wedding will bring color to this land."

Poppy shot Hasan a look. "Aren't they already wearing color?"

"The color is for our benefit," he explained readily. "We cannot name the gods and goddesses in our lyrics, because of the law. So we use visual cues to distinguish them. At the time this tale takes place, color had not yet come to Viryana."

Onstage, the musicians beat their drums into a hard frenzy as Rukmini went into labor. She and Neelam slipped off the stage as the drums crescendoed, then went silent. Rukmini reemerged onstage, a child-sized bundle in her arms. "The stars have given me a daughter," she announced. "Her laughter brings the rain; her wailing rouses a monsoon. She will water the earth with her storms." With that, she disappeared back behind the curtain.

When the next song began, Rukmini still appeared pregnant, but with a little girl in tow. Anticipating Poppy's next question, Hasan said, "Another visual cue. Rukmini is always portrayed pregnant."

Onstage, mother and daughter bonded, the former braiding the latter's hair. Poppy's chest constricted at the sight. Demetria had never done Poppy's hair herself, leaving that for Nanny to do—she always said Poppy had too much hair, and besides, it was a maid's task. Yet here was a goddess, doing something as trivial as grooming her daughter.

"Mama," the little girl sang in a clear and strong voice, "may I go out and play?"

"No," Rukmini answered. "You are safest with me, child."

"I want to be like the other girls," the girl cried.

"My darling Savana," Rukmini sang back, "no other girl is quite like you." To the audience, she turned and sang, "I will not let my daughter fall into the wrong hands. A century of safekeeping, if I must. That is my duty as a mother."

With that, Rukmini wrapped Savana into her arms and dashed back behind the curtains.

For the next song and scene, a teenage girl took the stage alone, dressed in a gray salwar kameez. As the audience watched, an adolescent Savana sang about her solitude, about the hobbies she had mastered in her time alone: archery, music, academics. But nothing she did filled her ache for freedom.

If Poppy had felt emotional at the sight of Rukmini brushing Savana's hair, then this song nearly undid her. Savana's solitude reminded her of her time in Welkland spent mastering the skills of a lady in her free time, unable to staunch the loneliness weeping from the hole in her heart, a hole created by the missing piece back home in Viryana. Hyperaware of Hasan's and Harithi's presence in the tent, she clenched her teeth, swallowing back the memories.

Finally, the scene shifted, and a new, fast-paced song began. Rukmini took the stage again, along with a young woman, dressed in the same grays as the teenaged girl. She was Savana, grown at last.

Rukmini sang of her plan to invite every eligible male to compete for her daughter's hand: "There will be three contests. To ensure she has the fiercest warrior to guard her, a contest of marksmanship. To ensure that she has the most sensitive of souls to cherish her, a contest of art. And to ensure that she has the most intelligent of minds to advise her, a contest of wits. Only the one who succeeds at all three trials will win my daughter's hand. These are the rules, and I vow that I will honor them."

Men climbed the stage, dressed in browns and blacks, but there was one man in white and yellow, a large gold crown settled on his hair, who stood out among the rest. When Rukmini called for entrants, he stood at the front of the line.

"The sun god, Altan," Hasan said. "Prince of the stars, master of fortune."

"He's going to win, isn't he?"

"What makes you say that?"

She rolled her eyes at Hasan. "Even if you hadn't told me that destiny was his domain, he's the only one in an elaborate costume. Of course he's a main character."

Onstage, the men in line had all moved to the back, leaving Savana in front of her mother, the pair of them singing lines back and forth in a furious volley.

"Wait," Poppy said. "What's happened?"

"Savana has entered her own name in the contest," Hasan filled in. "Rukmini is protesting that she is destined for an auspicious match and is not meant for a life of solitude."

"You vowed to honor the rules, and nothing about my entry violates them," Savana argued. "You seek a warrior, a sensitive soul, an intelligent mind. I am all three."

Unable to refute that logic, Rukmini grudgingly allowed her daughter to enter the contest.

Poppy marveled at Savana's daring—and envied her freedom. Savana didn't need a husband, not when she was a goddess. Her powers came from within.

As the contest began, Savana and Altan battled each other

through every round. During the marksmanship contest, their arrows split each other's, neither willing to concede even half a hair to the other. During the artistry contest, Savana fashioned her own flute by hand and played a melody so sweet it brought even Aganath, the war god, to tears. Altan, on the other hand, painted a perfect rendition of her while blindfolded. And during the battle of wits, the other competitors were hard-pressed to get a word in edgewise while the two sparred in a verbal flurry of parries and thrusts.

The chemistry between Savana and Altan was so riveting, Poppy hardly noticed when Rukmini took center stage. She started as Rukmini sounded a horn, then announced, "The contest is concluded. The champion is none other than my daughter, Savana."

Though Rukmini did not seem pleased, she tied a red ribbon around her daughter's wrist.

"Old Virian wedding tradition sealed the marriage bond with a red ribbon," Hasan explained. "It's tied around the wrists of both parties, to signify the joining of their bloodlines."

Onstage, all the other competitors began slinking away, disgruntled. Only one man remained: Altan, who had paused to cast one last look at Savana. Her back was to him, but the audience could clearly see her face as she examined the ribbon. The triumph in her eyes was clear, but then she looked up, peering over her shoulder at Altan. The music slowed to a lull, a sweet, tentative song where the yearning notes of the sitar overtook the drums.

From opposite ends of the stage, Altan and Savana stared at one another. Then Savana approached Altan. "In this contest, I won my own hand," she told him, "but you won my heart. If you are not opposed, prince of stars, I would have you as my husband."

Altan's answering smile was radiant as he extended his wrist to her. "Princess of rain," he sang, "it would be my honor." He held still, allowing her to tie a red ribbon around his wrist. As she did, the stagehands reemerged with banners of cloth, running in circles around the couple until the colors blurred and merged with each other, giving the appearance of a rainbow.

Rukmini appeared onstage, looking satisfied. "Thus, the prophecy is fulfilled," she told the crowd directly. "The marriage of rain and sun has brought color to Viryana. Under their rainbow banner, crops flourish, and the country prospers."

The music came to a grand finish. As the actors and musicians lined up onstage to bow, Poppy blinked, then hastily brought her hands together to applaud. "It's over?" She couldn't keep the disappointment out of her tone.

Harithi stretched. "Unfortunately," she said dryly, then slipped out of the tent.

Hasan rolled his eyes at her exit. "Harithi prefers the bloodier epics. I tried to persuade the troupe to perform more of the legends, but this was the only one they were willing to do. It's one of the ones my grandfather used to take us to see every Bahaari."

"Bahaari?"

"The beginning of the spring planting season," he elaborated. "The farmers celebrate the marriage of Savana and Altan with a festival of colors. The entire village attends. It's not unusual for there to be archery contests, artisans, and recitations by scholars and poets."

Poppy tried to picture that: the streets full of celebration, merriment and mirth swirling in the spring air. "I've never been to a festival," she yawned. Without the music and the story to keep her engaged, sleep beckoned to her, the warm summer night and her full stomach making her drowsy. Perhaps that was why, in a moment of thoughtlessness, she added, "You'll have to take me next year."

Immediately, she bit her tongue. There would be no *next year,* if all went to plan. She'd be back in society, her father's daughter and heir, and he would be reunited with his brother, free to resume his life of crime.

For one long, mortifying moment, Hasan said nothing, not meeting her eyes. *Stupid,* she admonished herself. He was likely thinking of ways to let her down gently.

Then, he said, "If you insist."

Somehow, this unsettled her far more than a rejection.

Mercifully, Hasan changed the topic. "Today was a bad start, I'll admit. But I meant what I said: I believe in our deal. I'm not giving up. Not unless you want to."

She bit her bottom lip, both heartened and intimidated by his words. She was so used to having to earn other people's faith. Hasan's conviction weighed on her like an obligation, a debt she couldn't repay.

"You're putting a lot of pressure on me," she said.

"It's nothing close to the pressure you'll face as vicereine. Are you up for this or not?"

Poppy turned over the question in her mind, doubt crawling over. Even with Hasan's alliance, this would be an uphill battle until the very end. She wasn't a goddess like Savana. She didn't have a century to prepare. But when she thought about the bleary damp of Welkland, of Richard's laughter as he discussed murdering daivyakt, her resolve hardened. No matter what it cost, he had to be stopped.

"I am," she said.

Satisfaction gleamed in his black eyes. "Then I'll see you first thing tomorrow."

Chapter Twenty-Six

Nothing to Sacrifice

The next morning, Poppy stood, holding her breakfast at the foot of the pantheon. Hasan waited upstairs, respecting her request. She needed to speak to the gods alone, without trying to imitate his behavior.

She chewed on her lip, staring at the idols. Many of them still looked unfamiliar, but now she recognized a handful: Altan, crowned in gold, perched at the peak of the volcano. Pregnant Rukmini, sitting on the fields of Sanivali. And finally, Savana, a bow in one hand and a sitar in the other, dressed in silver and blue. Poppy focused on her. Savana had not been afraid to claim her own power, and neither would she.

"We both know what it is to feel isolated," she told the statuette. "I can't go back to that."

With that, she kneeled and put the plate down. After a moment's hesitation, she recited, "My veins are a vessel for the divine power of the gods. If they find my sacrifice worthy, may I be filled with their cosmic energy." Instead of focusing on her pronunciation, Poppy held eye contact with the idol, praying, *Please, Savana. Even a fraction of your strength would be enough.* Her skin tingled—or was she imagining it?

She forced herself to leave the pantheon and head out to the yard, where Hasan and Harithi waited with a bucket of dirty, soapy water. Poppy glanced at Hasan first. His expression was neutral, his face relaxed. If he thought she'd failed again, he did a good job of hiding it.

"We're going to start simple today," he said. He gestured to Harithi, who dumped the bucket of water into the grass. It seeped into the hard earth, the dry soil drinking it greedily.

"Try to summon it back," Hasan instructed. "Draw the moisture back into a puddle on the surface. Once you master that, you can try to put it back in the bucket."

Hold a puddle. How hard could that be?

She closed her eyes, slowly reaching for the power. Trepidation came over her. She hesitated, mental fingers outstretched. What if the prayer hadn't worked again? This time, she'd have no one to blame but herself.

Hasan's and Harithi's curious stares weighed on Poppy. It occurred to her that the longer she stalled, the more concerned they would become. Hasan took a step closer, stirring the air beside her.

"Miss Sutherland—"

"No!" She threw out a hand to keep him from coming closer. "I'm fine. I'm just concentrating."

Before she could lose her nerve, she reached for the daivyakhi, splaying her fingers wide. In the soil, the water was trickling down quickly, heading toward the groundwater reservoir deep below them. Snapping her fingers into a fist, Poppy caught it with her powers before it could sink any farther. After a moment of fumbling, she managed to pull the water up through the earth again, like a sieve in reverse, drawing her arm upward as if hauling a bucket from a well.

The top layer of soil sprayed everywhere as a miniature geyser of water shot out of the earth. Harithi swore using a creative string of filthy words, both Virian and Welkish. Hasan jumped back, lifting a hand in a futile attempt to shield himself from the muck. Poppy tried to funnel the water into the bucket, but the geyser struck the tin, punting it toward the house with a clank.

"Okay, stop!" Hasan shouted. "Stop, stop. Let's not use all the energy at once."

She let go immediately. The water slumped back down into the earth, trickling away. She waited for the nausea to hit, for the earth to spin. Nothing. Her senses remained clear, her pulse racing with excitement, not exertion.

"I did it!" she cried, elated. She spun around to Hasan, eager for his approval. "Did you see that? It worked!"

Hasan wiped mud off his face as he tried to gather his composure. "It was kind of hard with the water in my eyes," he deadpanned, "but yes. I saw it. You did well."

Warmth spread through her at the praise.

Harithi laughed, raking clumps of dead grass out of her dark mane. "It was fucking great." She grinned. "Let's do it again."

Poppy got two more rounds of practice with the power from her breakfast sacrifice before her daivyakhi ran out. On her last try, she even managed to get some of the water into the bucket, which was now badly dented, although most of it had splashed everywhere else. Harithi headed inside, loudly proclaiming that she wanted to use the bathtub first. Hasan's kameez was soaked, the wet fabric plastered indecently to his skin. Poppy averted her eyes, focusing on a clump of mud stuck in his hair.

"Good job," he huffed, wringing out the tail of his shirt. "We'll work on it. Control will come with practice."

"That's one thing I don't understand," she said. "How did the rulers of old maintain the island if they got such little mileage out of each sacrifice?"

"Well, they were sacrificing more than just their breakfasts," Hasan pointed out. "But beyond that, you're right—our sacrifices aren't as potent as theirs used to be. We think that the gods' power and influence has diminished since their temples were desecrated in the fall of Viryana." His expression grew distant as he recalled, "There used to be massive, grand temples built around the island. There were always two on any royal compound: one meant for the use of all the palace inhabitants, and then a small, personal one for the maharaja's use. These temples housed grand, life-sized statues of the gods."

"Wait, I've seen those statues," she realized. "In a museum in Welkland. The headmistress took us on a trip there once."

A muscle in Hasan's jaw ticked. "They were stolen," he said. "After Jagat Rai died and the Welks finally annexed Viryana, they ransacked the temples, then built cathedrals to their own god atop the skeletons."

She shifted from foot to foot. How vile, that the statues Hasan's ancestors had worshipped were trapped in glass cases on a continent across the sea, where their descendants would never see them again. "Is there a solution?" she asked.

Hasan shook his head. "The gods have been banned, so we can't build new temples. Most Virians hide their pantheons in subtle ways, but the power from these makeshift altars is limited. For many, it's not worth having them at all. Under the imperial edict, the penalty for having them is up to five years imprisonment."

"But it's still worth it for you?"

"Miss Sutherland, I run a criminal organization," Hasan reminded her. "Household idols are the least of my concerns."

She rolled her eyes at him but remained quiet, expectant.

He rubbed at his chin. "My grandfather was adamant that we remain faithful to the old ways," he said. "The idols were his prized possessions. He believed firmly that one day, the gods and their chosen people would have control over Viryana again. I used to think it was the wishful thinking of an old man, but now . . ." He glanced at her as his sentence trailed off.

"Now?" she prompted.

"Now, I think I'm a little more optimistic than I used to be." He looked away. "Okay, that's enough. Let's go inside and get cleaned up. Tomorrow, we'll try again."

• • •

By the time the pair of them had washed the grass and mud from their skin and changed into dry clothes, the others in the house had already eaten lunch. They had left portions for Poppy and Hasan in the kitchen, where the two sat together and ate. Privately, Poppy considered the absurdity of her reality: Not even a full month ago, she and Richard had been dining in the best restaurants in the city of Marnapur. Now, she was in Sanivali, a rural village, eating lunch with her hands with a notorious criminal for company, after a morning of using unnatural magic she'd gained by praying at an illegal altar.

She'd had some time to reflect more on what Hasan had mentioned earlier, that the sacrifices made through these small altars did not yield the same amount of daivyakhi as the grand temples of old Viryana. It had certainly given her more insight into the current social climate—despite Hasan's earlier notion that the people had the power to choose or reject a ruler, the diminished strength of divine magic was further evidence as to why Virians had not yet revolted against imperial rule. Using one's daivyakhi against the empire was virtually ineffective, even with training, and would only result in steep personal consequences for the wielder. But it did not explain a blind spot in her education that was becoming increasingly obvious the longer she dwelled on it: Why hadn't the daivyakt of old used their power to stop Welkish colonizers, before it had been outlawed and reduced to the shadow it was today?

"Hasan?" she asked, fiddling with the edge of her placemat.

He looked over at her. "What is it?"

"I was wondering if you'd tell me the story of how the Welkish people came to rule Viryana. Not the version that my tutors taught me. Your version, the one your parents told you."

Hasan pushed his empty plate away from him, sitting back. "I'd wondered about that, at the museum," he said. "If you only knew their version of our history. Why are you thinking about that now?"

Poppy explained her question, about why the old daivyakt had not fought to preserve the independence of the country.

"They did fight," Hasan said, "but in the revised history that the Welks tell, they are both villainized and minimized. The true story starts, funnily enough, with the dry season.

"Dry seasons in Viryana were not so devastating for the population as they are now, I'm told. Daivyakt, both nobles and priests alike, would raise water from the aquifers beneath the island, similar to the exercise you did today with the bucket, and distribute it to vasudhakt in exchange for tithes or taxes."

"Shouldn't they have given it for free?" Poppy traced her finger on her own half-full water glass. "I thought the gods gave daivyakhi to people so that they could care for others."

"The daivyakt had a kingdom to run," Hasan said. "Everyone

had to contribute, daivyakt with their power, and vasudhakt with their labor. It was a fair system in theory, though maybe not in practice. The Welks exploited this inequality. Their first expedition built their own well and gave the vasudhakt water for free, no tithe or tax required. All they had to do was listen to the Welkish missionaries preach about the Founder. They claimed their mission was to create a world where all peoples were equal, and how these wells were part of that mission to ensure that all could drink regardless of caste or color. Vasudhakt began to convert, realizing they had more value as servants of the Founder than as followers of the pantheon."

As Hasan spoke, Rohini entered the kitchen, accompanied by one of the widows, both of them bearing a sack of produce. They dumped their haul on the counter and began to sort the different fruits and vegetables. Hasan didn't let that interrupt them, continuing his story.

"At the same time, the maharaja, Zeyar Rai, passed away—yes," he said, laughing at the look on Poppy's face, "Zeyar is named for that king. Explains his ego, doesn't it?"

Poppy thought she heard Rohini smother a snicker in the corner, and fought to restrain a giggle of her own.

"Zeyar's son, Jagat Rai, ascended the throne. Jagat had the misfortune of being the first king born without magic."

"How?" Poppy interrupted. "I thought being daivyakt passes from parent to child?"

"Jagat was a bastard," Rohini cut in, unable to pretend any longer that she wasn't eavesdropping. She left the task of unpacking groceries to the widow and came to sit at the table. "His mother, the maharani, was sleeping with one of the vasudhakt palace staff."

"Really?" Poppy asked.

"Zeyar Rai forbid open speculation, and of course the queen denied it, but many believed that Jagat was illegitimate," Hasan said.

"It doesn't matter why he was impotent." Rohini waved a hand impatiently. "His reign was doomed from the start. Who wants a king who has been snubbed by the gods? It would have been better for everyone if Zeyar Rai had named Narayan as his heir."

"Narayan?" Poppy asked. The name was familiar to her, though she could not place its significance.

"Jagat Rai's maternal cousin," Hasan said. "He was from the noble Sovan family, descended from a long line of water-wielders, and had the strongest affinity for the gift in living memory. His popularity made Jagat paranoid, and was probably one of the things that drove him to meet with the Welkish missionaries. Word of the Welkish missionaries' growing influence on the vasudhakt had reached the royal court, though no one took it seriously until Jagat met with their leader, none other than Charles Sutherland."

This was where Poppy's Welkish tutors and professors at Thornhaven had always started the story, with Charles Sutherland's alliance with Jagat Rai. Clearly, the Virians did not consider their union as beneficial as the Welkish did.

"Charles sold Jagat on a vision of Viryana without magic, where he would not be considered lacking simply because he had been born 'normal.' Jagat took Charles into his confidence and established a Council of Lords to advise him."

"A council of Welkish vipers," Rohini interjected. "He removed everyone who had ever dared to question him from positions that had been held in their families for centuries, and then he replaced them with turncoats and colonizers that his council endorsed."

"Eventually," Hasan continued, shooting his mother an exasperated look, "the Welkish missionaries convinced him to convert to the fellowship of the Founder. When Jagat converted, he also ordered the destruction of the temple within the royal compound, demanding that a cathedral to the Founder replace it. This was when Narayan confronted him, along with several other noblemen who were concerned about the direction of the country."

"Too little, too late," Rohini said. "Most of the original officials under Zeyar's rule had already been replaced, the administration of the country pawned off on traitors and strangers."

"Ma," Hasan said, "can you let me finish, please? I'm almost done."

"Fine," Rohini grumbled. She picked up their empty plates and took them to the sink, where she began washing them.

"To Jagat, the confrontation was proof that Narayan had been trying to usurp him all along. War broke out, during which the Welkish Imperial Army took Jagat's side. The Welkish historians call this the Unnatural Coup. While the daivyakt had immense power, they simply did not have the numbers to fight back against both the Imperial Army *and* the vasudhakt converts. Jagat targeted the compounds of his opponents, particularly their temples, which crippled the daivyakt's ability to fight. The war finally ended after Jagat found Narayan and his family, and ordered their execution—Narayan, his family, all household servants, and priests."

Poppy gasped. "Even the children?"

"Especially the children. Jagat did not want to leave the door open to be challenged again by another member of Narayan's family ten years later."

"That's horrible!" She shuddered.

"With the 'insurrection' quelled, Jagat continued to rule with the help of his Council of Lords. His health started failing, and in his final years, he gave more and more authority to the Council. When he finally died, the Council selected Sutherland to continue leadership of the country. Jagat had already handed off most of the workings of the country to the Council of Lords, making the transition of power nearly seamless. The emperor formally annexed Viryana and declared it a new territory claimed in the name of the Founder, with Charles Sutherland the first viceroy. The remaining temples—of which there were few—were destroyed."

"Did no one dissent?" Poppy asked.

Rohini shut the water off, her dishwashing complete. "Those who did were taken care of," she answered, swinging a dish towel over her shoulder as she turned back to face them. "My grandfather told me stories of those days. Protestors were arrested, interrogated, and, in some cases, publicly executed. Sometimes, even if your only crime was knowing a dissenter, you would be taken in. Neighbors turned their backs on one another, not wanting to be targeted by association. People learned pretty quickly that if they wanted to survive, the best thing to do was keep their heads down."

Poppy couldn't disagree with that. After all, wasn't that what she'd been doing all her life? Keeping her head down, reciting scripture she didn't necessarily agree with, trying desperately to become a success story so that she didn't have to return to the streets?

"Thank you," she said to both Hasan and his mother. "I've never heard that story told like that before. The way the Welkish tell it, the vasudhakt were being taken advantage of by the daivyakt, and they worked with Jagat to subdue the daivyakt and introduce the Founder to Viryana. When he died, Viryana joined the empire voluntarily."

Hasan snorted. "Voluntarily. That's a good one."

"Had me fooled," Poppy said. "But no more."

• • •

The next morning, Poppy sacrificed her breakfast again, and got in three more practice rounds before her daivyakhi sputtered out. She still hadn't been able to fill the bucket with water.

Hasan sighed. "We'll have to sacrifice again."

"I don't have anything else to sacrifice," she said. "I already gave up breakfast." As if to prove her point, her stomach grumbled.

"Cut off a lock of your hair. That might get us a couple more attempts. Or give a little bit of your blood. Blood always gets me a long way." He offered her his blade.

"Are you mad?" Poppy cradled her long, shiny braid protectively. "I'm not hacking off my hair. Nor am I going to resort to *bloodletting*."

"Then *you* think of something else to sacrifice! You can't fulfil your end of the bargain if you can't even fill a single bucket of water. I don't have much more time to teach you, and if you can't even practice . . ." He ran a hand through his hair, eyes distant.

"I could make more sacrifices if I had access to more of my things," she said, thinking back to her possessions at home. "I have a lot of money."

"Unless it pains you to part with that money, then it doesn't count as a sacrifice." Hasan put his knife away, exasperated. "If a rich man gave ten crowns to the gods, but a widow with a single crown to her name sacrificed that lone coin, then the gods would favor the widow."

"Okay, but I can't start giving up things I *need.*"

Hasan rubbed his temples. "Miss Sutherland, I don't think you know what it means to sacrifice something. Have you ever had to go without in your life? Before I kidnapped you, was there *anything* you wanted that you didn't get?"

Poppy balled her fingers into fists. How dare he pretend that he knew her? She had been separated from her home and family for seven years, consistently reminded of her deficiencies. She hadn't been enough for the nobility, and now even in the eyes of criminals, she was falling short. She hadn't forgotten Hasan's lecture over the cutlery.

She tilted her chin up, refusing to let him see the depth of her frustration. "You have no right to reprimand me when you don't even know the first thing about me."

"I have every right." He stepped closer, eyes flashing. "*You* made a deal with *me*. You promised me water for my people and an open door once you became vicereine. But now that it's time to make sacrifices, you've gotten cold feet."

"I didn't realize the price for this would be my blood!"

"The cost of revolution is always blood." He spread his arms. "Did you really think you wouldn't have to give anything up to win? Or were you expecting me and my family to make all the sacrifices?"

What Hasan didn't seem to understand—and what Poppy would never confess—was that she couldn't make sacrifices because the few things she had were tainted by loss. She had been adopted into a rich family at the cost of losing her birth parents. She had gained an education but had lost her Virian roots and would forever be barred from Welkish culture. Poppy could claim neither flag. No matter how hard she tried, she'd always be an imposter in both camps. In the end, she was a nobody with nothing. A lump formed in her throat, but she swallowed hard. She would not cry in front of Hasan.

"What do I have to sacrifice?" she demanded. "You think just because my family has money and status, my life has been easy?"

"It certainly couldn't have made life *hard*."

"But my life *was* hard," Poppy insisted. "You have no clue how challenging things were for me, because you insist on thinking of me as a pompous princess. When I asked if it was rude to eat with my hands, I wasn't disparaging you. I spent years in Welkland literally having the habit beaten out of me."

She held her hands up to his face, the faint scars visible in the full sun of the morning.

"They hurt you?" Hasan asked, his voice low. A shadow fell across his face, one that looked less like a man and more like the canine his moniker evoked.

Poppy shivered, pulling her hands back. "It's in the past now," she said. "But I have a hundred more scars, most of them invisible, which couldn't have been prevented by all the money or status in the world."

He pressed his lips together, visibly struggling to formulate a response. "Perhaps your life was not so idyllic as one would think," he allowed, choosing his words carefully. "I won't take your struggles from you. I haven't forgotten what those women said at your engagement party. I can't imagine the other, insidious ways the nobility's disdain for you and your race must have played out in your childhood. But just because you didn't have it easy doesn't mean that you didn't have it *easier* than the vast majority."

Poppy stared at her feet, humiliated and enraged all over again at the reminder of that accursed engagement party. She didn't want his judgment, but she didn't want his pity, either.

Neither acknowledged her for who she was: someone who worked hard, constantly fighting against odds, and always came out on top.

Hasan raked a hand through his hair, the dark circles under his eyes more pronounced than before. "We should stop for today," he said finally. "We won't get any further without another sacrifice. Go in and help the other women."

Poppy balked. Quitting went against her nature, and ending the lesson early felt like giving up. But Hasan was right: Without another sacrifice, this would go nowhere. And she had nothing left to sacrifice.

"Fine." She set her jaw. "As you wish."

With that, she turned and strode into the house, head held high.

Chapter Twenty-Seven

Sheltered

Samina's conversation with Hasan about Poppy had knocked loose a deluge of memories she'd repressed for nearly a decade. For the past week, flashbacks and dreams of her time in the state-run orphanage assaulted her, day and night: the matrons, quick to strike with their canes when she spoke in Virian or failed to perform her chores to their satisfaction; the patrons, especially the male ones who put their ghoulish pale hands on her changing body; the prospective "parents," middle- and upper-class Welks who were not looking for a child but an unpaid servant.

All this, Samina had endured for the sake of her brother, Sanjiv. For the regular meals, for a roof over his head, for clothes on his back. But as he got older, stronger, the prospective parents began to eye him with a hungry gleam in their eyes, one that Samina couldn't abide. She'd reached her womanhood, had unlocked her daivyakhi. The night before Sanjiv was meant to go to his new home, Samina opened the floorboards where she kept her statuette of Rukmini—the last thing she owned of her mother's—and made a cut on her palm.

Samina and Sanjiv left the orphanage together, slipping away in the chaos of crying children and sirens.

She had no regrets about leaving that place in ashes. She'd done what had been necessary to protect her brother, and she would do it again. Even now that they were both older, she worried for him. He was vasudhakt and a boy of nearly fifteen, even if the hardships of life had forced him to mature faster than she'd have liked. Samina needed to return to the city—to her brother—as soon as possible. She hadn't wanted to go home after the fiasco at the museum. Sanjiv would have insisted on taking her to a hospital. But she'd recovered enough in Sanivali, and it was time to go home.

Yet one question held her back: Had Poppy really turned her in? Had she knowingly sent Samina to that bleak hell? Had she thought of her at all, when she was off touring the grand cities and idyllic villages of Welkland?

Samina had thought she didn't care to ask—she would have sworn on her life that Poppy had intentionally betrayed her. She'd asked Hasan not to tell her that she was in the safe house so that Poppy wouldn't show up at her sickbed with a posy of excuses. But after days of recovering alone, Samina found she couldn't lie to herself any longer. She needed the truth, and she needed to hear it from Poppy Sutherland. She owed it to her, daivyakt to daivyakt, orphan to orphan.

She'd found her in the kitchen, standing beside Rohini as the Devar matron tried to teach her how to make aloo parathas. Slipping in, she laid a hand on Poppy's arm, causing Poppy to jump. "Can we talk?"

It took Poppy a moment to register who Samina was. Then she lit up, beaming widely. "Samina? You're here! You survived the museum!"

"Barely," she said. "Can we please talk outside?"

Poppy washed her hands quickly in the sink, then followed

Samina out into the hallway. Samina tilted her head up to look at her, resenting their height difference. Poppy stood at least half a foot taller than her. She opened her mouth again, but Samina interrupted, determined to be the one leading this conversation. "Did you turn me in?" she blurted.

Poppy's mouth snapped shut, then opened again, then closed. Then, she asked, "Are you referring to the necklace?"

"Obviously," Samina said. "What else could I be referring to?"

Poppy's fingers strayed to her collarbones in a subconscious gesture, as though reaching for a pendant. "I didn't turn you in. I would have never done that."

"Then how did they know to come and arrest me?"

"The pawnshop owner reported you."

Samina exhaled. Closed her eyes. One of the biggest grudges in her life had been completely unfounded, but the weight off her chest didn't feel like relief. Instead, she felt unmoored, a rowboat cut loose from the docks. She barely even remembered the pawnshop owner. She fervently wished she could go back and burn that bastard's store to the ground for what his big mouth had cost her.

"What happened to you?" Poppy asked. "When I asked Father if you'd be sent to jail, he told me you'd be going to an orphanage instead—was that true?"

Samina forced herself to look Poppy in the eyes. "Yes," she said. "It's true."

Poppy's shoulders relaxed.

Samina stared at her. "Are you fucking *relieved*? That place was *hell*, Poppy."

"At least you didn't go to jail," Poppy said.

Something about the way she said it—smoothly, like a stone she'd turned over again and again until all the edges were soft—made Samina realize that this was the justification Poppy had carried with her all these years, the story she'd used to console herself at night.

"At least jail is honest about what it is," Samina said. "The orphanage was nothing more than a glorified prison. Our every minute, every word, was policed by the matrons. If we fell out of line, we were beaten so badly that some children couldn't even lie on their backs at night."

"Okay, but they fed you," Poppy argued weakly. "They clothed you. They educated you. Surely there were benefits?"

Samina tasted bile in the back of her throat. "There were no benefits," she said. "It wasn't fucking *college* in Welkland."

Poppy reared back as though Samina had struck her. "You know nothing about what that was like for me," she said. "At least you had other Virian children to watch your back. I was *alone*, in a foreign country, surrounded by girls and women who thought me less than human for the color of my skin."

Samina's lips curled with the bitter taste of irony. "So you can tell me how lucky I had it in a Welkish-run organization that dehumanized me, but I can't tell you the same? What makes us different, Poppy? What makes your struggles more important than mine?"

Stricken, Poppy said, "I don't think mine are more important than yours."

"But you do!" Samina all but shouted. "You continue to justify what I went through to make yourself feel better about the hand you played in it. You didn't even mean for me to get caught, so there's no reason for you to continue to deny the abuse I faced after that. But you minimize it anyway."

She stepped close to Poppy, her anger making her impulsive. "You know what I think? I think you're so used to being the most marginalized person in the room, you don't know how to recognize that other people have it far worse than you. Maybe you were an outcast—but being an outcast in a Welkish school for fine ladies is still a hell of a lot more privileged than being an orphan in a shoddy human-trafficking sham."

Samina's eyes burned, the memories threatening to consume her again. Poppy reached for her, but she jerked away. An embrace would only serve to comfort Poppy, not Samina, and Samina was done serving the illusion that Poppy had held for the last seven years.

• • •

Hindered by Poppy's insistence that she had nothing to give the gods, Hasan had refocused his lessons on her language skills. She made quick progress, and her Virian improved exponentially. Even here, sitting on the front porch, he could hear her in the kitchen, chatting with the other women in Virian. Her accent had become smoother than it was a week ago, the words confident, less stilted.

Her lessons in summoning daivyakhi, though—she'd stalled there. After the play, she'd managed to forge her own connection to the gods, harnessing her powers with more skill than he'd have expected from an adult beginner. However, she lacked finesse and control, two things that would only come with practice—and they could only practice if she made sacrifices.

Her past had complicated things far more than Hasan had anticipated. On one hand, her time in the countryside had made her acutely aware of all the things her upbringing had deprived her of, her self-pity blinding her to her privilege. On the other hand, she was equally ignorant of the biases that she still carried with her, subconscious instincts that manifested in careless comments. Just the other afternoon, she'd complained about being outdoors, fretting that she would "become too brown" if she stayed under the sun for any longer. Harithi put her in her place before Hasan could intervene, demanding to know what the problem was with being brown. Poppy had fallen quiet, but the atmosphere had changed after that.

He couldn't blame Poppy for the way she thought—not when her biases had been so deeply ingrained during her childhood. But if she couldn't challenge those biases, then there would be no difference between her and Richard. And if there was no difference, then Zeyar was right: Richard *was* the favored choice, and they'd have more to gain by courting his favor.

Hasan would rather eat his own entrails than side with Richard. But Zeyar would return by the end of this week, and he was running out of time to get through to Poppy.

The front door swung open, startling him. Samina stepped out into the amber light of the sunset. She'd recovered slightly from her injuries, the swelling gone, the bruising less lurid. Still, she wore her arm in its cast, a cloth sling tied around her neck, and her awkward movements indicated that her ribs were still bothering her. Hasan's eyes fell to the bag she carried in her good hand.

Hasan opened his mouth to ask her where she thought she was going, but then she lifted her head, revealing a single tear streaking from her red-rimmed eyes.

He jumped to his feet. "What's wrong?"

"Nothing," she said. "I need to go back to Marnapur. I'm going to walk to Sanivali and catch a bus from there."

"You're not well enough." He reached for her bag. "Stay another week."

"Sanjiv is by himself." Samina sidestepped him neatly. "I am going, with or without your permission."

Hasan recoiled—Samina had always been forthright about her loyalty to her brother, but she had never spoken to him so defiantly before.

"Samina," he said, "what's bothering you? Really."

She turned her face away. "I can't be here with *her* anymore." She didn't have to say whom she meant. "It's bringing back these memories, things I never wanted to remember, and the worst thing is she doesn't even understand."

"I see," Hasan said. "You spoke to her."

Samina smeared another tear with the back of her hand. "Much good it did either of us," she scoffed. "There's no closure for what I went through, ever. I was stupid to think otherwise. And as for Poppy?" She turned, fixing Hasan with a piercing stare. "Teaching her to use her daivyakhi is a waste of time. You could train her to use every weapon in the world, and it would mean nothing if she didn't know whom she was bearing them *for*. She's so damned sheltered. The only injustices she's seen are the ones committed against her."

She struggled for a moment, a medley of emotions flashing across her face before it settled on frustration. "I know you want her to be a champion for us. But if she doesn't learn to put her struggles second, she'll be no different from a Welkish viceroy, justifying away anything that makes her uncomfortable."

With that, Samina stalked down the driveway, disappearing into the night. Her words settled like a stone beside Hasan's earlier doubts, weighting the scale against Poppy's favor. But speaking to Samina had also reminded Hasan of another anecdote she'd shared with him: sixteen-year-old Poppy, giving Samina a necklace off her own body. Samina was right: Poppy had been sheltered from the injustices her father had subjected this island to. But he had to believe that if she saw them firsthand, she would feel something—just as she had felt for her childhood friend.

He didn't know if it would work. All he could do was pray that her father and her time overseas had not snuffed out the spirit of kinship she'd once shared with her birth people.

Chapter Twenty-Eight

Blood for Better

Poppy clutched the grab handle above the passenger-side window of Hasan's car as he drove them both down the bumpy dirt road to the Sanivali village square. When she'd woken that morning, he'd announced that he wanted her to meet the villagers in person.

"Must we do this?" she asked.

"Absolutely," he said. "Remember what I said: The people will decide who rules. To get their support, you have to speak their language. You have to know their struggles. How else will they know that you're there to help them?"

Her stomach churned, and not just with car sickness. After the dressing down Samina had given her last night, she doubted she could persuade the villagers to see her as anything other than the privileged, pampered daughter of a duke. "What if *seeing* me is the thing that makes them retract their support?" She bit her lip. "My Virian is limited, and my daivyakhi is weak. It'll be so obvious that I'm an outsider."

"You have to be willing to try," he said. "Hiding is not a solution."

She prickled. "I'm not hiding."

"Prove it, then."

Unable to argue with him further, Poppy turned to stare out the windshield at the dusty road ahead.

Eventually, Hasan slowed, parking the car in a gravel lot.

She gave him a skeptical look. "This is it?"

Sanivali Square appeared rather bleak, composed of a handful of crisscrossing dirt roads bordered by weathered shops and stalls covered with sun-faded awnings. The tallest thing in sight was a massive banyan tree, which stretched so far into the sky, it hurt her neck to look. Hasan led her toward it, crossing through a patch of dead grass to approach the trunk. As they grew closer, she faltered in surprise. What she had thought to be the ridges and grooves of the bark were actually intricately carved faces and figures.

"This is the oldest tree in Sanivali," he said. "When the temples were ransacked, our ancestors carved the likenesses of the gods into the tree as an act of defiance. For those who don't have household shrines, this is where they come to make offerings."

As though summoned by his words, a widow in white came into view. She kneeled in a cradle of roots, arranging a small assortment of flowers and fruits. As they approached, she looked up, stiffening slightly when she noticed Hasan.

She started to rise. "Jackal—"

Hasan waved his hand. "It's fine, Lopa. May I introduce Miss Sutherland? She's the Duke of Cloudcliff's daughter, and hopefully, the future vicereine as well."

Lopa scrambled to her feet, bowing. "Miss Sutherland."

Poppy's cheeks flushed. No one had ever bowed and scraped before her like this—*especially* not while using her common title. She had no idea how to respond. Fumbling, she managed, "You don't have to do that. Don't let us interrupt your naumya."

This time, Lopa turned red, looking down. "I wasn't—I can't—I'm vasudhakt, miss."

"Really?" Poppy blinked. "Why do you leave offerings, then, when you can't receive divine energy?"

Lopa's eyes lifted back to hers. Her earlier reverence had faded, seemingly marred by Poppy's question. "Not all prayers are answered in power. Just because the gods do not grant me control over the elements does not mean that I have not been blessed for my faith." Her gaze darted back to Hasan's face, and she added, "It's okay—I was done anyway." Making haste, the widow lifted her empty basket and left.

Poppy watched Lopa's retreating figure, her white dupatta fluttering gently. "Why are there so many young widows around here?"

Hasan traced a finger over the trunk. "When Jagat Rai surrendered administrative powers to his Council of Lords during his illness, they abused their powers in a coordinated effort to reduce competition. They gave themselves tax breaks and increased taxes on independent farmers. When farmers went bankrupt, Welks bought the land and expanded their yield of commercial crops, such as tea leaves and cotton—things that fetched a good price in Welkland but couldn't feed Virians. They hired Virian farmers to tend the land and paid them in meager wages and rations of imported food. Despite the corruption, some Virian farmers still own their ancestral farmland, but they are under contract and must surrender a fixed amount of their crops after the harvest, regardless of how bountiful it is—which means some families are literally left with nothing.

"Without daivyakt to summon rains, the island has become increasingly prone to droughts, particularly within the last two decades, making groundwater an essential resource. Welkish-owned companies were able to fund the construction of deep wells on their own land, but contracted farmers, who had been underpaid for years, had to take large loans to fund the construction. Some couldn't secure financing and had to sell their land to the Welks. Others took loans and couldn't repay them. Many took their own lives."

Poppy's throat grew tight. "So all these young widows—"

Hasan's mouth tightened into an unsmiling line. "Their husbands were farmers, mostly. Starvation is the most common cause of death. Your father's export targets have forced farmers to grow cash crops instead of edible crops, but there're not enough food imports from Welkland to go around."

Poppy recalled every dinner she'd attended, satin tablecloths barely visible under loaded silver dishes, servants whisking away half-eaten porcelain platters of food. There *was* enough food to go around, but the distribution had been intentionally clogged in one place. Clarence Sutherland boasted a legacy of growth and prosperity. For the first time, Poppy saw her father's life's work for what it really was: a legacy built on the corpses of the nation he'd sucked dry.

"And the maharajas of old," she asked carefully, "they'd have been able to stop the drought? With their daivyakhi?"

He nodded. "Daivyakt leaders would have maintained the earth, keeping the villagers protected from harsh elements. Like I told you before, they didn't do it for free—greed and brutality existed on this island long before the Welks—but it was our way of doing things, and Welkish imperialism robbed us of the chance to grow ourselves."

She grimaced. With her subpar control over her daivyakhi, she wasn't certain she was in any position to protect anyone.

"Come on." Hasan led her away from the banyan tree. "There's more we have to see."

• • •

Hasan walked Poppy through the village streets, introducing her to the villagers as they came upon them: wizened old men; gaunt, bony children; and young widows hunched over from carrying the weight of the world. They all looked at Hasan the same way—like they were trapped in a pit, and he was standing at the top with a rope, but they weren't sure if he planned to haul them up or hang them with it. At first, they regarded her with the same suspicion as they did Hasan—but when he explained who she was and what she might become, many of them were willing to talk. Though Poppy's Virian was rudimentary, the villagers were patient, many of them just relieved to have someone to talk to.

"Baron Redbriar is in charge of this region," one of the widows told her. "He's not visited us *once* in the last three decades, let alone during this drought."

People came in motley groups, patchwork families missing key family members who were either deceased or had gone to find work in the city. They showed her account books with faded pages, battered plastic jugs full of yellow water, empty warehouses with holes in their ceilings. They brought their problems to her like patients bringing their wounds to a doctor. As she examined each one, her heart sank lower and lower.

Her father was supposed to be caring for these people, but all of them were suffering. While the duke hosted lavish dinner parties and made damning statements about the inferior nature of Virians, people died of thirst, watering crops with their blood while companies bought up the fruits of their labor for a fraction of their worth.

One elderly man invited Hasan and Poppy to his home for lunch. At first, Hasan tried to decline, insisting that they had to be on their way, but the old man persisted. His home was a small, two-story farmhouse that looked as though it had stood for the last century, though Poppy wasn't sure if it would make it to the end of the decade. The paint was chipped and faded, and the storm shutters on the windows hung crookedly or were missing altogether.

The old man introduced himself as Kanav. His elderly wife, Mishika, showed them to their dining room. Three children, aged four, six, and seven, sat around a low wooden table, where six plates of food had already been laid out. Beside them, a man sat in a flimsy wheelchair, his right pant leg tied in a knot just below the stump of his thigh.

"These are my grandchildren," Mishika said proudly. "And that is my son, Ganak. He's one of the village schoolmasters."

"Pleasure to meet you." Poppy smiled at them all and settled onto a stout wooden stool. In front of her, a plate of rice, dhal, potato bhaji, and spinach steamed, the fragrant scent eliciting a rumble in her stomach. She looked around, surreptitiously counting the number of seats. There were eight of them, and yet only six plates had been fixed. Were Mishika and Kanav going to serve them now?

Misunderstanding her searching gaze, Ganak whispered in Welkish, "Their parents won't be joining us. My brother and his wife are no longer with us."

"I'm sorry to hear that." Poppy glanced at the children again. A bitter thread of kinship tugged at her heart as she beheld the other orphans, chattering among themselves in rapid-fire Virian. "Was it some time ago? If you don't mind my asking."

"Their mother passed a few years ago," Ganak said. "She was a seamstress, and the workshop she worked in collapsed. They'd moved to Andhra for the opportunity, but the cost of living there was too high for my brother after she'd passed. Without her income, my brother took to stealing to make ends meet. Not long after her death, he was shot by a policeman."

Once, the news that a police officer had all but executed a man without a trial would have shocked Poppy. Now, she barely blinked at the fact.

At that moment, the two seniors returned. "Why is no one eating?" Mishika asked. "Come on, eat."

"What about you?" Poppy asked. "Aren't you joining us?"

Kanav waved a hand. "Oh, we are not hungry. At our age, our appetites are hardly there."

"Not like a growing child," Mishika crooned, sitting beside her youngest grandchild so she could pick up a small ball of rice and stuff it in his mouth.

Poppy observed the interaction between grandmother and grandchild longingly, another tender moment that her privileged upbringing had not afforded her. The Imperial Family had rejected her. Demetria had been raised in Welkland, and her parents rarely visited. But then Poppy observed details in the tableau that she hadn't noticed before: the gaunt, jagged angles of Kanav's and Mishika's bodies, carved by hunger; the undersized, delicate bodies of the children, shrunken from lack of nourishment.

Guilt filled any space that jealousy might have once held. The viceroy—her own father—was responsible for the deaths of these children's parents. His failure to enact labor laws, and his empowerment of a corrupt law-enforcement system, had created three forgotten orphans. And now, with his current export laws, there wasn't even enough food for everyone to eat.

Poppy took the edge of her plate in hand, ready to insist that either the grandparents or the children eat her meal, but Hasan caught her wrist.

"Don't," he whispered in Welkish. "Hospitality is essential in our culture. If you refuse to eat their food, you will insult their honor."

"Honor won't feed them," she hissed.

"You can, once you're vicereine," he shot back. "Offending them does not inspire support, however."

Fuming, Poppy pulled her plate to herself and took a reluctant bite.

Intrigued by their exchange, Ganak asked, in Virian, "Do you intend to succeed the duke, then, Miss Sutherland?"

Poppy and Hasan exchanged startled looks. She hadn't been aware that Ganak had been eavesdropping.

"She does," Kanav answered when neither of them spoke. "She was in the village all morning, listening to our problems."

"I'm here to help," Poppy said, recovering herself. "People are struggling to survive here. If I can learn more about what challenges you're facing, I can address the problems at the root."

"Oh, but we aren't staying," Mishika said.

"You're selling?" Hasan asked, incredulous. "But where will you go?"

"Marnapur, or maybe Indrabad up north," Kanav said. "Wherever we can find the best schooling for the lowest cost."

"Why?" Poppy asked. "Forgive me, but both your son and daughter-in-law died as a result of moving to the city. Wouldn't it be best to stay here?"

"An education is the most important thing," Ganak declared. "If I had a certificate from one of the Welkish schools, I would not have had to work in the factory. I'd still have my leg."

Poppy bit her lip, her next question on her tongue, but she wasn't sure if Ganak would be offended if she asked.

Seeing the question on her face, he explained, "I left the village to find work, to help support my brother after his wife's passing. Although I am literate, many companies refused to hire me as a bookkeeper or tutor because of my lack of formal education. I joined a factory, but there was an accident, and I was let go because I was no longer of use to the company. I couldn't afford the rates of a doctor in Andhra, and the wound got infected. Eventually, I returned home, where the village healer had to amputate it."

"So you see," Mishika said, "selling the land makes the most sense for us. It will sustain us until the children finish school and find steady, safe jobs. The Welkish academies are expensive—but they're worth it."

Poppy didn't want to disagree, not when the old woman spoke with such conviction. But her own experiences at a Welkish academy had nearly broken her. She doubted the schools on the island, run by Welkish administrators, would be any more welcoming to Virian students.

Carefully, she said, "The Welkish schools don't focus on Virian history, aside from the colonization of the island. The lessons are . . . biased. Are you not concerned that your grandchildren will lose your traditions and culture?"

"Culture couldn't have saved my son or daughter-in-law," Kanav answered. "But an education could have. It's not an easy choice to make—we are not selling our ancestral home lightly—but we cannot lose a future generation to preserve the past."

"It hardly matters." A hard edge entered Ganak's tone. "A lot of Virian history is biased too. Against vasudhakt. An unfortunate by-product of daivyakt nobility gatekeeping education, I suppose."

"Biased, how?" Hasan asked. His cool tone was layered with skepticism.

"For one, when daivyakt tell the origin story of how they came to wield divine power, they like to say that daivyakhi was given to the holiest of Virians, implying some sort of spiritual shortcoming on the behalf of vasudhakt. If it's not piety, then usually there is some other trait that vasudhakt lack that supposedly made them unworthy: Intelligence, bravery, athletic prowess, the list goes on. Tales like this have enabled daivyakt to treat vasudhakt as inferior for the entirety of our history, when in reality, no one knows why the gods chose the people they did. Daivyakt judge Jagat Rai for what he did, but none of them are willing to acknowledge the role that casteism played in driving him into the arms of the Welkish missionaries."

His speech was met with silence. Poppy wasn't sure what to say. Hasan's face had become stony.

Catching sight of Hasan's expression, Mishika immediately scolded Ganak. "Don't bring your politics in front of the guests!"

"Tell me where I lied, Ma. Is it offensive to speak the truth?"

Mishika snapped at him, a series of fast lines in a flurry of Virian. Poppy had gained enough fluency to understand that she was reprimanding her son for showing poor hospitality, and insisting that he either retract his statement or leave the table.

Face pinched, Ganak put his empty plate in his lap and wheeled himself out of the dining room in a huff, the chair bumping against the wall and on the other chairs in his haste. The sight stirred something in Poppy's chest.

Hasan must have seen her face shift, because he bumped her gently with his arm. "What are you thinking?"

"I feel terrible that he lost his leg, especially so young."

He shook his head. Meeting her eyes, he told her in Welkish,

"Don't pity him. He's still alive in a world that wants him dead. He may have suffered greatly, but in the end, he's lost nothing."

In a way, Poppy understood. Surviving in a racist society was an act of resistance in and of itself. But she wished it didn't have to be.

• • •

By the time they'd left Kanav and Mishika's house, Poppy knew she had been wrong when she'd said that she had nothing to give up. She'd been wrong when she thought that she had the most to lose. If she lost her challenge against Richard, the worst thing she could face was exile, but these people would continue to suffer and die under the regime of another indifferent viceroy.

Hasan's words about Ganak resonated with Poppy deeply. Every single person she had met today had survived in a society that had been designed to profit from their lives, individual coals destined to burn up in the fire of imperial greed. Their survival had not been an accident—it was by choice, a series of decisions that they had made every day: to sacrifice, to give something up in exchange for another day, another year on this earth. Mishika and Kanav traded meals for the growth of their grandchildren, were willing to trade their ancestral land and traditions for generations who would eventually forget them.

Poppy had faced her own hardships, but they paled in comparison to the battles these villagers fought every day, a reflection of the greater war to survive that spanned the island. Admitting this did not belittle her own struggles. Yes, she'd known racism—but she hadn't realized how deadly it could be when one didn't have wealth or an education to shield them. Hot shame spread through her as she recalled how she had insisted she had nothing more to sacrifice. What a fool she'd been, to think that she could fight this war without spilling blood.

When they returned to the car, Poppy turned and looked at the banyan tree. To Hasan, she said, "Give me your knife."

He eyed her suspiciously. "What are you going to do?"

"I'm going to try," she told him. "Trust me."

She held her breath as Hasan gave her a long, evaluating look, searching her gaze with his coal-black eyes. Wordlessly, he took out his dagger and handed it to her. She crossed the grass and circled the base of the tree, gazing at the gods carved into the ancient trunk, searching until she found the one she was looking for: Rukmini, the mother.

Before she could lose her nerve, she nicked her thumb with the edge of the dagger, drawing a thin line of blood. Behind her, the sound of footsteps crunched on dead grass as the villagers' curiosity drew them closer to her.

Poppy ignored the crowd as she gently smeared her blood on the bark below Rukmini's face. As she did, she prayed, *You are the mother of this island, and a mother protects and provides for her young. My father has failed to care for the people of this island. With your blessing, help me to become what these people need.* Silently, she finished with the prayer Hasan had taught her. *My veins are a vessel . . .* Hoping that Rukmini had heard her, she closed her eyes and reached for her daivyakhi.

Moisture flooded her senses, deep in the soil, plentiful in the air around her. It would take more energy to condense it from the air, so she pulled from the soil instead, funneling it up in a thin stream that burst from the soil at the base of the banyan tree. Poppy's palms grew sticky with sweat as she forced the stream to remain calm and steady, a fountain instead of a geyser.

A ripple of amazement ran through the villagers. "Poppy,"

Hasan whispered, his tone awed. Her control slipped. The spring faltered, losing its shape.

"Shhh!" she hissed. He quieted.

"Get a bucket, quick!" one of the villagers barked. A scuffle ensued, and a woman rushed forward with a bucket. Poppy traced her hand in an arc. The spring shot higher. A hollow, tinny sound filled the air as the stream drummed on the bottom of the empty bucket.

When it was filled, two more villagers came forward with containers. Holding her breath, Poppy maintained the flow, until not one but six buckets had been filled. When her knees grew soft and her vision blurred, she forced herself to stop. The spring burbled as it seeped back into the ground. Poppy's skin felt clammy; she'd run on the edge of using her mortal energy.

"Poppy, you did it!" Hasan shouted, running into the square. He grabbed her shoulders, grinning ear to ear. "I knew you had it in you."

"It only took a little bit of blood," she deadpanned, though it had taken a lot more than that—humility, connection, and sacrifice on her part. But she hadn't gotten here alone. She had failed multiple times on her own, and would have remained a failure if others hadn't helped her: the widows, Harithi—even Samina's brutal honesty had contributed to this moment. Most of all, Poppy owed this moment to Hasan, who had been given multiple opportunities to cry off, and had stayed true to their deal regardless. Despite her failures, he believed in her—perhaps more than she deserved.

She would not let Hasan down. She wouldn't let any of these people down. She would become vicereine, and then she would change the fate of this island.

Chapter Twenty-Nine

Bitter Reunion

Hasan held Poppy by the shoulders. Beneath his touch, she trembled—with excitement, or maybe exhaustion, or perhaps both. She had done it—no, she had *excelled* beyond any expectation he had had of her. Her breakthrough today had allowed her to tap into a much deeper, controlled level of her daivyakhi. The villagers murmured and stared, the respect in their eyes a shallow reflection of the reverence taking root in Hasan's chest.

Poppy had come a long way from the cowed woman she'd been at her engagement party. Nor was she the haughty, demanding maharani she'd been in the cells. In front of him was a lady who had humbled herself to learn about others, who could summon springs and save lives. Another rush of fierce pride ran through him. He blinked. When had Poppy Sutherland become someone he admired?

Grumbling rippled through the crowd as it parted for a newcomer. A man in a wrinkled gray suit pushed to the front, his usually tidy black hair mussed, as though he'd run to get here.

"Hasan?" Zeyar asked, bewildered. "What are you doing here? Is that Poppy? Why isn't she at the house?"

Hasan whirled away from Poppy. "Zeyar!" He laughed, still

giddy over Poppy's display of daivyakhi. "You're back early! Oh my gods, Zeyar, you would not believe—"

Zeyar caught him by the arm, dragging him away from the banyan tree. "Hasan, you shouldn't be here." His eyes flashed, darting from Hasan to Poppy to the crowd.

Hasan inhaled, his mood deflating as he remembered he'd done this all behind his brother's back. He had opted to beg forgiveness over asking permission, and now it was time to get on bended knee. He squared his shoulders. "I have something to tell you."

"We'll talk," Zeyar said, hustling Hasan along even farther. "But right now, you need to go back to the safe house. Quickly."

Zeyar had managed to steer them back to Hasan's car. Hasan opened his mouth to protest—Poppy was still back at the tree—but a chorus of screams cut him off. Lightning quick, he darted around Zeyar and sprinted back to the banyan tree.

"Poppy!" he shouted, pushing through the crowd of villagers. They stampeded past, and he doubled over, coughing from the dust they left in their wake. When he straightened, he spotted her, still standing by the banyan tree. "Poppy," he called again, but she didn't turn her head. Her gaze was locked on the lithe figure approaching her from the other direction: Montrose.

Though he'd come out the victor in his brawl with Samina, Montrose looked like hell. On the right side of his face, he sported a black eye. On the left, scabbed-over nail scratches marked his once-perfect ivory skin from cheek to collarbone.

"Poppy!" Hasan yelled once he finally caught up to her.

She turned to him at last, her wounded gaze searching his. "What is this? I thought we had a deal."

"We do," he said. "It's an ambush! Zeyar must have been tailed."

He reached for his dagger, but he'd given it to Poppy. Opening one hand, he hurled his good arm forward and sent a ball of flame at Montrose's head. Montrose ducked, scowling. Hasan shot another jet of flame his way. The arm of Montrose's uniform caught fire; he stripped his jacket off, tossing it to the ground.

"Zephyr, control your man!" he shouted, stomping on the jacket until the flames died.

Hasan didn't know whom Montrose was addressing until Zeyar seized him, wrapping his arms around him tightly. His gunshot wound throbbed from the pressure, but he struggled anyway.

"What are you doing?" Hasan kicked backward, making contact with Zeyar's shins, but Zeyar didn't let him go.

"He's giving us Paranjay," Zeyar said. "Stop it! Stop."

Hasan froze, his mind racing as he processed Zeyar's words. "You bartered with him behind my back?"

In front of them, Richard lunged at Poppy. She flung herself at the knife discarded at the base of the banyan tree, but Richard seized her first, arms wrapping around her waist.

"No!" she screamed, thrashing. Her eyes met Hasan's, and the look of raw betrayal took his breath away. "You said you'd help me!" Her voice broke. "I thought you believed in me."

"I do!" Hasan said, frantic, twisting in Zeyar's grip once more. "I didn't do this, I swear. My brother—"

He stilled for a moment as something occurred to him, a detail that hadn't quite clicked in the chaos of the moment. Twisting as much as he could to see Zeyar, he asked, "Where's Paranjay?"

Zeyar didn't meet his gaze. "He's in a secure location in the city. The deal depends on the *peaceful* transfer of—"

"So you don't even have him." Hasan laughed in disbelief. "You fucking idiot, Zeyar—"

Zeyar bellowed as Hasan clasped one flaming hand around

his forearm, burning his handprint into his suit jacket. Reflexively, he let go. Hasan tore free, chasing Poppy to where Richard had dragged her, close to his car.

"Poppy!" he shouted. He glared at Montrose. "She's not going with you."

"Step down," Richard said. "This doesn't concern you. I've already arranged this with your brother."

Hasan flinched as his words drove the knife of Zeyar's betrayal in a little deeper. "Let her go!"

He seized Montrose's arm, the one holding Poppy, with flaming fingers. Montrose lashed out with his free hand, striking Hasan in the jaw. His head snapped back, his teeth cutting into his cheek, but he didn't let go. He swung back, punching Montrose in the gut. Montrose grunted, but the other police officers had caught up to them, tearing Hasan away before he could land a second flaming punch.

"Hasan," Zeyar shouted. He'd almost caught up to them, clutching his scorched sleeve. "Let's go. This isn't our business anymore."

Hasan tried to twist out of Montrose's minions' grasp, writhing like a serpent. "Get off me!" Blood seeped from the wound in his cheek, and he spat a mouthful of it at Richard. "You can't take her! She doesn't want to go with you!"

Richard stopped, pinning Zeyar with an icy look. "Zephyr, silence your man, or I will."

Hasan flipped both palms upward and channeled the last of his daivyakhi into twin columns of flame. The officers holding him cried out and stumbled back, clutching at their singed eyebrows. He charged at Montrose. Before the captain could move, the whistle of metal cutting through air sang out behind him.

The nightstick smashed into Hasan's skull with a crunch. The last thing he saw was Poppy's feet, disappearing into Montrose's car, one at a time.

• • •

"We need to talk."

It was the first thing Richard had said to Poppy since they'd left Sanivali. Night had fallen over the island. She gazed out the car window, counting the stars in the sky to keep herself from crying. *I will* not *cry in front of Richard.* She would die before she let him slake his thirst for power on her tears.

"About what?" she asked evenly, still gazing out of the window.

"Don't act innocent. Something's happened. Since you were kidnapped, you've been different. I thought you were in shock, at the museum. But your kidnapper claimed you didn't *want* to come with me. What's going on?"

The best strategy would be to lie, to buy more time to plot against Richard. But after the last couple of weeks, Poppy found she could no longer go back to playing the demure, toothless fiancée Richard thought she was. She was a threat—and it was time he feared her.

"Will you not speak to me?" Richard reached for her hand.

Poppy whipped her head around, yanking her hand away as she locked eyes with him. "Drop the act," she said. "I know about your plan, Richard."

Shock spread across his face—genuine at first, followed by a mask of innocent confusion. "What—"

"No more lies," she said. "I heard you at the engagement party, how you intend to dispose of me once we're wed. You never intended to honor any marital vows to me."

Richard's face crumpled, wide eyes shining with hurt and disbelief. His act was so seamless, she nearly doubted her own memory. "Poppy, love, maybe you misunderstood—"

"The only thing I misunderstood is the depths of your evil." She held her ground. "You cannot trick me; I know what I heard. I know you're working with the Alderforts. I know you'll accuse me of drug smuggling, and I know you intend to have a witness from Welkland falsely testify against me. I *know*."

Richard stared, his blue eyes almost black in the darkness of the car. Then, finally, he smiled, his lips stretching as he bared his teeth.

"Okay, so you know. Very good! But what are you going to do about it? Tell someone?" He laughed. "The whole city saw the way you were mooning after me. Who do you think they'll believe set out to entrap whom?"

When Poppy didn't answer, his smirk grew even sharper. "I thought so. Face it—you're powerless."

She glared at him. She wasn't powerless. She had Hasan's support—

No, you don't, a snide voice in her head reminded her. Perhaps she never had. Either way, now that Zeyar had retrieved their brother, who knew where Hasan's allegiance would lie? The lump in her throat swelled. She dragged a shallow, painful breath from her lungs. But she didn't cry.

"I won't marry you," she said. "Your plan will only work if I marry you; otherwise, the succession will fall to a vote."

Richard scoffed. "You *will* marry me."

"Or what? You'll expose me?" She huffed out a humorless laugh. "You'll do that anyway. There is nothing you can threaten me with that won't harm you as well, so long as we remain unmarried."

He leaned in. She jerked back, bumping her head against the window. "You'll marry me," he said, "or instead of being exiled to some idyllic Welkish countryside, I'll have you swinging from the gallows."

Her heart skipped a beat. "On what grounds?"

"Treason," Richard said, his voice laced with venom. "Conspiring with the Jackal, a *known* unnatural, to extort the viceroy, not to mention arson. There's a certain curator at the museum who will testify to seeing you together the night it burned down."

"You arranged that meeting," she said.

"Unofficially," he corrected her. "The curator thought he was communicating with the Jackal from the start. According to official records, the police only arrived after the Jackal did, and so we were too late to stop him, alas. If only the Marnapur police had a better budget, we could have protected the museum."

Outmaneuvered, again! Rage rendered Poppy speechless. She twisted her head away, her heartbeat hammering against her rib cage. How was he always several steps ahead? He had backed her into a tight corner. But he would *not* hold her there for long. She would claw her way out of this wedding, by any and all means possible.

And then Poppy would see to it that he could never threaten her again.

Chapter Thirty

Hypocritical

Hasan woke with a pulsing headache. Eyes closed, he grimaced. Pain ebbed and flowed from his left temple. Without opening his eyes, he brought his hand up to the side of his head. When his fingers came away sticky, his eyes flew open.

Though it was dark, he knew exactly what the metallic-smelling substance on his hand was: his own half-congealed blood.

He blinked at the sight, dazed. Had he had an accident while he'd been out with Poppy? They'd been in Sanivali Square. She had finally come around, demonstrating excellent control over her power. For a moment, the memory filled him with warm pride. Then he flinched as he recalled what had happened next.

"Zeyar!" Hasan flung away the cotton sheet someone had draped over him, stumbling out of bed. A wave of dizziness washed over him. He staggered into the wall, knocking one of the paintings to the ground. He paid it no mind, lurching toward the door.

He was going to find Zeyar. And then he was going to kill him.

"Zeyar!" he shouted again, tripping into the hallway.

Heavy footsteps pounded up the staircase. Zeyar's head

appeared first, followed by the rest of him. He wore a white button-down shirt and the same gray slacks from earlier, dirtied from where Hasan had kicked at him. The sleeve on his burned arm was rolled up, clean white bandages wrapped around the wound.

Hasan launched himself at his brother without a second thought. The two of them flew backward, crashing into the wall behind the landing, denting the drywall.

"What's wrong with you?" Zeyar wrenched him into a headlock.

"Took the words right out of my mouth," Hasan said, thrashing furiously. "How could you deal with Montrose? Without telling me?"

All this time, he'd thought Zeyar had gone to the city to take care of Vinay's family. He'd authorized him to act on his behalf, trusting him to keep his interests at heart, and then he had gone and done the very last thing Hasan would have wanted. He twisted out of Zeyar's grasp, dancing back before swinging at him.

"There was no point discussing it with you!" Zeyar dodged the blow. "You wouldn't have understood." They separated, circling each other like lions.

"Because it was the wrong choice!"

Hasan lunged for Zeyar again. The two of them hit the ground with a heavy thud, each one scrambling to subdue the other.

"You act like there *was* a choice," Zeyar said, his chest heaving as he held Hasan down. "What did I tell you, Hasan? There is no white or black, only shades of gray. Men like Richard Montrose will *always* win. We'd only be damning ourselves by supporting the losing cause."

"Poppy could have done it." Hasan panted, the strain on his old injuries catching up to him. "I spent all week training her. You should have seen how quickly—"

"You trained her?" Zeyar stared at Hasan. He looked down the remaining flight of stairs, where their ma had appeared, summoned by the sound of violence. "Did you know he was training her?"

"The girl is daivyakt," Rohini declared, hands on her hips. "She deserved to know how to commune with the gods."

Zeyar turned back to where he had Hasan pinned, eyes blazing. "You broke your promise. You said you'd stop acting out based on your personal moral code."

"You did the exact same thing!" Hasan snapped his head forward, bashing his skull into Zeyar's nose with a sickening crunch. Zeyar grunted, lifting his hands to protect his face instinctively, allowing Hasan to throw him off at last. Zeyar rolled down the remaining flight of stairs, forcing their ma to jump back.

"Hasan!" she said, her eyes flashing with a warning.

He didn't heed it. He leaped down the flight before Zeyar could rise, grabbing him roughly by the collar. He shook him once, hard. "Tell me what he promised you."

"I did it to bring Paranjay home," Zeyar said, blood staining his teeth. "I did it for both of you. He'd have raided every holding of ours, razed every safe house, until he found Poppy. Even if we had the numbers to defend ourselves, we're no match for his weaponry. We lost *eleven* men at the museum. We lost Vinay—"

"Don't you fucking talk about Vinay," Hasan said.

"You yourself almost died. I got him to *stop*!"

"You got *nothing*." Hasan shook Zeyar viciously. "You say you did this to bring Paranjay home? Well, where is he, then? Where is he?"

Zeyar closed his eyes. Then, finally, he said, "He's in the city."

"He's still in jail?" Rohini covered her mouth.

"As part of the bargain, Montrose moved Paranjay to a third

location and gave me the address and the key when we arrived in Sanivali. He didn't trust me enough to bring Paranjay here until he knew it wasn't an ambush." Zeyar tossed Hasan a dirty look.

His words bothered Hasan, though it took him a minute to realize why. "Tell me what else you got from him."

"What are you talking about?"

"*Part* of the bargain," he repeated. "You said *part.* What were the other parts?"

"I got immunity, for all of us." Zeyar shoved him away. "We won't be charged for Poppy's kidnapping, so long as we don't provoke the police further."

"And that's all?" he asked. When Zeyar hesitated, Hasan said, "Swear that that's all he promised you. Swear it on our grandfather."

Zeyar relented, running a hand over his hair. "His father, the marquess, has agreed to sponsor me as one of his picks in the House of Representatives."

The revelation was like a kick to the teeth. Hasan's shaking hands curled back into fists. "How could you?"

"I told you," Zeyar said. "We can only protect ourselves if we have a voice in the system. Paranjay would never have been taken if we'd had someone to guard our interests."

"Poppy could have been our voice!" Hasan exploded. "That was my whole *point*, but you refused. What makes you different from Poppy, Zeyar? What makes you think you can survive the machine that you profess will devour her?"

"Because, unlike *her*, I'm not reaching for a position that I could never keep," Zeyar said, pointing at himself. "I only play games I know I can win. The girl has bitten off more than she can chew. She is *one woman* vying for the top office in the colony. No one will support her."

"I support her!" Hasan shouted. "I'd already told her we would back her, and then you went and ruined it."

"That was a choice you made without me," Zeyar said, "which is ironic, given that you're upset that I made a choice without you. What makes us different, Hasan?"

He recoiled. "Because the person *I* chose to back doesn't have a history of violence against us!"

"So, personal opinion." Zeyar's dark brow lifted, the twin to Hasan's scar standing in stark relief. "Your personal opinion on the matter is what makes it okay for you to act on your own, whereas if I do the same, I'm the bad guy?"

Hasan's head throbbed, though it had little to do with the wound on the back of his head. He couldn't find the words to describe *why* what Zeyar had done was so wrong when it so closely resembled his own actions. He'd known supporting Poppy meant breaking his promise. He'd chosen to ask forgiveness over asking permission.

But in that moment, he found it hard to get down and beg forgiveness at the feet of the same man who had planted a knife in his back.

"You could have told me your plan. At least I was honest about where I stood on supporting Poppy."

"And I was always honest about *not* supporting her," Zeyar retorted. "I told you she was the weaker choice. You don't listen, Hasan. Even if I'd told you what I was planning, you wouldn't have listened. All you care about is what's morally correct. You don't understand how the world works."

"It doesn't matter what's morally correct," Rohini said. "You secured a political role for yourself before you secured your own brother's freedom. What kind of man are you?"

For that, Zeyar had no answer.

Hasan couldn't look at him anymore. "You should go."

"You can't tell me to leave." Zeyar stood his ground. "This is my home too." He turned to their mother. "Tell him, Ma."

She tilted her chin up, the cords of her throat prominent as she clenched her jaw. "You can come back when you get Paranjay."

Zeyar stared at her. "Are you serious?"

Their ma did not flinch.

His face went slack. He dusted himself off, adjusting the bloodied collar of his button-down shirt. "Very well. You're upset; I can tell. When I return with Paranjay, I hope you'll be ready to apologize to me." Zeyar reached for his blazer, slung across the banister. His movements were slow, as though he were hoping Hasan or their ma would change their minds.

They didn't.

Zeyar buttoned the jacket, his eyes blazing. "I did this for you. For us I've won a seat in a House that has never opened its doors to Virians before. Now we have a seat at the table where they wouldn't even toss us scraps. But you want to cast me out? Fine!" Zeyar wrenched the door open. "Promise me this, Hasan: Don't go after Montrose. Don't try to rescue Poppy, or storm the precinct, or any other shit like that. Stay out of trouble."

"Fuck off," Hasan said. "I owe you nothing. I only make oaths to my brother, and the only brother I have is rotting in a Marnapur jail."

Zeyar flinched. It was a tiny, fleeting gesture that betrayed his proud indifference, but he covered it quickly with that ice-cold confident facade that Hasan hated most.

"When you get over yourselves, call me," Zeyar said. The door slammed shut behind him.

And with that, the second Devar brother was lost.

Chapter Thirty-One

Zephyr Devar

The drive back to Marnapur felt twice as long as usual. Zeyar simmered in silence. He'd known the moment he set out to strike a deal with Montrose that neither Hasan nor their ma would approve of his plan, but he hadn't expected them to hatch their own plot behind his back, either. He should have known better. Hasan had always had vigilante tendencies, delusions of heroism that likely stemmed from some sort of warped guilt over what they did for a living. Their mother, on the other hand, had always been superstitious. The moment Poppy had revealed she was daivyakt, it had changed everything. But Zeyar knew best, and he would prove it—right after he cleared up this latest misunderstanding.

The Montrose family butler showed Zeyar into Captain Montrose's study. "Captain Montrose will be with you shortly."

Zeyar sat on one of the chairs, tracing an idle finger over the ornately carved handrest. Though he'd been to Montrose Manor several times now, the sheer mass of their generational wealth never failed to gut him. The Montrose line had always been wealthy, but their fortune had ballooned over the last two centuries through investments in tea and cotton exports.

He jumped up as Richard entered the room. He walked over

to the side table, pouring a finger of Welkish whiskey for each of them. He handed one glass to Zeyar. "I appreciate your assistance in retrieving my fiancée, Zephyr."

"I am glad we could come to an understanding." Zeyar bowed his head to hide the annoyance on his face. "And it's Zeyar, Captain. Not Zephyr."

"Why are you here?" Richard asked.

He held up the key. "For my brother, Captain, as we agreed. I arrived at the destination you gave me, but he wasn't inside."

Richard sipped his whiskey, clicking his tongue once. "Actually, if you recall, our deal hinged on the *peaceful* return of my fiancée," he said. "When your brother attacked us, you forfeited that."

"He wasn't meant to be in the village." Zeyar gritted his teeth, his temper flaring as Montrose reminded him of Hasan's hypocrisy. Hasan had acted without the consent of the family, too, but somehow, it was he who had been cast out of the group. He forced himself to take a swallow of the whiskey, the sharp burn bringing him back to the conversation. "Besides, he barely did any damage before I subdued him."

Montrose tilted his glass. "A deal's a deal."

His nonchalance reminded Zeyar of a dealer in a gambling den, sweeping the chips away from the poor fool who had put them all in the center of the table, betting recklessly. He had seen similar scenes on countless occasions, but for the first time, he was the one crushed by the loss.

He clenched his teeth even tighter, swallowing hard as bile rose in his throat. "My brother was never inside that second location, was he?"

Montrose leaned forward, dropping his voice. "May I speak honestly with you?"

Zeyar knew from experience that this phrase was often the harbinger of bullshit, but he nodded anyway.

"I cannot let the smuggler go yet. In a couple of months, Poppy will go on trial, and he will be a key witness."

"I understand that things are sensitive right now," Zeyar said slowly, "but to wait a couple of *months*? Captain, you assured me that I could bring him home tonight."

"Plans change." Montrose examined one shirt cuff. "The best I can do is promise not to have him moved to a high-security prison. So long as he agrees to testify against her, of course."

"He will," Zeyar said. "But—"

"Is there a problem?" Richard locked eyes with him. "Remember, to join the House of Representatives, you need to be sponsored by one of the lords on the Council—and last I checked, my father is the only offer you have."

He hesitated, still seething at Richard's duplicity. *As if I have any other choice.* "No, Captain."

Richard beamed, pouring him another ounce of whiskey. "Excellent. I knew I could count on you, Zephyr."

He smiled painfully. "It's *Zeyar*, Captain."

"Zeyar," Richard drawled, butchering the pronunciation. "When my father formally sponsors you as representative, do you want him to stumble over your name? People in the House will whisper to each other, trying to figure out what he said, and then you've lost your chance to make an impression right out of the gate. Your lack of status and legitimate wealth already alienate you from the other representatives. This can't be helped, but a name is easily replaced. You can either be flexible, and give them a strong, Welkish name that they will remember, or you can continue to be Zeyar. Who are you going to be?"

He balked. As the first-born, his grandfather, Manoj Devar,

had been the one to name him. He'd chosen *Zeyar* for the second-last maharaja of Viryana, a powerful man who had brought the country to its peak. *You will be a great man, a leader just like the maharaja,* his grandfather had prophesied. Zeyar fought the urge to bite his cheek. *Great leaders made sacrifices.* That was another one of his grandfather's maxims. *This is a sacrifice,* he told himself. *He would understand.*

"Zephyr," he said. "But I'm keeping my last name. That, I won't budge on." He wouldn't relinquish his grandfather's last name, not after the promise he had made to him.

"Suit yourself," Richard said. "If there's nothing else you need?"

Zeyar knew a dismissal when he saw one. "That's all, Captain." He bowed his head. "If it's acceptable, I'll take my leave."

He walked back to his car, his hand hovering over the handle. Normally, he'd have gone to the apartment that he shared with his brothers. But now that they were estranged, whom did that space belong to? He had a key, and just as much right to the property as the other two, but the thought of returning to that place didn't sit right.

No. He could go home when he proved the others wrong. He could go home once he'd achieved what he'd set out to achieve: winning back his brother and securing a place of power for his kin in the House of Representatives. He'd spend tonight in a room somewhere. Tomorrow, he'd start looking for a new place for himself.

As he unpacked his bags in the sparsely furnished inn, it occurred to him that he was alone—truly alone. Paranjay was still incarcerated, he'd broken Ma's heart, and his only free brother had disowned him. And Harithi . . . Zeyar wasn't sure what she would make of his actions when Hasan told her, but he knew she would react with the same indifferent countenance that she usually wore. He wondered if she would pardon him eventually, or if what he'd done was unforgivable to her as well. He shook his head. Her forgiveness didn't matter.

Hasan, their mother, Harithi—they didn't understand. None of them did. Their life of crime would not protect them, though the money had insulated them as much as possible. The only viable move was to join respectable Welkish society. The only other person who'd even come close to understanding had been his grandfather, who had spent most of his last days bemoaning the way he was to go: quietly, without the royal fanfare he believed he was due.

"We are daivyakt! We can trace our ancestry back to the Rais," he'd raved to Zeyar in one of his final, feverish fits. "The Welks, they've stripped this country of its agency. Our forefathers would weep to see it as it is . . . to see me as I am. Don't let them strip us of what little dignity we have left. Promise me, boy: You will not let this family fall any lower."

"I promise," Zeyar had vowed, clutching his grandfather's hand until he stilled at last.

As he curled up on the hard mattress, he took comfort in the fact that he was one step closer to fulfilling the promise he'd made to his grandfather. It didn't matter if his family did not want his help—he would still use his new position to uplift their name.

Chapter Thirty-Two

An Offering of Anger

Hasan kneeled in front of the pantheon at dawn, his hands empty in front of him. Normally, he'd give the gods coin or food. But for what he was planning, he'd need far more power than what his usual offerings got him.

It was unfortunate, then, that he had nothing left. He'd lost Paranjay. He'd lost Poppy. And now, he'd lost Zeyar.

No, that wasn't true. Zeyar had betrayed Hasan, and Hasan was the one who was lost.

He burned to go back to the city, find Zeyar, and ruin him. He'd raze his elder brother's political aspirations until they were nothing more than ash. Zeyar deserved to lose everything, just as he had.

The only thing he had left to offer the gods was his anger.

He pulled out his wallet, removing a creased photograph of himself, Paranjay, and Zeyar as boys, taken at their grandfather's request. It must have cost the old man a small fortune to hire a photographer, but he had insisted on having a picture of the next generation of Devars.

"Every royal family has a set of portraits," Manoj Devar had claimed.

"We aren't royalty, Baba." Hasan's father had laughed. "We're criminals."

The old man hadn't found it funny. "We can trace our ancestry back to the Rais," he said. "Our people ruled this island once, and they will again. Mark my words."

Hasan studied the small sepia faces in his hand. Paranjay laughed in the center, effortlessly carefree. On his left, Hasan wasn't looking at the camera—what a waste of film he'd been—but to the right, Zeyar stood unsmiling, his expression severe for a young boy, as though their grandfather's words were a heavy mantle on his slim shoulders.

Slowly, he tore the priceless photo. He tucked the two-thirds of the picture with himself and Paranjay back into his wallet, and then laid the piece of photograph with Zeyar at the foot of the gods.

As he released it, he forced himself to loosen his grip on his anger. *I will not exact my revenge on Zeyar. I forfeit this to the gods.* "My veins are a vessel for the divine power of the gods," he chanted. "If they find my sacrifice worthy, may I be filled with their cosmic energy."

Though no breeze brushed through the underground room, goose bumps rose on his arms anyway. He rose to his feet, turning his back on Zeyar's serious expression.

The gods had granted him the power he needed. And while he'd promised not to go after Zeyar, he had another brother to pursue.

Hasan packed cash and a spare set of clothes before borrowing his mother's car keys. As he opened the door, her voice rang out.

"Where are you going?"

His ma stood at the top of the stairs, hands on her hips, brows knit together.

"I'm going to do what I should have done a long time ago," he said. "I'm going to get Paranjay. And then, I'm going to burn that police precinct to the ground."

She lingered a moment longer at the top of the stairs, then came down to stand in front of Hasan. She put one hand on his cheek. "Go then," she said, a reluctant blessing. "But promise me this: You will come home. Even if it's without your brother."

"Ma," he protested, but she shook her head.

"I cannot lose three sons." Her voice broke. "I would rather lose two than three. Promise me."

He hesitated, recalling the last time he had made a promise to a family member. He would not be bound by any more oaths. Instead, he bent and kissed his mother's cheek. "Have faith in me," he said. "I won't let you down."

As Hasan drew back, his mother caught his eye. His words weren't a promise, and she knew it. But she let him go anyway.

• • •

Hasan arrived in the city at sundown, taking the long way around. Though he'd been born in the countryside, he'd been raised on Marnapur's streets, growing and changing alongside it. The city was as familiar to him as a brother. He knew its nature by heart, was familiar with all of its moods.

But as he entered Marnapur that evening, he found it in a crisis that he had never seen before. For one, his beloved city was perpetually noisy, day and night, a symphony with a range of instruments: the clamor of seagulls screaming and sailors shouting as they unloaded the ships at the docks, the clash and clanging of products being assembled at the factories, and the rumbling of car engines deeper in the throat of the city, punctuated by honking and the occasional squeal of tires. Under it all was the constant thrum of *people*—talking, haggling, begging, laughing.

Tonight, Marnapur was silent, save for the wail of sirens, illuminated by blue and red flashing lights that blinded him if he dared look directly. He had never seen the police assembled like this before, lining the streets and rooftops. And while some might see the golden badges and silver pistols as symbols of order, Hasan saw them for what they were: a sign that the city had fallen into chaos.

As he drove deeper into the city, he encountered a new checkpoint on the road ahead. Cars slowed ahead of him, lining up as the officers went to every window, checking identification and asking questions. He eased down on the brakes, mind racing.

From this side of the city, the checkpoint was the only way to go forward by car. There were a dozen other ways to go on foot, but then he'd lose the advantage of speed and the anonymity of tinted windows. For a moment, he considered fighting his way through the checkpoint, but he couldn't afford to act rashly. If he fought the officers here, he would alert Montrose to his presence, and the police would certainly relocate Paranjay.

He turned off the main road, parking his mother's car in an empty lot. This far on the edge of the city, where the poorest residents resided, the car would likely be stolen by the time he got back. But if the car was the price for Paranjay's freedom, so be it.

In the blue light that preceded nightfall, he slipped into the streets, slinking into the city on foot, leaving the checkpoint—and the car—behind. He cut through the back alleys, careful to avoid major roads. Though muggers and pickpockets prowled the backstreets, Hasan was better equipped to deal with them than the police. But the lanes were empty, save for the occasional beggar. Even the street food stalls were deserted, rusty metal shutters pulled closed by vendors who had once been fixtures on this street.

He arrived at his first destination, Kaushal's home. As he approached the single-level house, the hairs on the back of his neck stood up. The windows, though filthy, were intact, but what bothered him was that they were dark. Night had fallen, and with the curfew, Kaushal should have been home. Even if he had left the house, he *certainly* wouldn't have left his front door ajar.

Hasan pulled his knife from the waistband of his belt, holding it aloft as he pushed the door open with his free hand. He didn't call for Kaushal—not when he already knew his cousin wouldn't answer, not when the advantage of surprise would be twice as useful as the knife in his hand against any would-be attacker.

He stepped forward. Something crunched under his shoe, sharp even through the thick sole. He flicked on the light, lifting his foot away to reveal the shards of a mug. His gaze followed the rivulets of dried coffee down to where the wooden table had been split in half, as though a heavy weight had been dropped—or shoved—onto it. The chairs lay overturned; one leg had been split off and lay discarded by the faded couch. Hasan bent down to examine it. Blood stained the edge.

He checked the bedroom next. Although it appeared to be ransacked—dresser drawers open, sheets wrenched back—the main struggle had taken place in the kitchen. He returned there, dragging his finger across the coffee stain on the floor. Thoroughly dried. Whoever had taken his cousin was long gone.

Montrose must have him. If it had been Virian burglars, not even the furniture would be left. Hasan growled, kicking the shards of the coffee mug, sending them skittering across the kitchen tile.

"Get it together," he breathed, pressing his fingers to his head. Kaushal wasn't the only fighter he knew. He would just have to find another man.

He found Jayendhra's house intact on the outside, but completely bare on the inside. Hasan pulled out drawers and tore open closets, finding them devoid of all personal effects and clothing. Unlike Kaushal's place, there were no signs of struggle. Jayendhra had clearly gone on the run, perhaps after having heard what had happened to Kaushal. He discovered a similar scene at Raman's house—empty cabinets left open, nonessentials left behind, as though he'd only had a minute's notice before he'd fled.

"Is *everyone* in this gang a traitor?" Hasan slammed one of the cabinet doors so hard it bounced back open. How was it that in a matter of weeks, everything he'd built his life upon had fallen apart? He'd put family first only to be betrayed by his eldest brother, the one who was supposed to watch out for the rest of them. He'd prioritized the needs of his gang, only for them to turn tail when things got difficult.

Outside, the sun was starting to rise. With the city crawling with police, Hasan would have to continue the rest of his search tomorrow night, under cover of darkness. Taking one last look around Jayendhra's place, he left, headed back to the apartment. As he stepped into the empty apartment, it occurred to him that he did not know where Zeyar was staying. In a way, he was relieved that he hadn't already been inside. But where else could he have gone?

It didn't matter, he told himself. Zeyar's whereabouts didn't matter. But as he headed off to sleep, he couldn't help but pause in the doorway to Zeyar's room, staring at the neatly made bed within.

Chapter Thirty-Three

Birthright

It was no secret that every woman out in society would murder their own fiancé for the chance to have their own custom Agatha Lark wedding dress. As Poppy looked in the mirror, she found it wasn't hard to see why. Agatha had outdone herself, crafting a masterpiece out of ivory silk the same shade as the elephant tusks that hung in the Sutherlands' sitting room.

Long bishop sleeves puffed below the elbow before tightening in a long cuff down her forearm. Half a dozen buttons fashioned from Welkish pearls adorned each one. A silk-and-pearl choker concealed her scar from the museum. The skirt, puffed up with layers of tulle, was further weighted down by handcrafted silk roses in Montrose scarlet.

Poppy's gown would be as coveted as the man she would marry, if not more. She'd be the envy of every woman in the chapel, yet she'd trade with any of those ladies in a heartbeat. Despite her resolution to end her engagement, her parents had dismissed her pleas, writing them off as a case of cold feet. It did not help her cause that she couldn't give them a sufficient reason beyond the flimsy excuse of incompatibility, but she wasn't confident that they would believe in the truth.

As Agatha arranged the bridal veil over her face, she couldn't help but feel as though she were being fitted for a burial shroud instead.

"There," Agatha said, stepping back. "It's simpler than I would have liked, but . . ."

The couturiere trailed off awkwardly, leaving the end of the sentence hanging in the air: *But I didn't have enough time.* Poppy didn't begrudge Lark for her grievance; if anything, she felt the same way. In less than a week, she'd be married to Richard, her place cemented at his side. The thought didn't inspire the satisfaction that it used to.

When it became obvious that Poppy did not intend to reply, her mother cleared her throat. "It's perfect. We are both so grateful to you."

"Of course." Agatha pinched Poppy's cheek. "Anything for the future marchioness."

She flinched backward. Agatha took her hand away quickly.

"Madame Lark, do you mind giving me a moment alone with my daughter?" Demetria suggested. "His Grace is in his office down the hall. One of his staff will give you the final check."

The couturiere looked relieved by the suggestion. She gathered up her pins and measuring tape and hurried out of Poppy's bedroom. Once Agatha closed the door behind her, Poppy's mother rose from the settee and came to stand behind her. In the mirror, Poppy's gaze met her disapproving stare. Though her face was mostly obscured by the lace veil, she kept her features cold and impartial. Mother and daughter stood like that for a moment, each sizing up the other.

"I don't know what's gotten into you," her mother said. "It's one thing to have cold feet. But must you be so sullen and ungrateful in front of the couturiere?"

"Forgive me, Mother," she bit out. "I will endeavor to better conceal my discontent at being forced to the altar."

Her mother gave an aggravated sigh. "Where is this coming from? It was *you* who rushed to get married. We are not forcing you!"

Poppy couldn't argue with her there. She had pursued Richard, chasing respect and security, but she now knew better than to expect either of these things from him.

"I've changed my mind," she said. "Yet you insist on going forward with this. What is that, if not forcing me?"

"I still don't understand *why* you wish to end the engagement." Her mother softened her voice, coaxing, "Be honest, now: What has changed?"

The truth perched at the tip of Poppy's tongue, but Richard's voice whispered in her head: *Who do you think they'll believe?* The rules of this game had been written by men like him, putting all the cards in his hand. He was a white, wealthy, attractive man who was well respected in the community. Meanwhile, Poppy was a brown woman who had been exiled for seven years over a single necklace. The truth didn't serve people like her.

"I've changed," she answered honestly. "I returned to marry Richard so I'd have a place in the nobility, as a marchioness, and as the viceroy's wife. But I don't want that anymore."

"Why not?" Her mother's bewilderment was plain on her face. "It's your birthright."

Poppy turned, lifting the veil away. "No, Mother. A birthright is something you're entitled to, not something you have to marry someone else to receive. By this definition, the only birthright I have is vicereine."

Her mother's confusion gave way to realization, which morphed into disbelief. She thrust a reprimanding finger into Poppy's face, parting her lips, but a familiar voice spoke first.

"What's going on in here?"

Her father stood in the hallway. He surveyed the scene: Poppy standing on the tailor's box like a cold statue on a pedestal, her mother on the ground, reaching up as though to tear her down.

"Madame Lark has outdone herself," he said. "But it seems as though neither of you is happy."

Her mother spoke first. "Poppy doesn't want to marry Richard!"

Her father rubbed one hand across his wrinkled forehead. "This again? I thought we were clear. You must marry Richard, Poppy. Your reputation is precarious after your abduction, but no one would dare impugn the honor of the next Montrose marchioness."

"I don't wish to be marchioness," she said, just as her mother said, "She wants to be vicereine, Clarence."

He grew still, knuckles tightening on the cane. Though Poppy still stood on the tailor's box, he was tall enough to look her in the eye as he said, "Poppy, it's true you have succeeded where most would fail. But the office of the viceroy?" He shook his head. "That is truly impossible."

His lack of faith burned like acid. "Why not?" She kept her chin raised. "I am your heir, and the role is always inherited by the heir. Am I being passed over because I am a woman? Or is it because I am Virian?"

"Both," he said, unrepentant. "I have always been honest with you about the hurdles you'd face as my adopted daughter. There are very few people who would not challenge the legitimacy of a lowborn woman, especially one without a title."

"I am prepared for adversity," she said. "At least the struggles of being vicereine would come with a measure of power. A viceroy's wife is nothing but a glorified broodmare."

Her mother gasped, paling.

He slammed the butt of his cane against the ground. "Apologize to your mother."

Poppy blew out a breath. "Mother, I apologize. I meant you no slight. But the position is essentially that—to provide an heir for the viceroy's office. She has no title, no official duties, no political power, no purpose other than to provide a male child."

"I'm sure you can have Richard delegate some official duties to you once he's inherited the role," her mother said. "He gifted you an orphanage, after all. I'm sure he'll include you."

Like hell he would. She fought the urge to roll her eyes. "That's not what I meant. Why must I rely on the Montrose name to give me power when I am a Sutherland? I should be vicereine. Anything less would be to rob me of my inheritance."

"Do you think that we seek to rob you?" her father glowered. "We saved you from a life on the streets. I've spent a fortune on nothing but the best governesses, tutors, even the best college for you. Everything I've done has been to enrich you, to give you the skills you need to survive in the world. You can read, write, and do sums, which is more than most Virian women can say, but you are ungrateful to the very end."

Shame stung Poppy's cheeks. Her father's lecture reminded her of Samina's, the flip side of the same coin. "I am grateful," she said, thinking of the families in Sanivali. "Don't think I'm not aware of all the ways in which I've benefited from my upbringing. But just because I gained much doesn't mean I didn't lose much as well."

"Lose?" her father repeated, as though it were a foreign word. "What could you have possibly lost?"

All the bitterness Poppy had felt in Sanivali came bubbling

to the surface. "My language." Her voice broke, but she raised it louder. "My culture. You raised me to speak your language, uphold your values, practice your traditions. I never learned my parents' traditions—"

"*We're* your parents," Demetria cut in. "We raised you."

"After you took me from another city," Poppy said. "I know nothing of my birth parents."

The duke sighed deeply, dragging the heel of his hand down his face. "We have been over this, Poppy. You've asked us this before, and no one knows who your birth parents were—the factory that killed them did not keep accurate records of the workers it employed. Finding out who they were was impossible."

"So you say," she said. She had believed that answer as a child, but her time in Sanivali had shattered the way she saw her father. "You have control over the police division, so forgive me if I find that difficult to believe. Did you even try?"

"We tried where it mattered!" her mother cried. In her corner of the room, she had started shaking violently, her face pale, as though the intensity of her emotions were physically taking a toll on her. "You had *nothing* when we found you, but we gave you a home, even gave you our names: *Poppy Demetria Sutherland.* We loved you like you were our own, because to us, you are our own. We adopted you with the best of intentions, and you could not have had a better life with anyone else."

The pain in her voice cut Poppy deeply, guilt and yearning welling up in the wound. She hadn't meant to make her mother cry. For a moment, she debated dropping the issue to avoid distressing her further. But now that she had seen the world that she had been taken from, she couldn't ignore it. Until her kidnapping, she'd been the version of herself the Sutherlands had chosen for her. But in captivity, Poppy had found there were multiple versions of herself—some lost to the past, and some that were still shrouded in the future—and she refused to let her choice be taken from her again.

Her father took another step forward, taking one of Poppy's bare hands and patting it between his. His wrinkled skin felt soft as suede. "I know the grass always seems greener on the other side. But remember—Virian culture is inferior and primitive. They ascribed value to a person based on the circumstances of their birth, limiting the social mobility and economic opportunities of those who had no magic. We raised you better than that, with the values of the Founder. All men have purpose. Anyone can rise based on their merit and hard work."

Poppy looked down at him. "If that's true, then name me as heir to the viceroy's office. If all are equal, then the title ought to be mine, because my rights would be equal to any natural-born male heir of yours."

He hesitated, his lips parting as he struggled with this. Finally, he relented. "I will give it thought, Poppy. But your wedding will take place as planned."

"But—"

"No," he declared. "It's not up for debate. To back out now would cause both families immense embarrassment and would only fuel speculation about what happened during your abduction. *If* you become vicereine, then you will need the support of the First Families to achieve anything. A viceroy is only as powerful as the allies he keeps."

Or she.

With that, he beckoned to his wife, who took his arm. They walked out of the room together, her father leaning more heavily on his cane than when he'd entered.

Poppy stared at herself in the mirror as Lark's assistants

came back into the room to unbutton the gown. If her parents would not help her end the engagement, she'd find her own way out. The assistants undid the last button, and the wedding dress slid off Poppy's frame, freeing her from its horrible weight.

Chapter Thirty-Four

Conditional Covenant

Two days after the fitting, Poppy secured permission from her parents to visit Catherine under the pretext of seeking marital advice. Thoroughly satisfied that she was making efforts to accept her fate, her parents agreed readily.

Catherine and Theodore ushered her in, calling for iced lemonade and sweets. As they waited for the refreshments, Catherine's anxious gaze roved over Poppy, darting from the scab on her thumb to the pink line of new skin across her throat. "You must have been terrified," she fretted. "Poor thing."

"It was . . . unpleasant," she said. She recalled her days in the cell, the slow pressure of fear building in her chest, to the blank terror of the fire and blood of the night at the museum, to the desperate panic when Hasan's knife had bitten against her thumb. All of these things had been horrifying, but the original danger still remained: a future bound to Richard Montrose.

Catherine took Poppy's hand, running the tip of her finger below the wound on the base of her thumb. "The Jackal must be a real brute."

The corner of Poppy's mouth turned up. "He was," she said, "and I told him so too. Several times."

But when she thought about it—*really* thought about it—the wounds Hasan had inflicted on her were transactional, blood for his brother. Richard's hatred was violent and personal. Only one of the two men was a monster, and it wasn't the one who had abducted her.

"Well, I'm glad you're safe now." Theodore sighed. "The last few weeks have been tense, to say the least."

Poppy looked down at her lap. "I fear that your relief may be premature."

Theodore and Catherine exchanged a look. "What do you mean?" Catherine asked.

Here was the part she had been dreading: telling Catherine about Richard's plan. She knew her friend would believe her—after all, she had tried to warn her off him from the beginning. What she feared was being blamed for her predicament. She would take responsibility for pursuing Richard, but his violent racism could not be laid at her feet.

"Richard plans to betray me, once we're married," Poppy said.

Both of them gaped. Whatever they had thought she was going to say, it clearly wasn't that. Without mincing words, she told Catherine and Theodore exactly what she had overheard the night of the engagement party. "And in case you think I misunderstood, he all but admitted it to me in the car ride on the way home."

"I believe you," Catherine said. "In a way, this is my fault—if I had been more adamant, perhaps I could have prevented you from getting tangled in all this."

"No, I would have found some other way to pursue him—which is one of the reasons my parents, and the rest of society, would likely never believe me. I should have listened to you. But I need to get out of this engagement. I cannot allow Richard to become viceroy."

"What are you planning to do?" Catherine asked.

Poppy bit her cheek, holding back her next words. But if she could not voice her ambitions to her best friend, the one person on this island that she trusted, then she might as well not do this at all. "*I* have to succeed my father, not him."

Poppy saw Theodore shoot a glance at Catherine. Catherine didn't return his look, but she hadn't been able to stop her eyebrows from shooting up her forehead. Poppy held her breath. How her best friend responded now would change the course of her life.

"Poppy, there's never been a vicereine," Catherine said cautiously.

"I'm aware."

Catherine chewed her lip. "Do not think me insensitive," she said, "but why not just break off your engagement, weather the storm, and marry someone else? Someone you trust to become viceroy instead?"

"I cannot trust that the same thing wouldn't happen again," Poppy said. An edge of bitterness laced her words. "I doubt there is a single man in the nobility who would court me if not for my father's station."

Theodore put up one hand. "To be clear, you intend to put yourself next in the line of succession as a single woman, thus thwarting any attempt by any man to take the office through marriage and abuse his power over you."

"That sums it up."

"Is there no other reason?" Theodore asked. "Why go to all this effort to take an office, if all you want is to avoid being controlled by a husband?"

"Because I'm the best fit," Poppy snapped. "It's not just about my husband controlling me. It's about my husband commanding this colony. I am the child of the current viceroy. Why should my blood and my gender make a difference? This is my right, both by birth and by parentage. I am just as qualified, if not more, to inherit my father's office. But I cannot work alone. I need allies. Will you help me?"

Tentatively, Catherine said, "You know I will support you, Poppy, as your friend. But in a bid for vicereine? What could we even do for you? We are not even part of the First Families."

"Then I want you to introduce me to the Second Families," she said. "The First Families will likely side with Richard, but if I can gather enough connections within the Second Families, my father may see merit in my case."

"I'm not sure how familiar you are with the history of the Second Families," Theodore said, pushing his glasses back up his nose, "but I'm sure you've realized by now that there's not a lot of goodwill between us and the office of the viceroy."

There had always been a palpable divide between First and Second, but Poppy had never thought about why. "I'm afraid I'm not familiar with this."

"The Second Families came from Welkland at the same time as the First Families, but we came with trades, not titles. We were shipbuilders, weavers, craftsmen, and as such, we were looked down on," Theodore explained. "Over the years, the Second Families leveraged their craft into businesses, building wealth that rivals that of the First Families. But the Council of Lords, the patriarchs of the First Families, continue to gatekeep legislation. If the House of Representatives passes a motion that is favorable to us, then the Council will shoot it down. We've asked the viceroy to expand the Council to include men without titles, but he has refused."

Poppy's brow creased. "Why?"

"The First Families resented the idea of our joining." Theodore scowled. "Our Founder wrote about the potential of all men to become equal, but all they've done is stratify society into subgroups to protect their own power. The system they've created here is equally brutal, if not more, to the one that they replaced."

"I see that we have common ground, then," Poppy said, seizing on that. "Both of us know what it is to be denied something we are entitled to because it makes people in power uncomfortable."

Theodore considered that. "We do. But common ground doesn't always make for common interests. Speaking candidly, there's a good chance that even with our backing, your bid will fail. For one, your father hasn't shown much respect for Second Families, so he may not even recognize the support. And from our perspective, unless the reward outweighs the risk, the odds of bringing others on board are low."

Poppy narrowed her eyes at him, picking up on his evasion. "Are you going to help me make connections or not, Theodore?"

He glanced at Catherine, whose jaw had fallen open at Poppy's latest response. She shut it quickly, but she couldn't hide her smirk. "Sorry," Catherine said, "but you weren't nearly so assertive when you left. It's refreshing."

Theodore chuckled. "It *is* refreshing, especially after hearing your father make pleasant, empty statements for the better part of the last decade. Since you've been straightforward with me, allow me to be blunt with you: I'll make the necessary introductions and brief you on the interests of the Second Families, but you will have to negotiate with them yourself. I am only a liaison. I will not try to influence any of them on your behalf. This way, if you lose your bid, I won't go down with you."

"Fair," Poppy agreed, hiding her unease. How would she win

over the Second Families if she couldn't even secure Theodore's endorsement?

Sensing her concern, Catherine leaned over to Poppy. "An introduction is an endorsement," she whispered. "It's just far more implicit."

She brightened. "Very good, then. But how are we going to call off the wedding?"

"That"—Theodore put his hands up—"is your own challenge. Based on your own account, you have everything to gain by breaking off this engagement. But by going against the Montroses, we stand to lose everything, especially if he ends up becoming our viceroy."

Her spirits plummeted. "But surely you—"

"No," he said. "There's only one thing I'm sure of, and it's that I won't stick my neck out in front of all of society. That is a risk that outweighs the reward, every time."

"But my brother is a monster," Catherine protested. She cast Poppy a desperate look. "We can't allow her to marry him."

He put a hand on her shoulder. "You know I loathe your brother, love. But this is bigger than us. If I contest the wedding, it will invoke the wrath of the Montroses and their allies for generations. We tried to protect Poppy from the start, but she insisted on pursuing Richard. She got herself into this. She can get herself out."

Poppy flinched at the firm pronouncement.

"Okay," Catherine said, though her lips were pressed in disapproval. "But if Poppy *does* escape, then she stays with us. We'll shelter her from her father and the Montroses."

Theodore balked, but the expression on Catherine's face told him it wasn't worth the argument. He nodded once. "Then let us recap the terms of our agreement. If you succeed in extricating yourself from the wedding, I will help make introductions to the Second Families. And"—he hesitated—"if you can turn them to your cause, I will make my support for you public. Are we agreed, or is there anything else?"

"We're agreed." Poppy extended her hand across the desk to Theodore, who shook it once. "Thank you," she added grudgingly. He hadn't provided everything she had wanted, but Poppy had one more ally than she'd had this morning, and that in itself felt like a miracle.

Chapter Thirty-Five

Police Business

After several nights of searching for his men without success, Hasan finally tried Samina's home. He hadn't wanted to bother her at first, especially since her injuries would not yet have healed. But everywhere he went, he found nothing. The police presence didn't help with the search, either. He'd almost run into them twice, which was two times too many. He could not understand whom or what they were looking for. Paranjay was still in custody. Zeyar had joined their side. So what were the police doing in the Virian quarter of the city?

He hadn't figured it out yet, but once he rescued Paranjay, perhaps they could solve that mystery together.

Samina lived in a small, single-room flat with her brother, who was one of the gang's vasudhakt runners. The flat had been ransacked, just like Kaushal's. The bed had shifted, the sheets rumpled and pillows slashed. The closet doors gaped, clothes strewn over the floor. The window was unlocked, but when Hasan opened it and looked out onto the roof, no one was there. He had almost resolved to leave when he heard it: labored breathing, coming from inside a vent in the wall. He took a single step backward, squinting between the grills. Sure enough, a shadow lurked within. He clenched his fist, daivyakhi at the ready. Then he tore open the vent cover.

A dark, blurry shape hurtled past him. He lunged, taking the other person down with a grunt. They kicked and squirmed, but he managed to grab both their arms and pin them down. Now that the person had stopped wriggling, Hasan realized his catch was a skinny boy no older than fifteen, all knobby knees and elbows, like a foal.

"Sanjiv?" he asked, astounded. "What on earth were you doing hiding in the vent?"

"I thought you were the police," Sanjiv said. "I thought they had come back for me."

Hasan let the boy up, brushing the dust off his shirt and hair. "Come back for you?" What would the police want with a fifteen-year-old boy, especially one who was merely a runner? "Where's Samina?"

Sanjiv's eyes grew glassy. "The police took her first." He sniffed. "That's why I thought they had returned, to take me too."

Hasan froze. "They've arrested Samina?"

"Just yesterday." Sanjiv's voice trembled. "She opened the window and told me to hide outside, on the roof. When I climbed back in, she was gone."

Hasan could picture it easily—Samina had left the safe house before her wounds had fully healed. When the police had come for her, she wouldn't have been able to fight or run as well as she normally could, and she would have never allowed Sanjiv to try and defend her.

"Do you know if they've taken anyone else?"

"I don't know. Samina told me it's too dangerous to go out, so I haven't. The police are stopping everyone. There's a curfew on our side of the city, and they set up checkpoints everywhere."

Sanjiv blinked furiously, fighting back tears. "It was already hard enough to survive."

Hasan loosed a ragged breath, patting the boy on the shoulder awkwardly. Samina would kill him if he left her brother here alone, but he couldn't possibly take Sanjiv with him. "You should leave Marnapur. There's a safe house in Sanivali."

"I won't leave without Samina," Sanjiv insisted fiercely.

The boy's sense of loyalty lodged in Hasan's chest, twisting in the wound Zeyar had left. "I'm looking for her," he said. "Go, and I'll find her." *I'll find them both.*

• • •

Hasan had to reconfigure his plans. With most of his daivyakt fighters missing or arrested, he didn't have the manpower required to overwhelm the police. He couldn't leave Marnapur empty-handed, but charging the police station on his own would be a suicide mission.

Tired and hungry, after another full night of disappointment, all he wanted was a warm meal and the comfort of his own bed. He returned to the flat. Inhaling slowly, he flipped the lights on, bracing himself for the rush of melancholy.

What he *hadn't* been bracing himself for was the figure sitting on his couch, flipping through one of Zeyar's old newspapers. Hasan whipped out his pistol, but the person holding the newspaper responded to the safety being clicked off by merely turning the page.

"Relax." Harithi rolled her eyes over the top of the paper. "It's only me."

He lowered his gun in disbelief, putting the safety back on. "How'd you find me?"

"After you ditched me at Sanivali, you mean?"

"No one knows about this apartment. Who told you?"

"No one did." Harithi tossed down the newspaper. "I have my ways. You're avoiding the question. Why'd you leave me behind?"

"I didn't need you with me," Hasan retorted. "Did Zeyar tell you about this place?"

"He didn't! I told you, no one told me." Harithi straightened her back, glaring. "What's the big deal about me knowing, anyway? I've been a part of this gang almost as long as you."

"You're not a Devar," Hasan snapped. Harithi flinched, the expression of pain on her face so rare that it took him a moment to recognize it. He backtracked, lowering his voice. "It was a promise we made to each other, as brothers—we'd never tell anyone else about this apartment. No friends, no lovers—no one. I never doubted that the others followed the rule, but ever since Zeyar—"

"I get it." Harithi softened. "What he did tore a thread loose—and now you can't stop pulling, even if it means unraveling everything."

After a long pause, he tucked his gun back into its holster. "I'm sorry." Then he frowned again. "Why did you follow me back to Marnapur?"

"Because you obviously have a plan," Harithi said, "and I'm going to be part of it."

"You don't even know what I'm planning."

"And whose fault is that?" She pointed at him. "Get me up to speed."

He balked. Given the way his plan had gone so far, he hated to admit that there wasn't much left of it at all.

Meanwhile, Harithi had interpreted his silence differently. She rose from the couch, punching her finger into his chest. "The problem with you Devars," she said, "is that you never share what you're thinking. When things get tough, all of you run off and do your own thing, trying to be the hero that saves the others instead of working collaboratively. If Zeyar had shared what he was thinking with me—if I had followed *him* to the city—"

Jaw clenched, she broke off, looking equal parts angry and mortified that she'd revealed so much of her thought process. Hasan didn't attempt to soothe her. She'd take any sympathy he offered her as pity, and if there was one thing that she hated, it was pity.

"I didn't bring you because you disagreed about attacking the precinct when I first suggested it." Hasan ran a hand through his hair, then added, "It's starting to look like a suicide mission, anyway."

Briefly, he explained his plan to recruit his fighters and storm the police precinct to free Paranjay. Then he recounted how every daivyakt fighter's house he'd been to had been raided or abandoned.

"So you've been out there all night?" Harithi demanded.

"Yeah." He yawned. "I need a new plan. This one isn't going to work."

"What you need is sleep."

He opened his mouth to protest, but she stamped her foot. "No. Go and sleep. You're useless to Paranjay if you're not at your strongest."

Hasan sighed. "Fine. But when I wake up—"

"We'll make a new plan," she said. "Now go rest."

• • •

When Hasan woke later that afternoon, he found Harithi eating in the kitchen. A second plate sat covered beside her.

"Feel better?" she asked, pushing the plate toward him. "I made some rice and dhal, but the meat and vegetables were spoiled. I had to toss them out."

"I haven't really had time to do groceries," he said wryly. He pulled his plate closer. "Thank you."

As he ate, Harithi caught him up to speed with what she had learned since returning to the city. "The Marnapur curfew was mandated by the viceroy himself," she said. "It flew through the House of Representatives and had the signatures of all four men on the Council of Lords."

"What was the rationale behind the bill?"

"Sutherland said the city had fallen into a level of chaos that wasn't conducive to the economy." Harithi rubbed a hand over her eyes. "I think what we did, setting that fire at the museum, has scared a lot of people."

"What about the arrests?" Hasan asked. "Any word about why they're taking our men?"

"No," she said. "But now that you mention it . . . have you realized that all the gang members they've taken are daivyakt? Have any of our vasudhakt members been taken?"

"I—" He hesitated, his face warm. "I didn't think to check on the vasudhakt ones."

"Hasan," she said, her voice full of reproach.

"I wanted fighters, not informants or runners," he said defensively.

"In case you haven't noticed, the Welks are doing just fine fighting without divine energy," she huffed. "Maybe it's time we started giving more importance to vasudhakt members."

"I can look for them tomorrow," Hasan said.

"No need. When I returned, I searched for you at several of

our hiding spots. Everywhere I went, the vasudhakt gang members are still around. Some of them are scared—a bunch of them have left the city—but, for the most part, the police haven't bothered them at all."

"What could it be?" Technically, the use of magic was not illegal, but the act of making naumya was. And all of his daivyakt members were no fools when it came to hiding their pantheons.

"It can't be that they're looking for us," Harithi said. "Zeyar said he got us immunity."

"Unless he was lying about that," Hasan said sourly. "Wouldn't be the first time he was dishonest with us."

"He's lied about many things, but I don't think he lied about this. If he hadn't gotten you immunity, Richard would have had you arrested at Sanivali. He had no reason to spare you otherwise."

"Fair," Hasan said. Maybe Zeyar *had* done him that one favor. "But then what could it be?"

"I don't know," she admitted, "but what I *do* know is that the arrests were made by members of Montrose's squadron."

Somehow, this didn't surprise Hasan. "What the fuck is Montrose up to now?"

"Well, at first I thought he was being paranoid because of the wedding," Harithi said. "But then why would they increase security in the Virian neighborhoods?"

"Wedding?" he repeated. "What wedding?"

She rolled her eyes. "I swear, Hasan, it's like when you put your mind to something, you get tunnel vision. I don't know how you managed to block out everything else, but Poppy Sutherland's wedding is all anyone is talking about. The wedding of the viceroy's only daughter would have been a large enough affair, but this one is laced with so much scandal. Her origin story, but also the fact that she was missing for nearly *three weeks* after her engagement party. The tabloids have been minting money for a month."

"I thought . . ." He'd thought what? That Poppy would protest? Richard had not gone to all that effort to get her back just to listen to what Poppy wanted. He had seen how she'd struggled against him, how he'd dragged her toward the car carelessly. Men treated donkeys with more care.

"She's being forced," Hasan said quietly. "I know there is nothing we can do for her now, but I vowed to be her ally. It feels wrong to allow it to continue."

Harithi sighed. "You said it yourself. There is nothing we can do for her now, Hasan. We have to stay focused on Paranjay. Poppy will have to save herself."

He snorted, and she gave him a sharp look. "Don't underestimate her. She was a pawn in a game, but she bargained her way into being a player. She's craftier than she looks."

"I suppose," he said, but he didn't see how Poppy would be able to work her way out of her current dilemma without allies. "So how do we find out what Richard is really up to?"

"The maids inside Montrose Manor may know something," she said. "They tidy office spaces, bring tea and refreshments whenever there are guests. I'd wager many of them know more than we'd think."

"With all these new checkpoints, I won't be able to cross Morning Bridge, let alone infiltrate Montrose Manor," he scoffed. "They'd arrest me in a heartbeat."

"No, you can't." Harithi smiled, teeth flashing. "But I can. Give me some time, and I'll figure out how to get through those checkpoints. Sounds like a plan?"

"Barely." Hasan grimaced. "But it's as good as we're going to get."

Chapter Thirty-Six

Divine Vessel

When Agatha Lark's girls rang the doorbell, it echoed like a death knell. The dreaded morning had arrived, and Poppy still had no plan to escape. The assistants moved quickly, putting her into the stockings, underskirt, and hoop frame that would support the overskirt, working on her with the cool, impersonal air of styling a storefront mannequin. They yanked on the ties mercilessly, constricting the bodice with every pull, squeezing Poppy's ribs and limiting her movements. As they bound her hair into an intricate braid, they tugged with the same force they'd used to lace the dress. Poppy winced, tears forming at the corners of her eyes.

After the girls had finished braiding, they retrieved a basket of red roses and baby's breath. They threaded the flowers into a crown on Poppy's scalp, weaving them into the braid. They then departed, leaving Demetria with the final task, traditionally left to the bride's mother: pinning the veil.

"You look lovely," her mother sighed. She was already dressed in her mother-of-the-bride outfit, a green dress the shade of rice paddies. Gold embroidery ran over the silk, curling around emerald and diamond embellishments that glittered when she moved.

"Did you know that white is a mourning color among Virians?" Poppy asked, examining one cream sleeve.

Demetria pursed her lips as she stepped forward, reaching over Poppy to settle the veil on her hair. "Come now, Poppy, don't be morbid. It's your wedding day."

"It's not *my* anything," she snapped, wrenching her head away. "*I* don't want this."

"If you knew any better, you would!" Two bright-pink spots of color bloomed through her mother's powder. "Who do you think you'll be, without your father's authority behind you? Richard can give you a name, a title, a permanent position in society even after your father and I are gone."

"What kind of society have you created, that your only daughter can be so easily discarded? That the only power she has is the name of her husband?"

Her mother flinched, but then her face softened. When she spoke again, her voice was gentle. "I understand how unfair it seems. When your father and I learned that I would never carry his heir, well, there was talk. Many people suggested that he should divorce me and take a new wife. Being spoken about like that, like I was disposable . . . it added stress in a period of loneliness and grieving for me. But I had to shoulder it. That's simply how things are."

Poppy sneered. "You mean to say that you and Father couldn't have done *anything*, all these years, to give the position of a viceroy's wife a little more power? A little more security?"

Her mother's tone became patronizing. "It takes more than just two people to create change, Poppy."

"You weren't just two people—you are the highest-ranked nobles on the island!"

"Perhaps together, you and your husband can work to repair

what you feel your father and I overlooked," she suggested, her voice frosty.

She moved again to pin the veil, but Poppy pulled away a second time. "I will not be ignored," she said. "I am the true heir to the viceroy's office, not Richard."

"This again?" Her mother rolled her eyes. "Poppy, when will you learn to be grateful for what you have?"

"What I *have* is the right to rule," Poppy insisted, "just as much as any other natural-born child you might have had." Desperation rose in her chest. Each second brought her closer to the wedding. She only had one more card to play: the truth. It was a weak one, but she tried anyway: "All Richard wants is the office. As soon as we're wed, he plans to be rid of me."

Her mother hesitated, holding the veil uncertainly. "You don't know that."

"I do." Poppy's eyes burned. She blinked once, hard. "He told me as much."

"Perhaps you misinterpreted," her mother said. "Richard is an honorable man. He'd never harm you."

Poppy sucked in a breath. Her own mother believed Richard over her. He hadn't even needed to be here to smooth talk his way through it. Though she had known this was the most likely outcome, her mother's dismissal landed like a kick to the sternum. *Stupid girl, did you really think you'd be believed?* She was furious—not at her mother, whose betrayal she'd expected—but at herself, for harboring hope like contraband. No one here would fight for her. If this marriage took place, no one would even care when she got exiled.

She tried one last time, forcing herself to breathe despite her tight rib cage. "If you take me to that cathedral today, know that he'll be shipping me off before the month is over. You'll never see me again."

Her mother pinched her lips together. "Things will be okay, Poppy. You'll see."

No, they won't be. The lump in Poppy's throat had grown dangerously swollen, but she couldn't show up at the cathedral with a tear-stained face. She hardly cared about looking joyful, but she refused to look afraid. Poppy remained still as a statue as her mother pinned the veil behind the crown of flowers on her head.

"Come now," her mother cajoled. "The car will arrive any minute now."

She settled the veil over Poppy's face, as absolute and suffocating as a shroud.

• • •

The sun rose behind the cathedral as Demetria and Poppy arrived in front of it. Not a single cloud marred the pastel sky. The sight rivaled the dusk of Poppy's first night back in Marnapur, but she could not enjoy it at all.

As the two women got out of the car, Founderson Harold stood waiting on the steps to greet them, the dawn light winking off his embroidered robes. Foundersons were scholars and protectors of the Founder's sacred texts. Though they were ineligible to hold any title or position of political power, they still had a great deal of influence and often pooled information among themselves. In theory, any man could become a founderson, but it took almost a decade of intense study to qualify for such a position, and not many finished.

"Good morning, Your Grace, Miss Sutherland." Founderson Harold winked at Poppy. "By lunchtime, we won't be calling you that anymore."

Poppy stared mutely at him.

He faltered, then addressed her mother instead. "The Montroses have yet to arrive, but the room for the bride is ready. Second floor, west wing. One of my acolytes will take her. Your Grace, if you'd follow me, I have a few questions about payment for the service. . . ."

The two of them began to walk to the founderson's office. A warm hand touched Poppy's shoulder. She jumped with a curse, whirling around to see a Virian boy of around seventeen, dressed in a simple brown robe.

"Oh." She eyed his brown skin. "*You're* the acolyte?"

"Founderson Harold takes in orphans sometimes," he explained, crossing his arms over his chest in a defensive shrug. "It's better than the orphanage."

She flinched at the inadvertent reminder of Samina's words: *The orphanage was nothing more than a glorified prison.* "Right," she said. "Show the way, then."

As he turned, a six-inch utility blade swung from where it had been tied to his belt, bumping against his hip. It wouldn't be hard to grab it from him, she thought. He was skinny, no taller than she.

She could stab Richard. Poppy stumbled, tripping over the intrusive thought. "Are you okay?" the acolyte asked, taking her arm to steady her. "Sorry, I should have warned you. The floors are a little uneven in this wing. This part of the building is really old."

"I'm fine," she said, brushing him off, her heart racing. "I'll be more careful."

The thought had lodged itself in her skull like a barbed thorn, and she couldn't pull it free. In her mind's eye, she reached forward and pilfered the blade from the acolyte, tucking it into her sleeve until it was time to say the vows. She would shove it between Richard's ribs, twisting hard, blade scraping bone, his blood blooming across her dress.

If he was dead, she wouldn't have to marry him.

But if Poppy killed him here, in front of everyone, then she would be executed, forget exiled. The successor for the viceroy's office would go to a vote. Richard would lose, but so would she. And as much as Poppy hated him, she wanted to win far more than she wished for him to lose.

Killing Richard was out of the question.

Poppy followed the acolyte into the bride's room, which was nothing more than a glorified storage room, bare walls and weathered tiles that looked centuries old.

"Fancy," she remarked, looking around.

"It's not much," the acolyte said apologetically. "Like I said, this part of the building is ancient. You can tell because it's built in a completely different style compared to the rest of it. See? There's no wooden paneling, and the walls have these hollows, like little alcoves. The roof is also curved, whereas the main chamber and the new portions of the building have flat roofs."

In other circumstances, Poppy would have tuned the boy out, but she clung to his rambling, using it to remain afloat as the panic began to rise around her like water in a tank. She strode to the far wall, looking out a dusty window between two of the alcoves. Outside, a motorcade of police cars arrived, one by one, carrying officers in ceremonial uniform. The last car in the chain was a silver Peregrine sedan. She turned away, gut churning.

"Where are the statues for the alcoves?" she asked, desperate to keep the acolyte talking.

"We've never kept statues here." The acolyte shrugged. "This is just a spare room, really. We don't use the west wing much."

Poppy dragged her fingers over the dust in the alcove, the thick layer proof of what the boy was saying. Her eyes widened. In the path that her fingers had cleared, the stone was two shades—one dark, the other faded several shades by the sun. She swept her hand through the dust in a wide arc, revealing circles of stone darker than the surrounding area. It looked as though multiple items had been arranged in the alcove, protecting the stone underneath from fading under centuries of sun.

Something about the placement of the circles, combined with what the acolyte had said, jostled a memory in her brain.

They ransacked the temples, then built cathedrals to their own god overtop the skeletons.

"How old is this building?" Poppy whirled on the acolyte. "Was it here before the Welkishmen arrived?"

He took a step back, overwhelmed by her vehement interest. "I don't know. They don't tell us much about before."

Poppy's mind raced. She was almost entirely certain she stood in one of the temples of old. If she asked for power now, would the gods still hear her even though the idols had been removed?

"Give me your dagger."

"What?" the acolyte asked, putting a hand on the hilt, startled. "Why?"

Poppy lifted the veil off her face, looking the boy directly in the eyes. "What's your name?"

He hesitated, wary. "Samuel."

"Samuel," she repeated, forcing her voice to be calm, coaxing. "I need you to trust me. Give me the dagger. I won't harm you."

He eyed her. "What about yourself?"

"I won't harm myself either," she said. "I'll give the dagger back when I'm done."

Samuel sighed. He took the dagger from his belt and turned it around, offering her the hilt. With the knife in her hand, Poppy tore the veil away and placed the sharp edge of the blade at the base of her neck, between the braid and her skin.

"Hey!" he protested. "You promised you wouldn't harm yourself."

She ignored him, sawing through the braid, working furiously through the thick strands of hair. Her soul cried out for her to stop. It had taken over a decade to grow her hair to this length. Her hair was the only feature that Welkish women had openly envied. But a sacrifice like this—her hair, her femininity, her vanity—the gods could not ignore. As Poppy hacked through her hair, she prayed fervently, calling out to Savana, the rain goddess.

My power is not in my husband's name, but in my connection to you, she thought. *Give me the strength to win my own hand.*

Two hard raps on the door startled her from her prayer. The founderson's voice came through the wood. "Miss Sutherland, Captain Montrose has arrived. Are you ready to come down to the main chamber and start the proceedings?"

"One minute!" she shouted, sawing faster. *My veins are a vessel for your divine power. If my sacrifice is worthy, fill me with your cosmic energy.*

"The ceremony will start soon," Founderson Harold called. "Acolyte Samuel, what's going on?"

"I don't know, sir." Samuel wrung his hands together, eyes wide. "She's—she's cutting her hair?"

The knob started turning. "I'm coming in!"

The knife broke through the last of the strands as the door burst open. The braid fell to the floor like a dead snake, rose petals fluttering gently to rest around it.

"Poppy!" Her mother burst in from behind the founderson.

Her gaze dropped to the braid coiled on the stone tiles. She pressed shaking fingers to her lips. "What have you done?"

Poppy ignored her, closing her eyes and reaching inward. Her hope was fragile and dangerous, but she had faith.

Please.

For a moment, she found nothing. Then the air in the cathedral lit up around her. She could locate every drop of moisture with perfect clarity; she could move them as easily as flinging a handful of sand. It was like she'd had a sixth sense all her life, one that had lain dormant until now. Her every nerve tingled, hypersensitive to the water around her. Was this how the maharanis of old had felt?

Her mother seized her arm with one hand. She opened her eyes, releasing the daivyakhi.

"Oh," her mother whimpered, fingering the short, ragged locks of hair.

"Oh," Poppy repeated, still drunk with the amount of power she had, an ocean compared to the puddles she'd been working with before. *This* was her birthright. She had been born with the gods' favor long before she had been dressed in silks and the Sutherland name. Her father's legacy couldn't give her the right to power. Poppy already had power—and with it, a responsibility to care for those without.

She drew from her well of daivyakhi slowly to avoid getting overwhelmed. She didn't need to reach for the groundwater; she could move the very particles of moisture in the air at will. As she concentrated, she could feel the clouds above the cathedral begin to knit together.

Poppy didn't resist as her mother refastened the veil into her ragged hair, nor did she fight back as the duchess threaded her arm through hers and guided her firmly back into the hall, until they reached the arched doorway of the main chamber. Demetria walked her onto the raised platform in front of the pews.

Ripples ran through the crowd: first, one of appreciation at the magnificent dress, and then one of discomfort as they noticed what Poppy had done to her hair. Only Catherine and Theodore did not look disturbed by the change. Poppy locked eyes with Catherine and gave her a slight nod. Catherine touched her own blond locks and smiled. Even though Catherine did not know what was going to happen next, she understood enough: This wedding would not be allowed to continue.

Poppy turned her gaze back to the front. Her father stood at the top of the stairs beside the lectern. On the floor below him, gold as a false idol, stood Richard. He wore the black ceremonial dress of the police force, epaulettes and badges gleaming. At his hip, the Montrose family sword lay sheathed against his thigh, the infamous rose sigil inlaid with rubies and emeralds in the pommel.

When he saw Poppy, he didn't react. Under the veil, she gave him a wide smile, baring all her teeth. His brow creased a fraction.

Richard's parents stood behind him in the front pew, practically vibrating with anticipation. After today, it would be their family in the viceroy's office, and everyone in the room knew it.

But all of them were wrong.

Flanked by her mother and the founderson, Poppy stood on the step below her father. Though she still had the higher ground, Richard gave her a cold look, one that gave her the distinct impression that he was looking down at her. She curled her fingers into her palms, sharp nails digging into the soft skin. They stared at each other, locked in a silent battle of wills as Founderson Harold began to address the congregation.

You've lost, his smirk seemed to say.

You underestimate me, Poppy glared back. *And that will be your downfall.*

The founderson called Richard's name, ending their standoff. As Richard began to speak, Poppy tuned him out, dialing up the power. The air in the chapel thickened, dense and humid, as rain started to fall outside, hitting the roof softly.

"Poppy Demetria Sutherland," the founderson announced. "You are here today because Richard Montrose the Second seeks you as his bride. In exchange for your hand, he has vowed to your father that he will protect you, provide for you, and remain true to you."

A high-pitched ringing started in her ears. Lies. Richard Montrose had come to the altar to offer nothing but lies. The only vow she knew he would keep was his oath to dispose of her once he had taken everything he needed. The rain fell harder, pooling on the flat rooftop of the main chamber. The rush of divine power numbed and electrified Poppy all at once.

"Miss Sutherland?"

Her vision refocused directly ahead of her. Founderson Harold stared at her expectantly. "Pardon me?"

He didn't hide his exasperation as he repeated, "Richard Montrose has made vows to you. To complete this union, you must make oaths in kind. Do you, Poppy Demetria Sutherland, vow to conduct yourself with wifely grace and servility, in a manner befitting the Montrose name?"

The idea had never sounded less appealing. With two words, Poppy would become a voiceless figurehead, an easily discarded docile wife, a means to a legacy that would devour then forget her. How had she ever believed that this was the best the world could offer her? She channeled the power of the gods. The rain itself would bear witness to her rage.

She took another step down so that she could be eye level with Richard. Quietly, so that only he could hear it, she whispered, "I won't."

My veins are a vessel for the divine power of the gods. Now Poppy knew why, after all those years of searching, she'd never found truth in the Founder's writings. The Founder was only a man, power hungry and persuasive, just like the man who sought to use her, just like the man who had raised her. She would not be the page on which they wrote their legacy. *If they find my sacrifice worthy, may I be filled with their cosmic energy.*

She lifted her hand to her chest and closed her fingers in a fist. Water burst in through the roof, pouring through the ceiling onto the crowd. The guests screamed, a cacophony of confusion and terror, scrambling to get out of the way as the main chamber began to flood. Poppy screamed as well, her elated cry cutting through the shrieks of fear.

I did this. She had destroyed the roof, soaking the nobility with frigid rain. She reached for the pipes in the walls, tugging on the water. Bursting a pipe had nearly drained her life force in Hasan's cell, but now it was as effortless as snapping a twig. The guests crowded against the wall screamed again as jets of water punched through the wooden paneling, drenching them a second time. Giddy with power, Poppy craved even more destruction, but she had to save her energy for the next portion of the escape. In the pandemonium, she took off, elbowing her way through the flurry of panicking guests.

Founderson Harold recovered his wits. "To the west wing!" he shouted, trying to corral the crowd. "We must take shelter." He waved them up onto the platform and through the arched door Poppy had entered from, going back toward the west wing. Poppy pushed through the water, dragging the heavy mass of her wet wedding dress and heading toward the doors in the opposite direction.

"My daughter!" Her father's roar echoed off the cathedral walls. She froze. "I won't leave without her."

"You must get to safety," the founderson said. "We'll find her, Your Grace, but you must go. We must protect you as viceroy, first and foremost."

"And I must protect Poppy!"

Her heart twisted. It took every ounce of her strength to resist turning around. She needed allies, friends who believed her, and her father had failed to be that. Ignoring the ache in her chest, Poppy threw her weight against the front door of the cathedral and pushed it open. She ran out onto the streets, water gushing over the steps behind her. The storm outside welcomed her into its arms, pulling her away from the wedding at last.

Chapter Thirty-Seven

Alliance of the Overlooked

Coverage about the freak storm that had disrupted Poppy's wedding dominated the news in the following days. Though every newspaper remarked on how bizarre the storm had been, each of them attributed it to the hot and humid summer, many of them deciding that this was the natural apex of the season. None of them suspected anything else.

Poppy scoured every newspaper that Theodore dropped in front of her for a week, until the journalists began to move on. He and Catherine had kept their promise. In the aftermath of the storm, they'd driven through Marnapur until they found her, soaking wet and shivering as she came down from her power high, the storm fading into a drizzle as the last of the daivyakhi dissolved in her veins.

Once she'd settled into their place, she'd sent her father a letter, informing him of three things:

First, she was alive. Second, she was not going to marry Richard. And third, she would not return home until he formally named her his successor.

The viceroy's response came lightning quick, the letter firm and chastising, scolding Poppy for scaring him and her mother, scolding her for being unreasonable, scolding her for being petty. He threatened to have the police drag her from Theodore's house immediately.

She didn't respond to that letter.

Not a single police officer arrived, exposing her father's threat for the bluff it was. He could not have her arrested for the same reason that he hadn't been able to call off the wedding: If Poppy had to be dragged to the altar in chains, it would be incredibly humiliating for both the Sutherlands and the Montroses, even more so than a dissolved engagement.

The letter that came the next day had changed remarkably in tone. Her father apologized for being short, then repeated his request for Poppy to return home, this time avoiding the topic of succession altogether.

To this one, she penned a short response:

> *I understand that you care deeply about my well-being, which is why I do not understand why you refuse to acknowledge the fact of the matter: If I had been your natural-born male heir, you would not have been so quick to give my inheritance to another person. Until I know you are willing to regard me as equal—truly equal—I will not come home.*

After that, no more letters arrived.

Though she had known that convincing her father wouldn't be easy, it still broke her heart each time the mail arrived without a letter for her. She buried the shards somewhere deep, throwing herself into her work with Theodore. As promised, he'd scheduled meetings with several of the Second Families, giving her time to prepare beforehand.

Until this week, Poppy had known *of* the Second Families, but not *about* them. She knew their names and their patriarchs, but not their industries, not their investments, not their histories. Surprisingly, it was Hasan's advice that had spurred her to do her research: *The people will decide who rules. To get their support, you have to speak their language. You have to know their struggles.* Poppy had spent countless hours cramming everything she could learn about her potential allies into her head. She learned about their histories, both in Welkland and in Viryana, about their business ventures and alliances with the other families, about their successes and—more importantly—their failures.

Today, she'd meet the head of the Greenwoods. They had the second-most connections, with the Oakbury family being first. Two of the men in the immediate Greenwood clan held representative seats in the House and had built a network of alliances during their time there. Most compellingly, they were the most likely to side with Poppy, having hired Virian managers in their company, a rarity in Welkish companies, who typically relegated their Virian employees to manual labor.

But this didn't guarantee anything. Just because they didn't mind having a brown man work to increase their profit didn't mean that they would be okay taking orders from a brown woman as their vicereine.

The Greenwood patriarch arrived on time. Theodore made the introductions. "Miss Sutherland, may I introduce Mr. Blair Greenwood, head of the Greenwood family."

Blair stepped forward, lifting a brow at Poppy's offered hand—a masculine gesture—but he shook it nonetheless. She used the moment to size him up. He was tall, of slim build, with meadow-green eyes and a dense mop of chestnut hair streaked with white in the front.

"Pleasure to meet you," Blair said.

"The pleasure is mine."

Theodore, true to his word, stepped out of the room once the introductions were complete. Her heart raced as he left. Though she wished fervently that he would have stayed, she forced herself to think practically. If she needed someone to intercede for her consistently, she would never survive as vicereine.

She turned her attention back to Blair Greenwood.

"So, this is Montrose's fiancée." He looked her up and down. Poppy stiffened, years of smiling through the Hawk's slights the only thing keeping her from flinching. If she wanted to establish herself as a serious contender for the viceroy's office, she needed to shed the Montrose name—fast.

Ignoring his comment, she extended her hand to the seat across from Theodore's desk. "Please, won't you sit?"

As Greenwood sat, Poppy sank into Theodore's chair. He opened his mouth, but she beat him to it, setting the tone of the conversation before he could bring up Richard again.

"I appreciate your coming today. I'll keep things straightforward. I seek to be formally named in the line of succession to the viceroy's office. However, given that having someone like me assume the role is . . . unprecedented, I am garnering support to prove that there *are* those who would follow me. When this goes to a vote in the House—because it will—I need to know there are men who are willing to vote for me. These men will not go unrewarded, of course."

Greenwood snapped his mouth shut. Then he chuckled dryly. The sound set Poppy on edge. *Was that a* no*?*

"I have to admit, whatever I thought you had called me here for, it wasn't *that*." Blair smoothed the lapels of his coat. "I suppose it's my support you'd like?"

"Yours, and that of the other Second Families," she elaborated. She switched tack, easily slipping back into her role of assimilated Virian girl. "Since returning to the island, I've noticed that life here is different based on the name and skin you wear. It's a perversion of what the Founder envisioned."

Greenwood waved a dismissive hand. "Oh, don't quote scripture at me. I'm afraid I'm not nearly so refined. My family members were shepherds in Welkland before we came on the first voyage, did you know?"

Poppy *had* known, thanks to her preparation, though she hadn't considered how that would have affected the man's attitude toward the Founder. She kept silent, allowing Greenwood to continue.

"When my forefathers landed, they soon learned that there was no place in the hot island climate for wool. They had to pivot to weaving cotton and other textiles, learning new methods of dying fabric."

"The quality of your fabric is unmatched," she said, gesturing at her attire, which Catherine had rush ordered from her seamstress for this very meeting. "In fact, this dress is made from Greenwood cotton." Noting the flash of approval in his eyes with satisfaction, Poppy continued. "Yet your business is the *second*-biggest manufacturer of finished cotton on the island."

Greenwood's smile bent into a scowl. "Size is one thing"—he sniffed—"but when it comes to quality, we are the leader."

"I don't disagree," she said, "but your company has been forcibly prevented from growing. By Gordon Alderfort, isn't that right?"

Gerald Alderfort's brother, Gordon, also owned several textile factories back in Welkland, the Alderfort Cotton Company. However, the quality of their fabric was hardly comparable to that of the Greenwoods'. Rather than improve their output, they had hiked the price of raw cotton, making it expensive for the Greenwoods to purchase from them. While the Greenwoods could try to find another supplier, the Alderforts had owned the majority of cotton farms on the island since early colonization, and if their behavior went unchecked, it would only encourage them to further bully the Greenwoods' business.

Greenwood gritted his teeth. "Alderfort is a cheap and dishonorable man. He would rather put his resources toward throttling other businesses instead of improving his own."

"I understand that my father has allowed his friendship with Lord Alderfort to cloud his judgment," she began carefully. "But I agree with you. Alderfort's unethical business practices not only throttle other businesses, as you so aptly put it, but outsource labor that could be used to keep our own citizens gainfully employed. If I become vicereine, I will reduce the raw cotton exports and require an increased domestic production."

"You would challenge the Council of Lords?" Greenwood did not look convinced. "Do you not need their support to see bills passed to your desk?"

"I do," Poppy said, "but I intend to review the membership of the Council. See, having grown up without a title, I certainly don't believe it to be a requirement for upward mobility at all."

She let him mull that over in silence.

Finally, he said, "If I might ask a . . . delicate question."

She inclined her head, shoulders tensed as she braced herself for the worst.

"Even if you are named heir, do you still intend to marry Richard Montrose?"

Poppy couldn't help herself; she flinched backward. *What concern is it of yours?* She wanted to snap. *Would you have asked me this if I were a man?* But she needed Blair Greenwood to like her. Instead, she sorted through what she knew, trying to understand the motivation behind his question.

Then she remembered: Blair had a son, Liam. He wasn't the heir, but he was three years older than her. Evidently, it had not escaped Blair that if he played his cards right, the next dynasty of viceroys could bear the Greenwood name. The thought of marriage—to anyone, not just Richard—made Poppy's palms sweat. If she had learned anything, it was that to share a name with a man was to give him power over you. Liam might have been a perfectly fine man, but she recoiled at the thought of marrying him. Still, Greenwood didn't need to know that.

"No," she said, as pleasantly as she could manage. "Richard Montrose and I are no longer engaged."

Greenwood's satisfied smile told Poppy that she had guessed his motivations accurately. "Well, Miss Sutherland," he drawled, "I think your leadership may be just what this island needs."

Chapter Thirty-Eight

Rulers of the Slums

Harithi lined up at the checkpoint to enter the Welkish sector. The midafternoon sun bore down on her, but since the freak storm that had interrupted Poppy Sutherland's wedding a few days ago, the heat had lost its brutal strength. Hasan and Harithi had both known the storm was no act of nature. No matter what the papers said about the summer's peak or humidity or ocean currents, they knew the truth: Poppy Sutherland had summoned that storm, washing half the city with her wrath. They'd watched it from the window of Hasan's apartment, black clouds flocking to the Welkish quarter, the rain falling so thick and heavy that the cathedral was obscured from view.

"How is that possible?" Hasan had asked. "The amount of daivyakhi that would require . . ."

"I guess you weren't as poor a teacher as you thought," she quipped.

"You!" an officer shouted at Harithi. Her focus snapped back. "You're next."

She picked up her bucket of cleaning supplies, readjusting the cotton dupatta over her shoulders where it had slipped, and made a show of hurrying forward, showing the man her stolen identification card. For the last week, she'd observed the checkpoint at Morning Bridge. Only servants who worked in the Welkish quarters were being permitted through. Each of them had to present a card, which was cross-referenced against a directory by a police officer. Harithi had sent one of her vasudhakt runners to pickpocket one of the maids. He'd brought back the woman's purse, where she found the identification card she needed, as well as a paycheck written from the Wainwrights. She'd taken the identification card, considering herself lucky that the Welks had been too cheap to invest in adding photographs of servants to their cards.

The officer squinted at the card. "Nandini?"

She hid her wince at the way he butchered it—*nan DEE knee*—and smiled, bobbing her head. "That's me."

"What business do you have today?"

"I clean houses." Harithi lifted the bucket of supplies she'd pillaged from Hasan's bathroom.

"Who's your employer?" the officer asked, eyeing her up and down. "I don't think I've seen you around."

Of course, she'd ended up with the one chatty checkpoint officer. She scowled. "Do you think I'm new? I've been mopping floors and scrubbing toilets for years! I was here just two days ago, cleaning for the Wainwrights."

The officer hesitated, skimming the list of names under *Wainwright* until he found her name—well, Nandini's name. "Oh, that was you." The officer nodded. "I remember now. Yes, it's all clear. Go ahead."

"Thank you, Officer," Harithi simpered, her tone so sweet it was almost putrid. She sauntered through with her bogus bucket of cleaning supplies, heading to Montrose Manor on foot. When she got there, she peered through the gatehouse window.

The man inside was probably in his sixties, close to retirement, and deeply engrossed in a novel. She sauntered up to the glass, knocking twice before he opened his window.

"Excuse me," she said, "is this the Montrose residence? I'm here to clean." She held her bucket up so he could see it.

The gatekeeper scowled. "You're late. The other cleaners were all here before lunch."

Harithi cursed internally, but she improvised, forcing her bottom lip to wobble. "Do you think they've noticed I'm late? I didn't mean to be tardy. It's my first day, but it took so long to get through the checkpoint, and then after that, I couldn't find the house, and then I ran out of money to pay the rickshaw driver, so he made me get out and walk on foot, and I can't lose this job because my mother has—"

"Just go," the gatekeeper said, lifting his novel and smoothing out the dog-eared corner. "And don't be late again, girl!"

"I won't," Harithi said breathlessly, clutching her bucket as she hurried past him. "Thank you so much, sir."

She made her way around the back of the house, looking for the discreet door that marked the servants' entrance. It took her a moment, but she located it eventually, half-hidden behind a wall of ivy. Making sure her dupatta was still up around her face, she tried the handle—and found it locked. Cursing, she tried again, pushing, then pulling, but the door didn't budge.

She should have seen it coming. Montrose might have been an ass, but he wasn't an idiot. Still, neither was she. She reached under her dupatta and withdrew one of the bobby pins that held her bun in place. Harithi had just finished bending it into the shape of a lock pick when the door flew open on its own. She dropped the hairpin immediately, covering it with her foot.

"Who are you?" A matronly woman glared at her. Wisps

of gray hair had escaped her servant's cap only to get trapped against her forehead by a thin layer of sweat.

"I'm here to clean," Harithi stammered, gesturing to her bucket.

"I know every maid who's ever been hired here," the matron scoffed. "You're no cleaner." As if to prove her point, she added, "I would ask you how you made it across the checkpoint, but I suspect it has to do with the reason Nandini didn't come to work today, hm?"

Harithi sized up the woman again and came to the conclusion that there was no bullshitting her. "I'm here looking for information," she said, keeping her voice brisk and urgent. "Let me in."

The matron didn't move. "What information?"

Harithi narrowed her eyes. She wasn't used to being questioned by anyone other than the Devars, and definitely not by a woman who was almost certainly vasudhakt.

"Captain Montrose has been arresting daivyakt people around the city," she said. "The Jackal wants to know why."

The matron's eyes widened at Hasan's name, much to Harithi's satisfaction. Then, to her surprise, the matron's expression stretched into a smug grin of her own.

"The Jackal won't be running free for much longer. If I were you, I'd drop the attitude, girl."

"What are you talking about?"

"Captain Montrose has been pushing the House to introduce a bill to control your kind for a long time, but he's never been able to prove what a threat you are until your Jackal took the viceroy's daughter and burned down the museum. The marquess himself has introduced the bill to register and track every single daivyakt. The House is voting on it in a week's time."

Harithi's mind raced. Her little brothers were daivyakt. The thought of them tagged like cattle sent a spike of rage and nausea rolling through her, sharpening her tone. "If this is true, then we have to stop it. I need more information. Let me in."

She tried to take another step forward, but the matron shifted, blocking her path. "Why should I?"

"It's for the greater good." Harithi stared down at her. "Will you really side with your white employer over your own people?"

The matron laughed derisively. "Oh, so now we're the same people, hm? Were we the same people when we were dying of thirst, but you refused to give us a drop of water without a tithe? Were we the same people when you barred us from mixing with daivyakt in public spaces such as schools and temples under the pretense of purity? The Welkish treat us badly, but so did the daivyakt."

"These are grievances from centuries ago," Harithi said. "Will you really deny me aid because of the actions of ancient kings?"

"Very well, let's look at your actions today." The matron put one hand on her hip and the other against her jaw as she pretended to think deeply. "Daivyakt today interact with vasudhakt only because they are forced to. But several of them still uphold the old ways as much as possible, refusing to serve vasudhakt at their businesses or permit intercaste marriages in their own families. Daivyakhi is forbidden now, so instead of divine or royal power, the daivyakt hoard wealth and gatekeep the best jobs, leaving vasudhakt to fight over coins in backbreaking, dangerous careers. We've had activists protesting for better working conditions for decades. Not a single daivyakt has joined that cause, because none of you care about vasudhakt oppression. You'd rather be rulers of the slums than equals in battle with us. You can't claim we're all one race when you've spent the last five centuries keeping us at arm's length."

Harithi tried to come up with a rebuttal, but nothing the other woman had said was false. Though the Welks loved to pretend that they had "fixed" the caste divisions, the truth was that they had taken a new skin. The prejudices of ancient daivyakt had been passed down generation to generation, just as much an inheritance as the power that ran in their veins. If anything, the Welks had complicated it even further, bringing racism to the island. By allowing the Welks to divide them, Virians had made it easy for them to pick them off, one by one.

Harithi only wished it hadn't taken her this long to realize it. "You make a good point. But things are different now."

The matron laughed. "They sure are." With that, she closed the door in Harithi's face.

• • •

Hasan listened as Harithi caught him up to speed on what she had learned at Montrose Manor. When she finished, he rose to his feet, pacing back and forth as he processed the information.

"So you're telling me that in a week, the House of Representatives is going to vote on some sort of law that forces daivyakt people to be registered and tracked?"

"Exactly," Harithi said. "I don't know how that ties into the arrests, though it does explain why they're only taking daivyakt. Maybe they're registering them early?"

"Still doesn't explain why they haven't come home," Hasan pointed out. "Never mind. We have to stop this bill. If we're on a registry, we'll be consigned to a life of police surveillance. And that's just the beginning."

"You don't have to persuade me. I'm with you. But *how* do we stop it?"

"We can't let this go past the vote in the House," he said. "It could potentially die if it doesn't get two signatures from the Council of Lords, or if the viceroy refuses to provide assent. But if Lord Montrose proposed it, then he knows he has the support of at least one other lord, and Sutherland too. So we have to kill it," Hasan concluded. He stopped pacing, running one hand through his hair. "But how? It's not like we can petition all the representatives. And we don't have connections with any of them, either. They hold all the power in this situation."

He winced as the words left his mouth, a burning echo of those that Zeyar had flung at him in the kitchen with Paranjay, in a different lifetime, after he'd brought Daria home: *Our business will* never *have as much power as the legitimate hierarchy.*

"You sound like Zeyar," Harithi said, her criticism disturbingly close to the turn that his thoughts had taken.

He spun on her. "Don't make this about him."

"Well, it's true! He was always going on about *joining the legitimate power structure,*" she scoffed.

"Because he was right!" Hasan shouted. He dropped onto the couch beside her. He hung his head over his knees and laced his fingers at the nape of his neck. At a normal volume, he said, "He was right, okay? All Devar Brothers got us was control over other Virians. Tell me, Harithi, how is taking advantage of vasudhakt going to help us now? We deal in extortion and violence, not petitions and constituency meetings. Do you want me to kidnap the Council of Lords? Should we just burn down the House of Representatives, while we're at it?"

"Well," she said, "we could."

"Zeyar was right. We should have spent more time trying to—" He straightened up. "Wait . . . what?"

Harithi looked him right in the eye. "We could burn down

the House of Representatives," she said. "Seriously. Think about it. If they show up to a pile of ashes, it would buy us more time to find a permanent solution while they regroup."

"No." Hasan's mind raced. "The House shouldn't be burned before they arrive. That'll only buy us a week, maximum."

"Then what?" she asked. "What would get us more time?"

He looked at her, measuring his words before he said, "If we burned it after they arrived. When they're all inside."

For a moment, Harithi was rendered speechless. Then, she demanded, "Have you lost your mind? You're talking about mass murder."

"Like we've never killed before," Hasan scoffed. "I've burned men inside their homes for less," he added, thinking of Darsh.

"Not rich white men." Harithi shook her head vehemently. "Hasan, the consequences for burning the nobility . . . they'll slaughter us."

"They're already slaughtering us!" Hasan seized her by the shoulders, forcing her to meet his eyes again. "Don't you see, Harithi? They starve us, brutalize us, force us to labor in their prison camps. If they tag us like livestock, it's only a matter of time before they round us up and put us in a pen like cattle. We are all going to die. Will you die on your feet, with a gun in your hands? Or behind an electric fence, shackles around your ankles?"

Harithi closed her eyes, silent. When she opened them, the fire in her eyes matched the heat in her tone: "Let's cook some representatives."

Chapter Thirty-Nine

A Matter of Succession

"You're late."

Richard gritted his teeth at the duke's admonishment. "I'm *late* because of the protest, Your Grace," he bit out. "Another demonstration. For *her*."

He didn't have to say for whom. Word had gotten out to the masses that Poppy Sutherland was making a bid for vicereine, and suddenly, every uneducated street rat had a vested interest in the line of succession. The police had been breaking up demonstrations for the past week, but the number of protestors vastly outnumbered the number of officers. They would break up one protest, but a new commotion would coagulate somewhere else, clogging the arteries of the city.

The old man only sighed. "Sit." He gestured across the table to where another place had already been set.

Richard had chosen to meet Sutherland at Hazelwood Gentlemen's Club, an exclusive club for the upper class. It was a paradox of a place. Its members prided themselves on their good manners and impeccable breeding, but they often escaped to the club to indulge in their vices, be it drink or even laudanum. For this reason, the activities within the club were supposedly sacrosanct, though the comings and goings of each member did not go unnoticed. Men saw who visited and when, whom they came with, whom they left with. Word spread, one way or another. One went to Hazelwood for only two things: privacy or publicity.

When Richard had sent the invitation to the viceroy, he hadn't known which one he wanted more.

Once he was seated and had given his order to the waiter, he turned to the viceroy again. "Why haven't you brought your daughter to heel? She's still meeting with Second Families. Yesterday alone, she met with the Wainwrights and Bluefinches, negotiating bargains. Now, even the rabble is rising in favor of her."

Sutherland's mouth twisted in a rueful smile. "She's not a child anymore. I fear her education has worked a little too well. She is determined, confident, and persuasive."

He didn't like the sound of that. None of those adjectives was critical in the least. If anything, Sutherland sounded . . . in awe of his daughter.

"She can never be vicereine," Richard said. "You know that. It's cruel to let her carry on like this, as though she has a chance."

Sutherland tilted his glass of whiskey, rolling the bottom edge on the table, the tinkling of ice filling the space. Their food arrived, but neither man made a move to touch the steaming plates in front of them.

"I'll still marry her," Richard said. "But I—"

"Why?" Sutherland stopped fiddling with the glass and looked up, pinning him with a look.

He paused. "Why what?"

"Why would you still marry her? She's clearly not interested in marrying you anymore." His tone held no malice, only a matter-of-fact dismissal, as though Poppy had outgrown Richard like a girl does a doll.

"Because I love her," he lied smoothly, keeping his fingers flat on the table to prevent them from curling into fists. Sutherland didn't look convinced, so he added, "I made a mistake, earlier, rushing things. I should have insisted we further acquaint ourselves. We spent less than a month courting, and then I sprang a very public, over-the-top proposal on her. Of course she got cold feet. That's all this is. Cold feet."

Sutherland leaned back. "Tell me something. If she were to be vicereine, would you still marry her?"

Richard dug his fingers into the tablecloth a fraction. "But she *can't* be vicereine. There's no such thing."

"That's not the question. If she *were*, would you still be interested in marrying her? If there were no reward to balance out her flaws, would you still forgive them?"

"There's no point in discussing this." He narrowed his eyes. "Unless, of course, you intend to name her your heir. And you can't."

Sutherland tightened his jaw, the muscle twitching. "And who are you, to tell the viceroy what he can or can't do? You forget, *boy*, that I'm still in charge. And that, for all intents and purposes, you have not been formally named in the line of succession. You are not viceroy yet, and you may never be."

"Are you seriously considering this?" Richard asked. "It's unheard of. There's never been a vicereine, let alone one who's Virian. The nobility will never support her—not here, and not in Welkland, either. Do you think she'll receive royal assent when the Imperial Family wouldn't even give her a courtesy title? I give it a fortnight before she loses the office to insurrection."

Sutherland raised a finger. "Ah, but you love her, don't you? As your wife, she'd have your family's title, and your support. Yours, and that of all the allies she's making in the Second Families."

Richard had no response to that. He turned his glare on his meal, shooting daggers at the roasted waterfowl.

"She's sympathetic to her people," he said. "She would undo everything you've built. Is that what you want?"

Sutherland fell quiet. Ah, so the old man knew that his daughter's sympathies were still there. Seven years at a Welkish college had taught her only how to hide the rot inside her heart.

Richard closed in. "Give up the idea. She's not qualified, and no one will permit it."

"I'm the viceroy, and a duke besides." Sutherland straightened, pushing out his chest. "I don't *need* permission."

He stared at him in dismay. "So you're decided, then? You're going to name her?"

"I haven't decided anything." Sutherland ran a finger below his lineup of cutlery. "I could name any of the youth in the First Families, if I wanted. Admittedly, you were my top choice. But this last month has been very . . . revealing."

Richard stiffened. "What's that supposed to mean?"

"It means you're not the man I thought you were."

He jabbed his finger into the table, punctuating his words. "I'm the man who *found* and *rescued* your daughter!"

"For your own selfish gain!" Sutherland's eyes bored into the younger man's face. "You didn't care for her then, and you don't care for her now. And if you think I'm going to leave my office, let alone my only child, in *your* incompetent hands before I die, then you're not as smart as you think you are, boy."

Richard had been prepared for this. If he couldn't marry the bitch, he would have to eliminate her. He reached down the side of the table for the briefcase, where the forged documents and

Alderfort's cousin's written testimony were safely enclosed.

"I didn't want to do this, but you leave me no choice. Your daughter is not the person you think she is."

But the old man raised his hand, cutting him off. His guards came quickly, rising from the surrounding table.

"Your Grace?" one asked.

Sutherland sniffed. "I've had quite enough of Captain Montrose's company."

Conversation in the club had petered out as the attention of the other members converged on their table. Richard pinched the bridge of his nose. He'd gambled incorrectly when he'd chosen Hazelwood. Still, he tried to salvage the situation.

"Wait!" He thrust the pages at Sutherland. "Trust me. When you hear what I'm about to tell you, you'll be thanking me for warning you. You have to hear me out."

"How many times do I have to tell you?" Sutherland sighed. He picked up his cutlery, turning his attention to his steak. "I don't *have* to do anything you tell me."

The guards each took one of Richard's arms, yanking him upward with so much force, the chair toppled. "Hey!" he barked. "Don't touch me."

The guards didn't listen. The other patrons stared openly. Word about this would make its way around society like wildfire. The bigger the scene, the faster the rumors would ripple. The only option left to Richard was to retreat—quietly.

"Very well! I'll go," he relented. "Let go of me. I'm going."

The guards released his arms, though they made it a point to walk side by side with him until he reached the parking lot, where his Peregrine sat waiting.

He got into his car and tore out of the lot, the roar of the engine barely audible over the blood rushing in his ears. The smell of burned rubber filled the air, but he hardly noticed.

The duke could not name Poppy. After all this, if he lost the viceroyship to her, he would never live it down. He would rather die than be governed by one of her kind. What had the world come to, where the shepherds appointed the sheep to give them orders?

In front of him, traffic had slowed to a stop. He laid into the horn, venting his anger through the blaring noise.

"What's the holdup?" he shouted, craning his neck. The sound of the blockade reached him before he saw it.

"Poppy, Poppy, Poppy!"

A small group of people had gathered in the center of the road, with cheap cardboard signs riddled with spelling errors. Something about the sight caused Richard to snap. He yanked open his glove compartment, pulling out his badge and gun from within. Killing the engine, he leaped out of the car and advanced toward the crowd, brandishing both badge and weapon.

"Disband, by order of the police!" he shouted. "You are creating a public disturbance, and I order you to stop."

Some of the people stepped back warily at the sight of the badge, but others continued to chant, ignoring him.

He lifted the gun, firing two shots just above the crowd.

That got their attention. They scattered like a flock of pigeons taking flight, shrieking as they disappeared into the side alleys. He fired a final shot at the stragglers, then turned and got back into his car, fuming.

This was the result of weak leadership. The very foundations of society were crumbling. If Poppy became vicereine, it would shatter irreparably. The old man was delusional about his daughter. And if he wouldn't take Richard's warning seriously, then he would have to hear it from someone he couldn't ignore.

Richard made a sharp turn at the next intersection, heading east, toward the Marnapur Telegraph Office.

• • •

TO: LORD T. GRANFORT, GREENHART, WELKLAND

C. SUTHERLAND TO NAME DAUGHTER AS NEXT VICEROY. DAUGHTER HAS SUSPECTED TIES TO CRIMINAL ACTIVITY. THE EMPEROR'S INTERVENTION IS APPRECIATED.

FROM: R. MONTROSE, MARNAPUR, VIRYANA

Chapter Forty

Impossible Decisions

The day of the vote, Hasan and Harithi each took turns making naumya. Hasan had already forsworn revenge on Zeyar at his mother's pantheon in Sanivali, but to that sacrifice he added several drops of his own blood. They left the apartment before dawn, dressed in dark, unremarkable clothing, with one duffel bag and four empty canisters between them. The plan was simple: Get to the House of Representatives, break in, burn it to the ground, and get out, all before the vote began.

They stopped at the gas station first, where Harithi filled the canisters with gasoline. Then Hasan drove them a block away from the House of Representatives. They took turns changing inside the car. When the transformations were complete, both of them looked entirely different from how they'd appeared that morning. Harithi, in a drab beige apron with her hair tied into a tight knot under a hairnet, looked exactly like the maidservants who scuttled around the Lower House, keeping the desks dusted and the meeting rooms stocked with tea and biscuits. Hasan was similarly dressed, in a beige shirt and overalls, standard dress for the repairmen who maintained the plumbing and electrical lines within the building. Each of them picked up two of the gasoline canisters and began walking toward the House.

By now, the sun had fully risen. Sweat trickled down Hasan's spine. For all his impulsive deviations and improvisations, this was the first real job that he had ever done without the support of his brothers. Doubt and an impending sense of failure loomed over him like storm clouds. He shoved them back, marching harder, as though he could somehow outpace his worries, his knuckles white on the canisters of gasoline.

"Doing okay?" Harithi asked.

"Just fine," he said. "It's not like the fate of every daivyakt in this country depends on us."

"Stay focused," she urged him. "Don't get in your head about this."

When they got to the House, there were several other workers in uniform heading into the building. Keeping his head down, Hasan followed them, Harithi on his heels. When they'd initially planned this, she had suggested setting the building on fire from the outside. But the exterior was pure stone, and he did not have nearly enough daivyakhi to keep the fire burning long enough for the interior to catch.

Luckily, getting in was easier than either of them had expected. The servant tunnel opened into a room where the other servants went about storing their bags and personal belongings in cubbies before heading off to their respective tasks. None of them looked at Hasan or Harithi; if anyone thought they looked unfamiliar or wondered about the canisters in their hands, they didn't show it.

The two of them followed the signs into the equipment room, where they stashed their canisters of gasoline on one of the service carts.

"So far so good," Hasan said. "We should split up now."

"Meet back here when you're done."

She turned and left, heading out to warn the other servants to evacuate. While Hasan knew they couldn't inform everyone personally, he hoped to avoid killing any more innocents than he had to.

He grabbed the handle of the service cart, pushing it out into the hallway. They didn't have a ton of gasoline, so he would have to pour the accelerant in the corridors around the Central Chamber of the House, where the vote would take place. The wheels of his cart squeaked on the wooden floors as he made his way through the west wing. For the most part, the hallways were empty—the representatives were all in the Central Chamber by now—but occasionally, he would duck his head when another person passed by him.

Finally, he reached the foyer of the building, slowing in front of the double doors to the chamber. He cursed silently; a bulky Welkish guard stood stationed on either side. Hasan called out to them as he approached.

"Excuse me? There's a woman in the east wing spreading rumors. She says there's a man in the building who's trying to burn it down, and that we should all leave now." The guards exchanged skeptical looks, so he added, "She said it was someone called the Jackal?"

This got their attention. "Where did you say this woman was?" the guard on the left asked, his cold blue eyes alert.

"East wing, third floor," he lied. Harithi would still be in the west wing, where most of the servants worked. "She's short, light skinned, with straight brown hair," he improvised.

"You stay here," the left guard told the other. "I'll go check it out."

When the other guard had disappeared down the hallway, the remaining guard said, "All right, then, get back to work, now."

He tried to brush Hasan away, but he only sighed. "Looks like you're the unlucky one."

"What—"

Hasan swung his fist around hard, knocking the other man out. He dragged his body off to the side, propping it up against one of the potted plants in the hope that no one would come by and notice it.

With the hallway left unguarded, he unscrewed the lid on a canister and poured the accelerant on the floor, taking extra care to soak the runner. While he could do a significant amount of damage on his own, even he couldn't torch a building of this size. The gasoline would feed his fires, help them spread and keep them alive.

He finished dousing the foyer, then swapped out his canister for the next one. Moving quickly, he ran up and down the twin staircases that framed the entrance to the chamber, trailing gasoline behind him as he went. He returned to the cart for the last two canisters, then headed upstairs. He did the second floor and the next set of stairs with the third canister, discarding it on the landing of the third floor.

As Hasan went around the third floor, splashing accelerant on the wooden floors and paneling, he heard voices coming from behind a closed door. He tensed. Something was off. These rooms were smaller, designed for more intimate meetings. The House was in session already, which meant that none of the representatives would be having individual meetings at this time. And something about their voices . . . He strained his ears, trying to put his finger on it. *Wait. . . . Were they speaking* Virian?

He dropped the fuel canister and grabbed the door handle,

finding it locked. As he rattled the knob, the voices fell silent, piquing his suspicion further.

"Who's there?" he demanded as loud as he could without shouting. He pressed his ear to the door, listening intently.

Silence. Then, "Hasan?"

His blood went cold. He'd know that voice anywhere. But here, of all places? He must have been hallucinating. The gasoline fumes were clearly addling his senses. He released the door and took a few steps back. Before he could lose his nerve, he charged forward, turning at the last second so that his shoulder struck the wood first.

The door burst open on impact, the wood splintering as it tore from the hinges. He fell into the room, landing hard on his knees and palms.

"Hasan!"

He leaped to his feet, spinning around. Relief swept through him. He wasn't hallucinating. It *was* Paranjay. He stood in a cage, with several other Virians. Hasan recognized two other daivyakt: Kaushal and Samina. Both looked bruised and battered, sporting scabbed-over split lips and puffy purple eyes. Paranjay had thinned out completely, his once-muscular frame thin and angular. His usually well-kept beard was frizzy and uneven, and his black eyes, normally full of humor, had a haunted quality under the thick lock of overgrown hair that kept falling in them. His face was badly bruised, though from the looks of it, none of the injuries were fresh.

Hasan took a step toward the cage, curling one hand around the cold metal bars as he squeezed the other through. Paranjay reached for him, and they clasped hands. Paranjay's skin was warm, his callused grip weak but familiar. Scabs and bruises decorated the back of his hands, extending up into his sleeves.

Hasan's eyes filled with tears. He pressed his forehead against the bars. Since Zeyar had returned Poppy to Richard, Hasan had feared the worst. His nightmares routinely featured the false Paranjay, dead on the floor in the museum. Except when Hasan kneeled to pull off the hood, it was the real Paranjay instead. Finding Paranjay alive had lifted such a great weight off his chest, it left him dizzy. Only Paranjay's hand in his kept him upright.

"It's actually you," he whispered. Against all odds, Hasan had found his brother. After all these weeks, after everything he'd survived, here was his blood, in the last place he'd expected him.

"Of course it's me. Who else?" Paranjay teased, trying to bring levity to the situation, even behind bars. "How did you know I'd be here?"

Hasan frowned. "I didn't."

Paranjay opened his mouth, then closed it. He looked just as confused as Hasan felt. "Then why are you here? If not to rescue us?"

In that moment, a revelation dawned on Hasan, horror soaking him down to the bone. If he burned down this building, he'd burn his brother too.

"What are you doing?"

He started. He twisted around, fingers still locked with Paranjay's.

Harithi stood at the remains of the bashed-in door, her hands on her hips. "We were supposed to be—*oh*." Her face paled as she caught sight of Paranjay. She glanced at Hasan, his distress mirrored in her eyes.

"Harithi?" Paranjay perked up. "Where's Zeyar?"

Harithi and Hasan flinched simultaneously. They exchanged a glance, both of them on the same page: This was the wrong time to tell Paranjay about the hostage negotiations and Zeyar's betrayal. In the prolonged silence, Paranjay's expression morphed into wariness, his weakened frame tense as he braced himself for bad news. "Did something happen to him?"

"No," Harithi answered quickly. "He's fine. But he didn't come with us. This was not supposed to be a rescue mission. What are you doing here, Paranjay?"

"To be honest, I'm not even sure where we are," Paranjay said. "They put hoods over our heads until we got here. Am I in the courthouse?"

"No," Hasan said. "You're not here to be tried for smuggling opium." Briefly, he explained the concept of the Registry Act to his brother. "You're here as a prop," he theorized. "As proof of how dangerous daivyakt are. Each one of you in this cage has likely committed some kind of crime using their daivyakhi, which supports the rationale behind the bill."

"When are they voting on it?" Paranjay asked.

"Today," Harithi said.

"But you have a plan to stop it, yeah? That's why you're here."

Hasan and Harithi exchanged a glance.

Paranjay repeated the question, this time uncertainly. "You have a plan to stop it, right?"

"We did," Hasan said. "We were going to burn this building down, with everyone in it."

Paranjay laughed. When neither Harithi nor Hasan joined him, his chuckle fizzled out. He paled. "Oh. You were serious."

"We'll figure something out," Hasan said. "Where's the lock on the cage?"

Paranjay pointed. "Over there."

They followed him around the perimeter of the cage, where a dense padlock had been bolted to the door.

"Has no one tried to open it with daivyakhi?" Hasan asked.

Paranjay shook his head. "None of us has made a sacrifice in some time."

Hasan hefted the complex lock in his palm, feeling its weight. It would take an extraordinary amount of heat to melt it—daivyakhi he couldn't spare, not if he wanted to burn the building down too. Even with his most recent sacrifice, he wouldn't be able to do both. He wasn't even sure if he could do this.

"Well?" Harithi sidled up to him, keeping her voice low.

"If I do this, I won't be able to burn the building," he muttered. "Did you bring matches?"

"Of course I didn't bring *matches*. And even if we used them to start the fire, you'd need your daivyakhi to escalate the intensity and kill the representatives fast, *before* help arrives."

Hasan closed his eyes. He could use his energy to try to rescue the prisoners, but he would damn the rest of the country's daivyakt residents.

Or, he could burn the building down as planned.

In the end, there were only a dozen or so Virians inside the cage, and tens of thousands of innocent people out there who would suffer if this bill was passed. Logically, the right choice would be the one that helped the most people. If he made decisions based on his own whims instead, how did that make him any better than Zeyar? If it had been twelve strangers in this cage, Hasan knew what he would have done.

"Hasan?"

He opened his eyes to see Paranjay looking at him. Concern creased the lines of Paranjay's face, but his jaw was clenched in fear. Revulsion rolled in Hasan's stomach, and he shook his head furiously, trying to clear his mind. In the end, his choice wasn't oriented around justice. Paranjay would have justified his choice by saying Hasan had prioritized family, but deep down, a doubt lurked, a self-awareness that he was not ready to confront. A suspicion that perhaps his decisions had never been about doing what was right, so much as justifying his means to achieve his ends.

"Step back," he warned the Virians inside the cage. Paranjay lifted his arms, shepherding the other prisoners backward, as far away from Hasan as they could get.

Hasan released the padlock, pointing two fingers directly at it. Concentrating hard, he released the daivyakhi within him. A stream of blue fire engulfed the padlock. At first, nothing happened. His face contorted as he dialed up the intensity. The flame flickered from blue to white to blue again, wavering with his strength and concentration. He'd never summoned a flame this intense before. Though he could make himself immune to fire when he used his daivyakhi, the flame was so bright and hot, his eyes watered looking at it.

The lock warped, but it wasn't melting fast enough. The divine energy bled from Hasan faster than he could melt the lock. *No, no, no.* His power couldn't fail him now. He pushed, pointing the fingers on his other hand at the lock, adding a second stream of fire.

"Come on," he growled, but the lock didn't give. It continued to melt at a slow, leisurely pace, taunting him with its resilience. How could he be losing to a hunk of metal? He put one last burst of energy into it, the flame flaring white—right before his daivyakhi ran out. Hasan swore. For a moment, the flames faltered. He couldn't stop here, couldn't admit defeat. Not when he was so damned close to freeing Paranjay.

Just two more minutes of power. That's all this will take. If he had to draw it from his own body, then so be it. The flames started back up as he reached inside, pulling from his very core. An ache started in his head, but he ignored it. His fingers spasmed as a spike of pain rippled down through his body. The kanusakhi ground at his bones as it tore free from the marrow, squeezing every organ as it drew from his life force.

Just one more minute. One more minute.

"Hasan," Harithi said. "Hasan, stop."

He ignored her. "I've almost got it," he said. His words tasted like rust. A quick swipe of his tongue over his upper lip confirmed that blood was dripping from his nose.

"Stop!" Paranjay said. "Hasan, it's not worth it. We'll figure it out. It's fine."

Hasan ignored him too. He channeled more kanusakhi, pins and needles tingling in his fingers and toes. His vision flickered. For a moment, he became deaf, Harithi's demands and Paranjay's pleas cutting out altogether.

The flames died as his knees gave way. Harithi caught him with a grunt. His head spun, colors blurring in front of him, but he could still make out the molten lock. He scraped together an ounce of strength, reaching for it one last time, but Harithi seized his hand and wrenched it away.

"No," she said, restraining him. "It didn't work. You have to let it go, Hasan. We need to get out of here. Both of us are defenseless now."

"I can try something else," he rasped, throat raw. His body throbbed, broken and tender, as though he'd been beaten by a crowd of fifty men. "Give me five minutes."

"Hasan, it's okay," Paranjay said. He reached through the bars, putting his hand on top of Hasan's head. His fingers trembled against his hair. "I don't want to see you arrested. If you end up in prison with me, I'll never forgive you. *Go.*"

"Damn it, Paranjay, I can't abandon you." He locked eyes with his brother, gripping the bars hard. "I could never—"

"I know," Paranjay said gently. "I know who you are, Hasan, better than you know yourself, even if you don't like it. But you have to go now, okay? The last thing we need is for them to catch you and imprison you too. We will talk about it later, I swear."

Harithi pried Hasan away from the cage, dragging him out of the room. Hasan kept his eyes on Paranjay until he could see him no more.

Later.

As Hasan and Harithi fled the House of Representatives, that was the only thing keeping him going. The promise of *later.*

• • •

Crackdown on Unnatural Population: Bill 201 Receives Royal Assent

Early Monday morning, the House of Representatives met to vote on one of the last bills in this year's legislative session. As a response to the uptick in crime over the last decade, Lord William Montrose III introduced Bill 201, or *An Act to Register Unnatural Persons*.

The bill states that the use of magic is rising again, due to lax regulations around it. Until this point in time, being an unnatural was not a crime in Viryana's criminal code, though the glorification and promotion of heretic magic was. "Unnatural criminals have exploited this loophole for years," Lord Montrose said in his statement to the press. "The greatest victims are the innocents, those with no arcane ability to defend themselves. I am pleased that this colony's lawmakers are standing up for this country and its vulnerable population."

When asked what the government might do with such a registry, Lord Montrose said it would be up to those who administer the law. "The purpose of this bill is really to allow us greater visibility on the kinds of people who walk among us," he said. "Right now, the size and distribution of the unnatural populace is a blind spot. You could be putting yourself in danger every time you engage with a new person."

In Monday's afternoon session, all four members of the Council of Lords applied their signatures to the bill. It was then sent to the desk of the viceroy, who has been vocal about his support for the bill. "It is certainly a step in the right direction," the viceroy said when asked for comment. "By providing my royal assent on behalf of the emperor, I am doing my part to protect my citizens. Let me make this clear: There is no room for magic in this country. Those who wield it must learn to respect that, or there will be very, very grave consequences."

Chapter Forty-One

A Father's Duty

Theodore came into the dining room while Catherine and Poppy were eating breakfast. He held a stack of mail in one hand and an opened letter in the other.

"I've received a letter from my brother-in-law." Theodore's lips twisted around the word *brother*. "It accuses me of harboring and abetting a criminal in her quest for power."

"What are you talking about?" Catherine asked.

Theodore handed Poppy the letter. Catherine came to stand behind her, reading over her shoulder as she skimmed it. Poppy's breakfast churned in her stomach. Richard's letter openly accused her of participating in the illegal trade of opium in Welkland.

When he hadn't exposed her after the failed wedding, she'd hoped it meant he'd been bluffing. But here in her hands was Richard's "proof" of her crimes: a copy of the written testimony of a former Thornhaven student, attesting she had witnessed Poppy sneaking off campus multiple times, and a ledger from Hasan's family's crime business, with Poppy's name on several lines.

Richard had also accused her of coordinating with the Jackal to fake her own abduction, with the intent of extorting her father. He cited the testimony from the valets at the engagement party, who had seen Hasan leave the party shortly after her, and from the museum curator, who had noted that he had seen Hasan guide Poppy by the hand and not in chains or ropes like a *true* hostage. The letter creased in her grip as she realized how easily several truths had been twisted together to spin a falsehood.

"The ledger is forged," Poppy said, her words tripping out in a rush. "And the testimony—the Alderforts are working with Richard, the servants' quotes are being taken out of context, and it was *Richard* who asked the Jackal to bring me to the museum in the first place. I was not in chains because the Jackal had only ever treated me gently, up until that point."

"Of course," Catherine scoffed. "My brother has a whole deck of cards up his sleeve. This is what he does."

Theodore nodded. "I suspected that this was some trick of Richard's. I believe you, because I know what he's like, and I know what you're like. But many of the other Second Families don't."

Poppy lowered the letter. "What are you saying?"

"I think you know what I'm saying," he said. "If Richard starts sending these documents to our allies, they will withdraw support, even if you attempt to explain yourself. The Second Families may be resentful of the First Families, but to them the police are a respectable, trustworthy institution."

"I don't know how to stop this." She crumpled Richard's letter in her hand, crushing it. "His letter says that if I retract my bid for vicereine, he won't expose me."

"Surely you don't believe he would honor such a bargain?" Catherine asked.

"I don't. But I can't *do* anything to stop him from circulating letters or rumors about me. Even if I retract, even if I disappear, he still has that information."

"Do you have anything on Richard?" Catherine asked

Theodore. "Something that we could hold over his head?"

"Nothing with proof," Theodore answered. "And nothing that the other families would take too seriously, either. Police brutality is acceptable so long as the victims are sufficiently guilty in their eyes."

It was hopeless. The whole venture was over. Poppy had had to fight twice as hard as anyone else to get to where she was, and now she would lose it all anyway, because no matter how hard she studied or how well behaved she was, she would never be as credible as a Welkish man. She put her head in her hands, the weight of this truth too much for her to bear.

"I do have other news," Theodore added. "I'm not sure if it's good yet, but you'll soon find out."

She lifted her head. He offered a sealed envelope. "It's from your father."

Her hands shook as she reached for it. The envelope felt dangerously thin; whatever the duke had said, he had not provided any cushioning to go with it. There would be no beating around the bush, no gentle easing into his message.

Poppy took the letter opener from Theodore and sliced into the envelope. Catherine scooted backward as Poppy drew out a single page from within, giving her space to read the note privately. The room went quiet; no one even dared to breathe.

She read the letter once. Twice. A third time.

"Well?" Catherine finally said, breaking the silence. "What does it say?"

Poppy looked up, her mouth dry. "He wants to meet me."

• • •

Poppy sat in her father's office, holding her breath as she waited for the butler to fetch him. He hadn't given any inclination of his thoughts in the letter. Whom had he chosen as his successor? What would she do if he had chosen, and it wasn't her? If it was Richard? Her stomach churned.

Then the doorknob turned, scattering her thoughts. The door swung open silently on well-oiled hinges. The duke stood on the other side. For a moment, all Poppy could process was relief: Here was her father, ready to speak with her after weeks of silence.

Then she looked at him more closely, catching details she'd missed in her first inspection. Guilt filled her heart, weighing it down like a stone. He looked like he'd aged seven years in the last week. The skin around his eyes had darkened to a bluish black, and his suit—usually pressed into perfect lines—was wrinkled, his collar rumpled and sticking up at the back. His signet ring, engraved with the Cloudcliff seal, hung loose on his finger.

"Father," Poppy said, rising.

He hobbled into the room on his cane, using his free arm to bring her into an embrace that was surprisingly fierce, given how frail he looked.

"I was so worried about you." He gasped. "When they evacuated everyone from the cathedral, and you weren't there . . . I nearly tore the rubble apart."

The stone of guilt threatened to rip the fabric of Poppy's heart apart. She had barely given any thought to her wedding day. "I'm fine," she said. "I'm sorry I scared you. I wasn't thinking straight. All I wanted was to get away from Richard. I didn't mean to upset you."

"I know," her father soothed, stroking her hair. "You've never meant any harm, Poppy. I've always been hard on you, perhaps harder than was necessary, at times. But I think you know that, don't you? Come, let's sit and talk. We have much to discuss, and I fear . . ." The hand that leaned on the cane began to tremble.

Poppy immediately helped him to his chair before retaking her earlier seat on the other side of the desk. He took a handkerchief from his jacket pocket and dabbed at the beads of sweat that had appeared on his forehead.

"I didn't mean to alarm you," she repeated, forcing her voice to be stern. "But I need you to know that I'm serious: I will not marry Richard, and I fully intend to succeed you as vicereine."

"I know," her father said. "I've given this matter a lot of thought. I was particularly affected by what you said to me, about your being equal to any natural heir I might have had. Because you are right, Poppy. You have always been my child, regardless of where you came from. I have told you that my decision to adopt you was highly unpopular. Everyone told me that you would never be a true daughter to me. In fact, the Imperial Family even offered me a ward, so that I might have a true heir."

She flinched. She had known that the Imperial Family had never approved of her, but she had not known that they had attempted to replace her. Would her father use their disapproval as a reason to choose a different successor? Was he going to say that he had selected a candidate from Welkland, instead?

"If I gave the office to another," her father continued slowly, "I would be proving them right. I'd be a hypocrite to insist for twenty-one years that you were legitimate enough to be my child, but not legitimate enough for the viceroy's office. It would be a betrayal of our relationship. This is your home, your inheritance, and it cannot be substituted by anything else, just as I could not substitute you with another child."

Poppy twisted her hands in her skirt, not trusting her own

ears. "What are you saying?" she asked, slow and cautious. She didn't dare hope for anything.

"I've made you my heir," her father said. "I've written an amendment to my will and had it notarized. Not every lord has agreed yet, but once I've guaranteed their cooperation, we will vote on it immediately. I will make them all see reason," he added darkly.

Hot tears sprang to Poppy's eyes. She ran to the other side of the desk, bending down to embrace her father. His arms came around her in a reciprocal gesture. For a moment, they stood like that, each holding the other.

"I know you'll continue the Sutherland legacy faithfully," her father said, so quietly she almost missed it. "I put every effort into civilizing you. You are one of us, of that I have no doubt."

Poppy tensed. Though once his belief in her wholehearted change would have gratified her beyond words, she took no pleasure in it now. His embrace became uncomfortable with the sharp corners of his legacy now between them, the bones of his victims poking at her conscience. How could she love someone who had been responsible for so much suffering? How could he be so warm to her, and yet so cold to the plight of her people? Did he truly love her, or was his pride only for the civilized woman he believed he had created?

She withdrew uncertainly, opening her mouth—but then the door flew open with a bang, scattering her next words. She spun around. Her heart plummeted when she saw who the intruder was.

"Richard? How—how did you get in here?"

He looked more disheveled than her father—ivory face pale, golden hair wild, police uniform creased. "The butler let me in." Then he bared his teeth at her father. "I knew you'd make her your heir, Sutherland. For all your lies, you couldn't lead me astray."

He glared at Richard. "I already told you, boy. It is well within my rights to choose my own heir."

"And I told *you,*" Richard retorted, "she's not what you think she is. She's been working with drug smugglers for seven years, even going so far as to fake her own kidnapping to extort you."

His words struck Poppy in the chest, winding her. "That's not true!" She turned to her father and placed a hand on his arm. "He's lying."

"She's the one who's lying," Richard said. "I have testimony, proof from various sources."

Richard pulled a wad of folded papers from his breast pocket, presumably the same documents he had sent Theodore.

"Father—"

Her veins ran cold as her father silenced her with a look, taking the pages. She swallowed hard as he unfolded them slowly. Richard smiled like a cat with a songbird. Each second that her father spent reading over the pages agonized her. The sound of the paper shuffling chafed against her skin.

"Father," she pleaded, no longer caring if she appeared impudent, "I didn't do it. I promise."

"The proof is in front of you, Your Grace." Richard spread his arms wide, like a showman. "What are you going to believe? The flimsy word of your daughter, or the cold, hard facts?"

"Not facts, but falsehoods. Those documents have been doctored," she insisted, her voice rising an octave. "Richard only wants the office of the viceroy. He would accuse the emperor himself of treason if he thought it would get him anywhere. There's no lie too low for him."

"You're one to talk about lying with the low," Richard sneered. "Half your Second Family allies are only helping you for the chance to plant an heir on you. I wonder if they'd still want you if they knew there was a chance that they might be raising a mongrel pup instead."

The lecherous meaning behind his words made her body flush with rage. "The Jackal and I *never*—"

"Enough," her father barked. He tossed the documents onto the desk. "I've made my decision."

Richard and Poppy both swiveled their heads toward the duke. Her heart pounded in her chest, echoing in her ears. What her father had decided would speak volumes about their relationship: Either he had meant what he had said earlier, about her complete transformation, or he would forsake her now.

"Poppy, I trust you," he said. "You will be vicereine."

Relief rushed through her, so intense it was nearly painful. She wrapped her arms around her father again. "Thank you," she sobbed. "Thank you."

"You're my daughter," he said. "I know how I raised you."

"Touching." Click. "Step away from each other. Slowly."

A chill ran down Poppy's spine as she turned to face the barrel of Richard Montrose's pistol.

"Young man," her father said, "put that gun away." He released Poppy gently, taking a single step away.

"I don't think so," Richard said. "I'm calling the shots now." He smirked. "Get it? Shots?"

"You're a monster," Poppy spat at him.

"I'm the only reasonable person in this room!" Richard said. "I gave you so many outs, Poppy, but you kept pushing. I'll give you one last chance: Renounce the office, and I won't have to kill you."

"You wouldn't," she said loudly, trying to persuade not only herself but him as well. "Even if you kill me, the office won't pass to you automatically. It will go to a vote."

"Oh, I would. Don't underestimate how far I'm willing to go

to make sure the office isn't sullied by an uncivilized rat like you," he snapped. "One last chance. Give up."

"Over my dead body!"

He smiled. "So be it."

"No!" her father shouted, the end of his cry cut off by the explosive bang of Richard's bullet bursting free of its chamber. He moved with impossible speed and urgency, leaping in front of Poppy. She howled as Richard's bullet caught her father full in the chest, his body snapping back, thrown off its trajectory by the force of the shot. He collapsed, the smell of copper and gunpowder filling the air.

She fell to her knees, pressing her hands over her father's wound, trying to stem the bleeding with her bare hands. Blood seeped through her fingers, coating her hands and settling along her cuticles. "Father," she gasped. Her voice cracked as she cried, "Help! Help!"

Richard, who had been staring at the duke in disbelief, stirred at the sound of her cries. He lifted the gun and pointed it at her.

"Run," Clarence gurgled.

Though she was loath to do so, she released her father and scrambled back, just in time to avoid Richard's second shot by inches. He stepped over Clarence, pushing Poppy back toward the corner. He took aim once more. Just when Poppy thought her luck was truly over, servants burst into the room, rushing Richard and wrestling his gun from him. He tried to resist, but they had him outnumbered.

"You did this," Richard said, drinking in her pain even as they dragged him away. "This is your fault, Poppy. You chose power for yourself over his life."

He was right, she thought. He had pulled the trigger, but it was *she* who had courted the monster.

"No," Poppy said, choking on tears, salt burning down her throat. She blinked them back furiously, making sure her gaze was clear as she stared Richard down. "It was you, all along. I'll never forgive you for this. I'll kill you myself."

Her father coughed, blood staining his lips. "Poppy . . ."

She whipped her head back around. "Father," she said, rushing back to his side. "Stay with me. Help is on the way."

"My girl," he said with a weak smile. "My time has come. Don't cry. I will die doing what every father was born to do: protect his child."

She wiped at her tears, staining her own face with his blood. "You can't die. I've only just come home. There's so much we haven't discussed."

"I regret that we have not had more time, but I have no regrets about you." Her father smiled feebly. "You are strong, Poppy. You are proof that the Founder was right, that all nations can be made civilized. I am so proud of your transformation."

"I have so many questions," she said. Not just about leadership, but about their relationship. Some were questions that not even her father could answer but, rather, would be answered by time itself: Could her father change his values? Could he see the error of his racist ways? She would never have answers. She had been robbed of things she would never know.

To herself, she confessed, "I'm not ready for this." She cradled his cheek, smearing his face with blood.

His eyes fluttered, and he inhaled raggedly. Poppy kneeled on the bullet wound, the same way Zeyar had taught her to do for Hasan. The hot scarlet on his shirt spread by the second, staining Poppy's skin a color that she would see in her nightmares for years to come.

"No one is ready," he wheezed. His voice was strained, but he kept going. "But you are closer than most." He took another rattling breath. "My time comes. Take care of your mother. I should have . . ." He gasped. His voice was softer than a dove's wings. "I should have believed you. Forgive me."

Poppy stared at him, his final words striking a deep chord of unease within her. She knew she would reckon with his brutal legacy as viceroy for the rest of her life. Those sins weren't hers to absolve. But for his mistakes as a father? He hadn't earned her forgiveness, and now he never would. Still, it would be cruel to send him to his grave without the mercy he sought from her.

"I forgive you," she whispered.

Her father's face relaxed. His eyes went glassy and unseeing.

Clarence Sutherland, Duke of Cloudcliff, viceroy of Viryana, and Poppy's father, was dead. She closed her eyes, letting out a sob that rattled her bones. Tears leaked down her cheeks, dripping onto her father's bloodstained shirt. She wiped her hands on her bodice. Then, with trembling hands, she gently closed his eyes.

Chapter Forty-Two

Night of Possibilities

Duke of Cloudcliff Dies Unexpectedly Amid Questions About Succession

Late last night, the family of His Grace, the Duke of Cloudcliff, informed press of his untimely passing. While they did not reveal the cause of death, the *Times of Viryana* has discovered from a source that the viceroy did suffer a mild stroke earlier in the year. While he had no natural-born children, he adopted an orphan girl after the textile factory tragedy in Andhra twenty-one years ago. He is survived by his adoptive daughter, Poppy Sutherland, and his wife, the dowager duchess, Demetria Sutherland. Both of them have asked for privacy while they grieve.

The duke came to power early after his own father died prematurely, becoming the youngest viceroy in the colony's history. Despite his youth, he guided the country to an era of prosperity. The viceroy will be remembered by many for his revolutionary economic policies, which helped Viryana double its gross domestic product over his term in office. He was an advocate for the ability of all men to better themselves on their own merit, his belief in the equal potential of all men to achieve greatness rooted in the writings of the Founder.

The duke's unexpected death leaves the colony bereft of a clear successor for the viceroy's office. The office has always passed to a male Sutherland heir. Until recently, most assumed that Captain Richard Montrose, police prodigy, would inherit the role given his engagement to the duke's daughter. Though it is unclear if the two are still set to marry after a torrential rainstorm flooded the cathedral during their wedding ceremony, Miss Sutherland has recently expressed interest in assuming her father's mantle herself. While the common citizens of Viryana have rallied in her favor, sources say the Council of Lords opposes the idea. A successor will be chosen and voted upon at a formal hearing next week, following the late viceroy's funeral.

The Duke of Cloudcliff's legacy is one of greatness, growth, and prosperity. While it is still unclear who is set to inherit his position, the last celebration of his life will be hosted this weekend at the Andhra abbey while the Marnapur Cathedral is under repair. The public is invited to stand in the streets; however, due to the limited size of the abbey, only those with invitations will be permitted inside.

• • •

That night, if the gods deigned to look down on Viryana, they would have seen the island carved into two halves: one dark and solemn, the other lit with the fire-bright light of renewed hope. In the streets of the Virian neighborhoods, people celebrated, their joy and victory made even louder by the silence from the Welkish quarter. They beat drums and sang loudly, dancing through the streets.

After the last few weeks of being dammed up in curfew, they burst free, pouring into the streets. Hasan reveled among them, a bottle of lager in hand as he flowed with the crowd, moving through the streets freely. No police tried to stop them. The entire force had gone to guard the bridge into the Welkish quarter, protecting their neighborhoods from riots, but the Virians were content to celebrate outside their own homes.

For once, it had been the other side who had lost something.

For once, the death wasn't one of theirs. For decades, suffering had resided on the Virian side of the island, haunting them with increasing aggression as the viceroy increased the severity of his economic policies. Death had been the viceroy's attack dog, and now the beast had finally turned on him.

The celebration went on for hours. Hasan wouldn't remember most of it, but what he would recall was the dawn.

In the last hour before the sun went up, he staggered to a street food stall. He'd lost count of how many drinks he'd had, and he'd worked up an appetite after celebrating all night. The vendor sold kathi rolls, kebabs wrapped in parathas. He ordered three, ravenous. The stall vendor efficiently wrapped them in a newspaper and passed them over the counter.

He wandered down the street, perching on a stack of crates left at the side of the road. The parathas were soft yet flaky, and the vendor had added a fresh squeeze of lime to the kebab and caramelized onion filling, giving it a pleasant tang. Once he'd finished all three, he moved to ball up the newspaper and toss it away. He froze, his eyes focusing on the headline, stained with grease but still legible: "Duke of Cloudcliff Dies Unexpectedly Amid Questions About Succession."

Splashed on the front page was a picture of the viceroy, in the prime of his youth, before Hasan had been born. But what had caught his attention was a smaller picture at the bottom of the page. Poppy Sutherland's face stared back up at him. She looked different in this photograph, taken at her engagement party. Under her thick and striking brows, her eyes were wide and shy, her full, bow-shaped lips curved into an uncertain smile, as though she weren't sure if she was allowed to be smiling at all. This was an entirely different woman compared to the one who had bartered with criminals under duress.

Hasan's heart twisted unexpectedly. While he'd been celebrating, she'd been mourning the premature loss of her father. Having lost his own father to the sea over a decade ago, he knew the unique ache intimately. He'd never forget it, never forget the way it had torn a hole in the fabric of his family. He had never wanted to experience a loss like that again, determined to keep the rest of his family intact.

"And look how well that worked out." He'd aimed for light and wry, but his words sounded bitter and heavy, even to him.

While Poppy's loss had settled on his chest, weighing him down, he couldn't make himself feel remorse over the viceroy's death. Sure, he could empathize with Poppy, especially as someone who had known the unique pain of losing a parent early, but he couldn't sympathize with a man—a monster—who had never sympathized with Hasan or his people.

The paper had said his legacy was one of "greatness, growth, and prosperity," but all of these things had come at the cost of the Virian people. Sutherland had stolen their land, their labor, and their lives, and used them to fuel his success. But of course, that wasn't the only thing he had left behind.

Hasan ran his fingers over the edge of the newspaper, tracing the shape of Poppy's photograph.

"Someone looks glum."

He looked up. An unfamiliar man stood in front of him, holding his own kathi rolls tucked in newspaper. He smelled distinctly of booze and bonfire smoke.

"May I sit?"

Hasan shrugged, gesturing to one of the other crates. The other man sat, sighing with satisfaction as he dug into a kathi roll. Hasan took the chance to study him. He was on the shorter side, likely an effect of childhood malnutrition, though his build was solid, indicating that he'd since done better for himself. His hair and beard were trimmed short. If Hasan had to guess, he'd put the man in manual labor—nothing as backbreaking as the factories, but something that required heavy lifting. A construction worker, though he didn't appear sunburned. Maybe a delivery driver.

The other man looked up and caught his eye. "Everything okay?" he asked. "You seem subdued. This is a night of celebration, friend."

"You're quick to call me *friend*," Hasan remarked. "Does the word mean so little to you? Or do you not know who I am?"

He only smiled. "It doesn't matter who you are. I can see by your skin that we've lost a common enemy," he said. "We divide ourselves when we ought to be making friends and allies, but tonight, we all celebrate together. Daivyakt or vasudhakt, young or old, tonight, we are all friends. I'm sure that when the dawn comes and a new oppressor is chosen to rule us, we'll go back to fighting our own. But tonight, you're my friend."

"A pretty speech," Hasan quipped. The other man spoke like a politician. In a way, he reminded Hasan of Zeyar, but without the edge. He wondered how his brother viewed this latest development. Quickly, he shook his head. *I have no brother but Paranjay.* He glanced back down at Poppy. "What if they didn't choose a new oppressor?" he asked. "What if we chose someone else?"

The stranger glanced over at the newspaper. "If you're talking about the girl, then I'm afraid I disagree. Though she looks like us, she was raised like them. She's a tigress in sheep's clothing, nothing more. What does she know about our struggles?"

"She's capable of learning," Hasan said. "She's willing to listen."

"And you know that how?"

Hasan struggled with an answer, then sighed. "Because I'm the Jackal," he admitted, "and she was once my prisoner. I saw for myself how she was willing to learn."

The other man was quiet, studying Hasan again, this time with a sober gaze that allowed him to see what he'd missed before: Hasan's height and solid weight, the mark of a privileged childhood, his scarred knuckles, his pristine clothing.

"Who will she listen to?" he finally asked. "Maybe she's willing to learn. But we have no representation in the viceroy's office."

"Then we'll be the representation," Hasan suggested. "What's your name?"

The other man evaluated Hasan before answering. "Arun. Arun Dhamakha."

"Arun," he repeated. "Think about it—we don't have to go back to fighting each other tomorrow. We could form a council of our own—a delegation, maybe—and advocate for ourselves. We've never been able to do it before, because no one would listen. But Po—Miss Sutherland would."

"I never thought the Jackal would be an idealist!" Arun grinned. "Somehow, I thought you'd be more . . . nihilistic."

"A lot of things have happened recently that I could have never imagined," he said. "This is just one more impossible thing that's now possible."

"Even if she's willing to listen, the odds of her being actually chosen are low," Arun said. "They'd reject her for the same reason we want her—because she could be sympathetic to us."

"Then we don't give them a choice." Hasan gestured around vaguely. "Look at the way they sent all the police to the bridge tonight. They fear us. There are more of us than them, and they know it. Every tyrant needs his subjects, but no people need a tyrant."

Arun didn't answer, finishing his kathi roll instead. Then, he said, "If you sober up and you still feel optimistic, Jackal, come and find me. We'll talk about it then."

From his breast pocket, he took out a stub of a pencil and wrote his address on a grease-free corner of his newspaper wrapper. He tore it free, gave it to Hasan, and stood.

"Good night, Jackal." Arun smiled wryly. "I hope, when the dawn ends, we choose to stay friends."

Chapter Forty-Three

Silence for a Voice

Poppy couldn't get her hands clean. No matter how much she washed them, no matter how clean they appeared, they felt sticky, soaked in blood that wasn't hers but was the source of her pain nonetheless.

The family doctor diagnosed her with shock. He told her mother that she was merely numb.

She was not numb. She was trapped. Trapped in *that* moment. It was like being held underwater, in a deep bath. She could see the light coming through the surface, could hear voices and see shadows move as people continued to live their lives around her. But she was stuck in those last moments of her father's life, so much so that they might as well have been the last of her own.

The scent of gunpowder and copper still choked her. Blood still seeped through cotton, staining her fingers, smearing against the soft, wispy strands of her father's hair as she stroked it, trying to comfort a soul that had already left. The taste of salt and metal lingered on her tongue and in the back of her throat, raw from screaming, burning from swallowing her own tears. Her ears still rang from the shot, from the screaming that ensued.

She did not know how much time had passed while she was

like that, trapped in her underwater world. But one morning, her mother came and pulled the plug, bringing her back to the real world to face a nasty surprise.

"Get dressed," she ordered, her face ashen. "The marquess is here."

• • •

Lord William Montrose was the second-last person in the world whom Poppy wanted to see. He stood in the parlor, dressed in mourning attire. Her fingers curled, itching to tear the black fabric from him. He had no right to mourn, not when it was his monstrous son who had done this.

"Your Grace," Lord Montrose said. "Miss Sutherland, allow me to express my deepest condolences at your loss."

Poppy's nails bit into her palms, but she kept her jaw clenched tightly shut.

Demetria gestured. "Sit, please."

They sat, Poppy and her mother on one sofa, Lord Montrose on the love seat across from them.

"I'm afraid we weren't expecting you." Her mother pressed her lips together. "If you would like, I can ring for tea." Her terse tone insinuated that *she* wouldn't like tea at all.

"That's quite all right," Lord Montrose said, picking up on the hint. "I understand that this is an inconvenient time to meet. However, the subject is time sensitive. So far, we have been able to keep Richard's involvement in the viceroy's death out of the press—"

"Involvement?" Poppy interrupted, decorum be damned. "He shot Father. He wasn't *involved*; he was the cause."

The marquess gave her a sympathetic look, artful in how

artificial it was. "We wish to keep the matter private. However, if this goes to the court, it will inevitably make its way into the papers. Richard has been very remorseful over the way events played out that day, and he's been extremely cooperative under house arrest. I want to propose—"

"House arrest?" Poppy demanded, her voice rising. "The police just *let him go home*? He tried to kill me. What stops him from sneaking out and trying again?"

"Not now, Poppy," her mother said under her breath. "We'll talk about this later."

"Rest assured, he's no longer in Marnapur. He's being watched very closely at one of our properties on the northern side of the island." Lord Montrose waved a hand dismissively. "I understand he's committed a serious crime, one that has deeply harmed many people, most of all yourselves. I have decided that the best thing to do is send him back to Welkland, where he will live with our extended family and never return."

Poppy's blood had come to a rolling boil. "You've decided what's best? Your son has murdered my father—he's not even in the ground—and you want to send him off to Welkland, where he'll live a quaint life buying thoroughbreds on some country estate?"

"Poppy," her mother warned, but Poppy waved her off.

"Let me tell you what *I* think is best," she said, her tone sweet and scalding at once. "I think it would be best if we tried Richard in court, found him guilty, and then let him rot in a cell for the rest of his life."

"Are you so merciless?" Lord Montrose asked. "He has a long life ahead of him. Is it fair to force him to live it in a cell, just because he misfired his weapon?"

"He didn't misfire! He meant to shoot *me*. And if it's mercy you want, then we can sentence him to swing from a rope. I can be merciful."

"That's quite enough!" Two spots of color bloomed high on her mother's cheeks. "Lord Montrose, do you mind if I have a minute with my daughter?"

"Of course, Your Grace." He tilted his head. He was too mature to give Poppy a smug grin, but the impersonal smile he wore as he left the room was grating enough.

Poppy stared at her mother as though she were a stranger. "What are you doing? He wants to send Richard back to Welkland, without any repercussions. Even the house arrest—he should be in a high-security cell. How did you not know about that?"

"I knew about the house arrest," her mother said. "I chose not to say anything then. Just as you ought to keep your silence now."

The admission struck Poppy like a slap. "I don't understand," she whispered. "He's your husband. Don't you want justice for him?"

"We won't get justice, Poppy," her mother said. "You're a fool if you think we will. The officers who assessed the scene have been Richard's brothers-in-arms for years. The judges who will hear the case have dined, drunk, and hunted with Lord Montrose for decades. The best-case scenario is that he'll be pardoned on the grounds of an accidental misfire. The worst-case scenario is that they'll pin it on the only other person who was there—you. Your father died for your future. Do you think you're honoring his memory, throwing it away to pursue a case that's been decided before it's even been tried?"

"But I didn't do it," she said. "And it wasn't a misfire. I was there."

"It doesn't matter," her mother said. "It is your word against his. And you should know by now that your word doesn't weigh the same as his."

Poppy laughed. "Of course it doesn't," she sneered. "My word doesn't even mean anything to my own mother."

Demetria flinched at the reference to Poppy's wedding morning. "I should have listened," she said. "But it doesn't change the facts: No one else will believe you. The most important thing is that your father still saw fit to name you his successor. He knew what he was doing when he signed that document, and he knew what he was doing when he died to protect you. To me, fulfilling his dying wish—making you vicereine—is more important than justice." Her voice gentled at the tears brimming in Poppy's eyes. "Justice won't bring him back."

"He still deserves more than this." Poppy wiped her tears fiercely. Her father might have been a tyrant, one who had allowed the vulnerable citizens in his care to suffer, but Poppy meant it when she added, "He deserves more than Richard Montrose's living as a free man in Welkland."

"We don't get what we deserve. You of all people should know that." Her mother laid one hand on her back. "Listen to me: If you go against the Montrose family, you will fail. The marquess has more power than you—power you *need.* Don't start this era by making enemies. Make allies."

Poppy sat silently, rage and frustration and grief burning in her chest. She knotted her hands together, but the sheen of sweat on her palms reminded her of when they'd been slick with blood. She wiped her hands on her dress, gripping the fabric tightly. She wanted to see Richard behind bars. She wanted to see him swing. She wanted to see him on the ground, life bleeding from him slowly.

She closed her eyes, trying to dispel the image. Her thoughts were violent in a way she had never been, but she couldn't make herself feel remorse. *He deserves it,* she thought. He deserved to be destroyed, and she wanted to be the one who did it. Even if it meant destroying herself in the process. But she couldn't destroy the last thing her father had given her, the one good thing he had done for this colony: a chance to lead, to fix the mistakes he'd made.

Poppy exhaled, her rib cage so tight it was almost painful. Her mother had been silent the whole time, but she must have sensed the shift, because she reached out and laid her hand over Poppy's, easing her fingers free from where they'd been clutching the skirt of her mourning dress.

"Call him back," Poppy relented. When Lord Montrose was sitting in front of her again, she said, "I will not pursue a legal case against Richard, nor will I publicize his involvement to the press."

He relaxed. "See, I knew you could be reasonable—"

"I'm not finished," she snapped, her tone hard and icy. "In exchange for this, not only will you send Richard to Welkland, but you will also support me at the hearing next week, when we settle on a successor. If you renege on your word, I will reveal Richard's involvement to everyone. There won't be a soul on this island who won't know what he did. Are we clear?"

"No one will believe you."

"Perhaps not." Demetria gave him an ice-cold smile. "But they will believe me."

Lord Montrose stared at them both, then narrowed his gaze at Poppy. "How callous you are, using your father's death as collateral in your quest for control."

"I wouldn't have to bargain like this at all if your son hadn't murdered him in his own pursuit of power," she retorted. "Do we understand each other or not, Lord Montrose?"

He glared at Poppy, but she refused to wither. Finally, he spat out, "We are in agreement. I will see you both at the funeral."

Demetria and Poppy rose, forcing him to stand too. Neither woman volunteered to see him out. When he had left the room, Poppy collapsed back onto the couch, pressed a throw pillow to her face, and screamed.

She had made the best of the situation, scraping out a win in a scenario where loss was inevitable. But Richard would go free, and she would never forget it.

• • •

"Are you sure you know what you're signing up for?" Harithi hissed.

The two of them sat in Arun's cramped sitting room while he prepared chai in the kitchen. After the celebrations—and their hangovers—had subsided, Hasan and Arun had drawn up plans for a delegation, one that would represent the interests of the common people and coordinate demonstrations around the city. Arun already had experience with this, having been a labor rights advocate for years. Today, they aimed to recruit Arun's people to their cause.

"I don't know what you're talking about," Hasan whispered back. "Wasn't it you who said we should be giving more importance to our vasudhakt gang members?"

"I meant that about our gang activity," she said. "This is politics. This is a game that we don't know how to play."

"Well, we're going to have to learn"—he gritted his teeth—"because if we don't, then we'll never be free."

A knock on the door interrupted whatever Harithi was going to say next.

"I'll get it," Arun called. He brought the chai into the living room, putting the pot down on the coffee table before answering the door. A small group filed into the house, four in all.

"What's this about?" one asked.

"Sit, please." Arun gestured toward the living room. The newcomers froze when they saw Hasan and Harithi already there.

"Arun, do you know who that is?" one of the men asked, eyes flashing in warning.

"This is my friend, Hasan." Arun smiled pointedly. "Hasan, these are my friends, Tara, Maya, Akash, and Niraj."

Akash scoffed, thick brows lifting. "No, that's the Jackal."

"Both of these things can be true," Arun replied. "The Jackal is my friend, and I hope you can all keep your minds open enough to allow him to be your friend too."

"What's this about, Arun?" Maya's gaze never left Hasan. "Why did you call us here?"

He raised his arms. "As you know, the succession to the viceroy's office is still undecided. We've all heard rumors that Poppy Sutherland has been rallying for the seat, but Hasan knows her personally and has confirmed this to be true. He and I both believe that she is our best chance at a better life."

"We've talked about this, Arun." Niraj sighed. "You yourself have said it—how can she empathize with us when she's never lived among us?"

"You don't have to have the same experience as someone to feel for them, only the desire to understand," Arun said. "After meeting Hasan that first night, I spoke to some of the laborers in Sanivali. Poppy *was* there, earlier this month, learning about their struggles. Clearly, she cares."

"I also heard word from Sanivali," Tara said. "I have a cousin there. Is it true that Poppy is daivyakt?"

"It is," Hasan said. Seeing the way her face soured, he asked, "What? How can her being gods-blessed possibly be a negative thing?"

Niraj grimaced. "Perhaps we remember the age of daivyakt rulers differently. The maharajas used their power to extort vasudhakt, withholding aid from poorer regions who could not pay the taxes. Their wars ravaged landscapes and destroyed homes. Their obsession with blood purity and hoarding power barred vasudhakt from entering entire sections of cities. Is it so unreasonable, then, that we do not wish to return to an era like that?"

"Poppy only discovered her powers recently," Hasan said. "She didn't grow up with any entitlement, and even now she remains an underdog. If we refuse to support her, then we'll lose this chance. We'll never get another Virian viceroy. Our lives will be hell forever."

"Since when do you care?" Tara tossed her thick braid over one shoulder. "Do you know, Jackal, how many lives you and your brothers have made hell with your *business*?"

"Call me Hasan. I *insist*." His smile was dissolving rapidly. "And we never forced anyone to do business with us. If their lives were ruined, it's because they made poor decisions."

"Does the victim blaming help you sleep better at night?" Akash asked. "You make these loans because you know we're too desperate to refuse them. You know the banks won't give us the money, and so you hike up your interest rates, forcing us to agree to unethical terms. You and your brothers have only ever used your power against us, instead of fighting back."

Hasan bit his tongue. Defenses, half formed, floated through his mind. He didn't want to admit that he'd spent the past ten years doing more harm than good. But if he couldn't humble himself now, he'd lose their support. *Poppy* would lose their support.

"You're right," he said grudgingly. "I'm sorry. I can't take it back, but I recognize that what we did was wrong."

"Let's not let the past prevent us from looking at the future," Arun suggested. "Sit, and if you don't like what we have to say, then you may go."

The four newcomers exchanged skeptical glances but relented, taking seats across from Hasan and Harithi. "What do you have planned?" Tara asked.

"The hearing to confirm Poppy Sutherland is this Monday," Hasan said. "We need the Welks to know that we won't be silent about this. We have to organize crowds to come and rally outside the House of Representatives, really lay the heat on them. Let the representatives know that we won't follow anyone else."

Akash and Maya exchanged a look. "I don't know," Maya said. "We've heard what's happened to your daivyakt followers, Jackal. It sounds an awful lot like you're forming this delegation as a substitute for your gang."

He pressed his lips together. He couldn't deny that if he had the choice, he'd have much rather had his gang to support him on this. In his silence, the others came to conclusions of their own.

"Why are we here?" Niraj threw up his hands, turning to Arun. "You say it's about the girl, but I think it's really about the Jackal."

Hasan tilted his head up, closing his eyes for a moment. When he looked at Niraj again, he asked, "Answer me honestly: If Arun had been the only one to present this idea to you, would you have agreed to support Poppy Sutherland?"

Niraj hesitated. It was Akash who said, "Yes."

Hasan rose to his feet, heart heavy. "Then I'll be on my way.

I recognize that my untrustworthiness is the roadblock here. I've done things that I cannot expect forgiveness nor understanding for, but Poppy shouldn't have to bear the consequences for this."

"Hasan." Harithi reached for his hand. "Sit down."

"No," he said. "All that matters is that there's a show of support for Poppy. If the only way I can help her is by leaving, then I will."

He opened the door and left. He was a good way down the street when the door flew open again.

"Stop," Maya called. He turned to see her standing on the road outside the house, faded pink dupatta fluttering. "Come back."

He approached slowly, as though if he moved too quickly, he'd startle her into changing her mind. She let him back into the house, where Arun and Harithi wore matching satisfied smiles.

"We've decided to let you stay," Niraj said. "It seems like, at least for now, you truly care for the girl's interests, if not ours."

"And we'll join the delegation," Akash added. "But we *all* get an equal say. You don't get to order us around just because you're daivyakt."

"We'll do coleaders," he said. "One daivyakt, one vasudhakt. Me and Arun."

Tara nodded. "Very well. What do you have planned?"

"We have to organize," Hasan said. "We have to spread our messaging, reach Virians in the city and the countryside. There needs to be a massive turnout. Because if there's one thing we have to make clear, it's this: We will no longer be governed silently. Our voice will shape the rules we live by."

Chapter Forty-Four

An Arrangement

Zephyr,

I regret to inform you that Richard left Viryana at dawn. There will be no trial against the girl. As such, there is no longer a need for you to testify. We no longer have an arrangement regarding the House of Representatives. Do not contact me again.

WM

• • •

Lord Montrose's letter burned in Zeyar's breast pocket as he knocked on the door. He'd read it a hundred times: forty-seven words that left him with nothing. Despite the warning, he had tried to call upon Montrose Manor, but the guard at the gatehouse had chased him out. He had lost it all: his chance to free Paranjay, his relationship with Hasan, even his own name.

There was only one person in the city who might not slam their door in his face.

The door cracked open a fraction. He caught sight of one hazel eye and lifted the corner of his mouth into a cocky grin. "Hello, Harithi."

She flew out of the door, her dark ponytail streaking behind her. "You have a lot of fucking nerve," Harithi said, slamming him into the wall. "I told you, Zeyar. You don't come here, *ever*."

"Your brothers are at school," he said, ignoring her dagger resting on the tip of his sternum. "They won't see me."

She curled her lip at him. "Have you considered that it's me who doesn't want to see you, especially after that stunt you pulled in Sanivali?"

He flinched. "If you didn't want to see me, you wouldn't have opened the door," he said. "But you did."

Zeyar reached for her slowly, giving her enough time to move back if she wished. She didn't. He laughed, placing one hand at the small of her back, pulling her toward him. The tip of her dagger pierced his skin, crimson staining his shirt, but he barely felt the sting as he leaned down and kissed her.

"I hate you," Harithi said, but she was already dragging him into the apartment.

• • •

"Still hate me?" Zeyar teased, leaning over to wrap one of Harithi's curls around his finger.

"Yes," she said, though she let him continue to play with her hair. They lay in silence for a moment, their bare legs tangled under her bedsheets. Then she rolled onto her side so she could look him in the eye. "Why are you here?"

He leaned over the side of the bed, fishing a lighter and his pack of smokes from his pants, which were pooled on the floor.

After he'd taken a drag, he said, "I wanted to talk."

She snorted. "We don't talk, Zeyar. That was never part of the arrangement."

Ah, yes. Their arrangement, a set of rules that had defined their trysts for the past year. The cardinal rule: It could be nothing but physical. No talking, no attachments. This was fine with Zeyar—Harithi was arrogant, blunt, and willfully independent. Oh, she was good at what she did, but Zeyar had resented her loud mouth from the moment Hasan had brought her on. The arrangement only worked because each trusted the other not to stab them in the back while they were putting their clothes back on.

Zeyar exhaled a thin stream of smoke. "I have no one else to talk to."

"That's hardly my problem." She lifted his cigarette from his lips, taking a drag herself.

As she reclined, blowing a cloud of smoke out, he confessed, "Richard Montrose has left the country. His father won't honor his deal with me."

Harithi lolled her head over, unmoved. "Oh, I'm sorry. Am I supposed to be surprised?" When Zeyar glared at her, she spread her arms. "What do you want me to say?"

"I don't know." He gritted his teeth. "I gambled everything on this. And—"

"And you regret it," Harithi said. "What made you deal with him again, Zeyar? He'd already burned us once. We'd have found another way to get Paranjay back."

"It wasn't just about Paranjay." Zeyar took the cigarette back from her. "It was for Hasan too. What happened to Vinay at the museum could have just as easily happened to Hasan. When I saw him bleeding out in the back seat . . ." His stomach turned, and he forced himself to push the image out of his mind. "The police are too advanced—their weaponry, their technique. Paranjay can't escape them, Hasan can't defeat them, and I couldn't protect either of them—not unless I befriended Montrose. Becoming a representative was supposed to be insurance, for the future."

"Did you explain this to Hasan?" Harithi asked.

"Hasan doesn't want my protection." Zeyar flicked the spark wheel on the lighter absentmindedly, watching the flame wink in and out with each click. "Even before he cut me out, he was so damned bullheaded when it came to taking advice from me."

"You're one to talk. When you left for the city, did it even occur to you to talk about your plans before you made them?"

"Hasan would have—"

"Not Hasan. Me."

Zeyar's eyes snapped to her face. "You?" He hadn't meant for the word to come out sounding so incredulous.

She tilted her chin up defiantly, her hazel eyes hard. "Yes, me."

It hadn't occurred to him at all. "What could you have possibly said?"

"I would have said that when you took Richard to Sanivali to take Poppy, you should have left the key with *me*, and I would have fetched Paranjay from the neutral location before Montrose could have reneged." She rolled her eyes. "Honestly, Zeyar, I'm shocked that you didn't think of it. The solution was right fucking there."

Zeyar flushed with humiliation. That was the thing about Harithi. She rankled a man's pride, and right now, with his ego wounded, her scorn was like salt in a wound.

He dug his words in hard, trying to pierce her stone heart. "Yeah, well, talking isn't part of our *arrangement*, is it?"

Harithi glared at him. "You're right. It isn't," she spat. "You've overstayed your welcome. Get out."

Zeyar reached over, stubbing out the remains of his cigarette in the ashtray perched on top of a stack of *Miss Marnapur* magazines on the nightstand. He dressed himself in his pants and bloodstained shirt. As he bent to pick up his blazer, he noticed a scrap of newspaper sticking out of Harithi's blouse pocket. The name *Arun* was scrawled over the newsprint, followed by an address.

"What's this?" he asked, turning around to show her the paper.

Harithi's face paled. She leaped out of bed, snatching for the scrap. "It's nothing."

He yanked it out of her reach. "It doesn't look like nothing." Zeyar frowned. Their arrangement wasn't exclusive, but as far as he knew, neither of them had been with other people in the past year. "Who's Arun?"

"No one." She made another futile grab for the paper.

He shrugged, his heart pounding. "Maybe I'll visit this *Arun*," he said. "See what all the fuss is about. Is he ugly? Is that why you're ashamed of having him as your lover?"

"He's not a lover," she said. "Fine! I'll tell you, but you have to promise to stay out of it."

"I won't interfere."

She sighed. "This is Hasan's paper, not mine. Arun is a vasudhakt man who's helping him form the Delegation for Virian Interests. Their aim is to install Poppy Sutherland as vicereine, then advise her in office."

He almost laughed out loud. Hasan, playing at politics? Hasan, whose first instinct was to fight his problems with fire? He would never last. Either his own delegation would oust him, or he would ruin Poppy Sutherland with his idea of "advice" first. That girl needed someone rational, someone cool and logical.

The delegation needed Zeyar.

"It was good seeing you again, Harithi." He bent to kiss her on the cheek, but she caught him by the throat.

"Don't fucking come back here," she said. Then she kissed him once, savagely, and kicked him out of the apartment.

Chapter Forty-Five

The People's Vote

The House of Representatives reeked of gasoline. When Poppy had asked about it, staff had told her that vandals had done it some time ago. They had tried to shampoo the carpets, and mopped the floors a hundred times, but the pungent odor lingered. It made Poppy's head ache even more than it already did.

Today, she would find out if all her efforts and sacrifice would be recognized. The outcome of the vote would be a clear message on what mattered more to the Council: the viceroy's last wishes or their personal prejudices. She wished she could believe that they would vote on whether or not they believed in her ability to govern, but she knew by now that the only thing they were voting for was their own agenda. The pressure had built in her skull like a bomb, and she doubted if she'd even survive to see the outcome.

The representatives arrived slowly, many of them delayed by the crowd outside. Thousands of Virians of all genders and age groups had shown up this morning outside the House of Representatives, their sweaty bodies crushed against the makeshift barriers the Marnapur police had set up. They had cheered when Poppy had stepped out of the car, an overwhelming show of support so loud she had felt disoriented.

As more and more representatives arrived, the seats in the House began to fill up: a hundred chairs upholstered in green leather, with four extra ones at the apex of the curve upholstered in red, intended for the Council of Lords. Poppy had been given a makeshift seat in the center of the U-bend, where all could see her. The chair was hard and uncomfortable, but she refused to squirm. Instead, she smoothed out the folds in her black mourning gown, running through the Hawk's checklist for proper presentation: *hair bound—check, skirt straight—check, back straight—check, ankles crossed—check.*

When all the members had taken their seats, Lord Colwick rose and cleared his throat. "The House is now in session," he said. "Today we are debating and voting on a special topic: the succession of the next viceroy. Members will be given two minutes to speak. If a question is asked, then the respondent may only take two minutes to provide an answer. Who will start?"

Gerald Alderfort rose. "Good morning, gentlemen. My first question is for Miss Sutherland. Miss Sutherland, are you aware that succession laws stipulate that only a male can inherit the office?"

Poppy relaxed a fraction; she'd prepared for this. "While we've always interpreted the law this way, the actual wording of succession laws does not specify anything about gender. It stipulates that once the viceroy passes away, the seat must be given to the—and I quote—'designated heir.' My father frequently referred to me as his heir, even in public."

"That may be so, but the *legal* definition of heir refers to a male," Alderfort said.

"If I may intervene." Theodore rose from his side of the room. "That definition was written when women couldn't own land. Men *had* to inherit property, because no one else could."

"So now that women can legally own land, would fathers be able to name them as heirs?" Poppy asked pointedly.

"Absolutely," Theodore said. "And I would ask the House and Council to bear in mind that not only *could* the late duke name his daughter his legal heir, but he *has*. There is a signed document in which he wills not only half his funds and the entirety of his land to his daughter, but his office as well."

"That's preposterous," Lord Whitecliff spluttered. "He would have never done that."

"But he did. And why wouldn't he?" Poppy asked. "Is it so hard to believe my father thought me suitable? He publicly maintained from the very first day of my adoption that I have every right and opportunity as a trueborn daughter of his."

She made direct eye contact with Lord Whitecliff, then with each of the other lords. Their lowered eyes were an answer in themselves. Finally, Whitecliff said, "You have no training."

She raised one eyebrow. "What *training* are you referring to, my lord? I can read, let me assure you, and I am quite fast at sums."

"There's more to it than that," he said. "A viceroy must be educated."

Ice formed in Poppy's stomach, hard and cold. "Are you implying that I am without an education? In case you've not noticed, I spent the last seven years getting *educated*, at one of the most prestigious institutions for ladies in Welkland, no less."

"What about leadership?" Lord Alderfort asked. "You may have all the hard skills required, but do you have the prerequisite soft skills?"

"I'm sure my father, who inherited this role at only twenty himself, had minimal leadership experience as well. Just as he relied on his council, I trust that mine will work with me on matters of importance." She managed a smile. So far, this meeting was going as she'd expected: There was pushback, but nothing she was incapable of rebutting. Every protest so far had been something that she and Theodore had predicted and prepared for.

"We should still explore our other options," Lord Alderfort said. "My son is the eldest of the heirs, and the most experienced thus far. He would make the best viceroy."

Poppy tensed. "There—"

"Your son hasn't worked a day in his life," Whitecliff said, talking over her. "Andrew has completed not one, but two degrees. He has the necessary intellect and work ethic."

"A scholar does not a leader make." Colwick shook his head. "My boy, Edward, is still young and energetic. His Grace inherited early, and we saw how successful he was."

"There are no other options," Poppy shouted, capturing their attention again. She rose to her feet, curling her fingers into fists. "I am Clarence Sutherland's legal heir. He named *me* in his will, and so I will be vicereine."

"Miss Sutherland, be reasonable," Whitecliff said. "You are a woman, and unlike any viceroy this entire country has seen before. Who will follow you?"

Poppy turned to look at the other representatives, searching out the faces of the men from the Second Families whom she had met with. "I daresay there are several here who would follow me," she said. "Others who, like me, have been robbed of opportunities in order to placate those higher up. Others who were denied the chance to become anything more than their birth, despite the Founder's edict that all can become equal.

"But the people here are not the only people who matter. There are hundreds of thousands of people outside these walls who are not opposed to following me. Don't pretend you haven't seen them, the way they gather in the streets rallying for me. They want a Virian viceroy. Will you risk mutiny? Those are your workers, your servants, your farmers. No amount of formal education or leadership experience can make up for the loyalty of the people. You are in the minority, and you would do well to remember it. Will anyone follow Edward? James? Andrew?"

Poppy's question hung in the air. Though her nerves had stretched to their breaking point, she forced herself to make eye contact with each patriarch as she said their heir's name. Each of them looked uncomfortable, save for Lord Montrose, whom she had already dealt with. Lord Alderfort glared at Poppy, his open display of hatred clearly meant to be unsettling. Instead, it lifted a weight from her shoulders. *He was angry because it was the truth.* She had made a point that no one could rebut, and they knew it.

Lord Colwick rose to his feet. "Let us vote on the motion to confirm Poppy Sutherland as the successor to the office of the viceroy," he said. "If she can secure the majority of votes among representatives, the Council will then vote among themselves. She will need the votes of *three* lords. Should she secure those, she will be vicereine, pending royal assent, of course."

Poppy bit her cheek. She had gained Lord Montrose's cooperation, which would likely be enough to sway at least one other lord. But could his vote influence two others?

"If the majority rejects Miss Sutherland, where do we go from there?" one of the representatives called.

Colwick paused. "Though unprecedented in Viryana's history, the law says that it would fall to the lords to identify and interview the next set of eligible candidates."

"So your own sons, then," Theodore scoffed, loud enough for the rest of the room to hear.

Lord Colwick didn't acknowledge the jibe. "When the clerk calls your name, rise and say *aye* or *nay*. If your response is *aye*, remain standing so that we can do the final tally."

The House clerk rose, calling names off the list in front of him.

"Mr. James Alderfort?"

"Nay."

Though Poppy had expected that, the word struck her like a stone anyway. It felt like a bad omen to start the voting on a negative note.

"Mr. Ian Bluefinch?"

"Nay."

In that manner, the clerk went around the bend, collecting *ayes* and *nays*. Soon he'd made it almost halfway through the crowd, and the number of *nays* was overwhelming. Poppy clenched the black silk of her mourning gown so tight, her knuckles turned white. She would never get the chance to reverse her father's legacy. Her father had died for nothing.

Bang.

The House clerk paused. "What was that?" he asked, echoing the question on everyone's minds.

Bang.

The representatives in front of Poppy craned their necks, staring at the door. She turned, too, looking over her shoulder to see what they were all staring at.

Bang. Bang. The thick, heavy doors to the Central Chamber were trembling, shaking as an unseen force struck them from the other side.

Bang. Bang. Bang. The pounding continued. Between each strike, shouting came through the walls as well. Lord Colwick rose unsteadily, but before he could say anything, a deafening crash filled the room as the doors to the chamber flew open. A crowd of Virians spilled inside, filling the space of the Central Chamber. Poppy sucked in a gasp as she flew to her feet.

At the head of the group was none other than Hasan Devar, his knuckles bruised and bleeding, his clothes torn and in disarray, his brows drawn fiercely over his burning eyes.

She had not imagined she would ever see him again. She had so many questions: Why was he here, after he and Zeyar had betrayed her? What about his brother?

As the rest of the room dissolved into chaos, his eyes met hers. His split lip stretched as he gave Poppy a rueful, tentative smile. Then he shouted over the din, "For too long, you have made decisions without us, the people who are most affected by those same decisions. We demand the right to participate in the selection of our next leader. We're here to cast our vote for Miss Sutherland, and we won't leave until each of our voices has been counted."

The crowd roared in agreement with his words.

Poppy's chest and throat swelled with an emotion that lifted her up and rendered her impossibly vulnerable all at once. Hadn't Hasan told her? *Gods, blood, and kings do not decide who rules. The people do.*

And the people—her people—had chosen her.

"Everyone get out, *now*!"

Guards poured in, half of them splitting off to fight the sea of Virians who flooded the chamber, the other half escorting the lords and representatives out. Poppy's heart raced as one of the guards escorted her out, but fear didn't drive her pulse—joy did.

Just before the door swung shut behind her, she twisted, peering over the guard's shoulder to catch one last glimpse of the chaos within, Hasan at its core, teeth bared, fists flying.

She brushed her finger over the thin pink scar on her thumb, a strange warmth in her chest. All this time, she had been so consumed with fighting for the country, she hadn't dared to dream that the country was willing to fight for her.

Chapter Forty-Six

Appease the Masses

Protestors Released from Marnapur Jail After Ten Days of Riots

This morning, the protestors who broke and entered into the House of Representatives were released with all charges dropped. This comes after ten days of destruction and defiance from the Virian populace. Workers across the colony have abandoned the fields and factories, spilling over Morning Bridge to demand that their voices be heard in the selection process of Viryana's next viceroy.

"I think it's an outrage, frankly," James Alderfort said in a statement made earlier this week. "With these riots, we have no workers to tend the fields, plus the domestic supply chain has been disrupted by road closures and looting. The economic consequences can't be ignored."

Superintendent Nottingham refused to comment on whether the Marnapur police's inability to subdue the rioters had any impact on the decision to free the trespassers. "These delinquents have been emboldened by our viceroy's death," Nottingham told reporters. "Without strong leadership, we can expect more chaos."

The Special Committee will resume its hearing to select the new viceroy this Tuesday. In an unprecedented turn of events, six protestors will be permitted to sit in on the hearing and cast their own ballots. House Leader Colwick declined to make a statement on their inclusion. Only time will tell what ramifications this concession will have on Virian society.

• • •

Eleven days after the vote on succession was disrupted, the House of Representatives reconvened. In addition to the lingering gasoline fumes, stains shadowed the carpet, and the wooden desks and chairs were scratched and scarred.

However, not all of the changes were for ill. Six wooden chairs had been added to the U-bend for Hasan and his delegation. The representatives pinned them with outright hostile looks, but not a single delegation member faltered when they stood and asked the clerk to record their vote in favor of Poppy.

That being done, the rest of the representatives began to vote, starting from the beginning again. Some of the favorable votes, Poppy expected—the Greenwoods, Theodore—but others came as a surprise. There were *also* votes she had expected to have that she'd lost. She tried to keep her expression placid throughout, but each *nay* punched through her like a rod being shoved through her body, until she was riddled with holes.

Finally, the clerk finished with the Wainwrights, and the vote was over. Under her breath, Poppy counted the number of men still standing. She wasn't the only one. Theodore's lips moved in an echo of hers as he counted too. Even Lord Whitecliff had his neck craned, taking note of the number of people on their feet.

"I have now finished the tally," the clerk said.

Bile rose in Poppy's throat. This moment would decide her future. What would happen to her if she lost this? Desperate, she cast her gaze to Theodore, but Hasan intercepted her gaze. His face was composed, unbothered, but she still remembered the language of his body. His jaw was set, his limbs perfectly still: He was just as anxious as she was. Her heart beat so loudly, she feared she wouldn't be able to hear the numbers when the clerk said them.

"The number of representatives who voted *aye*: fifty-four. Majority rules."

Relief rushed through Poppy in a cold breath, so intense it was painful. Her entire body went soft and numb. She had never been so grateful to be sitting in her whole life. She had done it—against all odds, she had gotten the votes. Her eyes met Hasan's again, his expression mirroring her thoughts: If he and his delegation had not been here, she would have lost.

"Given the sensitive nature of the vote," Lord Colwick continued, "the lords will vote now, for efficiency and transparency. The representatives who are still standing may sit down."

She sucked in another breath. Of course. She'd nearly forgotten. There was one more round of voting to be done, and Hasan would not be able to influence this one.

The representatives took a seat, and the lords rose. Poppy's heart was now drumming so hard against her rib cage, she feared it would burst. She curled her toes in their slippers, unable to show any other sign of her immense stress without giving herself away.

"Lord Alderfort," the clerk called.

"Nay," Alderfort said.

She closed her eyes briefly. *Damn.* She was going to lose. She needed three votes, and she had already lost one. It was so bitterly unfair, that her father had named her his heir, the way his forefathers had named theirs before him, but she would be the first to get vetoed. The double standard was so infuriatingly obvious. She clenched her jaw so hard, she feared her teeth would shatter. But she wouldn't hide from her defeat. She would face it with her eyes wide open.

"Lord Colwick."

The other man studied Poppy, his expression blank. She wished he would just say *nay* and move on, instead of dragging out the disappointment. Then, he said, "Aye."

She blinked. *Aye?*

Lord Montrose was next. "Aye," he spat, but his cold look made one thing clear: This was not support. This was a fulfilment of their deal, his voice for her silence, and nothing more. If she lost her seat tomorrow, he wouldn't say a word.

Lord Whitecliff was openly staring at Lord Montrose,

surprise evident on his face. He'd been expecting Montrose to say no. Poppy could see him recalculating. His was the deciding vote, and the pressure was bone crushing. Poppy wanted him to say it—aye or nay, anything, just to release her from the agony of suspense.

"Lord Whitecliff?" the clerk prompted. "Your vote, please?"

"Aye," he said.

"What?" Lord Alderfort looked appalled. "Arthur, you—"

"Gentlemen," Lord Colwick said, "let's not forget that the House is in session. We must maintain a level of decorum."

"The vote is decisive," the clerk declared. "Poppy Sutherland will be the next—nay, the first vicereine of Viryana."

A wave of cold electricity swept through Poppy, snapping through cords of tension that held her taut like marionette strings. She slumped in her chair, boneless with giddy joy. The room was roaring—or maybe that was her pulse, rushing in her ears.

"Lords, gentlemen, this session is concluded," Lord Colwick said. "House dismissed."

The representatives rose, filing out single file. Poppy floated through the doors, weightless, suspended in disbelief. When she emerged into the foyer, Catherine and Demetria paused their pacing.

"Well?" her mother demanded.

Poppy ran and buried her face in the shoulder of Demetria's black gown. Sobs ambushed her, rendering her incapable of speech.

"She did it," Theodore said from behind her. "Poppy will be vicereine."

Chapter Forty-Seven

Imposter

Three weeks after her father's burial, Poppy returned to the same abbey where he'd been laid to rest, to take the oath of office. Though she had pushed to keep the affair small out of respect for his memory, the entire city had turned out to see the inauguration ceremony. They pressed against the barricades, nearly spilling onto the roads as they leaned over to wave and cheer. The sight was fearful and inspirational at once, for the same reason: All of these people expected something from her.

What if she failed them?

She'd tried to quash the thought several times, to no avail. It dogged her, haunting her like a shadow. She couldn't fail. Not when the entire island had come together for her right to succeed.

Poppy stepped out of the car to raucous cheers. The guards took charge quickly, hustling her into the abbey, to the front of the pews, where a temporary throne had been installed. It was symbolic, an echo of the emperor's throne in Welkland, a reminder that the viceroy was an extension of the emperor, who was an extension of the Founder. Poppy stood in front of the throne for a long moment, a chill trickling down her spine.

The last man who had sat in that chair was her father. She

would sit in his place, but she would not take on the role he had played. She had to pull his legacy apart, brick by brick.

A voice spoke, jolting her from her reverie. "Big crowd, Miss Sutherland. Not even your father had this kind of turnout."

She turned to see Lord Montrose standing by the front pew, his wife behind him. Richard had left the island three weeks ago, just before her father's funeral, but the injustice of his so-called *punishment* still brought a bitter taste to Poppy's mouth.

"The people believe in me." She tilted her chin up defiantly. "They're why I'm here."

"I hope you live up to their expectations," he said. "People tend to love an ideal far more than the person behind it. If I were you, I'd take care."

"Is that a threat?"

"Consider it advice," he said, "from someone who has been playing the game much longer than you. You are where you are today because of the alliances you forged. But will these people stick by you, especially when you're forced to make unpopular decisions? When you bargain with mortals, the terms can change at any time. Today, you have the faith of the people. But tomorrow? You may have nothing at all."

Leaving that bizarre warning hanging in the air, he turned and made his way to his seat. She stared at his retreating back, his words stuck in her chest like the blade of a dagger.

The ceremony went according to schedule. Poppy sat on the throne, holding a scepter in one hand and the works of the Founder in the other, repeating the oaths that the founderson read to her. When it was over, he took her hand, helping her out of the throne.

"Ladies and gentlemen, I now present to you, Vicereine Poppy Demetria Sutherland the First!"

Polite applause filled the abbey, but it was overshadowed by a loud cheer from outside. It swept through the open windows like a wave crashing on the sand. Poppy soared with elation, sailing on its high. But as Lord Montrose caught her eye, her heart sank. If she didn't find someone to teach her how to swim, she would certainly drown in this tide.

• • •

After the inauguration, the guests were permitted to line up and wish the new vicereine well. Lord Montrose had left immediately, to Poppy's immense relief. Catherine and Theodore were some of the first in line. She came down off the dais to embrace both of them.

"How does it feel to be officially the vicereine?" Theodore asked.

"I can't believe this is real," Poppy said. "The last half year has gone by in such a blur."

Catherine reached forward to squeeze her hand. "I'm here anytime you want a shoulder to lean on."

"Thank you," she said. "That means a lot to me."

Then the pair were off, making way for the next group in line. In that manner, she spent the next couple of hours making small talk with every person who approached her, until the line had mostly dwindled. Names and faces blurred, but some were welcome, friendly faces, such as that of Rohini Devar, who had squeezed her hand and said that the island was blessed indeed. Finally, a group of Virians reached Poppy. The founderson consulted his list, reading out the name of their envoy to her.

"The Delegation for Virian Interests."

She brightened, sitting up straighter as her eyes fell on

Hasan. "Let them come up," she said, the words worn from an afternoon of repetition. He introduced her to each member formally. The group clustered around her for a quick picture, Hasan and Arun flanking her. When the photographer had finished, Hasan turned back to Poppy.

"Congratulations," he said. "You pulled it off."

"*We* pulled it off. I couldn't have done it without you," Poppy said. "All of you," she added, her gaze touching the faces of the other members.

"Yes, well, we believe in you," Maya offered.

She flinched involuntarily. Though Maya didn't realize it, her words reminded Poppy of the conversation she'd had with Lord Montrose before the inauguration had started. She smoothed out her expression swiftly. "Is that so?" she asked, keeping her voice level. Her eyes flickering back and forth between the delegation members, she wondered how she could get them to leave so she could speak to Hasan alone.

"It was a pleasure meeting you," Maya continued, oblivious to the tension she had just created. "I hope we meet soon. We have so much to talk about."

"Indeed." Poppy dipped her head, her shoulders still tense. "I look forward to it."

Hasan and the rest of the delegation turned to leave. Poppy hesitated, then called his name.

"Mr. Devar. A moment, if you would."

Hasan turned around. The others in the delegation paused, then carried on without him. She tilted her head at her guards, indicating to them that she wanted a moment's privacy. They eyed Hasan warily but heeded her, taking several steps back. She rose, coming down the steps until she stood on one that was eye level with him.

"You've seen me at some low points in my life," she said wryly, "so I'm not going to mince words."

The corner of his mouth turned up. "Go on. I'll suspend any judgment."

"I don't think I can do this," she confessed, her words tumbling out in a rush. "I know that sounds bad, considering all we went through to get here, but . . ."

He stared at her as though she'd gone mad. "What are you talking about? You already *have* done it, Poppy. You became vicereine. You defeated Richard. You sent that bastard packing back to the homeland where he'll be kicking rocks for the next five decades."

"Don't get me started on that," she said, clenching her jaw. "If it were up to me, he'd be placed in front of a firing squad and shot."

"Someone's gotten more violent since the last time we met," Hasan deadpanned. "Though for what it's worth, I don't disagree."

"The last few months have changed me," she said. "But I need to change *faster.* Did you see how many people came today? How many Virians?"

"It was impressive." He grinned. "That's why the delegation was late. The streets were practically overflowing."

"All of those people are expecting something from me." She shook her head, her voice laced with panic. "They support me because they think I'm one of them. But I'm not, Hasan. What will happen to me when they realize that?"

"You are one of us," he insisted. "You have just as much right to call yourself Virian as everyone else. They can't take that from you."

"They can't take something I never had." She pressed her lips together in a firm line, holding on to her composure. "I'm trying, but it's hard. I was away from Viryana for seven years. Even when

I was here, I had no idea about the depths of my father's cruelty. He thought he was doing what was best for the colony, but his bias was a huge blind spot. I don't want to become like him, implementing oppressive structures out of ignorance. I need someone to help me. To explain histories and backgrounds, so that I understand the problems those people want me to solve. It was their support that got me here, and if I lose it, then this whole thing will crumble. I want your delegation to formally advise me—especially you."

Hasan opened his mouth, then closed it with a sigh. "I have to talk to Arun and the others," he hedged. "But I don't see why they would say no."

"Thank you." Poppy sighed. "I have something else for you as well." She beckoned to one of her guards, who approached her with an envelope in hand. Hasan took it from him. "What's this?"

"My first order as vicereine: an official pardon for Paranjay," she said. "If you go by the jail tomorrow, the police will release him for you."

Hasan looked up at her, holding the paper to his chest. "Thank you," he said, his voice fevered. "I can't wait to bring him home."

She inclined her head at him. "That's all."

He turned to go, but when he'd taken a few steps away, he turned around. "Poppy," he called. "You *can* do this. I believe in you."

I know, she thought. *That's what scares me most.*

When Hasan left, there was only one more person left waiting to speak to Poppy. She'd sat at the back of the abbey, but with everyone else gone, she rose and came to the front. Poppy regarded Samina evenly. Most of her injuries had healed since her fight with Richard, though her skin bore fresh new scars where wounds had closed. Her hair had grown longer, shoulder length now. Other than that, she looked the same, dressed in a clean cotton salwar kameez, her arms crossed over her chest as she sized Poppy up.

"I wasn't sure you'd come," Poppy said. "Hasan wasn't sure you would, when I asked him to pass along the invite."

Samina snorted. "At first, I wasn't planning to. He talked me into it. He said it was an important historical milestone for Viryana whether I liked it or not, and I would be stupid to miss it. But why did you invite me at all?"

Poppy bit her lip. "I wanted to apologize," she said. "First, for everything that happened. With your mother, with the necklace, with the orphanage—"

"Those things weren't your fault," Samina said. "You were a child. I judged you harshly, because I felt life had been soft on you, but really, neither of us had much control over those events."

"I might not have controlled them, but I'm still the one who caused them," Poppy insisted. "And though I was a child, I was an adult at Sanivali when I tried to downplay what had happened to you. I wanted to believe you were better off at the orphanage so that I wouldn't feel guilty about my father's sending you there. For that, I want to apologize. If there is ever anything you need from me, you can always come and ask."

"Oh. I wasn't expecting that," Samina said, shifting her weight. "I don't know if I forgive you yet. But I do appreciate the apology."

"You don't have to give me your forgiveness," Poppy said, and was surprised to realize she meant it. "But I hope you'll let me keep on trying to earn it."

Samina tilted her head. "We'll see," she said. "Fix the island first. Then we can talk."

• • •

Zeyar waited until the rest of the delegation had separated from Hasan. His eyes trailed Harithi, dressed in her best sari, as she walked side by side with the other coleader. *So* this *is Arun.* He was of middling height, average in every way, and yet something about him was distinct, an optimism that shone in a warm aura.

Harithi would eat him alive.

Zeyar got out of the car, strolling up the street to where the delegation was coming his way. Harithi locked eyes with him, stiffening.

She bared her teeth. *You wouldn't dare.*

He only smiled back at her. "Mr. Arun," he said, stopping in front of the other man. "Congratulations on your achievement. I heard the vote was tight."

Arun dipped his head modestly, but a small divot formed between his brows. "Have we met before?"

He shook his head. "I'm afraid not. I read about your delegation in the *Viryana Post.* I'm curious: What are your objectives, now that you've been able to see Poppy Sutherland seated in the vicereine's office?"

Arun's expression became guarded. "We'll have to decide as a delegation. Rest assured, we will advocate for the best interests of the Virians."

"Naturally," Zeyar said. "I assume your strategy will be less . . . intense than storming the House of Representatives? I was sad to hear about the casualties of that day. All power comes at the price of blood, so they say."

As Zeyar had expected, Arun's smile faded. Rushing the House of Representatives was so reckless and stupid; he'd known there was only one man who could have led that charge: Hasan.

And if the glower on Harithi's face was anything to go by, that one action had become a sore spot in the delegation—which was exactly why Zeyar had pressed on it.

Arun regarded him warily. "None of the major newspapers reported the deaths of the protestors."

Zeyar flicked nonexistent dust off the shoulder of his blazer. "I have more than one way of gathering information, which is why I'm here. I know things about the nobility that may be of interest to you. I'd be happy to share . . . if I were part of the delegation, of course."

He avoided looking at Harithi as he spoke the last bit, but her gaze seared into him anyway. He could picture her hazel eyes, hot with fury.

"Information such as?" Arun tilted his head, eyeing him with interest.

Zeyar cocked his head to the side, mirroring him. "We'd be here all afternoon if I were to say. Once I join the delegation, we can decide which parts of my knowledge are more advantageous to our objectives."

Arun glanced back at the other members. Zeyar tracked the way his gaze jumped from face to face, landing on Harithi's before turning back to him.

"We'll think about your offer," he said. "What's your name?"

He produced a calling card from his pocket, extending it to Arun. "Zephyr Devar."

Chapter Forty-Eight

Homecoming

The morning after the inauguration, Hasan waited outside the Marnapur jail, every limb taut. In one hand, he clutched the envelope Poppy gave him, his grip so strong that it had creased the paper. Printed in neat script on the page inside was an official pardon, from the new vicereine to one Paranjay Devar.

When the door swung open, his heart jumped painfully. An officer walked out first, followed by Paranjay, holding only the clothes and shoes he'd been arrested in, dressed in his prison uniform. A lump swelled in Hasan's throat. His brother was gaunt, dark circles prominent on his ashen face. For the first time in Hasan's memory, Paranjay no longer smelled like the sea he so loved. Paranjay wasn't merely haunted by this experience; he had become a wraith himself. The sight landed like a kick to the ribs. Hasan could live a hundred years, but he would never forgive himself for every single day that his brother had been a prisoner and he had failed to rescue him.

His hands shook as he reached forward to take Paranjay's clothes from him. "Let me get those."

Paranjay didn't protest. He let Hasan take the clothes, then moved obediently as Hasan draped one of his arms around his shoulders so that he could lean on him.

"Watch yourselves, Devars," the officer warned. His stare could have melted iron. "Weak leadership never lasts. And when we have a *real* viceroy in office, we'll come for you first. Don't forget; we have your number."

"Don't listen to him," Hasan told Paranjay, but deep down, the pig's words made his stomach twist. Clarence Sutherland had signed the Registry Act, one of the last things he'd done before he'd passed away, and Paranjay was now on there. Hasan himself had not yet been registered, as the police had not yet gathered enough evidence on him, but it was only a matter of time. He did not regret saving Paranjay's life—how could he?—but he wished fervently that he had been able to stop the Act from passing too.

Once they were out on the streets, Hasan paused so that Paranjay could tilt his face up to the sun. His elder brother closed his eyes, basking in fresh air for the first time in months. "I'm free," he said quietly. "I would think I'm dreaming, but my dreams of the sun were never this good in prison."

Hasan pulled him into a hug. He tried not to squeeze too hard, not until Ma had a chance to examine him for lasting injuries, but he held Paranjay close. "You're free. It's over now."

Paranjay nodded, sunken eyes shining. "I know," he said. "I . . . I can't believe it." Then he spotted the empty car parked curbside. His face fell. "Why didn't Zeyar come?"

The innocent question wrenched at Hasan's heart. He couldn't meet his brother's eyes. Now that Paranjay was free, there was no keeping the news from him. Silently, he cursed his bastard of an eldest brother for sullying Paranjay's first day of freedom like this.

"Get in the car," he said. "I'll explain it on the way to Ma's. She's positively frantic to see you."

"Gods"—Paranjay tilted his head back, smiling—"I hope she made fish curry."

Hasan chuckled at that. Their mother had been up since dawn, preparing every single one of Paranjay's favorite foods. Knowing her, there would be at *least* three different kinds of fish curry.

As they pulled away from the curb, Paranjay asked about Zeyar again. "Where is he? I thought he'd come."

Hasan sighed. He opened his mouth, trying and failing to find the right words. Finally, he said, "Zeyar's left our business, Paranjay."

Briefly, Hasan explained all that had taken place between himself and Zeyar. Paranjay listened mutely, which was unlike him. Normally, he'd chime in, always full of opinions and questions. But he stared at Hasan with haunted eyes, saying nothing until, finally, Hasan prompted, "Well?"

"It sounds like he didn't leave," Paranjay said. "It sounds more like you sent him away because you were upset with him."

Hasan bristled at the accusation in Paranjay's tone. "Because he betrayed us!"

How did Paranjay not get that? He'd been the prisoner. Was Paranjay not angry that Zeyar had bargained for himself instead of his brother's freedom?

Paranjay flinched at Hasan's raised voice, his hands shaking, the first sign of his invisible injuries.

Hasan lowered his voice hurriedly. "Sorry. I shouldn't shout at you. But are you honestly taking his side right now?"

"I'm not taking sides. I'm making an observation," Paranjay said. "I agree—Zeyar should have never made that bargain without you, just as you should have never agreed to back Poppy without asking him."

Hasan tightened his grip on the wheel. “Those aren’t the same, and you know it.”

“Maybe not in magnitude, but at its core, both of you made the same decision: to take matters into your own hands, and ask for forgiveness instead of permission. Did you try to see it from his point of view?”

“I would have understood if it had actually worked,” Hasan said. “Hell, I’d have packed Poppy’s bags myself if I knew it would bring you back. But in the end, it was *me* who had to free you. The only thing he gained from this was power.”

“Okay, and I’m back now.” Paranjay’s voice wavered as he asked, “Can’t we move past it?”

Hasan couldn’t believe this. He almost wanted to remind Paranjay that he was free because of him, not Zeyar, so no, they could not just *move past it.* But he looked at Paranjay again, and wondered if it might be worth it, if it would help him recover his spirits quicker. Then he remembered the way that Zeyar had restrained him when Richard had arrived at Sanivali, Poppy’s feet stumbling out of his line of sight before he’d blacked out.

“You can’t forgive someone where there’s no remorse,” Hasan said, his jaw set. “If you want to talk to him, you can. But I’m done. I don’t trust him anymore.”

“Hasan—”

“No, Paranjay.” Hasan stared ahead resolutely. He couldn’t look at his brother, couldn’t bear to see his sunken face crumple, couldn’t watch his bony shoulders slump, or his resolve would crumble. “I’ve made up my mind. If Zeyar wants to be forgiven, he’ll come and ask me. If it takes us until our senior years for him to humble himself, then so be it. Until then, I’ll keep my distance.”

“You’re making a mistake,” Paranjay said. “The chasm will

only widen with time, and with our line of work, growing old isn't guaranteed. Baba is proof of that." He struggled for a moment, searching for words or courage—maybe both. "When I was in jail, I was certain they would execute me. All I could think about was the things I had said—and the things I hadn't—to the people I loved, things I thought I'd never get to rectify. You don't want to have regrets like that, Hasan."

"I won't have any regrets."

Paranjay only sighed. "You're too stubborn," he said. "I won't push this issue any further. But think about it. Right now, he's out there missing you as much as you miss him. All it takes is one call."

"I don't miss him," Hasan lied. "Can we not talk about it?"

When they arrived at their mother's house, she ran out onto the lawn, tears streaking her face as she buried Paranjay in a tight embrace. "My son has come home," she wept. "I've invited the entire village to celebrate."

As Hasan surveyed the tables and chairs set out in the backyard, he reconsidered what he'd said to Paranjay. If he'd forgiven Zeyar, then Zeyar would have been here to welcome home Paranjay. It seemed unfair that everyone in Sanivali was here, but the trio was still incomplete. Hasan could have fixed this, if he'd forgiven Zeyar.

Hasan shook his head, casting off the thought. If Zeyar wanted to be here, then he shouldn't have betrayed them. It wasn't Hasan's responsibility to rebuild the bridge that Zeyar had burned. Zeyar would realize that, eventually.

And then he would come back and beg him for forgiveness, and the three of them would be together once more.

Epilogue

Roots

SIX MONTHS LATER

Hasan, Arun, and Poppy sat in the viceroy's office—Poppy's office—late on a Friday evening. While she'd been away on her inaugural tour, she'd ordered all the rugs and furniture changed, instructing the cleaners to scrub the floors twice. Though the room still reeked of wood polish, sometimes Poppy could have sworn she'd stepped in a puddle of blood, only to look down and see her own reflection in the hardwood floor.

Many had tried to dissuade her from touring, but her reasons were threefold: First, it was just before the monsoon season, so her storms in the farmlands could be passed off as an early start to the season. Her position with the lords and representatives was too tenuous to openly expose herself as daivyakt, and she could not lose the few allies she had if she was going to bring about change. Second, she needed the common people to see her, their new vicereine, and know that their voices had been heard. And last, the Sutherland estate was haunted.

The smell of rust and gunpowder followed her everywhere. Sometimes she would catch a glimpse of white hair reflected in the window, only to realize it was a cloud. The nightmares had subsided while she was on tour, but since her return, the visions had only gotten worse.

"Cotton exports are down another percent," Arun announced, bringing Poppy back to reality as he snapped the report closed. "But import figures are still high."

She'd expected that much. Since becoming vicereine, she'd been able to incentivize more local cotton growers to sell their yields to local factories instead of sending the raw material to Welkish factories. Theodore, newly appointed to the Council of Lords, had helped advocate for the law, though the Alderforts and the Montroses had fought it at every turn.

"We've also seen an increase in employment in the cotton industry," Hasan said. "We'll likely see more if we can get the labor reforms to go through. How's that coming?"

Poppy gritted her teeth. "It's not," she said. "We're talking thousands of crowns for safety inspections, plant maintenance, employee training. No one is willing to shell out, least of all the lords."

"What about Oakbury?" Arun asked. "Or Wainwright?"

"They're hesitant, but even so, they're a minority. Now that we have six council members, I need three signatures to pass the motion."

Arun sighed, and the three of them went quiet again.

In the silence, Poppy's gaze drifted down to a locked drawer in her desk. It contained just two letters, both marked with the seal of the emperor, one addressed to the office of the viceroy, the other addressed to her by name. The first one she had received only two weeks after her inauguration, too soon for it to be her royal assent. When she opened the letter, she realized that it had actually been intended for her father.

> *We have heard concerning rumors in Welkland that your Virian ward is campaigning to be named heir to your office. While we respect that the adoption was an extension of your devotion to the Founder's teachings on assimilation, we are greatly concerned about the future of the colony should it pass into the girl's hands, and will advise you strongly that if you name your daughter as successor, she will not be granted royal assent, and her rule will not be considered legitimate.*

The letter had been signed by a man named Lord Granfort, on behalf of the emperor.

When months had gone by without any royal assent, she feared that the emperor was serious. What would they do to her now? But then, three months after her inauguration, she received the second envelope, which, to her great relief, contained the royal assent. Her relief was short lived, for in the same envelope, Lord Granfort had written a letter to her personally. Though politely worded, his message had been sinister in nature. The royal assent had been provided not as a vote of confidence, but to maintain temporary stability in the colony of Viryana. While the emperor decided what was to be done, Poppy would be *permitted* to hold control of the island. Until then, the Imperial Family was watching, *very* closely.

She had told neither Arun nor Hasan about the letter, hoping that the emperor had chosen to leave it be and respect his late cousin's final wish. Lifting her gaze from the drawer, Poppy focused on the conversation again.

"There must be a way to crack one of the Council members," Hasan was insisting. "Poppy?"

“If there’s a way, then I don’t know it.” She spread her arms helplessly.

“Is there any dirt on the lords?” Hasan mused. “We could try blackmail.”

Arun cleared his throat. “I wouldn’t resort to underhanded tactics so soon. Let’s ask Zephyr,” he suggested. “He may have a more tactful way of dealing with this.”

Hasan and Poppy stiffened. Despite their trepidations, Zeyar had managed to join the delegation, winning over enough of its members for them to overrule Hasan on the decision. She’d never admit it to Hasan, but Zeyar’s plans had a subtlety that his lacked. Though his schemes had worked well thus far, she remained wary of them, unsure of whose ends they served—hers, or his.

“Okay,” Poppy sighed. “I don’t think we’re going to get any further. Go consult with the rest of the delegation. We can talk about this on Monday.”

Arun and Hasan rose obediently, gathering their papers. Arun left first, tipping his hat on his way out.

Poppy glanced up and saw Hasan lingering, his hand on the doorknob, his features taut. “Is there something you need?” she asked.

“Nothing,” Hasan said quickly. “I just . . .” His gaze searched her face. “Are you okay? I saw you lose focus during our meeting. You look . . . troubled.”

She shook her head. “I’m fine,” she said. “Truly. Just a little tired.”

Hasan hesitated, doubt clear on his face. “Well, if you need anything, I’m here.”

When she didn’t say anything further, he took the hint. After his footsteps faded away, she rose from the desk, stretching as she made her way over to the window. Night blanketed the island, moonlight cresting the waves crashing into the beach that backed onto the estate. For a moment, she recalled her childhood, walking along those same waves with Nanny and Samina as Nanny told them tales of magic and maharajas. Poppy had been too young and ignorant then to understand how courageous that act of storytelling had been, but now that she knew, it was her obligation to continue Nanny's work in preserving Virian tradition. She pressed her aching head to the cool glass, eyelids drifting shut.

No one ever talked about how hard it was to erase a legacy, only how hard it was to build one. If Welkish rule over Viryana was an invasive tree, then appointing Poppy as vicereine had only felled it on a surface level. The roots were still in the earth, tightly entrenched, choking the native plants, leeching water and nutrients.

Poppy opened her eyes, staring across the horizon, where the Welkish continent lay. No matter how weary she grew, she would tear every last root out. Even if it made her hands bleed.

And she dared someone to try to stop her.

ACKNOWLEDGMENTS

Writing a book is a solitary activity, but publishing it takes community. I would like to thank everyone who has been a part of my writing journey up to this point, starting with my parents, who gifted me with my love for books over twenty years ago. Thank you to my dad, who spent countless evenings reading Tintin comics with us. Thank you to my mom, who, when I told her I wanted to be an author, spoke to literally every person she could think of in order to try to understand the mysterious world of publishing. To my sister, Ayesha, thank you for reading all my early drafts and providing your (sometimes brutal) feedback. Because of you, I can spell zucchini now.

Thank you to my grandparents, especially my grandmothers, Anita Picardo and Indrani Basu, who never stopped asking me if I was still keeping up with my writing and when I was planning to publish a book. Here it is—I hope you like it ☺

Thank you to the rest of my extended family. Your excitement and support over this process mean a lot to me.

I am incredibly fortunate to have had Allegra Martschenko, the best agent in the world, to champion me through this process. Thank you for all your advocacy, for your unfiltered sidebars, and for translating legalese. Publishing is full of uncertainties, but I have no doubt that entrusting my career to you was the best decision I made.

Next, I would like to thank the team at Bindery, who gave this book a home. To Emma Skies, you loved this book and its characters to the point of cyberstalking. Your passion for my work and collaboration throughout this whole process has made this the best possible debut experience. Meghan Harvey and Matt Kaye, thank you for welcoming me and this book into the Bindery family. Thank you to CJ Alberts, marketing extraordinaire, and Shira Schindel, whose voicemail in September changed my whole life. Thank you to Charlotte Strick for your dedication to creating the cover of my dreams.

Dan Funderburgh, I'm convinced you must be a wizard, because you worked literal magic with the cover illustration. Every detail is perfect, thank you.

To my editor, Matthew Patin, I'm definitely not the first to say it, but you're a genius. Your feedback not only made *TBWM* a better book, but it made me a better writer. Thank you for your insightful editorial letters and making time to hop on calls with me to brainstorm solutions.

Thank you to the team at Girl Friday Productions. Emilie Sandoz-Voyer, thank you for managing all the moving parts so smoothly and for buying me an extra couple of days, or even a week, when I needed it. A special shout-out goes to my copyeditor, Jane Steele. Opening the style guide left me speechless in the best way. Thank you to Carrie Urbanic, who proofread the manuscript. Your attention to detail is appreciated.

Thank you to Brittani Hilles and Lavender PR for working so hard to get *TBWM* out to readers.

To my Pitch Wars mentors, Sarah Mughal Rana and Vaishnavi Patel, thank you for choosing to uplift both me and this book. Without your editorial vision, *TBWM* would not be what it is today. I am also incredibly grateful that even three years after the program ended, you were there to jump on a call with me at short notice and walk me through all of my concerns and questions. A special mention goes out to the rest of the Pitch Wars class of 2021, as well as all to the volunteers who made that program happen.

It's time to expose the title of my group chat. Thank you to The Real Manny Jacinto Fan Club (and to Manny Jacinto, on the off chance you're reading this): Zoulfa Katouh, Alina Khawaja, and Aliyah Fong, for the inspiration, the memes, listening to my hot takes, the late-night writing sprints, and being my sounding board during the drafting process and the multiple rounds of revision that followed. All of you are true friends, and I am blessed to have had you with me on my road to publication.

Sidrah Mughal, you believed in this book long after I declared it dead in the query trenches. Thank you for refusing to leave it behind and for sending me the link to Bindery's open call for submissions. You have an eagle eye when it comes to books, and it means all the more to me that you believe so strongly in this one.

To M.T. Khan, who read an early version of this book. Thank you for your friendship and advice throughout the years. There's no one else I would rather get Italian food with.

Thank you to S. Hati for answering all my questions about Bindery on short notice, for generously referring me to Allegra, and for always being down to order a sweet treat with me at the end of a meal.

Thank you to Alexander Kotsopoulos, former coauthor, current best friend. When we go on our first Sunday walk through the bookstore after *TBWM* comes out, I can't wait to pick up a copy and show this to you.

To Mahir Chowdhury, thank you for cheering me on throughout this process and for making dinners when I'm on a deadline and getting celebratory crème brûlées with me. I hope the future holds many more reasons to celebrate (and consequently, crème brûlées).

Finally, to you, the reader, thank you for taking the time to read my book. I sincerely hope you enjoyed it.

THANK YOU

This book would not have been possible without the support from the Skies Press community, with a special thank-you to the Producer members:

Abbey Grace
Alica D
Allie Christian
Amelia Armstrong
Andi
Ashley Wood
Brandon Odom
Brett Foster
Brittany Gunter
C Pagel
Carter Kalchik
Chester Scofield (LinkinBreak)
Christina Sultani
Daniel Pagan
David Zehder
Elisabeth Arritt
Elizabeth Serafin
Emily Gearhart
Emmy Sage
Hanna Flora
Haydn Woodward
Heather Meisch
Jamie Sadler Edwards
Janine Chambers
Jill Smith
Jonathan Negron
Joseph LaPorte
Joyce Irene
Kaitlin A
Kas
Katey Coull
Kathleen Levy
KayLee Besse
Kia Borner
Larissa Allred
Micah Burnham

Myriam B.
Nick Gonzales
Rachel Prince
Samantha Rush
Sara Bensaou
Sarah Boyd
Savaira
Selene Nicholson
T Throneberry
Taylor Case
Victoria Ann
Demno
ungrokkable
KTAinsworth
marina
nquery
AmandaBookCandleCo
kellidianne85
Nedpets
GabbyVegaa
Brigid
Cassanova
Scarlett
elleparwai
pawsitivevibes
HadesBaby
fairestfaee
luckyonesoph
SirAaronCarter
AjWill
BJBookworm
nerdykayleigh
bobthetrombone
Beckahhreads

ABOUT THE AUTHOR

R. A. BASU is an Indian Canadian author from Ontario. She graduated from the Schulich School of Business at York University in 2021 and works in app development. When she's not reading or writing, she can be found playing cozy video games, fighting for her life in Pilates classes, and searching for the best matcha in the city. She currently lives in Toronto.

Skies Press is an imprint of Bindery, a book publisher powered by community.

We're inspired by the way book tastemakers have reinvigorated the publishing industry. With strong taste and direct connections with readers, book tastemakers have illuminated self-published, backlisted, and overlooked authors, rocketing many to bestseller lists and the big screen.

This book was chosen by Emma Skies in close collaboration with the Skies Press community on Bindery. By inviting tastemakers and their reading communities to participate in publishing, Bindery creates opportunities for deserving authors to reach readers who will love them.

Visit Skies Press for a thriving bookish community and bonus content:

skiesreads.binderybooks.com

EMMA SKIES is a content creator from Northern California, reading, reviewing, and discussing genre fiction with over 200,000 followers across various social media platforms. Emma believes storytelling in all its forms is one of the most powerful and universal ways that we process the world around us. She loves few things more than hearing that someone has found themselves in a book she shared with them.

TIKTOK.COM/@EMMASKIES

INSTAGRAM.COM/EMMASKIES